Riding the River
of Dangerous Dreams

MEREDITH—Disguised in buttons and bows and the simpering manners of a Southern belle, she hid the inner woman possessed by a mission to find a half sister sold into bondage, obsessed with a man she didn't dare to love. . . .

QUINN—Hiding dark secrets of violence and imprisonment, he appeared to be a Mississippi riverboat gambler and a cruel slave master; but few knew the risks he took in freedom's name or the passion that drove him to Meredith's bed. . . .

CAM—Whipped for his pride, crippled for his defiance, he was doomed to die a slave's hopeless death until there was Quinn, freedom, and a chance to save the woman he loved. . . .

DAPHNE—Cursed by her beauty in a slave's world, she felt only hate and despair until she accompanied her new mistress onto a riverboat and met a gentle giant of a man who offered her a promise and a dream. . . .

*R*ainbow

Patricia Potter

BANTAM BOOKS
NEW YORK · TORONTO · LONDON · SYDNEY · AUCKLAND

RAINBOW

A Bantam Book / August 1991
Bantam reissue / May 1993

All rights reserved.
Copyright © 1991 by Patricia Potter.
Cover art copyright © 1993 by Wendi Schneider.
No part of this book may be reproduced or transmitted in any
form or by any means, electronic or mechanical, including
photocopying, recording, or by any information storage and
retrieval system, without permission in writing from the
publisher.
For information address: Bantam Books

ISBN 0-553-29069-X

Published simultaneously in the United States and Canada

Bantam Books are published by Bantam Books, a division of
Bantam Doubleday Dell Publishing Group, Inc. Its trademark,
consisting of the words "Bantam Books" and the portrayal of a
rooster, is Registered in U.S. Patent and Trademark Office and in
other countries. Marca Registrada. Bantam Books, 1540 Broad-
way, New York, New York 10036.

PRINTED IN THE UNITED STATES OF AMERICA

RAD   0 9 8 7 6 5 4 3 2

For the Potter clan, one and all

Prologue

Seaton Plantation,
Vicksburg, Mississippi, 1839

MEREDITH SEATON tried not to tremble.

She struggled desperately to stand up straight, to keep her lips from quivering, as she defied her father for the first time in her young life.

He was so big, so tall, and his mouth was frowning in an all too familiar manner. That expression was always the beginning of a rage, and rage meant punishment. Though she couldn't stop the fear that shook her legs, she had to let him know how important Lissa was to her. Perhaps, just this once, he would understand and relent.

Meredith had thought about it all day, ever since she found Alma in tears that morning, and was told she could no longer play with Alma's daughter, Lissa.

Meredith had listened in stunned astonishment. Lissa, who looked like her own self, had been her playmate since she could remember. They had done everything together except sleep. Meredith retired at night to a beautiful large room while Lissa shared a bed with her mother in the slave quarters.

They were only two years apart in age: Meredith was now eight and Lissa six. In spite of that small difference, Meredith had always felt motherly and protective about Lissa, giving her many of her toys and dolls, and directing their games. She loved Lissa, who looked up to her with faithful adoration, and followed her lead in everything. Meredith didn't really have anyone else. Her mother had died when she was a baby, and her father, who had never remarried, was distant and harsh. She had one older brother, but he thought her a nuisance and paid attention to her only when he scolded her for one mischief or another.

There was only Alma, who was the closest thing she had to a mother, and Lissa, who was almost as light as she and who had the same dark brown eyes. Only their hair was different. Lissa's was black while her own was blond.

That morning, when she ran downstairs to the kitchen, she did not find Lissa in her usual place beside Alma. And she saw that Alma's eyes were red with weeping.

"Where's Lissa?" she asked hesitantly, suddenly afraid.

The question brought a new burst of tears, and Meredith moved to place a comforting hand on the woman who had done the same to her so many times. But Alma jerked away and looked at Meredith as if she hated her.

Meredith stepped back. "Alma," she whispered.

The black woman glared at her through tears shining in dark eyes. "It's your fault," she said. "The master saw you givin' your new doll to Lissa and decided you were too familiar." She spit out the last word, bitterness flowing from her like lava from a volcano, boiling and deadly. "Familiar!" she said again, and laughed, but the sound was ugly to Meredith's ears.

"And why shouldn't sisters be familiar?" Alma continued in her vitriolic tone.

"Sisters," Meredith whispered. "But Lissa is a—"

"A slave," Alma said. "A slave to be sold. Even by her own father."

"Father . . . ?"

Meredith didn't understand any of it. She knew they had slaves, and many of them, particularly the house servants, were her friends. Some disappeared occasionally, but she had never questioned that. As for Lissa, how could she be her sister? They looked alike, of course, but Lissa was . . .

Lissa was what? Meredith had never thought much about their different status. Lissa was required to help her mother in the kitchen, while Meredith spent hours in the classroom. She had asked once why Lissa couldn't share her studies—it would be much more fun—but her governess had only said Lissa had other duties and changed the subject. No one had seemed to object when the two of them played, though, not if she had finished her lessons and Lissa her chores.

Until yesterday. Meredith had just given Lissa one of the dolls she received for Christmas and Lissa was hugging it to her when Meredith looked up and saw her father watching them closely, a grim look on his face.

"Go to Alma," he had directed Lissa. Then he turned to Meredith with a frown. "And you, miss, have you no studies?"

"I'm all through, Papa," she said.

"Then I shall have to ask Miss Wentworth to increase her efforts."

"Yes, Papa," Meredith said obediently. She couldn't remember when he had said something kind to her, or touched her with affection no matter how hard she tried to please him.

"Why does Lissa have your doll?" he asked abruptly.

"I gave it to her," Meredith replied, surprised at his attention.

"That doll was a present to you from your brother," her papa said.

"But I have others . . . and Lissa admired it."

"Lissa has no need of such things," he said. "It just gives her ideas."

"But—"

"That's enough, miss. Go up to your room and stay there."

Meredith recognized the tone of voice. It scared her. It always scared her, ever since the first time she had unknowingly angered him and felt his belt on her back. She retreated and went up to her room, wondering what she had done.

It was several hours later when, restless and unhappy, she had ventured carefully downstairs to get one of Alma's cookies. She heard voices in her father's office but didn't understand what they meant.

"We have to do it." Her father's voice came through the door. "She and Meredith look too much alike and they're much too friendly. It's not proper. I should have done it years ago before it went too far, but Alma . . ."

Her brother's reply was soothing. "You can always get another black wench. There's Ruby for instance. She's real fine in bed. Pretty, too, and eager." His tone hardened. "I don't fancy seeing a black half-sister here."

"It's done, then," her father said. "I'll send for Sanders in the morning."

"You better lock the girl up. Alma might try to take her and run."

"You're right. I would hate to have to punish her."

"She'll get over it. She's just a nigra. She always knew it would happen."

Meredith heard footsteps and scampered back upstairs. None of it had made much sense until now as she looked at Alma's ravaged face and blazing yet hopeless eyes.

"Lissa?" Meredith said, an enormous dread spreading from the pit of her stomach.

"The master's selling her," Alma said. "She's in the slave jail until the slave trader arrives."

Meredith backed away. "No. He can't. Not Lissa. She's my friend."

"Bein' your frien' is gettin' her sold," Alma said, sinking

into a chair. "God knows what will happen to her, pretty and light as she is."

"But . . ."

Alma's usually impassive face was ugly with pain and hate. "They will put her on an auction block, all alone and terrified. To be sold like a horse or a mule or . . ." She couldn't say anything else. Years of hiding her feelings, her hurts, her humiliation while she serviced a man she despised were ending in the final terrible tragedy. Nothing mattered anymore. She looked at the motherless girl she once pitied. She had tried to give the child love, and her efforts resulted in the sale of her own daughter, the only source of happiness in her hopeless life. And now she hated Meredith, as she hated the girl's father. "Go away," she said tonelessly.

Meredith felt her world crumbling. Alma and Lissa had been her only allies, their friendship the only haven in a lonely world.

"I'll talk to father," she said. "Maybe I can change his mind. . . ."

And Meredith, despite her fear, tried. How she tried as her knees quaked and her heart pounded.

"She's my friend," she said.

"Slaves aren't friends, they're property. To be bought and sold," her father said. "I'll hear no more about it."

"Please . . . I'll do anything. I'll be ever so good. I won't talk to her anymore, if you wish."

"That's enough," her father roared. "Get up to your room."

Meredith bravely stood her ground. "But—"

Her father picked her up roughly and carried her to her room. Once there, he pulled up her bulky dress and petticoats. Meredith bit her lip. *I will not cry. I will not.* She felt the heavy blows as pain coursed through her, but although tears formed in her eyes no sound came from her lips. The blows finally stopped and she heard his footsteps retreat, the door open and close, and the sound of a key turning in the lock.

For hours she lay on her bed silently, tears flowing, her heart hurting. Finally, she rose and walked over to the window seat where she could see the road in front. She tried to sit, but it hurt too much, so she stood there, watching through the branches of the tree that shaded the room.

Meredith didn't know how much time had passed before she saw a wagon come up the long drive. A man, unkempt and fat, stepped down and talked briefly to the overseer. Minutes later Lissa, her face streaked with tears, appeared and was placed in the wagon. Horrified, Meredith saw a chain locked around her ankle.

"Mama!" her friend screamed. "Mama!" Meredith saw Alma run out, only to be caught by the overseer who struck her to the ground.

"Miss Merry!" the terrified girl in the wagon yelled. Meredith felt her heart crumble. She had to go to Lissa, had to help her. She opened the window and reached out for one of the branches of the huge tree. In agonizing fear, she began to climb out. But her hand lost its grip, and she screamed as her body tumbled through the air, her own terrible screech mixing with that of Lissa.

Chapter 1

Lucky Lady,
New Orleans, 1855

QUINN DEVEREUX looked around the spacious cabin of the riverboat. After the eight years of hell he had endured, it seemed like Eden. He often wondered if he would ever become accustomed to its luxury.

He had personally designed everything in the cabin. A large bed dominated the room, reminding him only too well of the nights he had been squeezed together with other convicts in a portable prison wagon. Books, which he had craved during years of loneliness and boredom, lined the mahogany walls. Soft comfortable furniture welcomed the few visitors he permitted inside. A cabinet, filled with the finest wines, sat in a corner.

Windows lined two sides of the cabin, wide spacious windows that he could open to welcome the fresh breeze flowing in from the ocean or river. Centered on the back wall was an oil painting of a rainbow, and as his eyes hovered on the canvas, an odd dissatisfaction gnawed at him. The damned picture, at times, seemed to taunt him.

He shook off the melancholy feeling, trying, instead, to restore the usual pleasure he received when entering this cabin, a quiet but profound pleasure that had only recently returned to his life. He had once thought any enjoyment, any contentment, had been completely whipped and worked out of him on the Australian road gang to which he had been condemned. He had once been certain he would die without tasting freedom again.

Even after his miraculous escape, he had wondered if he would ever feel anything but hatred and bitterness. But slowly, very slowly, some measure of peace, if not happiness, had slipped into his life. His covert activities with the Underground Railroad for the past three years gave him a release from the terrible tension that had maintained its grip months after he'd arrived back in America. At times he even felt a renewed zest for life. But he was always cautious. One mistake, and he could well be back in prison—or dead. The latter, he knew now, was preferable to the former. He could never suffer captivity again. Never.

A knock came sharply on the door. Cam! Only Cam would knock in quite that impatient way and with the suppressed rage that was so much a part of the former slave.

"Come in," Quinn called out as he loosened the frilly cravat at his throat and threw it down on the chair in disgust.

A large black figure filled the doorway. Cam was huge, three inches taller than Quinn, who towered over most men.

"The special cargo's been stored," Cam reported.

"What kind of shape was it in?"

"Not the best, Capt'n."

"The passengers all boarded?"

"There's still a few coming."

"Anyone look suspicious?"

"Two of them. I seen them before, and they *are* looking."

"I'll just have to distract them with a little game of cards."

"Yes suh." Cam smiled slightly. It had taken him a year to smile after being purchased by Quinn Devereux. It was not until he received his manumission papers that he really believed he could trust Quinn's word. Now he would willingly die for his former owner. Captain Devereux, quite simply, had given him back his soul.

"Any other interestin' passengers?" Quinn asked with an air of indifference.

Cam regarded Captain Devereux with curiosity. The man wore a cynical facade, but Cam knew it hid a deep commitment to justice and a heart that bled only too freely for others. It had taken him a long time to discover that, and sometimes even he doubted when he caught the whip of Captain Devereux's savagely caustic tongue. He often thought he would never really understand the man. He wondered if anyone would.

Cam smiled suddenly. "A woman . . . pretty. But she giggles a lot."

Quinn arched an eyebrow over one of his deep blue eyes. "How far is she going?"

"Vicksburg."

"Any company?"

"An elderly lady and a maid."

"Is the maid pretty?"

This time Cam looked askance.

"The maid," Quinn said, pressing him. "There must be some reason that party caught your notice. You don't usually help me look for the ladies."

Cam's smile broadened. "I don't usually have to. However, recently . . ."

Quinn's crooked grin was quicksilver. Fast to come, faster to go. "What about her mistress? I'm sure you've discovered her name by now."

"A Miss Seaton. Miss Meredith Seaton."

"Meredith Seaton." There was surprise in Quinn's voice.

"Do you know her?"

For a moment, Quinn's eyes softened as he remembered a June day nearly sixteen years before. Or was it more? His life before Australia seemed centuries, rather than years, away. He remembered being twenty-one and ready to embark on the Grand Tour, but first he had stopped with his father to visit the Seaton plantation. Meredith Seaton had been a charming child: a little shy but still as bright as a new silver coin. He had built her a swing, and she had been embarrassingly grateful, as if no one had ever been kind to her before. Since he had returned to America, he had heard his brother speak of her, and she apparently had changed greatly from the enchanting child he remembered.

"I met her once . . . years ago," Quinn said. "My brother controls a trust in her name. He doesn't think much of her. An empty-headed flirt, he said, who runs through money like it was water." He grinned. "Just like me. He doesn't approve of either of us. He nearly agrees with you though. Says she could be pretty if she ever learned how to dress."

There was a touch of pain in his lighthearted words, and he'd stopped smiling. Quinn was aware of how much his younger brother disapproved of his life. Although Brett said little, Quinn knew he was considered a gambler, womanizer and profligate, and no credit to a father who had risked a fortune for him.

His lips twisted into a wry grimace. That was the hardest part of this charade: his brother's disappointment. He tried to shrug off his sadness. "I think I would like to meet this . . . female counterpart. Why don't you invite the lady and her chaperon to my table tonight, Cam?"

"I'll see it's done."

"Along with your two suspicious men."

Cam nodded, not even puzzling over the strange combination of dinner guests. Captain Devereux always had a reason for what he did. Even if it wasn't immediately evident.

"You can take care of everything below?"

"Yes, Capt'n." It was said with indulgent patience, and Quinn sighed at the hint of impertinence.

"I should have left you on the block in New Orleans."

"Yes suh, Capt'n, suh," Cam replied, thinking that particular day had been the luckiest in a life filled with unlucky ones.

Their eyes met, remembering the scene, and then their faces again became impassive as they had both learned to do so very well. Cam turned without another word, limping slightly as he walked out, and closed the door behind him.

Meredith watched as the new maid carefully unpacked her clothing. The girl constantly looked back at her mistress for approval and Meredith nodded reassuringly.

But Meredith couldn't rid herself of her own haunting depression.

It had been another wasted trip as far as Lissa was concerned. Her whereabouts continued to elude Meredith's best efforts. But she had found Daphne, and Daphne probably needed her as much as Lissa.

Her new maid was like a frightened rabbit. She had been at the slave jail, awaiting auction. Meredith, after her private detective told her a young mulatto girl was there, had visited the jail looking for Lissa, using the excuse that she'd needed a new maid.

Meredith had been searching for her half sister for the last three years, ever since she had enough freedom to do so. But she kept running against stone walls. No one knew of a Lissa, a light-skinned Negro slave.

Meredith had mourned her childhood friend since the day Lissa was sold, and vowed to find her and somehow free her.

As she had helped free others. As she planned to help free more.

But the mulatto in New Orleans turned out to be Daphne, not Lissa. Meredith had taken one look at the girl's terrified face and purchased her. She hadn't wanted to ask about the girl's past. Daphne's face told her more than she wanted to know.

Her companion had not approved, but then she approved of very little. But Meredith was twenty-four, and had her own funds, and "just loved visiting." The best her brother could do was send his wife's aunt with her, and hope his sister would not disgrace him and the family.

Robert's most fervent wish, Meredith knew, was to see her married. Preferably to another plantation owner, preferably to Gilbert MacIntosh whose plantation adjoined their own.

To escape, Meredith simply went visiting frequently, claiming she was looking over likely husbands. It was as good a reason as any, and one Robert accepted easily enough in his eagerness to rid himself of her and her giggles and often odd behavior. And her painting. Her "damned monstrosities," as Meredith had once heard him say to his wife. They were a terrible embarrassment, especially the way she pushed them off on friends and even acquaintances.

Robert had, Meredith knew, attributed her eccentricities to the fall she had had as a child. She'd been unconscious for two days and when she awoke she had never been the same. She had turned reclusive and silent, a quiet shadow who sat for hours with books and had little to say to anyone. Meredith had then been sent to a convent school in New Orleans where she had stayed for ten years. She had come home only twice during that time: for a disastrous visit over the Christmas holidays, and for her father's funeral.

When she returned home at the age of eighteen, there were still secrets in the dark brown eyes, but to her family she was gayer, even fanciful. She giggled and chattered aimlessly, and if the smile never quite reached her eyes no one seemed to notice. And if she disappeared at times, no one noticed because no one really cared.

When Meredith was twenty-one, she became an heiress in her own right. She discovered then that her grandfather, long dead, had established a trust in her name at the time of her birth. But her funds were administered by the Devereux Bank in New Orleans. She was able to draw on it in reasonable amounts, but it was structured to keep the bulk of the money from any fortune hunter. Large withdrawals had to be approved by the president of the bank. Presently that man was Brett Devereux.

Although no one said so, Meredith suspected she had never been told of the trust until there was no avoiding it so she would marry their neighbor. Money of her own might have given her ideas. And it had. That money had armed Meredith with another weapon she needed. Guile was the first, and she had honed that to a fine art. Even she herself sometimes had difficulty knowing who she really was.

She traveled frequently, agreeing to a chaperon only to quiet suspicions, and the good Lord knew that her companion was as dense and unsuspecting as a hen headed for the dinner table. No one had ever connected Meredith with the spate of slaves that ran away soon after she left her hosts. Nor had they associated her occasional shopping trips to Cincinnati with the Underground Railroad. No one would ever suspect the giddy-headed Miss Seaton drugged her aunt and slipped out to meet Levi Coffin, one of the most active abolitionists in the North, or Underground Railroad contacts in New Orleans.

And Meredith could be very giddy-headed when she tried, and frightfully silly. She often declared that she didn't marry because there were just "too many handsome men around, and they all just kept her little ol' head aswimmin'."

She sometimes tired of the role, hating the constant playacting and hiding her own intelligence, but so many lives depended on it. Including her own.

"Miss Meredith."

Daphne's soft tentative voice startled her. "Miss Meredith," the girl repeated, "which dress you like to wear tonight?"

Which dress? Meredith wished she cared. They were all ugly. Purposely ugly. Purposely misleading.

"Which dress you like?" Daphne said again with a patience born of a lifetime of servitude.

None, Meredith wanted to scream. *Dear God, I would like to be alone for a while.*

But then her aunt would worry. Meredith was usually eager to be the center of attention. Swallowing her distaste, she pointed to an overly fussy blue velvet with too much lace and too many bows.

She turned her back so Daphne could unhook her day dress when a knock came at her door.

"Yes?" she said.

A deep voice came from the other side. "Message from the capt'n, ma'am."

Meredith opened the door, not waiting for Daphne to do it. She stared at the huge man outside who held a note gingerly.

"Miz Seaton?"

"Yes."

"Wi' the capt'n's compliments, miz. He ask me to wait fo' an answer."

Meredith opened the note and read it carefully. She and her aunt were cordially invited to dine with Captain Quinlan Devereux tonight at eight o'clock.

She felt her spirits drop. It was the last thing she wanted. After three weeks of smiling brightly, of making silly observations and nonsensical chatter, she had hoped for a few days of relief. She looked at the note again. "Devereux."

Quinlan Devereux! Her heart started thumping. She had fallen madly in love with him when she was eight, and he had been her knight in shining armor in dreams ever since. She had met him just before "the day," the day her life had fallen apart. She could still see him. Tall, ever so tall, with laughing blue eyes and midnight-black hair that curled at the back of his neck. He asked teasingly what she wanted most in the world, and she had answered a swing. He had laughed, saying that was a most modest wish and one he could easily fulfill. And he had. A magnificent swing in the woods. He had pushed her, almost up to the clouds, his hands sure and firm. He had been the first man to pay generous attention to her, and she had held that brief time like a precious jewel in her memory.

Later, she had heard he had disappeared in Europe. And when he returned after ten years, everyone talked of Quinlan Devereux—the dissolute older brother of Brett Devereux. It was said he had, in some unknown way, disgraced his family. It was also said his father had disinherited him, and that he was a gambler and, worse, a coward. He had, several times, refused to race his riverboat, *Lucky Lady,* on the Mississippi, asserting only fools risked their lives on such ventures, although every other riverboat owner took pride in the races. It was also said he cheated at cards, although no one could ever prove it.

Meredith had listened, never quite believing. Such tales portrayed a rogue, so unlike the young man who had been so kind to her.

She looked at the man patiently awaiting an answer. Quinn Devereux. Her aunt Opal would be horrified. Meredith's brown eyes suddenly twinkled with golden lights, and a flicker of a smile passed across her lips.

"Oh how very sweet of him," she simpered. "Tell Captain Devereux we accept . . . with thanks," she ordered the tall man. Briefly she wondered whether he was a slave or freeman. Although he appeared polite enough there was something in his bearing that didn't quite fit. He must be a freeman, she finally decided. The riverboats plying the Mississippi favored free labor since it was easy for slaves to escape once they reached Ohio.

The man nodded with dignity and turned, walking away with a slight limp.

Now why in heaven's name did I do that? The last thing

she should do was spend the evening with a man who'd been on her mind for years. How could she possibly continue her masquerade as a spoiled ninny when her heart was pumping so abnormally? She remembered his eyes . . . as blue as the summer sky at dusk, she had thought then. Were they still that blue? Had they ever been that blue? Or was it just a child's dream? And if he was the rogue he was reputed to be . . .

Dear God, but she had enough problems already.

But he's Brett's brother, and it's only good manners to accept the invitation, scoundrel or not.

And she needed a change from pomposity. She had suffered so much stuffiness during the past weeks of traveling, not the least of which at the hands of Brett Devereux. He was frustrated with her spending ways, and had tried to instruct her on the wisdom of thrift rather than indulgence.

Where did all the money go? He had asked the question with exasperation. Why did she need more?

She had shrugged her shoulders indifferently. "A lady must have clothes . . ."

"You should have enough for six women," he said, sighing as he authorized another draft.

If he really knew . . .

It was difficult to imagine the very respectable Brett Devereux having a black-sheep brother. It should be immensely interesting, she told herself, and perhaps she could pick up some information of value. And maybe . . . he would remember her, remember that summer's day.

Now, Meredith thought, to convince Aunt Opal . . .

The saloon was one of the finest Meredith had ever seen. Gilded chandeliers sent glittering streams of light against the Brussels carpet and frescoes. The stained-glass skylights twisted the last colorful remnants of a setting sun against the silver and crystal set on snow-white linen tablecloths.

Meredith and her aunt were led to a large round table where six men were already seated. All stood immediately as they approached, but Meredith saw only the striking man who rose lazily. The movement was almost insolent in its slow deliberate manner, and the expression on his face was both amused and mocking.

"Why, how gallant of you all," Meredith chirped. "Please do sit down," she added as she settled herself awkwardly in a chair held out by one of the diners. She noticed her aunt wince at her clumsiness. She slid a sidelong glance to Quinn, who so completely dominated the table as he descended back into his seat like a sleek languorous leopard.

He was dressed in black, except for his white shirt and cravat and, strangely enough, gloves. She wondered about that briefly, but everything about him was so different, so striking, that what she might have considered an affectation on someone else seemed perfectly natural with him.

An inquisitive smile hung on his lips but his dark blue eyes were unfathomable . . . and cold. Nothing like she remembered. There was no smile in them, no warmth, no welcome. And perhaps cold didn't actually describe them. It was as if they were not eyes at all, but a rich blue curtain. She had a slight chill as she suddenly sensed that much lay behind them, that he had a reason for protecting himself so thoroughly.

Noticing her interest, he inclined his head. "We are grateful that you could join us," he said in a quiet, brandy-smooth voice that sent a current of warmth through her. "Let me introduce your dinner companions. I have the honor to be your host, Quinlan Devereux. On my right is Tal Simmons, a horseman from Tennessee. Next to him is Gerald Wright, a planter from Biloxi, and then George Brown, a businessman in Ohio. On my right are Ted and John Carroll from . . . Natchez, is it?"

The two roughly dressed men looked out of place at the table, and now they acknowledged the introduction awkwardly.

"Pleased to make your acquaintance, ma'am," one said, flattered by the arrival of a lady of quality as well as impressed at being seated at this table. He and his brother were usually considered outcasts.

Meredith noticed that Captain Devereux had not mentioned the two men's occupations. She fluttered the fan she had brought with her. "Oh my, what a distinguished company," she said. "Are you a businessman too?" she asked one of the brothers.

There was a moment of silence. "No, miss," one said slowly. "We are . . . well, you might call us lawmen."

Everything inside Meredith tensed. She should have known, should have sensed it immediately. Slave hunters. Indignation replaced sudden apprehension. Men of their stripe—though used widely by plantation owners—were regarded to be at the bottom of any social ladder, far below an overseer in fact. It was unthinkable they would be asked to dine with . . . with . . .

With whom?

She had to stifle a small laugh that was part tension, part irony, part something else, something that had infected her from the moment she sat down. If only Captain Devereux knew he had slave stealers and slave hunters at the same table.

She fluttered her fan. "How fascinating . . . Mr. Terrell, is it?" Beside her, she heard her aunt gasp with dismay at her choice of conversation partner.

"Carroll, miss," the slave hunter said, emboldened by her interest. "John Carroll."

"Have you caught any murderers lately?" Meredith asked, then felt her aunt jab her waist.

"Well, mostly we hunt fugitives."

"How dangerous for you." Meredith smiled sweetly. Everyone knew few fugitives ever fought back. "You must be very brave."

John Carroll puffed up like a bloated fish. "Well, a man has to be, miss."

The discussion ended as the waiter appeared, nodding his

head politely at Devereux. "Brandy smash, gin sling, mint julep . . ." he recited in a monotone. "What is your pleasure?"

Captain Devereux, his lips still twitching at Meredith's wide-eyed attention to the slave hunter, looked at his tablemates, his glance lingering on Meredith before moving to her chaperon. "Miss Frazier?"

"Nothing . . . nothing," Opal stammered. She was horrified beyond speech at her fellow dinner guests.

His lips twitching even more obviously, the riverboat captain turned to Meredith. "Miss Seaton?" he said politely.

"A small glass of sherry, thank you," she replied sweetly. She needed it. Badly. She wished she could gulp a shot of whiskey.

Captain Devereux's grin deepened, as if he'd guessed the direction of her thoughts, but his eyes remained remote, watchful.

She studied him as he pleasantly questioned his male guests. She could imagine no one more unlike the young banker in New Orleans.

Where Brett Devereux had dark brown hair and light blue eyes and pleasing features, his brother's hair was as black as a raven's wing, thick and curly and looking as if it resisted taming. There were streaks of white around the edges—premature, she guessed, since he couldn't be much more than thirty-six. Instead of aging him, the white endowed him with an air of intrigue. His facial features indicated no softness, and hard lines around his eyes and mouth belied the smile that frequently touched his lips. The impassive dark blue eyes were set deep, framed by long black lashes and heavy dark brows. High cheekbones were divided by a strong straight nose. His chin was square, stubborn, and it would have been most daunting if there had not been a deep cleft in its center that gave him a rakish look. And his mouth . . .

Was what? Fascinating was one word. Frightening another. Not the shape, which was masculinely beautiful and revealed perfect white teeth beneath, but the motions it went through. Motions and curves that had, she knew instinctively, nothing to do with what he was really thinking. It was, she thought with instant clarity, only a tool he used. As she did.

But more overpowering than the near perfection of his face was the air of raw vitality and danger he exuded. As he sprawled lazily in the seat across from her, his gloved hands moving in fluid motion, she wondered if anyone else noticed the tension within him. Probably not. But then she had been trained to observe . . . trained by excellent teachers.

When Captain Devereux completed questioning his guests for drinks, his eyes returned to her. Meredith could feel all his attention, and it was like being struck by lightning, so great was the impact. She forced out a small nervous giggle.

"Does this big old boat really belong to you, Captain Devereux?" she asked with her best admiring gaze.

"I'm afraid so," he replied, his mouth bending into the half-amused smile that she now expected. "The ill-gotten gains of a poker game."

"This whole boat? In a poker game?"

The smile widened. "The whole boat, Miss Seaton."

"And you run it all by yourself?"

"I have someone who does that for me," he said. "I prefer gambling."

"Oh," she said, seemingly crestfallen. In her society, a successful businessman was fair game; a gambler was not, not if he were a professional one.

His eyes crinkled with the first real amusement she had seen, and Meredith felt a surge of elation that her role as husband hunter was so readily believed. Yet mingled with that elation was a curious disappointment too.

But why? And why did her stomach feel so strange and unsettled? She lowered her eyes. She should feel nothing for a man like Quinlan Devereux who gambled for a living, who had shocked New Orleans with his reckless behavior, and who, most damning of all, entertained slave hunters at dinner.

He must approve of their activities, possibly even helped them in return for a percentage of their rewards. How could he have changed so much? He didn't even seem to remember her.

He laughed softly, almost silkily. "You see, Miss Seaton, I'm the black sheep of the family. I don't particularly care to work for a living. Playing poker is much more amusin'."

"But your brother . . ." she protested.

"My brother is a fool. Do you know him, Miss Seaton?" He already knew the answer but he was curious about her reaction. Why, he didn't know. This overdressed woman with the simpering manner interested him on some level he didn't entirely understand. Perhaps because she had been so different as a child, so open and unaffected. Apparently she didn't even remember that visit. But then he had heard something about a fall she had had as a child. Perhaps it had affected her mind.

Cam and his brother were right. Dressed properly and stripped of that infernal giggle, she would be attractive enough if not beautiful. She was tall and slender, but the bows and frills on the heavy blue velvet gown made her seem awkward, and although her hair color was a rich burnished gold, it was dressed in an unbecoming style that did nothing for the fine bone structure of her face. The mouth pouted or simpered, ruining an otherwise striking countenance. Her eyes, if they had conveyed any vitality or intelligence, would be quite remarkable. Golden lights hovered in their rich dark brown depths. But they were so damned empty now, drained of any life or passion.

For one second he'd thought he'd caught a glimpse of something more in them, something like a wary examination, but it vanished so quickly he thought he must have imagined it.

"Miss Seaton?" he prodded when she didn't answer his last question immediately. "Are you acquainted with Brett?"

"Oh my, yes. Such a fine gentleman," she gushed. "And so helpful. He's my banker, you know. Or I suppose you don't. Of course, he scolds me all the time about my spending.'' A sudden surge of mischief overtook her. She wanted to jolt him, to even hurt him for not remembering a small girl. His attention then had meant so much to her, but to him apparently nothing. "But I don't imagine he approves of you either, Captain," she trilled. "I mean . . . well . . ." She purposely stumbled, watching the sudden chill in his eyes.

But he recovered nicely. "I don't quite approve of him either, Miss Seaton. Entirely too respectable for my taste. Now *I've* never claimed to be anything but a rascal of the first order." There was a glint in his eyes that bored into her, and she thought she had better be careful. He wasn't quite as dense as he first appeared, as she had found most arrogant men to be. And he *was* arrogant. Everything about him spoke of it.

Quinn turned to the Tennessean, apparently losing interest in Meredith. "Tell me about your horses, sir. I understand you do some racing. Do you have a horse you would recommend betting on?"

After that, the dinner seemed fairly typical to Meredith. Courses of food arrived. Oysters and mussels, ham, chicken, mounds of potatoes swimming in butter, beans and peas and fresh biscuits. A selection of pies followed.

The conversation turned to politics, and Meredith noted that Captain Devereux seemed completely bored with it. He contributed nothing as he leaned back with a glass of brandy while the businessman from Ohio and the planter from Mississippi heatedly argued the merits of Republican John Frémont and Democrat James Buchanan in the upcoming election.

"Slavery's going to pull this country apart," Mr. Brown said.

"Not if the damned abolitionists will leave our property alone," countered the Biloxi planter.

"No one has the right to sell human beings," Brown said.

"Property, Mr. Brown, property. And because they are valuable property we treat them a sight better than you treat free workers in your factories."

Meredith only half listened. She knew the arguments. She had heard them a thousand times. But no argument, she knew, would ever quiet Lissa's cries in her mind. Or her own nightmares, which continued to this day. It had always taken iron control to ignore these conversations until she learned, finally, to block much of them out. She could not change things with words.

"Miss Seaton?"

She looked up, surprised. She had not heard Captain Devereux's amused drawl.

"I fear we have been boring you and Miss Frazier with all this talk of politics."

"Oh no. I just love listenin' to men. I don't understand it, but it all sounds so . . . so important."

Quinn used his fingers to cover the smile on his lips. She was worse than he had thought possible. He might just kill Cam tonight for arousing his interest. Or better yet, he'd condemn Cam to an evening with Miss Seaton.

Although he seldom demanded much from his women, he doubted whether he could tolerate her level of vacuousness. Even if it had been twelve years since he had truly shared a bed with a woman.

Despite the rakish reputation he had cultivated, he had had no opportunity to pursue amorous adventures for eight years. And in the four years he had been back in America, he had had only brief uninvolved encounters. Yet each had been fraught with danger. He could never let the woman see, or feel, his back or ankles, or there would be questions he didn't want to answer. And then there were even more complicated reasons he didn't care to explore. So on the few occasions he had allowed himself release he did so nearly fully clothed, and he chose women who would not ask questions and who asked very little in return.

"Don't you think, Captain . . . ?"

Now *he* could be accused of inattention, Quinn thought dryly as he tried to pay heed to his guests.

He raised an eyebrow in question.

"That we should protect our property?" said one of the slave hunters. "Your man, for instance, the one who delivered the invitation for dinner... Now he must be worth a lot. Or is he a freeman?"

It was an impertinent question, even for a slave hunter. The others at the table looked embarrassed, but Quinn merely looked disinterested.

"Two thousand dollars to be exact," he said, the answer almost as tasteless as the question.

"And you're risking taking him up North?"

"There's the Fugitive Slave Act," Quinn said carelessly. "And he tried to run once. He won't do it again."

The pure callousness of his tone sent a shiver down Meredith's back. She remembered the man's limp and she wondered if that was the result of an escape attempt. Looking at Devereux's cold blank eyes, she suddenly felt it was possible. Any attraction she might have felt for the gambler, even the childhood memory, disappeared, and only a chill remained.

"I'm afraid we're distressing our lady guests," Devereux said smoothly. "I think a change of subject is in order."

One of the Carrolls flushed. "Beg your pardon, miss," he mumbled.

It was John, Meredith remembered. The other was Ted. She would sketch their likenesses as soon as she returned to her room. She could pass the sketches on to the Parson near Vicksburg, and he would see them distributed throughout the Underground Railroad.

She jerked up as if startled. "I'm sorry, I've been daydreamin', I fear. I suppose it's been the long evenin' and all these fascinatin' politics. My little ol' brain can just absorb so much. If you will excuse my aunt and myself... Captain Devereux, and gentlemen."

Meredith rose, her aunt following with a relieved sigh, and

all the men stood as one, murmuring their farewells. She nodded her acknowledgment and they left the room, leaving Captain Devereux studying them with a strange gleam in his eyes.

He glanced around the table and noticed that no one else seemed to have paid mind to the woman's last sentence. He was the only one, apparently, who realized he had been excluded from the word "gentlemen," despite the presence of the two slave hunters.

He wondered for a moment whether it had been deliberate, and then decided it had not. Miss Seaton didn't appear to have the gumption or intelligence to fashion so subtle a barb. It was, he decided, his imagination again.

"Now who," he said, "would like to indulge in a friendly game of cards?"

Chapter 2

"I HAVE NEVER been so humiliated in my life," Aunt Opal said. "Those men. Can you imagine a Devereux inviting them to his table? I couldn't eat a bite."

She had consumed considerably more than a bite, in fact, but Meredith refrained from the observation.

"It was rather . . . bad taste," she agreed.

"Bad taste indeed," Opal huffed. "I'll tell his brother about it, you can be sure. And I'll not eat at that table again. And I'll not allow you to do it either."

"I have no intentions of doing so." Meredith soothed her aunt. "I was just as shocked as you."

"Well you didn't sound like it, talking to them like they were . . . were . . . decent people."

"Remember, Aunt, that Brett Devereux controls my trust fund. I didn't dare be impolite."

"Humph . . ."

"It's all over now," Meredith said. "I'll send Daphne to your room to help you undress."

"And that girl . . . you don't know a thing about her."

Meredith sighed. "She seems willing enough."

"I know but she's . . . well, almost white. She'll probably just take off like the others."

I hope so. The words were locked inside her, but she thought them nonetheless. Both Daphne and that man of the captain's. The thought brought back Quinlan Devereux's dark countenance and mocking smile. How could someone so handsome be so cruel?

But she reassured her aunt, and led her to the stateroom adjoining her own. Despite the older woman's protestations, Meredith always insisted on two rooms, claiming her aunt's proximity was chaperonage enough. Now Meredith shared her cabin only with Daphne, who slept on a cot.

Meredith needed her privacy. Required it. It was the only time she could really relax and think. Even with Daphne, she had to be on guard. Now she would have a few moments alone while Daphne attended to her aunt's needs.

When she opened the door to her cabin the girl was waiting inside. Meredith had ordered food for her earlier, but the plates appeared barely touched. She was still eating little more than a bird, drat it. No matter what she did, Meredith couldn't seem to tempt her into a better appetite. She was already so slender, so small. Daphne now curtsied nervously, then rushed next door to do Meredith's bidding.

Meredith sighed deeply, relishing the silence. She was able to unhook her own heavy dress, and she slipped quickly into a nightdress and dressing gown. She then unpinned her hair, brushing the long golden tresses as her mind wandered back to the strange scene at dinner.

Why did Captain Devereux have to be so confounded attractive? And so much of an enigma? A dangerous one, she reminded herself. He was probably every bit as ruthless as his reputation deemed him to be, and he obviously had few, if any, human feelings. What had happened in those missing years that had changed him so? What had made those laughing eyes into such closed ones?

She wished suddenly that she'd paid more attention to the rumors about the scandal surrounding him. Some said the law had been involved. Some said a woman. What was certain was that Captain Devereux had disappeared for a number of years, and in that time both his father and older brother had died while waiting for the return of the long missing middle son.

Well, it didn't really matter. She would be home in a few days, and she would probably never see the man again. She would take great pains to avoid the *Lucky Lady* in the future. There were certainly plenty of other boats.

She quickly made notes on the dinner conversation and on the Carroll brothers, then slipped into bed. She pretended to be asleep when Daphne came in and settled quietly on the cot.

But she couldn't sleep. She kept seeing those shuttered blue eyes of Captain Devereux and wondering what terrible things they'd seen. And much as she tried, she couldn't stem the swell of bitter disappointment that swept over her as she realized her knight's silver armor was only rusted tin.

Meredith woke to the sound of her own scream. The nightmare again.

Miss Merry! Miss Merry! The terror was as vivid as it had been so many years ago, as real. But as the cries had increased in volume with each nightmare, the voice had also grown in age, until it had become a woman's voice.

I have to help, Meredith thought desperately. *I must.* She reached out, and then she was falling . . . and the cries rose to a crescendo in her ears.

"Miss Meredith, Miss Meredith."

She felt gentle hands shake her, and the voice was soft, not the hopeless wail that shattered the peace of her night. Gradually, her heart slowed its frantic pace, and she opened her eyes.

Daphne was standing above her, her face creased with worry in the flickering light of the oil lamp she held. "Are you all right, Miss Meredith?"

Meredith wasn't altogether sure. Her body was rigid with tension and soaked with sweat. She put her hand to her cheek and felt the moisture, and knew she had been crying.

She swallowed painfully and put out a hand to Daphne, reassuring her. "It was just a . . . bad dream. I'm all right now. Go back to sleep."

Daphne hesitated. She had only been with her new mistress three days and she still wasn't sure what was expected of her. She was grateful that Miss Meredith had rescued her from the slave jail and auction, but she had learned painfully not to expect a great deal from those who owned her. She had trusted once. She could not trust again.

She knew only one thing now. Obedience. So she nodded and went back to her cot and lay down, grateful she was sleeping in this comfortable cabin rather than the slave pens below where many of the servants spent the night. She had spent time there, in another boat, when being taken to New Orleans for sale. Miss Meredith seemed kind enough, but Daphne knew she was subject to her mistress's every whim. And she knew nothing of the household to which she now belonged. She trembled as the future yawned so terribly frightening in front of her.

Meredith could almost taste the girl's fear across the room and wished with all her heart she could do something to alleviate it. She had made tentative efforts, but there was so much distrust in Daphne. Meredith would have to take one step at a time.

She waited until she heard Daphne's breathing relax and knew she was asleep. Then she rose soundlessly, carefully, and went to the window of the cabin. It was near dawn, the deep black of night was fading into a softer gray. The sun would not be far behind. She knew she would be able to sleep no more and she felt a great need to be completely alone, to taste the fresh air of morning and watch the sun rise.

She brushed her hair, leaving it down and free, and slipped on a petticoat and plain gown, not bothering with the stays. She would wear her cloak. She doubted if anyone other than a few tired members of the crew would be awake to see her at this hour.

Meredith blew out the oil lamp and slipped out quietly, passing several cabins along the narrow passageway. The *Lucky Lady* was like a ghost ship now, empty and silent. She opened the door to the deck, relishing the first whisper of a breeze.

The deck was wet; it must have rained during the night, although she had heard nothing. Only a few clouds remained above, and those moved quickly along. It was August, but the air felt fresh and intoxicating. Seeing no others on deck, Meredith shook off the hood of her cloak, and let the wind ruffle her hair as she looked east toward the rising sun. Lining both sides of the river were great oaks, and the first tentative rays of light shimmered over the drops of moisture on their leaves. The sky itself was awash in pale gold, then pink, and she exclaimed with awe as a rainbow appeared, its beautiful muted colors reaching down to tease the wide river. It was almost as lovely as the one she had captured on canvas months before, the one she had sent North for sale.

The rainbow of promise. She swallowed, the familiar lump catching in her throat. How meaningful those words had become to her. She had first heard them years ago in Cincinnati when she had visited Sally Grimes, her best friend at the convent school. Meredith had just finished school and her brother had been eager enough to get rid of her. He would not have been so pleased, she thought with some amusement, if he knew that Sally's grandparents were secret abolitionists, and she was visiting the very foundation of the Underground Railroad.

In Ohio, Meredith had attended a lecture by a former slave and read many narratives of fugitive escapes. Most moving of all was one by Frederick Douglass, who equated freedom to the "rainbow of promise."

Suddenly, her life had a purpose. Consumed by memories of Lissa and the need to do something, Meredith became more and more involved, particularly when she reached twenty-one and found she had money of her own. She was not a conductor on the Railroad; she did not shelter or shepherd escaping slaves on the way north, but she visited plantations, her painting giving her the excuse to wander about and talk freely with slaves. When she discovered those with the desire and will to escape, she gave them money, a compass, and names of stations along the Railroad. Some lines went overland, some by river, and the fugitives were passed from one conductor to another as they went north, mostly through Kentucky, Indiana, Ohio, and across Lake Erie to Canada. Meredith knew the names of some of the stations, but few of the conductors. The entire network was safer that way.

The rainbow was slowly fading, and Meredith noted the increased activity on deck. She replaced the hood over her hair and reluctantly walked back to her cabin—and back into her stifling role.

Quinn played poker until six in the morning. The Carroll brothers left hours earlier after losing nearly everything they had. Only the Tennessee horseman and another professional gambler had remained at the table.

Quinn was a superb poker player, partially because he had complete control over his facial expression. He knew just how to make it work for him. When he was bluffing, he would allow the smallest fraction of a smile, and those who had not played with him before would toss in all but the best hands. And he knew human nature. He could detect weaknesses within seconds of making an acquaintance.

He had, on several occasions, been accused of cheating. That had not dismayed him; he had simply ordered the accusers off the boat. He always refused to fight, which, along with his refusal to race the *Lucky Lady*, gave him somewhat a reputation of a coward. Although it galled his sense of honor and pride, it nonetheless reinforced his image as a man without principles or values, an image invaluable in his work. But he never cheated. He did not need to. He was a skilled player, and he generally knew when luck was running with him and when lady luck had abandoned him.

Presently, she had left him in the small hours of the morning . . . after the Carrolls had left. The Tennesseean was a very happy man.

Quinn shrugged off the loss. He won much more often than not, and the losers would be horrified to discover where a great percentage of the money went. He smiled grimly at the thought. God, but he was tired. He paused, enjoying the cool air of the morning before retiring to his cabin on the upper deck. He had just checked with Jamison, the pilot, and all was well. Jamison, a dour Scotsman, practically ran the boat and that suited them both. The Scotsman needed, and wanted, little interference from the owner who called himself captain.

Quinn paused at the mahogany railing of the upper deck and looked down at the one below. His eyes finally rested on the solitary figure of a woman. She was silhouetted against a golden sunrise, her hair, the color of spun gold, spilling in tangled curls down her back. Her head was tipped up toward a rainbow, her cheek flushed rosy by the wind.

She was wearing a cloak, which hid her figure, but it couldn't hide the grace or pride with which she moved. He saw her head turning toward his direction and instinctively he ducked back, not wanting to be seen. When he looked again, the hair was covered with a hood, and she was hurrying away.

He stood there stunned. She had looked like a goddess standing motionless at the railing. He couldn't remember when he had been so affected by the sight of a woman. Especially since he harbored a profound distrust for most of the species; one, after all, had caused him to spend eight years in chains. A woman, combined with his own stupidity and arrogance.

In prison his arrogance had been painfully crushed. And he hoped he had learned to avoid stupidity. He was wary of women on any terms but his own.

His thoughts returned to the woman below. He had only

glimpsed her profile, and for a moment he wondered who she was. His mind skipped over the passenger list, but there were only a few women on it, none of them attractive young women. The only unattached one had been the disappointing Miss Seaton.

The Seaton woman! Damn it, how could he have been so unobservant? *She* had blond hair—although he didn't remember it being that bright shining gold. Perhaps because it had been dressed in that ridiculous mound of baby curls. Nor had her complexion looked so fresh and glowing, but powder could easily conceal. And that damned dress. It would hide the most graceful of figures.

But why? Why would a woman deliberately make herself plain? And why would a woman who appeared so shallow be up at dawn to appreciate a sunrise?

It didn't make sense, and Quinn Devereux distrusted things that didn't make sense. Particularly when lives were involved, not the least of which was his.

Cursing fluently, he made his way to his cabin. For the next few days he would make Miss Meredith Seaton his prime piece of business.

Wherever Meredith went, she knew Captain Devereux was not far behind.

Thank the good Lord, in three days she would be home. For the first time, home seemed a refuge—if only from the captain's prying eyes, his sardonic tongue, and that damnable twisted smile.

She thought she had discouraged, if not disgusted, him that first night. But at noon the next day, she and her aunt received another invitation for dinner. She politely refused, saying they were both tired and intended to dine in the cabin.

The next morning he greeted them as they went into the saloon for the morning meal and asked if they would join him. There was no polite way to refuse.

Aunt Opal, much to Meredith's surprise, fell quickly

under a charm that was in full attack. Clearly, her aunt had forgotten the first night's insult, and blossomed under Captain Devereux's smooth questions and admiring eyes.

Damn the man. What did he want?

He virtually ignored her. And she was surprised to discover that that was a mammoth irritation. Why in heaven's name should she care?

She didn't.

She did.

She wished he would disappear.

And then he turned those dark blue shaded eyes on her and she felt as if she had been invited into some private maze where, if entered, she would be lost forever.

It was ridiculous. She abruptly excused herself from the meal, pleading a return of a headache.

He raised a rakish eyebrow, clearly indicating he didn't quite believe her, and that he understood the turmoil that had made her stomach resemble a whirling dervish.

But he stood and bowed, a little too exaggerated a bow for Meredith's taste. "Perhaps not enough sleep, Miss Seaton?" he asked solicitously. Meredith wanted to smack the smirk from his face while a shiver of fear ran up her backbone.

Could he possibly have seen her the other morning? But no, she reassured herself. She had been very careful, and she had seen no one. He just enjoyed displaying his bad manners, like a cat tormenting a mouse. Gambler, rogue, womanizer. She was just unfortunate enough to be the only eligible woman on board.

Meredith fastened a pout on her face. "It's . . . perhaps the company. There's just no one of . . . quality. Oh, excuse me, Captain, other than yourself of course," she added as she received a reproving look from her aunt. She left little doubt, however, that she included Quinn in that deplorable void of civilization.

"My apologies," he replied neatly. "I'll see if we can't remedy that complaint at our next stop and attract a bit more . . . what is it you require? Quality?"

"That would be most accommodatin'," she simpered, "and refreshin'."

He grinned. "I most definitely like to keep my passengers . . . refreshed, Miss Seaton. I hope you'll feel better soon." With that, he sat back down, and Meredith, hoping that he'd understood her subtle insult, fled before she said anything else unwise. She just didn't understand why she reacted so strongly to him, or why he prompted her to say things that were definitely taunting.

That night, Meredith stayed in the cabin, again pleading illness as she sent Daphne on deck to get some air. She took her sketchpad and drew the Carroll brothers and then, strangely compelled, she found herself sketching Quinlan Devereux. She drew two portraits. One was Quinn at twenty-one, and that she had to do by memory. As a handsome young face, with bright eyes and a warm smile, emerged on her paper, she wondered how much she had idealized him. Then she sketched the man she had seen last night, the hard lines around his eyes and mouth, the cynical smile and wariness in his eyes. Why, dear God, was she so obsessed? With an unfamiliar curse, she reached to crumple the paper with her hand. But something stopped her. Instead she hid it, with the pictures of the Carroll brothers, in the bottom of her trunk. Still, her thoughts ran maverick. Although he'd become everything she despised, those childhood images still intruded, and she couldn't quite equate the old and new Devereux. She kept reminding herself of his careless cruel words concerning his slave. She had even seen his cruelty for herself. As cargo was being loaded at one stop, the slave was helping lift some crates, and he was shirtless. She saw the deep whip marks on his back and again noticed the limp. From Captain Devereux's careless words at dinner she'd gathered he had been responsible.

But even if the captain didn't have a list of sins long enough to be the devil himself, Meredith told herself she wouldn't be interested. She had little use for the male species. She had seen her father and brother take mistresses—wenches, they called them—with no regard for feelings or consequences. None of the other "gentlemen" she had met appeared to have any finer scruples. She had been courted, and asked for her hand in marriage, but those proposals, she suspected, were intended for her fortune more than her charms.

She planned never to marry and, thanks to her grandfather, she would never have the need. No one would control her life, or her thoughts or her deeds, as her brother controlled his wife's. She was responsible only to herself, and that was the way it would remain.

So why did Devereux get under her skin?

Chapter 3

DAPHNE HESITANTLY went to the open deck, finding an inconspicuous place where she could hide in the shadows. It was evening, and a warm breeze ruffled the water. She looked ahead at the long ribbon of river that stretched out as far as her eyes could see. It was so free!

The knot that had originally formed inside her when her old master died tightened. Ever since she had been sold away from the only home she had ever known, she had been frightened. Not just frightened, terrified. She had suddenly realized how completely helpless she was.

Her childhood had been a lucky one, and she knew it now. Although Daphne didn't know anything about her parents, she'd been raised with the other slave children by a woman everyone called Granny. When she was small she had carried water to field hands; later she was trained as maid to one of the two daughters in the house.

Despite the heat, Daphne shivered now in the open air. She didn't know what she would face at the new plantation, although her mistress seemed kind enough. But what about the master there? She knew she didn't have any choices. She had been taught from the time she was a baby to accept her lot in life, to obey. She was taught she had no rights, no freedom. She was born only to serve others and, knowing nothing else, she accepted these teachings. She had willingly served her selfish young mistress for nine years, grateful she did not work in the fields and that the master of the house was a religious man who treated his slaves fairly if sternly. Runaways, slackers, troublemakers were sold, not physically punished, but the threat of sale alone kept most of his people hardworking and docile. There were worse masters, and they all knew it.

So if not content, Daphne considered herself lucky until weeks ago when the master died, and his family discovered they were near bankruptcy. The plantation was sold to a neighbor who planned to combine the fields. He had no need for additional house servants, and they were all sold.

She would never forget when the slave trader came for them. The women were loaded in two wagons, and the men, many of whom had been on the plantation all their lives, were ironed and chained to a long cable attached to the wagon. At night, the women too were chained, and Daphne could still feel the pinch of cold metal . . . and the overwhelming sickening fear.

"You hidin'?"

The voice, as deep as the rumble of thunder, made her jump and she felt a huge but oddly protective hand on her arm.

She looked up slowly, cautiously. It was the man who had delivered the invitations to her mistress on those several occasions. She kept looking up until her neck almost hurt. He was so tall. And the chest, covered by a straining cotton shirt, was so wide she could barely see beyond it.

He was looking at her with concern, and her heart nearly stilled at the gentle expression in his face.

"No . . . I . . ." Daphne stopped, not knowing what to say. Because of his size he would have been terrifying, but the teasing curve of his mouth and the softness in his eyes conveyed nothing beyond kindness.

"Don't be scared," he said now as if reading her mind. "I mean no harm."

"I know," she answered, surprising herself with the ease of her reply. She had never been comfortable with men. The male house servants had been much older than she, and already mated, and she had never been attracted to any of the field hands, had never wanted to be. It was not snobbery, but reluctance to give birth to new slaves. But she was around seventeen or so, and the master had been pushing her to take a mate for that very purpose. She had known, when she was taken to New Orleans for sale, she could probably escape it no longer. Then Miss Meredith appeared, almost like an angel. But when they arrived at Miss Meredith's home . . . ? The thought settled in her stomach like a stone.

"Where's Miz Seaton?"

"Restin'," she said, then added defensively, "She gave me permission to come up here."

He nodded, turning away from her to look at the river. It never ceased to fascinate him, this road to freedom. Although he had not needed to take it, he continued to help others along its way.

Cam slid a sideways look at the girl. She was so small, so frightened, and so pretty. When the captain had asked him to befriend the girl, he knew it would be no hardship. She had drawn his eyes and sympathy from the moment he had seen her. Perhaps the captain and he could purchase her. But right now the captain had asked him to find out as much as possible about Meredith Seaton, although he didn't exactly understand why the captain had requested him to do so. There seemed little unusual about her, and she certainly wasn't the captain's customary taste.

But if the captain asked him to fly, he would damn well do it, one way or another.

"My name's Cam," he said, keeping his voice soft. "What's yours?"

"Daphne," she whispered, her heart beating rapidly.

"Daphne," he repeated, liking the sound of the name. He felt tenderness seep into him and creep into places it had never been before. He had lived with hate for so long, it had taken most of the last three years to even realize there could be anything else.

"How long you been with Miz Seaton?"

"Just a few days," she answered in the same low voice.

He looked at her quizzically, his gaze so intense she felt she had no choice but to continue.

"She . . . bought me in New Orleans." Daphne had trouble with the word. When she had lived at the Dunham plantation, she had never actually thought of being bought and sold. She had just always belonged there. The last weeks—the chains, the dirty slave jail, the prospect of auction—had all brought the horror of her position to her.

Cam saw the hopelessness in her eyes, and his hand reached out to her. God, he knew that feeling. Only he had fought it while she apparently did not. He had come close to dying for that rebellion.

"Is she . . . good to you?" It was a difficult question to ask, but Quinn needed to know. And he, Cam, needed to know.

"She seems kind enough," Daphne said. Her mistress still puzzled her in many ways, and it made her wary.

"Where you goin'?"

"A plantation near Vicksburg. That's all I know." Daphne once more felt the fear of the unknown, and tears sprung to her eyes. She turned away, not wanting . . . Cam . . . to see them. She had seen his back. She knew he had gone through much more than she, and she felt terribly weak and cowardly for crying.

She felt a gentle touch, and she lurched away, afraid of it.

Cam slowly withdrew his hand and stood there, a silent still giant.

Daphne backed up even farther into the shadows. "I have to go," she said, her face tensing.

"Daphne," he said with a voice that once more sounded like distant thunder, muted but ominous in her suspicious ears.

"I have to go," she repeated and ducked under an arm that pinned her to a wall. She sped away as if all the ghosts in the world were after her.

"She's only been with Miss Seaton a few days," Cam reported to Quinn, who lounged in a seat across from him, his boots comfortably angled on another chair.

"She didn't say anything?"

"Only that she was 'kind enough.'" Cam snorted. "She's obviously too terrified to say much of anything."

"Of Miss Seaton?"

"No," Cam said slowly. "I don't think so. Just of everything that's happened to her."

Cam's dark eyes held a pain Quinn hadn't seen in a long time. He reached out a hand and grasped Cam's arm, and his lips firmed in silent sympathy.

"I have some money," Cam said slowly. "Perhaps you can buy her, Capt'n."

"Quinn, damn it. When we're alone, it's Quinn."

Cam shook his head slowly. "Then I might make a mistake some other time."

"You?" The word was said in disbelief.

Cam shrugged and smiled. "You will always be the capt'n to me."

"Don't ever forget it," Quinn said, a slight smile belying the meanness of the words.

"The girl?"

"I'll see what I can do."

"I don't care what it costs. If it's more than I got, I'll pay you back."

"Don't tell me you've fallen in love?"

"No . . . no, I . . . she's just so damned frightened of everything."

Quinn's voice softened. "I'll talk to Miss Seaton." His lips curved into a grin. "She must be very pretty."

Cam's body went rigid. For a moment he wondered if he would ever accustom himself to Quinn's teasing remarks. In his past experience, white men's interest in black women had always meant violation. But this was the captain, the man who had given him his life back.

"Yes," he said slowly. "She is."

Quinn watched Cam's eyes and knew what he was thinking. He felt a momentary melancholy that even after three years Cam was unable to trust him completely. But then Cam had had a lifetime to build mistrust and suspicion. He reached out his hand and put it on Cam's shoulder. "Well, by God, we'll get her."

"What if she refuses to sell?"

Quinn knew he meant Meredith Seaton. But why would she turn down a good offer for a slave? "She won't," he said, confidently enough. He had thought about her during the day and reached the conclusion that she was nothing more than she seemed. If it had been she that morning on deck, then the mist and the rainbow and his own fatigue had made her appear to be something she was not. He would talk to her this evening and offer a price for Daphne she couldn't refuse.

Tired of her room, Meredith ventured out on deck, sure that Devereux would probably be abed. Did the dratted man never sleep? It seemed whenever she appeared, he was there: breakfast, dinner, supper. Each time, his eyes seemed to bore into her, seeking secrets without giving any away himself. His eyes never changed, except to narrow every once in a while. His mouth changed often, but always in some maddening way: to look amused, mocking, or derisive.

She often thought of the sketches she'd made of him, of the warmth on the younger face, of none on the older one. Could a child be so deluded? She wanted to find out, to perhaps talk to him again, but there was something fearful inside her. He did things to her that no one else had ever done. He made her weak and jellylike inside, when she was usually nothing of the kind. She had never been cowardly before. She told herself it was merely caution, good judgment. He had a way of making her react in ways she knew she shouldn't, in ways completely alien to the Meredith she had tried so hard to create.

But she would be damned before she allowed him to force her to hide. She wouldn't hide from anyone.

The day was lovely, the sky an intense blue, the green of trees and grass the deep vivid green that comes only in late summer. The water was silver, not muddy, and the paddlewheels of the steamboat made soft music.

"Peaceful, isn't it?"

The voice, *his* voice, bit into her consciousness, and any peace she had felt turned suddenly into violent confusion.

"It was," she retorted, turning slowly, almost against her will, toward him.

He leaned nonchalantly against the railing, his lean body dressed in the same impeccably tailored black she was quickly learning was a trademark with him. Or an affectation, like the gloves he always seemed to wear. Or conceit. He must know how damnably handsome he was in that color, how it made his eyes so startlingly blue, and his hair so impossibly dark. The white of his shirtfront, on the other hand, contrasted with the deep bronze of his face. He looked amused at her sharp answer, and the blatant invitation to leave.

"Come now, Miss Seaton, surely appreciation shared increases the pleasure."

"Of some ol' trees?" she inquired disdainfully.

"I remember," he said slowly, "one old tree you once appreciated."

Meredith's stomach twisted painfully, and her hand clutched the railing. So he did remember. Why was he mentioning it now? Why not before? Some kind of trap? Some secret amusement of his own?

She allowed her eyes to flutter. "Why, Captain, I don't know whatever you mean."

"We met once, long ago, when you were a child. A delightful child, if I remember."

"I don't remember," she said. "I had a fall." Her lips said the lie easily enough. She hoped her eyes did. "Were you delightful, too, Captain?"

He grinned, but as usual it went no further than his mouth. His eyes were even wary. She wondered why. "I hope so. I try hard."

She couldn't prevent a raised eyebrow of her own, and she heard him chuckle. Be careful, Meredith, she told herself. That was a stupid thing to say. It's stupid to encourage him in any way. He's not like the others. She had the feeling he caught every nuance, and knew it for what it was. *Be very, very careful.* He's Brett's brother. He's a slave owner. He consorts with slave hunters. But his laugh was such an attractive sound, deep and resonant. Just as she remembered.

But he's changed, she told herself.

She stiffened her back, hoping it would also stiffen her resolve against his insidious charm. "Perhaps you should try harder, Captain," she said caustically despite her attempt to make her tone light, bantering, even flirtatious.

"You really think I should?" he said, and she knew he was laughing at her, even while his eyes probed hers.

"Most assuredly," she said, anger at his taunting and at herself once more driving her beyond caution. She wanted to wipe that smile from his face. "A gambler's charm . . . well, it's as worthless as fool's gold."

"A profound statement, Miss Meredith," he replied. "I'll take it to heart."

If you have one, she wanted to say, but she had gone as far as she should. Much farther, in fact. The last thing she'd intended was for him to deem her biting comment profound, even if he had done so mockingly. And there was still a glint of interest in his eyes.

She was saved by the timely arrival of Opal, who fluttered her eyelashes shamelessly at the captain. Meredith quickly excused herself.

"Weighty matters, Miss Meredith?" Quinn asked courteously.

Meredith, steeling herself against yet another barb she longed to throw at him, laughed lightly. "Of course, Captain. I must choose my dress for our arrival tomorrow, and Daphne's going to help me with a new hairstyle."

Daphne! Damn, Quinn thought. This was the perfect opportunity to mention the girl, but Meredith was already disappearing through the doorway, leaving him with Opal.

He turned his most charming smile on her. "I hope you and your niece will join me for dinner tonight."

"I'd be delighted," Opal said. "I'll ask Meredith."

He bowed graciously. "Eight, then."

Cowardly or not, Meredith was not going to have dinner with the blackguard. She knew foolishness when she indulged in it, and he brought out more than a little in her. He challenged her, and she longed to respond in kind, to meet barb for barb, and mockery for mockery, but she could not afford to do so. He had the damnable ability to slice her protective layers to shreds. If it was only herself involved, she might risk more. But there was Lissa to consider. And the Underground Railroad. And the people she could help.

So she pleaded fatigue and lack of appetite, hating herself for retreating, yet knowing it was the only wise course. She was relieved they would arrive in Vicksburg tomorrow. Relieved and yet regretful too. She wished she knew why she felt a ridiculous sense of loss.

Her aunt decided to accept the invitation, despite her niece's refusal and pointed comment about associating with gamblers. Opal's opinion of Captain Devereux had undergone a great transformation under his not inconsiderable charisma. He came from such a good family, she declared. And he was an absolutely charming man, even if he was a gambler. Many gentlemen, she justified, gambled.

It made Meredith sick. Devereux was an unscrupulous slave owner, and charm did nothing to alter that fact, she kept telling herself.

After Aunt Opal left for dinner, she nibbled at some food she had ordered for the room. She then sent Daphne to see to Opal's clothes since they would be disembarking the next day. But that was only an excuse. She wanted, more than anything, a few moments to go up on deck. Everyone, she knew, would be eating, and she would go to the rear of the steamboat, away from the windows and the gaiety of diners and the rapscallion smile of its captain.

Her sausage curls were still in place, her dress as frightful as the others. She smiled slightly as she thought of how carefully Daphne had implied that she looked frumpy.

"Perhaps," Daphne had said hesitantly, "I could do your hair another way."

Meredith's heart reached out to the girl. Meredith the woman wanted to say yes. Meredith the pretender had to say no.

"I like it as it is," she said testily, but her tone softened at Daphne's crestfallen expression. She wished she could confide in the girl, but Daphne was still too new, too frightened. It would take time—perhaps months—for Daphne to trust her. And she could do nothing until the trust was there.

Meredith put on her cloak over the dress. She didn't need it in this weather, but she felt partially invisible with it on. As she did the other morning, she slipped out the door and headed for the rear of the boat.

Meredith didn't know how long she stood there, watching the churning water, her artist's eyes appreciating the designs it created in the wake. Tomorrow, she would be home. There was some safety there, but little pleasure. Her brother would start nagging her again about marriage, and she and her tight-lipped sister-in-law would exchange insincere pleasantries.

"Your aunt said you were ill! I came to offer my assistance, to see whether my cook could prepare some broth, perhaps."

The voice, which had all the warm allure of soft running honey, immediately made her insides churn as fiercely as the water.

Drat her aunt. She had told Opal to merely say she was tired. "I needed some air," she said guardedly, not turning to face the man.

"I thought you might be avoiding me."

"Ah Captain, such arrogance. Why on earth should I bother doing that?"

"I'll be damned if I know," he said, mischief in his words.

Meredith didn't dare look at him, knowing that deviltry twisted those lips as well as raised one dark brow.

But she couldn't hide for long. Gloved fingers, strong persistent fingers, caught her chin and turned it upward until she was forced to look straight into bottomless indigo eyes.

Meredith twisted away. "You forget yourself, Captain," she said furiously.

"I felt it my duty, my *gentlemanly* duty, to see that you were all right." The emphasis on the word, gentlemanly, rendered her speechless. So he had caught her meaning the other night. She licked her lips nervously. The drawl in his voice was exaggerated, as if he were baiting her. But, dear God, it would lure a wild thing to eat from his hand.

"Consider your duty done then," she finally snapped, trying to prick the spell he was weaving.

"I had another purpose," he said softly.

Meredith turned and looked at him. "And what might that be?"

"I want to purchase your girl."

Nothing he said could have surprised her more. As if she would sell anyone, much less to him. She had seen his own servant's mistreatment. And why would he want someone as pretty as Daphne? There could only be one reason. Distaste, deep and repugnant, swamped her. Distaste and a bitter disappointment that was like a kick to her stomach.

"No," she said flatly.

"I'll pay a good price."

A lump settled in Meredith's throat, one she hated to acknowledge. She had discovered that he had become a rascal, an immoral gambler and scoundrel, but even then she had not expected this. Outrage, however, would not fit the Meredith Seaton he knew.

"Oh la, Captain, Daphne's the only maid who's ever been able to dress my hair correctly." She giggled, touched one of the abominable curls and coquettishly batted her eyelashes. "I just couldn't sell her."

She saw Devereux's eyes run over the mass of sausage curls and wince, and she felt a confusing mixture of satisfaction and regret. As she wondered at the contradiction, he moved closer, and she could smell the rich scent of sandalwood and bay.

She backed up.

Devereux considered her retreat. The last pink glow of the sunset caught the cream of her cheeks. She had not bothered with the layers of paint he had seen her wear at dinner the first night and in subsequent days, and her skin had the luster of pearls. Her eyes, dark brown with golden lights, now looked speculative, even angry, instead of vacant. He regarded her hair, and wondered how the mess could be the same flowing mane he had glimpsed at dawn several days earlier.

Without thinking, he reached out for a tightly wound curl and extracted one of the pins, letting a long silky strand of gold fall around her face.

"She does you a severe injustice," he said slowly. "You should definitely sell."

Devereux's gloved hand touched her cheek and even through the fine leather, Meredith felt the spot burn as if branded. She couldn't move, mesmerized by his voice, by his closeness, by his touch.

By his wickedness.

Meredith summoned every bit of control she had learned over the past years, straightening up, forcing her eyes from his. She slapped his cheek with a force made strong by her confusion. The sharp crack seemed to echo in the evening silence.

She had expected Devereux to step back, but he didn't, nor did he acknowledge the blow. Instead, his face came closer to hers and his arms pinned her to the wall. She felt like a trapped rabbit as his lips moved down, toward her own with dreadful purpose.

Meredith tried desperately to squirm away, but he had trapped her, his body tense against hers, and her own was responding in some strange unfamiliar way.

"No," she cried.

"Yes," he said simply, implacably, his eyes riveting yet completely unfathomable. His mouth touched her lips in a slow exploring way, and Meredith felt flickers of fire flame deep inside as she sought to remain stiff and cold.

His lips probed and teased and demanded while one hand held her in place and the other tumbled her hair, releasing it from the pins that held it in tormented fashion.

There was nothing tender about his kiss. It was searching and savage and demanding, and nothing in Meredith's life had ever prepared her for it, or for the feelings his touch aroused.

The kiss deepened and his lips gentled only slightly as they worked to open her mouth. And then his tongue slipped in, intrusive, questing, arousing. Without will, Meredith responded in the most primitive and instinctive way, her own tongue seeking to inflict as much painful exquisite sensation as he did, even though she didn't understand her own reactions. Something new and exciting and terrifying had taken over her body, and it was not the control that Meredith had honed to a fine art.

His mouth finally withdrew and he leaned back, his eyes almost black in the now deep dusk of evening. There was a questioning look on his face, for he had seen the flashes of fire in eyes usually void of any kind of passion, and there had been unexpected responses in her body. *Who are you?* he wanted to ask, but except for the tumbling hair there seemed nothing but a wood figure in front of him.

His eyes are what the devil's must be like, Meredith thought. So dark they were almost midnight black. And haunted in some strange way. She had not seen that before, but it was there now, lurking behind the curtain. She felt herself trembling and hated the weakness in her that caused it. He was her enemy. She had known it from the first moment she had seen him again. And yet something inside her was terribly drawn to him. What terrible flaw in her made her this way?

"How dare you?" she finally managed in a low furious voice, outraged at him for making her feel this way, enraged at herself for being so vulnerable to him.

Devereux bowed low, mockery in every movement, in the amusement in his face. "My pardon, Miss Seaton. Your charms seem to have overwhelmed me." His hand once more caressed a curl, bringing it to his lips and allowing them to caress it.

Even as anger foamed inside her at his obvious derision, another part, a detached analytical part, wondered why he always wore gloves. An affectation? His eyes narrowed slightly as he saw her staring at the glove. She caught his surprise, and she knew he had recognized the speculation and didn't like it.

But he merely smiled, a smile that touched nothing but his lips. "You didn't answer, my dear Miss Seaton. Do I have your pardon?"

Meredith thought about a number of things she could say, but withheld each one of them. She condemned herself bitterly because she had, at the end of the kiss, participated as much as he. She wished she didn't have so strong a thread of honesty running through her. It often warred with the other things she felt she must do.

She drew herself up indignantly. "You took advantage," she accused.

"So I did," he said lazily, his hand still playing with the curl. "I wanted to see your hair down. I did not expect it to be quite as . . . irresistible. Now I *know* you should find a new maid."

The words struck her to the core. So the kiss had been only a ploy to obtain Daphne. She had never felt such an utter fool. A susceptible idiot falling for practiced and superficial charm. Damn him. Double damn him.

"Daphne is not for sale," she said. "Not for any price *you* can pay." It was not a wise statement for it implied far more than she had intended, and Meredith knew it. There was a passion in the words that was uncharacteristic of shallow Meredith. But she felt such a rage inside that she could not control herself. He had not wanted her. He had merely been using her to get Daphne.

Quinn saw the flash of fury and didn't understand quite what had caused it. He knew, however, he had made an error, a bad one. He had mixed business with pleasure when he knew the two were incompatible. And he realized he had failed Cam.

He tried to recoup his losses and shrugged. "It's really of no matter. May I accompany you back to your cabin?"

Meredith looked at him in disbelief. "You, sir," she said, "are as wanted as the devil at a camp meeting."

Quinn grinned. "But it might be as interestin', would it not?"

His quick retort stunned her. And unaccountably she wanted to smile back. His lips were full of self-mockery now and nigh on to irresistible. Join me in laughing at myself, they invited her. Drat it, but she really wanted to smile at his impudence. But he was also a slave owner, and, apparently, a merciless one. Her amusement quickly fled.

"You, sir," she said in her most huffy manner, "are no gentleman."

"No," he admitted agreeably. "And you, Miss Seaton, what exactly are you?"

Meredith drew herself up, even as she felt a tremor of fear.

"A lady," she said frostily, forcing her lips into a pout. "And I will certainly report your despicable behavior to your brother."

"Do that." He chuckled. "I'm afraid it won't come as a surprise at all. I'm my brother's cross to bear."

"He has my condolences," she retorted quickly, knowing once more she was saying too much.

Quinn's eyebrows raised, and his mouth twitched. "I'm sure he will appreciate them."

"And be so kind as to shower your distasteful attentions on someone else."

"Your wish is my most honored command, Miss Seaton," he said in the most accommodating voice. "I bid you a good rest."

Meredith spun around before she was tempted to deliver another retort and stalked through the door to the cabins.

Quinn lounged against the railing, watching the door bang behind her. He tipped his head upward considering the sky above. He had not missed that unexpected gleam of amusement in her eyes. Damn but she was a puzzle.

Slowly he headed back toward the dining room. His mind was still on Miss Seaton, on the way her hair had tumbled gloriously down her back, at the quick flash of humor in her eyes, at the momentary passion he felt in her arms.

He shook his head at his own foolishness. Why was he

pricked by this notion that there was so much more to Meredith Seaton than anyone knew? Had a part of her just awakened, or was she just trying to hide something? Or was it simply his imagination? He hated to think it might be the fact that he had been alone too damned long and that any woman would have some appeal to him.

Damn it all to perdition.

Chapter 4

SWEET, SMOOTH KISSES.

Hungry, aching ones.

Quinn had intended the first and delivered the second instead.

He couldn't stop thinking about it, either, as he entered the dining room.

He disliked failure of any kind, most of all one of his own making, and he knew his actions had done nothing to help secure Daphne's freedom. And he didn't like the tenseness in his body, not to mention one specific part of his anatomy. How could such a spoiled woman do this to him? And that was exactly what she was—spoiled and empty-headed.

He rejoined the company he had left just thirty minutes earlier, and barely participated in the conversation for the remainder of the meal. His thoughts were in another direction, in another part of the steamboat.

The *Lucky Lady* would be docking at Vicksburg tomorrow, and the Seaton woman and her slave would leave. He needed to get his mind back on business because the *Lucky Lady* would be picking up additional cargo, including perhaps a new shipment for the Underground Railroad. He never knew in advance.

The secret room built into the cargo deck was already nearly full, and Quinn knew it must be miserable for the occupants. The tiny compartment had not been built for comfort but for secrecy and safety. It was, by necessity, long and very narrow so no one could detect a false wall. When it had first been constructed, Quinn had tried it himself for several days to see whether it was livable. It was, but only barely. The heat and darkness were suffocating.

There could be no candles, no lamp of any kind, and the only sanitation facility was buckets. But Quinn had found in the past several years that escaping slaves would—could— abide any discomfort as long as there was hope.

He himself knew. God almighty, but he even knew what human beings could endure without that hope.

"Captain . . . ?"

He shook the mist from his mind as he turned toward the speaker, the Tennesseean.

"Is there a game tonight?"

Quinn grinned. "There's always a game, particularly when I've lost to someone," he said.

The man smiled back. "You won enough from the others to more than compensate."

"Ah, but you present a challenge."

"I'll try to see I continue to do so."

"At ten tonight then," Quinn said. "I have some business to attend to before then."

The man nodded. "Ten."

With relief Quinn stood, bowing elegantly to Opal and another middle-aged lady traveling with her husband. "Thank you, ladies, for gracing our table tonight," he said to both, setting their hearts fluttering. He fastened all his attention on

Opal. "I'm sorry your niece hasn't been feeling well."

"It is so unlike her," Opal said. "She's usually flitting all around. She likes to paint, you know."

Quinn's attention was suddenly riveted on her. "No, I didn't know," he said.

Opal looked sheepish. She didn't want to mislead him, but neither did she want to say anything unkind about Meredith. "She's just an amateur, of course. Never has sold anything. Just likes to dabble at it."

"Have you been traveling with her long?"

Pleased at the change of subject, Opal gushed on. "Oh yes, years I suppose. Ever since she came home from convent school."

"Convent school?"

"Saint Mary's in New Orleans," Opal continued guilelessly. "Her brother—my niece's husband—keeps hoping she'll get married, but she's turned down all the proposals. She likes to visit though."

"She does a lot of traveling?"

"Oh yes. But there's a fine bachelor gentleman in our county, and her brother and I suspect she will marry him soon."

"I imagine you'll miss chaperoning her, then? You must be close, traveling so much together."

Opal fluttered the fan she was holding. "Well . . . yes. She can be a dear."

He gave her a sympathetic smile. "And difficult at times?"

"She can be a bit . . . headstrong."

"I never would have suspected," he observed dryly.

Opal felt guilty. "She really is a dear girl. It's just that she—" She stopped suddenly. She couldn't believe she was saying these things to a stranger, to a gambler. But he had such a nice way about him. And he was so handsome.

"Of course." Quinn nodded, knowing he had probably milked as much information as he could. So she had had proposals. She would have, of course. She was an heiress in her own right, and many of the young bucks had need of money, either because their plantations were draining them or because they indulged in a way of life in which spending money was more important than making it. It was easier to marry it. Money, he reflected, would be the only reason Miss Seaton would be in demand. But then, unwillingly, he thought of that hair. And those lips.

Disgusted at his own thoughts, he wished Opal a pleasant evening and went in search of Cam.

His friend was waiting in the cabin, anxiety showing on a face that was usually blank.

Quinn shook his head. "I'm sorry," he said softly. "She wouldn't sell."

"Why?"

"Something about the girl being the only one who could dress her hair properly," Quinn replied. "Properly. Hell, that's the best reason in the world to get rid of her."

He went over to a cabinet and took out a bottle of brandy, pouring a drink for each of them. Quinn then sat down, putting his booted legs on a chair and gazing into his glass morosely. It was the one drink he allowed himself before playing cards. During the game he drank colored water.

"Damn," he said, in reply to Cam's painful silence. The man asked for so little, expected so little. "We'll get her," he said slowly. "I promise."

Cam leaned against the wall. "We can't do anything on the *Lucky Lady*."

"No," Quinn answered. "But I know her family. Perhaps it's time I stopped at the Seaton plantation and inquired about the possibility of carrying their cotton. Perhaps by then Miss Seaton will be tired of her. She doesn't seem the type to stick to anything long."

"If she does?"

"We'll get in touch with the Parson. See what he can do."

Cam nodded. The Parson operated a very successful Underground Railroad station near Vicksburg.

"He'll find a way. . . ."

Cam sat down heavily, his eyes bleak despite Quinn's words. He didn't know why he felt so strongly about the girl he had seen so briefly. But something smothering and heavy settled around his heart.

"There's another agent in the area," Quinn continued, trying to ease the anguish he saw in Cam. "But I don't have a name. It's one they keep secret. Everything goes through the Parson. Between them we can get her out."

Cam's face was etched with frustration. "She's so young, and so frightened. If only I could say something . . ."

Quinn sighed. "We can't risk the *Lucky Lady*," he said. "Not for just one person. I don't think anything will happen to her with Miss Seaton."

"Daphne said she seemed 'kind enough.'" There was a hesitancy, a question, in his voice that sought reassurance. It seemed strange in this big man who was so terrifying in his anger and so gentle in his kindness. It was a miracle, Quinn thought, that the kindness had survived.

He had first seen Cam on the auction block. He was heavily chained, which was unusual. Most traders removed chains, knowing their presence indicated an unruly and troublesome slave. But perhaps the trader knew it would be obvious anyway because Cam's back was crisscrossed with both old and new scars.

Quinn had been back in New Orleans only four months when he had stopped by the slave auction. He would never know what drew him there for he usually avoided them. His family had several household slaves who, it seemed, had been with the Devereuxs forever, and they had always been more like family than servants.

But he had been frustrated and dissatisfied for reasons he didn't understand, and he had decided to visit his favorite tavern. It was a trip he took with increasing frequency, much to Brett's dismay. He had to walk past the slave market to get there. It was then he saw Cam's defiant stance, and it brought back all the deep agony of his own past. He looked into eyes that glittered with hate and a kind of hopelessness that struck Quinn to the core.

Much to his surprise, he found himself joining in the bidding, which climbed to unexpectedly high levels until there were only two bidders left. Quinn knew his opponent, knew his reputation for cruelty and working his slaves to death. He kept upping the bid, until he finally won.

His reward was a look of absolute hatred from his new possession.

Quinn ignored it, ordered the chains removed despite the trader's warning and asked his new slave whether he had a shirt.

"No . . . suh." The "suh" was hesitant enough to border on insolence, and Quinn barely repressed a smile, wondering all the time what in the hell he had done . . . and why.

That was four years ago, just after he had won the *Lucky Lady* in a three-day poker game. He had been restless since he'd returned from Australia, only to find his father and oldest brother had died in a yellow fever epidemic. Although Brett said nothing, Quinn knew they had stayed in New Orleans to await word of him, and guilt and self-hate had eaten at him like poison. They hadn't been the first to die because of him. It seemed everything he touched, every person he loved, suffered because of him.

He was next in line to take over the bank, but he couldn't bear the thought of staying in an office, of being confined in any way. And he felt immensely unworthy. His younger brother had selflessly worked in the bank while his own foolishness had cost his family a fortune. Brett knew and loved the banking business, and was well trained to assume leadership, so Quinn abdicated and went on a four-month binge of drinking and gambling, trying to submerge eight years of perdition. But they wouldn't go away, not during the nights when he would awake moaning, or even the days when the sight of a chain, or whip marks, sent his mind whirling back to Norfolk Island.

For some reason, the gods suddenly seemed to favor him

after so many years of desertion. He simply couldn't lose at gambling. He realized part of it was the fact that he now had the quintessential poker face, the hell-earned ability never to show emotion, but it was something else, too, for his luck went beyond capable playing. He won thousands of dollars and then, in one night, the *Lucky Lady*. But even that didn't satisfy him. Nothing seemed to sate the restlessness and emptiness inside him.

Until he purchased Cam and decided that Cam's liberation might be his own.

It had not been easy. Cam was so full of distrust and bitterness and hate that he had challenged each one of Quinn's overtures. But challenge was exactly what Quinn had needed. He thought about immediately filing manumission papers for Cam, but since the man had no skills and was nearly consumed with hate, Quinn knew that easy option would probably end in disaster. So he set himself the task of making Cam completely self-sufficient. Despite Cam's bitter resentment, Quinn taught him how to read and write and cipher, and together Quinn and his newly acquired property learned the mechanics of steamboats.

Cam learned with astounding quickness, and each bit of knowledge spurred an enormous hunger for knowledge that overcame his distrust of Captain Devereux. His feelings changed gradually from hatred to suspicion to grudging gratitude to a kind of reluctant acceptance. One year later, nearly to the day of his purchase, Quinn presented a speechless Cam with manumission papers.

"Now you can go anywhere, do anything you wish," Quinn said, holding out his hand.

Cam had stared at the papers. Quinn knew Cam had never even considered such a possibility. He also knew, from an occasional comment, that Cam had tried, by himself, to escape several times from previous owners, each time knowing that his odds were infinitesimal without help, and that if he did succeed there would be little awaiting a man who knew nothing but manual labor.

And now this white man was offering him the world. A man he had hated and despised and fought. Quinn had seen wetness on Cam's cheeks, and suspected that for the first time in his life Cam was crying.

Quinn had turned around, realizing how important it was to give him privacy, to respect the pride that he had seen grow day by day.

"I would like to stay with you, Capt'n," the low sonorous emotion-filled voice said, and Quinn turned back to him, grinning.

That had been the beginning. . . .

The first step on the road that had brought them both back from a very dark pit.

Now Cam paced the cabin floor, and Quinn watched him sympathetically, wondering at his friend's unusual impatience. They had both learned caution and patience during the past few years. It was why they were so successful as conductors, why they hadn't been caught as others had. Of those captured, some had been killed outright. Others were serving terms in prison; several had died there. Because Cam was black, he and Quinn had no question as to what fate awaited him. On the other hand, a long prison term was Quinn's likely future if caught, yet he knew he would favor death.

"We'll get her," he said again.

Cam looked sheepish. "I don't know what there is about Daphne . . ."

"You've been alone too long, Cam."

"Maybe," Cam said. "She's a pretty thing."

Quinn looked at Cam speculatively. He himself did not want a deep commitment with a woman. He had been betrayed once, and the result had been disastrous. Maybe Cam was different.

"Aye, she is," Quinn agreed. "And I swear to you we'll have her free within three months."

Cam smiled, a slow movement of lips that still came much too rarely. He nodded. The captain had never disappointed him.

"And our guests below?" Quinn sought to change the subject.

"I checked on them an hour ago. They're doing as well as can be expected. But it's mighty miserable down there."

Quinn also knew that the tiny hidden room was only one of the many discomforts his secret passengers would endure. At Cairo, they would be transported in crates to a river packet that would carry them along the border of Illinois and into Ohio. The Railroad went from there up to Canada. It was a long dangerous journey, and on this particular route they could not take young children. One sick child, one cry, could destroy the whole network.

Daphne combed out Miss Meredith's hair, once more wondering why her new mistress insisted that such a lovely head of hair be hidden by ridiculous curls and pins. But she was not brave enough to say anything. White people were different, she had discovered, and often did strange things. She had learned long ago not to question, not even to think about the orders she'd been given. Just obey them. If Miss Meredith wanted her head to look like a plateful of sausages, then she would do her best to accommodate. She would do anything to keep from being sold again. Every time she thought of the auction block, she went faint with fear.

She did summon the courage to ask Miss Meredith if she could go up on deck if she was no longer needed. It was a monumental act of bravery, but they would be leaving the boat tomorrow, and she did so want to see that huge gentle man again.

"Of course," Miss Meredith said with a quick smile.

"Thank you, miss," Daphne said and darted out the door before her mistress changed her mind.

Once outside, she breathed the fresh air gratefully. She looked up, noticing that the sky was a dark rich blue. Stars were shining brightly, and a full moon hung high in the sky.

She wondered where the man named Cam was.

She remembered the scars on his back, and she hated the man who put them there, the man who owned this boat. She had seen Cam work harder than anyone else, his muscles straining the cheap cotton clothes, his eyes dark and secretive. Until he had talked to her. And then they had been kind.

Daphne knew it was unwise for her to think of Cam. She had no say in matters of love. She was an owned thing. Tears crept down her cheeks and she closed her eyes, willing her crying to stop.

A hand, callused in its strength, tender in its touch, wiped away the drops, and Daphne opened her eyes. *He* was there.

She hadn't known until this minute how much she wanted him to be there, how afraid she was that he would be.

"I mus' go," she whispered, taking a step back.

"Not yet," he said, taking her hand. He led her to the back of the boat where stacks of cotton were piled, and he moved forcibly through them until he found a hidden, protected spot.

He guided her down, then sat, his large form awkwardly folding itself. But he didn't let go of her hand.

His other hand traced a pattern on her cheek. "You're very pretty," he said finally.

She stiffened, and Cam could feel her withdraw to someplace deep inside herself.

"It's all right," he soothed. "I won't hurt you."

She squeezed up into a tight tense ball. She was afraid of him, of the way he made her feel, of the fact that after tomorrow she would never see him again.

Daphne felt his hands on her and she was afraid they

would start groping, as others had, but they did not. Instead, they were comforting. She felt a sudden aching in the deepest part of her soul. She could stand anything, she thought, except to taste tenderness that would too soon be gone.

In a quick birdlike movement, she jumped to her feet but Cam, despite his size, was just as quick.

"Daphne?" he asked.

"Won't your master want you?" she parried.

There was a short silence. "He's in the saloon."

Soft brown hurting eyes went to him. "Don't you hate him?"

Cam's hand went to her shoulder. "I hate anyone who keeps slaves," he said tensely.

"Did he do . . . that . . . to your back?"

Cam's features went hard, his eyes like burning coals. There was no trace of gentleness in him now. He didn't say anything, but his expression and the tense silence seemed to answer Daphne in the affirmative.

"I hate him too," she said fiercely. "I hate 'em all."

Cam winced. He hated to mislead her about the captain, but it was part of their protection. When the whole business started, he and the captain had decided that Cam would continue to play Quinn's slave. The stripes on his back were only added proof of Quinn's firm commitment to slavery.

"I know," he finally said softly.

Daphne looked around carefully before she put her thought into words. "Have you ever . . . thought about running away?"

Cam laughed, and he didn't have to pretend the bitterness in it.

"Twice," he replied. "The first time brought me a whippin'. The second time, they cut a tendon in my ankle, so I couldn't run again."

"Him!" Daphne exclaimed with horror, again referring to the steamboat captain.

Cam shrugged. He disliked seeing the hatred in her eyes for the only friend he had ever had, but there was no help for it now. Later, she would know. Later when it was safe.

"Will you . . . try again?"

Again, Cam hesitated. How much to say? He wanted to prepare her for the day the captain could make arrangements. At the same time, he didn't want her to do anything on her own. It was too damned dangerous.

"Not without help," he said finally.

"Is there . . . help?"

"I hear talk of it."

Her eyes grew large. "How do you find them?"

"Keep your ears open, little one. It's called the Underground Railroad. They say they will help you all the way to Canada."

"White folk?" she asked with disbelief.

"White people and freemen," he said.

"If you know so much, why don't you go?" Daphne said, hesitant to believe.

Cam smiled to himself. She was a bright little thing. "I haven't found the right people yet. But I will," he promised.

"White folk?" she repeated in amazement.

"There are some who don't like slavery," Cam said slowly.

"I don't believe it." Her words were filled with sorrow. "How can you? After what they've done to you?"

"I have to," he replied simply.

Daphne didn't understand how anyone could feel that way. All she felt were defeat and hopelessness. She lowered her eyes, glancing away from the strength of his face, the fire in his eyes.

"You have to have hope," he said in a low voice that carried conviction.

"I don't know how," she whispered.

He bent down and lightly touched his lips to her forehead. So lightly that Daphne was surprised at the waves of emotion that surged out of control within her.

"Trust me," he said.

"I don't know how," Daphne repeated, as she fled once more. She tripped on a rope and started to fall, but suddenly strong arms were around her. For the first time in her life, she felt protected.

But there was no protection outside of his embrace, she thought bleakly. "Let me go," she said desperately, afraid to believe his words, to believe in anything because to do so would be to know bitter disappointment. Better not to hope. Better not to feel. "Let me go," she said again, twisting away from him and running into Miss Meredith.

Meredith had come up for some air when she saw Daphne run from behind some bales as if the very devil were after her. Captain Devereux? But then she saw a large black man come after her. It was Devereux's man.

"Leave her alone!" she shouted in anger.

Cam stopped abruptly, carefully reestablishing his pose of servitude. "Yes ma'am."

Meredith looked at Daphne. "Did he hurt you?"

Stunned, Daphne could only shake her head. Had her mistress heard any of the conversation?

"Are you sure? You don't have to be afraid."

"No ma'am," Daphne said. "I just . . . I just saw a rat, and it scared me. He just kept me from falling, that's all."

Meredith saw the girl's shoulders shaking, and she looked sharply at the large servant. He obviously took after his master, thinking he could take with masculine strength what he couldn't win with persuasion.

The man lowered his eyes, but Meredith didn't fail to see the flare of hatred in them, the spark of rebellion against being docile. She thought about reporting him to the captain, but she neither wanted to see the arrogant rogue again nor did she really want to see this man receive any more punishment. Quinn Devereux obviously had a vicious streak if this man's back were any indication.

"What's your name?" she said sharply.

"Cam."

"I won't say anything," she said, "unless I see you near Daphne again. If I do, I'll see you punished."

"Yes ma'am," he said softly, but Meredith noted his hands balling with suppressed rage.

She stared at him until his eyes fell once more, and then she turned to Daphne, her voice gentling. "Come, Daphne. We both need some sleep."

When they arrived at the cabin, Meredith lit the oil lamp and saw the dried tears on Daphne's face. The girl looked so incredibly forlorn. "He *did* do something," she accused.

"No ma'am," Daphne said.

"Then what?"

Tears that Daphne couldn't stop rolled down her face.

"I will talk to Captain Devereux," Meredith decided out loud, wondering if the words would prompt more information from the girl.

"You mustn't," Daphne cried. "Captain Devereux will . . . he'll . . ."

"He'll do what?"

"Something terrible," Daphne said. "He already had him crippled." Daphne hadn't meant to say it, but the words spilled out, her fear for Cam overcoming her fear of Meredith.

Meredith stood still, horrified. She had heard of such a thing although it had never been done at her plantation. And she *had* noticed his servant's limp. But she never thought a person could actually order such a punishment. She remembered her response to Captain Devereux's kiss and felt sick. Nausea rose up in her, and she had to sit down.

"You won't say anything, will you, Miss Meredith?" Daphne pleaded. "He was just trying to be kind."

"No," Meredith said. She felt dirty, violated, and she knew a swell of hate against the man who could be so cruel. How could she have felt any kind of attraction? Any feeling?

Thank God she would never see him again.

Quinn wasn't playing well. His famed concentration was gone. He looked at the damned cards, but his mind was on soft lips and eyes that flashed golden fire. She *had* responded to that kiss and with a passion he never would have expected. It stirred a want so deep and so painful within him that he could barely breathe.

He was astounded. During his eight years in British prisons and chain gangs, he had gone without the pleasure or comfort of a woman, and since his return he had felt little need for more than quick physical relief, certainly nothing close to what was bedeviling his loins now.

After losing steadily for two hours, he left the table and went to his cabin. He took out a bottle of good scotch whiskey and poured a large amount into a glass. He didn't savor it, as he usually did, but just swallowed, wanting the oblivion it used to bring.

Brown eyes. Blue eyes. Green eyes. Damn, they were all the same. Traitorous and deceptive.

He remembered Morgana's. They had been blue. As blue as the midsummer sky. Her lips had been like fresh berries with the same tangy sweetness.

And she had cost him eight years and three lives. He would never let another woman do that.

Quinn gulped another glass of whiskey, knowing it would take more than this bottle to forget. He threw it against the wall of the cabin, realizing that this would be another night he wouldn't sleep.

The *Lucky Lady* docked at Vicksburg early the next morning. The day was bright and clear and the sky a deep rich shade of blue. There was music in the air; the boat's musicians often played on deck as they reached a major landing. This added a certain gaiety to the occasion.

Quinn stood on the highest point, near the pilot's house, and looked on as the passengers disembarked. Among the first were Opal Frazier, Miss Seaton, and Daphne. He felt Cam's presence before he heard him, and simply nodded to him as they both watched the Seaton party approach a buggy. The luggage was loaded and the ladies were helped aboard.

Daphne's face turned back to the steamboat, her eyes searching until they found Cam. Misery was written all over her face before she looked ahead once more. The buggy was well down the main street before Miss Seaton also turned. Her back arched up and her chin tilted upward. Quinn couldn't see her expression due to a fussy hat that shielded most of her face.

His lips moved into a half smile. "We're not through yet, Meredith Seaton," he murmured. "Not by half."

Chapter 5

BROWN EYES. *Blue eyes. Morgana's had been as blue as the midsummer sky.*

Quinn had been immediately intrigued with Lady Morgana Stafford, and not a little flattered when the lady seemed to prefer his attention to that of the heir and only son of the Earl of Sethwyck. Quinn had been in London two months after touring the continent and was using the last of his funds to rent a townhouse in the most fashionable part of London.

He was in no hurry to go home to America. The bank awaited him in New Orleans, and the bank was duty and responsibility. He was not ready to lock himself in a cubicle and parcel out loans to people who had no need of them. If they had, they would not get them, he thought cynically. Instead loans went to the rich to make them richer and were denied to the poor who needed them to get ahead. He sneered at the hypocrisy of it, but was not ready to take it upon himself to change it. At the moment, his only concern was milking every moment of this freedom, exacting every second of pleasure.

And pleasure lay in the rooms of Lady Morgana.

She was spectacularly beautiful: ash-blond hair flowing to her waist, large clear blue eyes, skin the color of rich ivory, and wide full lips that knew every trick to bedevil a man. He was a most willing pupil.

He had been warned. His friends told him she was private property, that she belonged to young George Dunn, only son of Sethwyck, that she was only using him to make Dunn jealous and force him into a proposal. But Quinn was in love by then, madly, crazily, blindly in love, especially when he experienced the joys of her bed.

Until the night Dunn burst in on them with several of his friends. The young lord had slapped Morgana, and Quinn had gone after him, beating him badly. Dunn demanded satisfaction, and Quinn's pride and anger made him accept.

The duel took place in a field outside London. As the challenged party, Quinn had the choice of weapons and he selected pistols.

It was dawn, a pretty day for late in the year in London. A pink and persimmon glow lit the sky, and the birds sang happy songs . . . until the shots rang out. Quinn was nicked by a premature shot. The next shot was his. He aimed to the right of Dunn, but just as he pulled the trigger, George Dunn sought to avoid the bullet and moved straight into its path.

It was the first time Quinn had ever shot a human being. He watched disbelievingly as the young lord crumpled to the ground, blood spreading over his chest. Then there was a flurry of activity as a group of horsemen pounded down on them. Two dismounted and grabbed his arms while the third, an older man, leaned over the fallen heir. When he looked up at Quinn, his face held a mixture of grief and fury. "You'll pay for this . . . I'll make you wish for hell . . . ."

". . . Wish for hell."

• • • •

And Sethwyck had, Quinn thought.

Blue eyes. Brown eyes. Stay away from them all.

Quinn had told himself that each moment for the past week, ever since they had left Vicksburg. What confused him most was that Meredith Seaton was not even pretty, except possibly for those eyes and hair, and she certainly wasn't the type of woman who had ever appealed to him before.

Perhaps, he told himself, his desire was only the result of abstinence. Any woman with two eyes, two hands and two legs would look good to him. Or perhaps the growing hunger in him was for something more, for the soft touch of a woman who wouldn't care about his past, or even his present. Few southern women, he knew, would forgive his current activities. In the South, a slave stealer was worse than a thief; he was a danger to a whole way of life.

But the ache in his loins was more insistent than it had ever been, and he knew he had to have some relief. Perhaps it would take his mind away from the woman who was the very embodiment of everything he had come to detest. If only he hadn't seen her that morning against the rainbow. It had put fantasies in his head, and he had no room for them there.

He heard the loud clanging of the boat's bell and knew they were approaching Cairo. In minutes the band would start playing, and there would be a cacophony of sound: steam hissing, bells ringing, musical instruments blaring. He felt the familiar tension build within him, although he knew neither his face nor stance indicated it. Cairo was probably the most precarious station along the Railroad.

There were two routes leading from Cairo, one heading north up the Mississippi to Minnesota, the other east over the Ohio River and along the border of Illinois and into Ohio, and finally Canada. This particular shipment was to go the second route, and the transfer was risky. Because of Cairo's position on the border between slave and free states, it attracted a fair number of slave hunters and marshals, and they paid particular attention to boat traffic.

As the *Lucky Lady* inched up to the wharf, Quinn's eyes searched and found the Carroll brothers, both of whom were on deck, their own eyes weighing every passenger preparing to leave. Quinn's eyes then went down to the people on the wharf below. His stomach tightened as he noticed two wore badges.

With a nod, he summoned Cam, who quickly responded, understanding his message without words being spoken. Quinn knew he would fill the empty crates with the bolts of cotton they kept in the hold for just such a purpose and warn the fugitives to stay very still in the hidden room.

Quinn turned back to the Carroll brothers. He couldn't help but notice the furtive looks of the two slave catchers. They were very definitely searching for something or someone. Perhaps, he mused, they were seeking to recoup a portion of the small fortune they had lost to him on this trip. It had probably not been wise to pull their tail that way, yet he had been unable to resist the temptation, particularly when he had earmarked those funds for the Railroad. Levi Coffin, the reputed leader of the Railroad and a member of the Society of Friends, would not approve, he knew, but still it made the game a bit more interesting.

Sometimes too interesting, he rebuked himself. He should not risk others for his own sometimes whimsical desires.

He continued to watch as the gangplank lowered, and the roustabouts lifted sacks of sugar and dye destined for the Northeast. At another nod of his head the roustabouts quickly ran down the gangplank, preventing anyone from coming aboard. Quinn smiled at the frustrated looks of the marshals below.

Finally, the two men elbowed their way up, cursing as they came, and made their way to Quinn. They knew him well and had even shared a few drinks with him in the saloon.

"There's been a spate of runaways reported," one said curtly, annoyed at the delay. "We have orders to search all riverboats."

"Of course," Quinn said easily. "I can just about guarantee you won't find anything. Everyone knows the way I feel about runaways."

"Yes sir, Captain," the second man said, "but we're checking every boat, packet or barge going upriver. We've been getting a lot of pressure, damned abolitionists stirring everyone up."

Quinn shrugged. "Go ahead. They'd be damned fools to try the river, but you're welcome to look."

"We also have to see the papers of your crew," the second man said, his tone more agreeable. Most captains weren't as accommodating as Captain Devereux. And he knew he and his partner could expect a damn good brandy afterward. Captain Devereux was a gentleman. He didn't get testy like the others.

"You'll find them all in order," Quinn said with a disarming grin. "I see to that."

But the harmony ended when the Carroll brothers approached. They were obviously known to the two marshals who, equally as obvious, didn't like them. It was an attitude Quinn had seen and used frequently. The lawmen, while not a bit loath to do their duty in apprehending fugitives or those aiding fugitives, despised those who did it for money alone.

Their eyes, which had lost their annoyance with Quinn, now focused on the Carrolls with hostility.

Completely oblivious to the sudden strain, Ted Carroll addressed the marshals. "We've heard rumors about this boat. We want you to search it and check some of those crates."

One of the marshals turned an icy expression on him. "Lost some money, did you?" His question was directed more at Quinn than Carroll, and Quinn merely shrugged easily while the Carrolls flushed angrily. All their grateful

cordiality of the first night on the *Lucky Lady* was gone, lost
in the succeeding nights of card losses.

The marshals looked at Quinn. "Go ahead," he said and
called a man over to fetch some tools. When they arrived, he
took them and looked inquiringly at the Carrolls. The fugitives were always the last to be unloaded, remaining in their
hiding place until Quinn believed it completely safe.

The Carrolls eyed the various crates, then pointed to three
in separate locations. Quinn handed the tools to them. "You
want to look, you do the work. And be sure to nail them back
securely again."

He leaned nonchalantly against the boat railing as the
Carrolls pried open the crates and looked through them,
finally giving up in disgust. They started to walk away, but
one of the marshals stopped them. "You heard the captain.
Nail them shut again."

"We want to see below deck too," Ted Carroll said, his
face full of frustration as his brother started nailing the crates
back together.

"Of course," Quinn said. "I want you fully satisfied.
But while you're repairing the damage, I'll show these two
gentlemen the crew's papers." He stressed the word "gentlemen," and remembered fleetingly how Meredith Seaton had
excluded him from such company days ago. Why in the devil
did he keep thinking about her?

Quinn led the way to the office he and Jamison shared and
took out the papers, then offered the marshals a glass of
brandy. They accepted without hesitation and downed two
glasses each as they slowly perused the papers. As on most
riverboats, each roustabout and deckhand was a freeman,
except for Captain Devereux's large black. The marshals had
never understood why the captain kept the man around; he
looked and acted rebellious and dangerous. Upon being
asked, Devereux had merely laughed and said it was a
personal whim and challenge to break the man's spirit. There
were no more questions. It seemed entirely within character
of the mercurial gambler.

Besides, Quinn had added, Cam was readily recognizable by his size and his limp. He would be very easy to recapture if he dared to escape.

When Quinn knew Cam had had more than enough time to load the empty crates, he suggested they rejoin the Carrolls and go below. The brothers, sweating and obviously furious, were just finishing closing the final crate, when Quinn and the marshals appeared. Their mood was not improved as the marshals sent challenging looks toward the Carrolls. Would a guilty man invite a search, even eagerly lead it? The expressions on the Carrolls' faces became grimmer.

Quinn led the way to the cargo hold. When he met Cam on the steps, his easygoing manner disappeared. His eyes narrowed, and his lips grew tight. "You lazy bastard," he said angrily. "You're supposed to be on deck, unloading."

Hate crept into the black man's eyes. "Yessuh, mastah. Jest come to see how much more needs unloadin'."

"Others will do that," Quinn said roughly. "You're to handle the heavy crates, damn you. I catch you sneakin' off again, I'll have you whipped."

Cam lowered his eyes, but not before the others saw the sudden blast of fury in them. "Yessuh," he said and went up the stairs.

One of the marshals looked at Quinn. "He'll try to kill you some day. You would be wise to get rid of him."

Quinn shrugged. "He knows what would happen to him." He took out a match and lit a candle lamp hanging on a peg on the wall. Turning to the Carrolls, he spread his arms wide. "Look where you wish. Just remember you have to crate it back up."

The Carrolls looked at the two lawmen for help. One of the marshals grinned. "I'm satisfied."

Ted turned to his brother. "Hell, I ain't going to spend the rest of the day inspecting and securing these damned things. It's obvious there's nothin' to the tale." John wasn't quite so ready. His eyes went slowly around the hold, visibly measuring the walls and the number and sizes of the crates. Suspicion radiated from his eyes, and Quinn had the sudden feeling that he was not finished with these two. It was as if John smelled something he couldn't quite pin down, and wouldn't give up until he did. But for now, Quinn saw the slave hunter's eyes surrender. He nodded.

Quinn invited them to the saloon for a drink, but the two brothers looked at each other's dirty, sweaty clothes, and curtly refused. A glint in John's eyes told Quinn that he was aware the invitation might be a barbed one.

The Carrolls nodded to the marshals and took their leave. Quinn turned to the marshals. "You're sure you don't want to look any further? If there's anyone hiding down here, I sure would like to know about it. Wouldn't mind getting some of that reward money myself."

One of the marshals, a man named Bill Terry, laughed. "Damned fool slave hunters. They see fugitives in every closet. Other day, I heard they took a freeman by mistake, and the man's employer raised holy hell. Had them arrested, and rightly so. Greedy vultures."

They reached the saloon. "Another brandy before you go, gentlemen?"

"Don't mind if we do," Terry said.

It took Quinn another hour to get rid of them. When the two men finally wove their way happily off the boat, he searched the boat and wharf. The Carrolls were nowhere to be seen.

Cam was busy unloading the legal cargo when he caught Quinn's eyes and with insolence strolled over to him.

"Yessuh?" he said with a gleam in his eyes.

"Lazy bastard," Quinn said again, but amused regard had taken the place of anger now that there was no one within hearing range. "I think the cargo below is ready to move."

Cam's face was impassive, but his eyes warmed as he nodded.

•   •   •

Sophie's Parlor for Gentlemanly Pursuits stood on one of the back streets of Cairo. Unlike the saloons on River Street, it had a regal air and boasted of some of the finest ladies of joy along the Mississippi.

Quinn had first visited Sophie's on Underground business several years ago, and now often returned if the boat remained overnight. He seldom used its most obvious attraction, but enjoyed the rich luxury of the parlor itself and the ready availability of the best liquor, cigars, and food. He also liked Sophie, who, in addition to her role as hostess and madam, was a member of the Underground Railroad. Her establishment was often the ideal spot to hide runaway female slaves who could pose as Sophie's new girls. Authorities, who often used the facilities, would be loath to see it closed, much less raided and their own sins revealed. Sophie's was regarded as "sacred" by the politicians and the police.

Quinn had remained on board the *Lucky Lady* until the last of the cargo had been transferred. He had then decided to visit Sophie's and asked Cam if he would like to accompany him. Sophie was one of the few people who knew everything about Cam, and there was a certain mulatto girl at Sophie's who welcomed Cam's visits. But this time, uncharacteristically, Cam declined. Quinn had noted the lines of strain in Cam's face and wondered if they came from worry about Meredith Seaton's young servant. He was afraid it was so, and once more he vowed to himself that he would do something about it.

Sophie welcomed Quinn warmly, ordering the best whiskey for him and inviting him into her office where plush chairs were gathered around a small table. It was here that she enjoyed discussing business.

"I saw the *Lucky Lady* come in and wondered if we would be favored with a visit."

"Whenever I have time, Sophie. You know that."

"Not always," she said with a small frown. "And never enough. All the girls ask about you."

"As if you didn't keep them busy enough already," he said, the corner of his mouth crooking in a particularly attractive way.

"And Cam? He's all right?"

Some of the half smile disappeared. "He's brooding. A personal project."

"A girl?"

"Ah, you've guessed it," Quinn said.

Sophie frowned slightly. "It's dangerous . . ."

"To get personally involved," Quinn finished for her. "But the damage is done. He saw her on this last trip upriver."

"Sarah's going to be bitterly disappointed. She was hoping . . ."

"I know," Quinn said softly. Many of Sophie's girls ended up married, particularly to men headed west where there was a shortage of women and old rules didn't apply. Sarah was a particularly attractive mulatto girl who had been freed when her master had died. But she had had no place to go. She was suited only as a ladies' maid, and few ladies wanted such competition around. Nearly starving, she had ended up at Sophie's as a maid but had gradually become "one of the girls." She had planned to earn enough money to go north and start a small clothing store of her own—until she met Cam. Then her dreams started to change. Both Sophie and Quinn had seen it in her eyes, but Cam had not.

"And you, Quinn, still no lady in your life?"

"Only you, love," he said teasingly.

"Ah, but I'm old enough to be your mother."

Quinn looked at Sophie closely. From everything he had heard, she must be in her late fifties, but she looked fifteen years younger. Perhaps it was because of the sparkle in her eyes and the compassion in her face. Her hair, always neatly bound in a chignon, was as blond as it must have been in her twenties, and her skin showed few wrinkles, only laugh marks around her eyes.

Yet she, like all of them, faced danger every day. He hoped it showed no more on him than it did on her.

"You didn't answer my question," she reminded him.

"Ah, Sophie, you have told me time after time that no one in our business should get involved. It's too damned distracting."

She looked at him thoughtfully. She had known him three years now, and she was an extraordinary judge of character. She had to be, just to survive. She didn't think she had ever met a lonelier man than Quinn, although it had taken her a while to discover that. He hid his emotions extremely well behind a mask of cynicism. She regularly tried to tempt him with one of her girls, and God knew they were all more than willing, but only twice had she succeeded, both times with Alicia, who had black hair and a slight form.

Alicia had been hesitant to say anything to her later, only that he was a considerate tender lover and that, oddly enough, he didn't want her to undress him, as many of the clients did, nor did he even wish to discard his shirt.

Sophie had often wondered about Quinn. Few wealthy Southerners were involved in the Railroad. She knew of only two, both Virginians, one a Samuel Smith, who had been caught and sent to prison, and John Fairfield, who had once dropped off a delivery at her place of business. But then there was so much secrecy that she did not know more. She knew about Quinn only because they had worked together.

She had tried to prod several times ... to no avail. He would talk about anything but himself and the reason he was involved in the Underground. If she hadn't seen the affection between him and Cam, she would wonder if he had any heart at all. And then she started to see the loneliness behind the self-confident facade, and she hurt for him.

But she could not press him for explanations. It might mean losing his friendship, and that she was not willing to risk.

"And tonight?" she pressed. "Alicia's free."

Alicia was one of the reasons he had come. Passionate

Alicia who never asked questions. The relief, he'd hoped, would take his mind away from the nagging image of Meredith Seaton. But somehow, he knew it wouldn't. Not tonight.

He shook his head. "I'm tired, Sophie. Your company, a good glass of wine and dinner—that's all I require."

Sophie shook her head. His eyes were tired, his mouth grimmer than usual. "You need more than that, Quinn."

"Perhaps," he said, "but it will do for the moment."

"Any trouble?" Her question came as an afterthought. Quinn Devereux never had trouble.

He lifted an eyebrow. "Ever hear of the Carroll brothers?"

"Them!" Sophie nearly spat the words out. "You heard about Toombs?"

"I was told about him. I've been wondering if there's anything I can do. . . ."

"Don't," Sophie said shortly. "They're hoping someone will try to help him escape, so they can discover more of us. We can't afford to lose you. In any event," she said, "it was the Carroll brothers who discovered him and a shipment of slaves. They're smarter than they look."

"You've met them?"

"No," she said. "But we've had various reports about them. Be careful around them."

"They were on the *Lucky Lady*."

"They must have had a reason. Be careful, Quinn."

"I'm always careful, darlin'," he said. "Now what about that dinner?"

From that moment on, the conversation turned light, to the foibles of local politicians, to a new singer who was to come to Cairo, to new books, especially Charles Dickens's *David Copperfield*, which had recently reached America and which Quinn had just finished reading. It was, as usual, an enjoyable visit, yet Quinn couldn't quiet a restlessness he hadn't felt this strongly in years.

When he finally took his leave, he wandered down to the river. Then, still restless, he returned to town, ending up at the furniture and art studio that he had visited a month earlier. It was here that he had found the rainbow painting that so intrigued him. He knew the proprietor often worked late and decided to stop by and inquire whether any more of M. Sabre's paintings were available.

A light was on in the back of the store, although the front door was locked. He knocked with more force than he intended.

The stocky proprietor, a man named Davis, came into sight, his eyes and face anxious and growing more so when he saw Quinn. He quickly unlocked the door, urged Quinn inside and locked it again, this time drawing the shade.

"My God, what are you doing here? Trouble?"

Quinn felt immediately apologetic as he eyed the man whose hands were trembling slightly. He had never before come here after hours, and he knew he probably shouldn't be here at all. Casual contact between stations and conductors was not encouraged.

"No," he replied soothingly. "I just . . . wondered if you had any more paintings by that artist."

The man's nervousness noticeably lessened, although there was a trace of anger in his response. "No," he said shortly. "We receive very few, no more than three a year, and they go very quickly."

"The artist—what do you know about him?"

"Nothing," Davis said. "The paintings are sent by one of our stations in New Orleans. I asked once whether I could get more, and the answer was no. I also asked for information about the artist, but there was none."

"What . . . are the other subjects . . . ?" For the life of him, Quinn couldn't understand why he had become obsessed with M. Sabre.

"Usually the Mississippi. There was one—dawn over the river—that nearly equaled the one you bought."

"Can you try to find out more?"

"I can try, but I doubt I'll have any luck. The artist obviously wants to remain anonymous."

"If any more paintings arrive, I'll purchase them . . . regardless of price."

"I'll save any, then."

Quinn nodded.

"When will you be back?"

"We'll reach St. Louis tomorrow night and then start back. Ten days, no more."

"Any special cargo this time?"

"Ten. They're safely loaded on Cameron's keelboat."

The storeowner studied his visitor's hooded eyes. He was more than surprised at Devereux's visit. Earlier visits had always been strictly business. "I'll let you know when they reach Canada."

Quinn smiled. The storeowner didn't know about Sophie, nor Sophie about the store. As far as Quinn knew, Davis and Sophie were the only two Underground stations in Cairo, and he couldn't imagine two individuals less alike.

Davis, he knew, was a deeply religious man who was involved because he believed slavery was an abomination to God. Sophie, on the other hand, was simply a compassionate woman whose own tragic early life made her sympathetic to others. He wondered, with just a touch of sardonic amusement, what each would think of the other. Or, for that matter, what they thought of him.

Unwilling to guess, he simply nodded his head in farewell and waited for Davis to unlock and open the door.

But Quinn still wasn't ready to go back to the boat.

He thought he had defeated this dissatisfaction, this damnable craving for something he didn't quite comprehend. For three years now, his restlessness had been tamed or at least submerged, but now it was once more rearing its ugly head. And it was worse than ever.

"Build a wall around ye, lad . . . and stand tall inside. They no ken tetch ye, then."

It had been good advice eleven years ago. It had helped him survive, those words from Terrence O'Connell, the Irish rebel who had shared his cage on the transport to Australia. Quinn had built that wall, heavy stone after heavy stone, and it had withstood the assault of his captors. But now, for some reason, it was crumbling.

It was just too damned lonely inside.

Chapter 6

MEREDITH RELUCTANTLY made her way down the winding mahogany staircase to her brother's study. She had been summoned and she knew there was no refusing. She had been home several weeks, and she felt trapped, eager for another trip.

Since she arrived, disapproving eyes always settled on her, accompanied by condescending words.

"Don't you think, dear, you could do something with your hair?" Her sister-in-law.

"Damn it, make yourself useful for once in your life, and stop that infernal giggling." Her brother.

And though she brought censure upon herself, and planned everything exactly this way, inside there was something hurtful and aching and yearning. Something reaching out for more. The feeling was especially sharp since she had left the *Lucky Lady*.

She paused outside the study doors, hearing the voices inside.

"Strangely enough," she heard her brother say, "Gil is pressing his suit."

"It must be the money," she heard her sister-in-law Evelyn muse.

"If it were anyone but Gil, I would agree," Robert said. "But he has more than enough of his own."

"Well, I don't care why. I'll just be glad to get her and those horrible paintings out of here. She's insisting we put that . . . that bowl of fruit in the dining room. It will give everyone indigestion."

"It was that fall," Robert said. "She's never been quite right since then. Poor Gil. He doesn't know what he's getting into."

That fall. Meredith leaned against the wall next to the door leading to the study. That fall. It had changed everything, but not in the way Robert thought.

She remembered the pain. It had been excruciating: as if a hammer were being struck haphazardly in her head. Every place hurt, and as one sharp pain receded, another took its place. She cried out, wanting the comfort of a word or a hand, but there was none. When she opened her eyes she saw only the cold hostile stare of her father.

"You made a spectacle of yourself," he said in his harsh voice.

"Lissa?"

"She's gone."

"Where?" That was the only important thing.

His eyes grew even colder. "I don't know, and I don't care, Missy. There will be no more mention of her."

The pain came stronger, and Meredith closed her eyes against it . . . and against her father. She would find Lissa. She didn't know how, but she would. Someday she would. She swallowed against asking more questions, knowing it would accomplish nothing. Something inside her hardened, and tears, which had been in the back of her eyes, froze. She would not give him the satisfaction. She turned to the wall, away from him.

During the days that followed the pain receded, but she did not speak. She didn't complain. She didn't question.

A week later, she overheard her father and the doctor talking when they thought she was asleep.

"She's acting very strangely. She hasn't said a word since she first woke up."

"It could be the blow to the head," the doctor said. "It could have affected her mind. . . ." His voice trailed off.

"You mean she might never be . . ." Her father's voice trailed off. There was disgust that he made no attempt to hide, and Meredith's stomach contracted. He had always valued perfection.

"I don't know," the doctor said. "We just don't know much about head injuries. We'll just have to wait and see."

Meredith adapted quickly in the next few days. Her father visited less and less, and when he did she looked at him blankly. She had found an exquisite punishment for him—and for herself, for she couldn't help blaming herself for the catastrophe that had befallen.

If only she hadn't given Lissa the doll.

Four weeks later, she was sent to Saint Mary's, a Catholic school in New Orleans. There was no hug or kiss good-bye.

The tears that had frozen in the back of her head solidified. She had not cried since.

Meredith shook her head to rid herself of the memories and knocked at the study door. The voices stopped. She heard her brother clear his throat, then bid her enter.

He was at his desk and Evelyn was standing at his side.

"You asked for me?" Meredith said tentatively.

Robert cleared his throat again. He was a handsome man, or would have been, Meredith often thought, if his face had been stronger. But there was a weakness about it, a dissatisfaction that tugged his lips downward and dulled his brown eyes. His hair was light like hers, but more a chestnut than blond, and he wore it long. A mustache added distinction to a weak mouth, and he wore sideburns that he believed gave him a rakish air. For a moment she compared him with the riverboat captain, who wore his hair shorter than fashion and kept his face clean-shaven. The strong harshly sculptured face fixed itself in her mind. Strange that such a reprobate could have such determined features. Devereux had needed no facial hair to mask weakness. He had needed no sideburns or mustache. Arrogance and roguishness were a natural part of him.

She swore mildly to herself. Devereux was like a frustrating fly that constantly buzzed around her ears. She couldn't escape him, she thought, thoroughly annoyed with herself.

But she kept her face blank as she looked up innocently at her brother. "You wanted to see me?" she repeated.

"Gilbert MacIntosh is coming for dinner tonight. I want you to look your best...Evelyn's maid will tend to your hair."

Meredith stared at him blankly, although her mind was rapidly turning over possibilities. Of all her suitors, Gil was by far the most persistent and, she had to admit, the least objectionable. She had never understood why he continued to pay court to her, when she was purposely obtuse and giggly when he came around. Gil owned the neighboring plantation and was financially self-sufficient, so money should not be much of a factor to him, she thought. But perhaps he had unknown debts.

"I like the way Daphne does my hair," she said stubbornly. Then she pursed her lips. "I could show him my paintings," she said slowly.

Her brother and sister-in-law exchanged looks, and Evelyn hurried off. Meredith smiled to herself. Many of her pictures, she thought, would become mysteriously misplaced in the next several hours. But she would make sure her bowl of fruit was quite evident.

"Gil has asked my permission to marry you, Meredith. You couldn't do any better than he . . . and you know you're getting, well . . . older . . ."

Meredith's lips pouted. "It's unkind of you to remind me . . . you know I have lots of beaux . . . I just can't seem to decide. And I do so like to travel. And then, I would just hate to leave you and Evelyn. She's just like a sister." She gave him a bright smile.

Robert flinched visibly. "Gil—"

"Mr. MacIntosh is most admirable," she said prissily, "but he's so dull. He never talks about anything but that old plantation of his."

"It's the biggest plantation in the parish," Robert broke in impatiently. "And the union would benefit us both."

Which was, Meredith suspected, why Gil wanted her. Together the Seaton and MacIntosh plantations dominated the parish. She thought about Gil MacIntosh. He was tall and thin, serious in demeanor, and almost painfully shy with women. He was also, she knew, a good horseman, and a natural farmer. But she would never marry a plantation owner, never wed a man who owned slaves. Never. She would, in fact, never wed any man.

Meredith had her own dream. When this was over, when she had found Lissa, they would go to Canada together, and she would paint. Openly, gloriously paint. She would not hide behind another name. Painting would be all she needed. Painting and Lissa. A true friend. She would never place her life or destiny in the hands of another, especially a man.

But she looked guilelessly up at her brother. "I'll ask Daphne to do her very best, and I'll wear the . . . lilac dress."

Robert blinked rapidly. "Why don't you wear the wine-colored dress Evelyn had made for you?"

"Oh, it's too plain. Yes, I think the lilac dress." She gave him a broad smile and bounced out the door, knowing he was tapping his desk with frustrated fingers. Poor Gil. Poor, poor Robert.

Meredith returned to her room, dismissing Daphne. She

wanted to be alone. She sat in the window seat, the same one where she had watched Lissa being taken away, and looked over Briarwood. Home. A home in which she was a stranger.

Meredith felt racked with the old pains of loneliness, with the yearning for a gentle touch, a loving glance. She felt her lips tremble. These . . . spells came occasionally and unexpectedly, yet they were fierce in their devastating impact. Only one thing ever helped. Painting. The creation of a world not as lonely, not as alien. She left the window and fetched her satchel of paints. She had sketched from the window before, painted the great oak tree that was her sentinel, the fields with their harvest. They were white now, full of small cotton balls, looking like the rare snow she had once seen in New Orleans. She could see the figures bending over, and she knew their hands were darting quickly from plant to plant. The workers—men, women, and children as young as seven—would return at sunset, backs bowed by the constant bending.

Her hands now captured the movements but not the faces, which were shielded by bonnets or worn brimmed hats: protection from the unmerciful late afternoon sun. When all the cotton was in, there would be a celebration with extra rations for the slaves, liquor supplied by Robert, and dancing and laughter, perhaps even a marriage or two. At the plantation, Robert would hold his annual ball, which attracted growers from miles around, and the other owners would compare yields. And then work would start again, preparing the fields for the next crop. The cycles never changed, the work never lessened.

Meredith glanced down at the canvas. It was good. She knew it was good. There was a weary strength in the figures, an indomitable pride in one woman who, unlike the others, stood straight up, her face toward the sun. Although her features were indecipherable, there was an unmistakable challenge in her stance.

You can chain the body, but never the soul.

Levi Coffin had said that at a lecture she had attended in Cincinnati, and she had never forgotten it. The words were indelible in her mind, because they applied to her as much as to those she helped.

She heard Daphne's knock at the door. Two hours already! She quickly placed the painting in the ornate trunk at the foot of her bed. It would be quite safe there. She turned the key, then slipped the small piece of metal under the armoire. She seldom risked painting here, but that sudden wave of melancholy had prompted it, nay demanded it. She already felt better. Elias would be pleased to have another painting, and the fee it would bring. She would finish it tonight after everyone went to sleep. The anticipation would make the evening bearable.

The table glittered and gleamed with the best china and crystal, lit by the chandelier with its hundreds of pieces of glass that danced with the light of the candles. Ever hopeful, Evelyn had dressed as if she herself were the bait and not her unwelcome sister-in-law.

Gil looked uncomfortable in his conservative blue waistcoat and trousers, his kind hazel eyes regarding her inquisitively as she demonstrated her abysmal knowledge of politics.

"Mr. Frémont is so handsome and bold," Meredith rattled on aimlessly.

"He's a Republican." There was horror in her brother's voice. He turned to Gil and shrugged. "Women . . . it's a damned good thing they don't have a vote."

Meredith bit her lip to keep from making a sharp retort.

"I agree with one thing," Gil said mildly. "He is bold. He helped win California for us."

"As a free state," Robert said bitterly. "Mark my words, we will go to war over slavery. Kansas and Missouri are already running with blood. The damned North won't be satisfied until they ruin us all."

"Oh war," Meredith said. "Sounds excitin'. Uniforms and balls, and trumpets, and men marchin' off to fight the Yankees."

"There's nothing exciting about war," Gil said quietly.

"Oh la," she said carelessly. "I think war would be mighty romantic. I believe y'all would look so handsome and heroic." She looked at them both dreamily. "Don't you, Robert?"

Robert studied his neighbor cautiously. Gil MacIntosh seldom said much in a group, and Robert wasn't sure where his sympathies lay, although he did own slaves. His neighbor was, in fact, one of the largest slaveholders in this part of Mississippi. "What if it did come to war, Gil?"

Gil carefully laid down his fork. "Half of my estate is tied up in slaves," he said. "They are collateral for loans my father and grandfather made. I don't have much choice but to use them, or go bankrupt. Then they would simply be sold and be worse off than now. But I don't like slavery. I never have, and if I could see a way out of it, I would take it. I wouldn't fight to keep it."

"The devil you say," Robert blustered as Meredith stared at Gil with utter disbelief. The statement was akin to treason in Mississippi.

Gil shrugged. "Sometimes I think I'm more of a slave than they are. Perhaps we all are, Robert."

Evelyn changed the subject abruptly by asking Gil to the ball she and Robert would give after the cotton was in.

"I would be delighted," he said simply, then turned to Meredith and added, "if Meredith will honor me with some dances."

She felt a funny twist inside, as if he saw more of her than anyone else did. Tipping her head, she kept her dark eyes curiously blank as she had trained herself. There was more, much more, to Gil MacIntosh than she had imagined. But even he would frown upon what she did. It was, in his eyes and others', no less heinous than stealing money from them.

At Robert's suggestion, she walked Gil to the door, wondering all the time what he saw in her that stirred his interest. It frightened her that perhaps she was not playing her role well enough.

A few moments later, she decided she had been mistaken,

because he merely bowed at the door, saying it had been "delightful," and left. She watched him swing up on his horse that was waiting outside, some of his earlier awkwardness disappearing.

Robert came and stood beside her. "Perhaps I was wrong about him," Robert muttered. "Didn't care for that kind of talk at all."

"Ah posh," Meredith said. "You men. One takes one side and the other feels he has to take the other. Just to argue. I would much rather talk of parties and who's courtin' whom."

Robert looked at her strangely and swore beneath his breath. God only knew what would happen to Briarwood if Meredith inherited. It was essential that she marry.

That night Meredith finished the painting, but her mind was wandering. It was well that the major strokes were in place, that she needed only to fill in the sky, and the river in the background.

She was twenty-four years old, and until this summer had never taken particular notice of a man. Now she couldn't sleep without thinking of Quinn Devereux, and tonight Gil MacIntosh had also stirred something in her. It wasn't the thunder and lightning Devereux seemed to create just with his presence, but something milder, something pleasant.

She stared at the painting in her hand, at the pride of the central figure. Unconsciously her head went back in the same pose, her chin jutted at the same angle.

Meredith locked the painting in the trunk. Perhaps she would visit the Parson tomorrow. He was always a fountain of comfort. If only those blasted blue eyes of Quinn Devereux didn't haunt her so relentlessly.

The morning dawned clear and bright. Meredith felt drugged with lack of sleep, but she summoned Daphne to prepare a hot bath, and then dressed quickly in one of her many riding costumes. Like her other clothes, the red was too bright, the ornate buttons too gaudy, the material too heavy. Everything was a little off. Tasteless, she thought with a certain perverse satisfaction.

But instead of immediately riding off to her destination with her satchel of paints and sketchbook, she found herself making a detour. She had avoided this particular section of the woods for years, for it reminded her too much of Lissa and the few happy days she had spent as a child. Meredith quickly found the tree. The swing was gone, most of the rope and the board rotted away and the small clearing overgrown. But she remembered.

Meredith heard the laughter. Her own. And his. They had mixed with the song of the wind, as she flew higher and higher into the sky. She closed her eyes, trying to capture the sound of his voice. Not yet cynical. Not yet mocking. It was rich and carefree and exuberant. As was Lissa's when it was her turn. Lissa had been afraid to go as high as she, and Quinn Devereux had been gentle and careful, calming her fears and teasing shy Lissa into giggles.

She saw him in her mind's eye, so tall even then, with an easy smile and eyes that creased with fun. She felt a flood of warmth as he stood proud in her memory, handsome and kind.

A sudden cold wind brushed her skin, jerking her back to the present. She looked again, and the children were gone. There was only a frayed piece of rope hanging from the tree, swinging forlornly in the gust of wind. Illusion. She was seeing what she wanted to see, not what was real. She was remembering what she wanted to remember, nothing more. He must have shown signs of cruelty then, but the child hadn't wanted to see them.

Meredith shook her head. She had to rid herself of this obsession. She had to. He was of no more substance than that rotting piece of rope.

Without looking back, she found a fallen log and used it to help mount. It would be a long ride to the Parson's.

His name was Jonathon Ketchtower, but everyone just called him the Parson, and he and Elias, a Quaker in New Orleans, were Meredith's only two direct connections in the Underground Railroad. They kept her supplied with the list of stations for runaway slaves and kept her aware of what was going on through the network. They also gave her the encouragement and courage she occasionally needed.

The Parson was, quite simply, the best person she had ever met, and the bravest, for it was he who often braved the dogs and slave catchers to personally ferry slaves to safety.

As she rode up Meredith heard one of his dogs barking and knew he was home. She whistled as he had taught her, and the dog quieted immediately. Meredith had often wondered how he had accomplished that, but then the Parson was a miracle worker with animals.

He wore a broad grin as she reined in her horse and dismounted, and she couldn't help but smile back. His hair was long and straight and lanky, often pushed back from his forehead by impatient hands. He had a wispy beard, which made him look somewhat benign and innocuous, and he had eyes that changed rapidly from piercing to empty on a second's notice. No one could look more harmless, when he needed to, and no one, she suspected, was more effective.

"Merry," he said with delight. "Come in. Have you had anything to eat?"

She shook her head. She had left before breakfast, before Evelyn could capture her to extol the virtues of Gil MacIntosh.

"Good," he said. "I have fresh bread and some honey one of my friends has given me."

He led the way into the small, neat hut. A braided rug covered the floor that Meredith knew opened into a large secret room beneath. There was a bare cot, neatly made, a table and two chairs, several hooks with black clothes hanging from them, and a large fireplace. That anything so small and spare could be so warm often amazed her. This rough

shelter seemed more like home than her own plantation
manor.

He soon had hot tea ready, and they ate comfortably
together.

"Tell me about your trip," he said as they finished, and
he leaned back, lighting a pipe. Smoking, and the animals,
were his sole indulgences.

"I found one man on the Graves plantation and gave him
the first station, a compass, and some money. He should be
going through any time," she said. "He promised to wait a
month. There might be another going with him."

"No word of Lissa?"

"No. But I found another girl, Daphne. She was a maid
at a plantation that was sold. I think the experience of being
transported frightened her. She's very shy and uncertain.
Perhaps in a few months you can help her North."

"It's dangerous," the Parson said. "You know we don't
advise helping slaves from one's own home."

"I know," she said. "But I look at Daphne and think of
Lissa and what she must have gone through."

"Can she make it on her own?"

Meredith shrugged helplessly. "I don't know. Not now.
But perhaps a little time . . ."

The Parson leaned back and regarded her fondly. He had
not been so certain of her when Levi Coffin said she would be
talking to him. The Underground included few members of
slaveholding families; the system was too ingrained within
them, too much a part of their lives for them to challenge it.
He knew there were a few who did, and they were uncommonly effective for they could usually move around more
easily than the others connected with the Railroad.

Meredith had been a part of the system for five years now,
and he had never been disappointed. She was exceptionally
bright and mature, and she had a commitment rare in someone her age. Few young women would willingly pretend to be
an addlehead and give up what should be among the richest
years of their life for a friend . . . and an idea.

The Underground Railroad was informal, with one person learning the sympathies of another and enlisting him to help the fugitives. There was no formal organization, no written list. A member knew of another, and that second person of a third, and on and on. Several, like the Parson, were aware of a complete network and passed on information to those who needed it. He kept Meredith advised of those who might help in the areas she visited, no more. Talk was not loosely bandied about. There had never been a betrayal of the Underground Railroad, and the Parson meant to keep it that way.

"When did you get back?" he asked.

"A few weeks ago . . . on the *Lucky Lady*."

His dark bushy eyebrows met in a slight frown. "The *Lucky Lady*?"

"You know anything about it?" she said with an interest that surprised him.

"Just rumors."

"About the captain, no doubt," Meredith said disdainfully. "Or whatever he is."

"You didn't like him?"

"A more arrogant cruel man I've never met," she answered heatedly.

The Parson leaned back in his chair, obviously waiting for her to continue.

"He has a slave. He's been crippled and whipped."

"How do you know the captain did it?"

"He as much as admitted it," she replied. "And the slave told my maid."

"I've heard tales," the Parson remarked thoughtfully. "You said he admitted it? You talked with him?"

"He invited Opal and me to dinner. With slave hunters."

The Parson's bland expression didn't change. "That must have been interesting," he observed.

"More like loathsome," she replied.

His mouth cracked a small unusual smile. "Who were they?"

"Brothers, name of Carroll. I drew pictures, and wrote descriptions for you to pass on." She pulled out the sketchpad from her satchel and handed him two sheets. He looked at them carefully, noting the bold strokes, and admiring her work. She had a wonderful eye for both people and places. That she hadn't seen more to the riverboat captain than she had surprised him. She was usually very intuitive.

He leaned back. "Tell me more about this captain."

"He's obviously a rogue and a blackguard in addition to being a gambler," Meredith said, a small flush mounting her cheeks as she remembered his kiss.

"He didn't . . . try to take advantage of you?" the Parson asked hesitantly.

Meredith deliberated. Could that angry, mocking kiss be considered an advance? She knew he had done it only in retaliation for her slap. And why had she slapped him? Not for anything he had actually said or done, but more for the naked invitation in his knowing eyes. An invitation some vulnerable part of her had wanted to accept.

"No," she said finally, but the pause made the Parson wonder.

A silence hung between them for a moment, and he said a quiet prayer. He knew Quinn Devereux, just as he knew Meredith Seaton, and he recognized the simmering emotions both held in check. They were both of a passionate nature, or they wouldn't be doing what they were doing. But they concealed that fervor under a cause, a very worthy cause to be sure, and he feared what might happen if the cover unraveled.

He would, he realized, have to keep them apart. Already, he knew from Meredith's flushed face that sparks had flown between the two. He raised his eyes heavenward in entreaty. He *must* keep them apart. Somehow. The problem was that both of these agents were uncommonly stubborn. God help him if they got stubborn together.

But, the Parson was devious. He had learned to be so in the ten years he had been involved in the Underground

Railroad. "I think Captain Devereux could be very dangerous," he said slowly, conviction dulling the stab of guilt at
his deception. "It would be wise to avoid his boat from now
on."

She nodded. "He wanted to buy Daphne. . . ."

For the first time, she saw surprise flicker in his eyes, and
she wondered about it.

But he changed the subject and said no more about the
Lucky Lady or Captain Devereux. Instead, he took her out to
the small shed and watched her as she fed the red fox he had
rescued from a trap two months earlier. It was almost well,
and soon he would release it back into the wild. Then he
studied her in interested silence as she sketched the playful
animal and handed him the result.

"I'll treasure it," he said slowly. "Have you finished any
more paintings?"

"I gave Elias one to sell several months ago." She
grinned suddenly, and the Parson thought how pretty she
looked on the rare occasions when she smiled. "It was a
rainbow . . . our rainbow."

"You finally found one, did you?"

"I hated to send the painting away."

"Perhaps you'll find it some day."

"Or another rainbow," she said.

"Or another rainbow," he agreed.

Chapter 7

QUINN SHIVERED in the unusual chill of the morning as the deckhands loaded dry goods bound for New Orleans. The wharfs in St. Louis were, as always, a beehive of activity. In addition to the *Lucky Lady*, one other steamboat and a number of smaller crafts, ranging from makeshift rafts to flatboats, were docked there.

He should have taken time to put on a coat, but these past days he had been seized by an impatience, even to the matter of rising in the morning.

God, but it was bloody cold for early October. He caught himself. He had tried to train himself against using "bloody," that particularly British oath, even in his mind. But too many things were coming back now. Why, damn it? Why?

Perhaps it was the cold. The bitter, familiar cold.

He had felt little else during the months at Newgate. . . .

• • •

It was easy to lose track of days, since he was locked up alone in a tiny cell with no window and no difference between day or night except for the changing of his guards. Letters were against the rules, he had been told, and he had bartered away his waistcoat in exchange for having a missive delivered to friends. He did not know whether it had been sent, although the guard said it had. But no one came.

He felt buried alive. The money he had with him was confiscated when he arrived at Newgate, and he couldn't purchase any comforts, not even food or a blanket. Because he was charged with murder, heavy leg-irons were clamped around his ankles. Lighter ones were available but these were denied Quinn, for they cost a certain sum he no longer had.

Weeks after the duel, Lord Sethwyck appeared and viewed him with both hatred and satisfaction. Quinn knew he was filthy and pale and awkward with his chains. The man's gaze moved slowly around his cell, to the hard bench that was its only furniture and the odorous can that served as a chamber pot.

A guard held a lantern that almost blinded Quinn after the darkness. He rose and walked the few feet to the bars that caged him.

The earl's face told him he could expect no mercy.

Quinn stood defiantly under his gaze, knowing that he little resembled the immaculate American of a few weeks before. His clothes were filthy, and his face covered with whiskers. His hair, he knew, hung lank and lifeless. And yet his chin lifted with defiance.

"Your trial is tomorrow," the earl said softly. "At Old Bailey."

Quinn's hands clutched the bars of his cell. He'd been charged with murder and, with the earl's influence, he would most likely hang.

"I have an offer to present."

Quinn looked at him skeptically.

"I don't want my son's name, my name, dragged through scandal," Sethwyck continued. *"Plead guilty, and I'll see that you're transported rather than hanged."*

"Like hell I will," Quinn said. *"I want an open trial. Your son challenged me in front of witnesses."*

The earl's voice was cold, full of hate and venom. *"It makes no difference who challenged whom. Duels are illegal in England. Besides, you will find that all the witnesses have disappeared except one who will testify you shot my son in a jealous rage . . . without justification. You think an English court will believe . . . an American against an English lord?"*

Quinn's fists tightened in frustrated rage. *"You're bluffing. Why else would you want me to plead guilty?"*

"Because," the earl said softly, *"I don't want my family name tainted. I don't want . . . any unfounded rumors."* It was clear to Quinn then that the earl was afraid word would circulate that his son shot early, before the count ended. Even if the earl's witness perjured himself, someone might believe Quinn.

"It's a chance to live, Devereux," Sethwyck continued. *"Your only chance."* He paused at Quinn's silence, then his thin lips curved in a mocking smile. *"Have you ever seen a hanging? It's not pleasant. And you will hang, my boy, if you go to trial. I have seen to that."*

Quinn believed him, believed that he could do anything he wanted. After the past months in Newgate, he didn't question the man's influence. But to plead guilty to something he didn't do, to give away his freedom . . .

Or hang. Dear God, he didn't want to die. Particularly that way. He closed his eyes, trying to think.

Quinn had heard of transportation, of Australia, and knew that many of those sent there had stayed after their sentences had been completed. It was a vast land, mysterious and . . . a prison colony.

But to live! He was twenty-two years old and he did not want to die. He particularly did not want to die publicly at the end of a rope. His father, his brothers, would eventually learn of it. And that he could not bear.

After sleepless hours, he made his decision. Once in Australia he could escape and get word to his family. He was a gambler. And now he was gambling he could beat the earl . . . and Australia.

The next morning he sent a message to the earl, one, he realized sardonically, that would actually arrive at its intended destination. Hours later, he heard a judge, garbed in black robes, sentence him to "transportation for the term of your natural life . . ."

"Capt'n?" Cam's voice brought him back to the present. Quinn looked up, his blue eyes dark and brooding.

"Mr. Jamison . . . he said to tell you we're leavin' now."

Quinn nodded. The whistle would sound, and the *Lucky Lady* would slowly pull from the wharf and turn around, heading downriver again. Toward New Orleans. Toward Vicksburg.

Cam looked at him curiously. He had never seen Captain Devereux as distracted, as brooding as he had been in the past weeks. The captain seemed lost in a world that precluded even him, and despite their different situations he thought he knew Quinn Devereux better than most.

He had seen the scars on Quinn's back, thin scars that were barely visible now, but he knew they came from the same source as his own: a whip. He didn't know the particulars. He hadn't asked, nor had Quinn told him. But he suspected they were part of the reason Quinn was involved in the Underground Railroad and the main reason he, Cam, was now free. Their suffering had created an unspoken bond between them, although they retained a certain distance. There were too many shadows, too many wounds, in his own life and, he suspected, in the captain's life, for either to be entirely comfortable with other people. Although Cam knew he would willingly die for Quinn Devereux, he had, by necessity, protected his heart and soul too long to surrender them easily, even to friendship. And Captain Devereux had never asked for more than his loyalty. Or, for that matter, even that. Cam had just given it. Out of gratitude. Out of respect.

But there were things that, because of the raw pain they caused, were always kept hidden. Not buried, but hidden. Even from each other. Perhaps, particularly from each other.

"Breakfast, Capt'n?"

Quinn's eyes lost their faraway look, and he grinned crookedly at Cam, sensing the concern under Cam's words.

"Aye," he said. "It's damn cold for October. Let's go inside."

But Quinn's memories didn't disappear, and he didn't understand why. He had often had nightmares at night, but usually sheer determination kept them at bay during waking hours. Something was happening to him, and he damned well didn't like it.

Perhaps he needed a challenge. A new challenge. He looked at Cam, and remembered Daphne. And his pledge to Cam. They would be back in New Orleans in two weeks. He would visit his brother and gather all the information he could about the Seatons. Perhaps the Seatons had cotton to be shipped; that would give him a good excuse to visit the plantation. And possibly Meredith Seaton's brother would be more amenable to selling Daphne. It was worth a try.

And it would be damned interesting to see what Brett knew about Meredith Seaton.

Now that he had plotted a course of action, Quinn felt better. And, damn, but he was hungry. He heard the *Lucky Lady*'s whistle and felt the boat creak under him as the ropes, binding it to the wharf, were released. The boat strained toward the middle of the river where it belonged.

Where he belonged. If he belonged anyplace at all.

Brett Devereux regarded his brother warily. As a boy he had worshipped Quinn. He still loved his brother, but he no longer regarded him with the single-minded devotion of a young lad. He saw the faults and, while he restrained from commenting, he nevertheless could not quite conceal his disappointment.

Brett, like his father and brother, had worried over the missing brother during the years when every attempt to locate him met with failure. Their father had spent thousands of dollars on private detectives; after nearly seven years they found Quinn; it took another year to bring him back.

And when he returned his father and his oldest brother were already dead of fever in an epidemic that had swept New Orleans. Brett had temporarily assumed management of the bank. He had expected Quinn to take over the bank's leadership when he returned, but to his amazement, Quinn showed no interest. After months of gambling and drinking, Quinn had obtained the *Lucky Lady*, which he treated like a toy.

Brett knew only a little of what had happened to his brother. Quinn's eyes grew icy cold whenever Brett had tried to find out more.

It hurt, damn it. It hurt badly, for they were the only Devereuxs left.

Quinn still smiled as easily as he had as a boy, but now there was a curious emptiness about the gesture, which never quite reached his eyes. Nothing seemed important to him, not their home, or their heritage. Nothing except pleasure.

"Why," Brett asked now, "are you interested in the Seatons?"

"Cotton," Quinn said. "We need to increase our shipping."

"Don't tell me you're getting interested in business?"

"Don't you approve, little brother? Your profligate brother finally settling down."

"Then come into the bank."

"Ah, Brett, the bank's yours. I told you that years ago."

"I would be delighted to have you back. A partnership."

Quinn shook his head slowly, something inside him hurting as he watched the light leave his brother's eyes. "The *Lucky Lady* is one thing, the bank something else. You may like staying in an office all day, but it's too much like a cell to me."

Brett leaned back, taking his eyes from his brother's face. Quinn had made the allusion before.

"You wouldn't be locked in it, you know," he said carefully. "You can leave whenever you want."

"Not for me, Brett. I like the river. And as much as you disapprove, I like gambling. And I'm damned good at it. A whole sight better than banking."

"You could do anything you tried," Brett said in one last attempt.

"But I wouldn't, little brother. I wouldn't try, because I don't give a damn about the bank. I never have."

Brett searched his brother's face, seeking something but not finding it in the ruthless, hard visage before him. They shared the same facial features, although Quinn's coloring was darker than his own, but the resemblance ended there. Brett sometimes envied Quinn's lean saturnine handsomeness; he knew his own girth was spreading comfortably, and he didn't really regret it. He realized he knew a contentment that had evaded Quinn. Although often office-bound, Brett loved banking, and he adored his wife Betsy and their three children. The only burr in his life was Quinn, and that was because he wanted his brother to be happy, and he knew Quinn was not, despite his protestations to the contrary.

"The Seatons?" Quinn reminded him gently.

Something within Brett rang like a fire-alarm bell. "There're many cotton plantations," he observed. "Why the Seatons?"

"I met Miss Seaton several weeks ago on the *Lucky Lady*. I was told her family owns one of the largest cotton plantations in the Vicksburg area."

Brett's gut tightened. Surely Quinn couldn't have any interest in Meredith Seaton. Dear God, the silly woman would be putty in his hands. Brett didn't particularly like, or admire, Meredith, but she was under his protection, to a certain extent.

"Don't worry, Brett," Quinn said, reading his thoughts. "She believed me perfectly odious."

For some reason, that did not comfort Brett. "What did *you* think about her?"

Quinn shrugged. "What you said. Overdressed. Self-indulgent. Not very bright."

Brett felt better. He relaxed a little. Of course, someone with Quinn's eye for the ladies wouldn't be interested in Meredith. Maybe his brother was changing. Perhaps if he became more interested in the shipping business, it might lead him to the bank. Working with Quinn was Brett's fondest dream. And respecting him again as he once had.

"What do you need?" Brett asked.

"An introduction to Robert Seaton. I met him long ago, but I doubt he'll remember."

"I can do better than that."

Quinn arched an eyebrow in question.

"I'm always invited to their annual ball. It's a tradition after the last of the cotton is harvested. But Betsy's in the family way again...."

Quinn grinned. "Again?"

Brett looked pleased with himself, and nodded. It would be their fourth child. "You should consider it, Quinn."

"Me, a papa?" Quinn's brows rose with amusement. "Surely you wouldn't wish that on a helpless child."

"You do rather well with mine."

"That's because I can leave at any time," Quinn said, suddenly feeling awkward.

"They adore you."

"Because I bring them presents."

"No," Brett said firmly. The way his sardonic, sarcastic brother enchanted his children had always surprised him. Even more astonishing was the way Quinn's cold, closed eyes warmed in their presence. It gave Brett hope.

Quinn saw the brief glow in Brett's face and knew he had to snuff it out.

"You were mentioning a ball?"

"Ah, yes. I could send you in my stead. I usually stay at their home." Brett didn't like the sudden feral smile that appeared on Quinn's face. He was struck with misgivings. But it was too late now.

"When is it?" Quinn asked.

"October thirty-first."

"All Hallows' Eve?" Quinn smiled with the cold amusement Brett had learned to dislike. "How appropriate."

"Remember, Quinn, they are my clients, and I'm Meredith's trustee. I'm relying on you to honor that."

"I'll be the very epitome of respectability and courtesy," Quinn replied solemnly, one side of his mouth twitching. Then his eyes softened. "I won't do anything to disgrace you, Brett. I swear."

Brett looked a bit abashed. He stood and went to Quinn, putting his hand on Quinn's shoulder. "I know, Quinn. It's just that..."

Quinn stood. "I know, Brett. We just think differently... want different things."

"Do we?" The question was soft and probing.

"Ah, I'm afraid so. You're all for hearth and home and bank, and me... well, give me a deck of cards and an easy woman. I like my freedom, Brett. And I won't change. Not for you, nor for anyone."

Brett sighed. "I'll send that letter to Seaton."

"Thank you, brother. And I must be on my way."

"Won't you come over for dinner?"

Quinn wanted to. God, he wanted to. But he had to keep his distance from Brett in order not to hurt him. If he were ever caught, he didn't want his brother implicated. It was better if the brothers were believed estranged. "I have a previous engagement, Brett. Sorry. But give Betsy my best and give her my congratulations."

Brett nodded, his blue eyes, much lighter and clearer than Quinn's, regretful. "You know, of course, you're welcome anytime."

"I know," Quinn said softly. And left.

• • •

"My brother's arranging for me to attend a ball at the Seaton plantation," he told Cam upon his return to the boat. Watching his friend's eyes light with expectation, he added, "You will accompany me, of course."

"When?"

"All Hallows' Eve. A good time to spirit someone away, wouldn't you say?"

Cam permitted himself a small smile for the first time in weeks. "The Parson?"

"Aye. We can't be connected to it, but I can put a plan in motion."

"And I'll have a chance to see her, to reassure her."

Quinn nodded, pleased at the way everything was falling so easily into place.

"Any special cargo?" Cam asked.

"Not this trip, I expect," Quinn replied. "Elias said the recent increase in runaways has made the plantation owners particularly watchful. He never knows, of course, when someone might show up, but right now he's urging most of his contacts to be very careful."

"A dull trip, then."

"It's seldom dull, Cam. We'll leave the boat at Vicksburg and stay there a few days until it's time for the ball. We'll take two horses with us."

"Marigold?" Cam asked. Quinn had picked a fanciful name for the great gold stallion that he kept at his townhouse on Jackson Place.

"I think Marigold would be the most impressive, don't you?"

"And you want to impress someone?"

"Only for Daphne, Cam," Quinn retorted quickly.

"Hmm," Cam said with the impertinence of familiarity. "Couldn't be your pride, Capt'n?"

Quinn's eyes narrowed. "Pride?"

"Women don't usually say no to you, no matter what you want."

Irritation rose within Quinn. The suggestion that Meredith Seaton had, in some way, bothered him was not welcome. "Don't you have something to do?"

"Yes suh, master, suh. I could always scrub the decks, haul yore crates, fan yore body."

"Go into town, Cam." A wry glance accompanied his words.

Cam gave him his rare smile. Never in his life had he thought it would feel good to tease a white man.

"I'll do that, Capt'n. I think I'll just do that." It was still magic to him that he had choices. Magic.

Perhaps in several weeks he could give that same magic to Daphne.

Chapter 8

MEREDITH NERVOUSLY smoothed the satin material of her gown.

Damn her brother!

Why in the name of all that was dear had he invited Quinn Devereux to the ball?

She had been looking out the window yesterday when he arrived. He was unmistakable in his black clothes and white-streaked black hair. So was the slave, Cam, who rode a little behind him.

Meredith had stared with fascination. She hated to admit it, but Captain Devereux was a superb rider. He sat his stallion with ease, although it pranced nervously coming up the road. If it had been anyone else, she would have loved to paint them—the lean straight figure in black on such a spirited gold-colored mount. Instead, she swore in a most unladylike fashion.

What was he doing here?

She left her room and found Evelyn. Her sister-in-law was standing in the middle of her bedroom while the dressmaker was making last minute alterations on her ball gown.

"Captain Devereux is coming up the road." The statement was obviously a question as well.

"Oh, didn't we tell you?" Evelyn said. "Brett Devereux sent his regrets and asked if his brother could substitute for him. Opal is delighted. She said he was very pleasant."

Meredith searched for something to say. "He's a gambler... he just isn't received."

"Well, if Brett says he's a gentleman, then he is," Evelyn said complacently. "Anyway it's too late. He's been invited. He'll have dinner with us tonight." She looked at Meredith critically. "Try to wear something nice."

Outrage flooded Meredith. For weeks she had tried to rid herself of images of Quinn Devereux and the way she had felt when their lips had met—even though she now realized the kiss had been only part of a plan to buy Daphne.

Daphne. Suspicion started building in her. Perhaps that was why he had wrangled an invitation. Well, it would do him no good. Daphne belonged to her, not to Robert.

And she would be blasted before she shared another meal with Devereux. She put a hand to her head and swayed. "I think I'm getting the vapors," she said. "My little ol' head is just pounding away...."

Evelyn did not look sympathetic. Meredith often had the vapors. Usually very conveniently. "It would be very rude."

"Why should I care about being rude to a gambler? His reputation... well, it's plain unsavory. I just can't believe you'd invite him. We'll be the talk of the whole state." She fanned her face with her hand.

Evelyn's face suddenly creased with worry. "You really think so? I mean Brett is so respected. He would never ask anything compromisin'."

"He was probably forced into it," Meredith said slyly. "Everyone knows Quinn Devereux just isn't received."

"Oh dear," Evelyn said, forgetting she usually didn't put much stock in Meredith's opinion.

"But if you must, you must," Meredith said. "But I plan to eat in my room."

"Well . . . I think I should go and talk with Robert."

So Meredith had dinner alone in misery. She kept thinking of Quinn Devereux sitting in the room below, so damnably handsome and arrogant while she was a prisoner in her own room. And she kept Daphne with her, although the girl seemed unusually tense.

Still, she got through the evening and most of the next day. There was no way, however, she could avoid the ball. It was one thing to snub him at dinner, quite another to ignore the major social occasion of the year. She comforted herself with the knowledge that there would be more than a hundred people there, including Gil, to serve as a buffer between her and his aggravating smile and derisive observations.

She chose the yellow gown. It made her skin dreadfully sallow and did nothing to enhance either her hair or her eyes, her two best features. The dress had a high bodice and was decorated with hundreds of rosettes and numerous ruffles, which made her look twice as big as she was. She commanded Daphne to curl her hair into tiny little screw curls that hung over her cheeks, hiding the clean oval lines of her face. When her hair was done to her satisfaction, she dismissed Daphne.

And now she stood in the middle of the room, hesitant to go down although she knew she should be receiving with Robert and Evelyn. But her stomach felt sick and her hands trembled.

She had faced danger repeatedly, calmly, had even been nearly caught once handing money to a slave. And she had certainly never felt this kind of nervousness with a man. Gil was comfortable, and she respected him. But the tingling that started in her body whenever she thought of Quinn Devereux, the assiduous assault on her most protected feelings, astounded her. And frightened her in a way she had never been frightened before.

She knew, deep inside, that he was very, very dangerous to her.

Meredith took one last look in the mirror. She was comforted by the fact that a very plain, frumpy woman returned the steady gaze. Perhaps, he would ignore her. There would be many very attractive young girls here tonight. Strangely, the thought sent a wave of desolation through her.

Fanciful fool, she accused herself. The path she had chosen years ago allowed no fantasies or personal feelings. Especially for a man who personified everything she hated and worked against.

She straightened her back, left her room, and joined her brother and sister-in-law.

The room was full when Quinn Devereux descended the stairs, and suddenly it seemed as if there was no one else present. Her legs trembled and her fingers tightened painfully around an elderly woman's hand, exacting a tiny cry of protest.

She heard a nearby gasp and knew she wasn't the only one so affected.

Dear Lord, but he was strikingly handsome. His dark elegance made every other man look like a schoolboy. The white hair around his sun-browned face disappeared into an inky rich blackness that boldly invited touching. The icy dark blue eyes swept the crowd below him with something like contempt before a curtain descended, hiding all emotions. They found her and locked with her own eyes with a relentless power, and once more Meredith felt her whole body responding in a rebellious way. By sheer force of will, she moved her gaze from him and turned back to the woman whose hand was nearly broken by now.

"I'm so glad you could come," she said somewhat apologetically, her fingers gently massaging the white knuckles of her victim.

"Yes, yes, indeed," the woman said, jerking her hand away while she had the chance. Odd child, she thought as she moved quickly away. Poor Robert.

Meredith smiled wryly. Then she turned to her brother as

she saw Devereux approach. "I'm just about to faint with the heat, Robert," she drawled. "I'm goin' to get a glass of punch." She fled before he could object or Devereux could reach them. But she had the surest feeling that his amused eyes followed her. Damn him.

She found Gil, who had been one of the first to arrive. She couldn't help but compare him to Devereux. Although Gil had little fat on him, he was heavier than the gambler, stockier in build, although not as tall. He smiled, his mild hazel eyes lacking the intensity of those that had just pierced her.

"Meredith," he said warmly. "May I have this dance?"

She smiled at him. "I would be delighted."

Like everything about him, he was a comfortable dancer, doing nothing unexpected, nothing exciting. Now why did she think of that? She forced herself to relax, forced herself to keep her eyes from the hallway where she sensed Captain Devereux was, with *his* eyes following her across the floor. She stepped on Gil's foot and she apologized profusely, much to Gil's discomfort. There, she thought with hidden satisfaction. Quinn Devereux will never ask her to dance now. If he'd even planned to.

When she spun around again, she saw him talking to Vinnia Fields, one of the prettiest girls in the district, and she felt an agonizing and incomprehensible streak of jealousy. Her hand tightened on Gil's, receiving in return a corresponding pressure. Dear God, what was she doing? For the first time in years, she felt totally out of control, unable to harness either her emotions or her actions.

Meredith felt a bump at her back and she turned. It was Devereux, who was dancing with Vinnia. He bowed low, his eyes laughing at her as he apologized. Her gaze went to Vinnia, who was obviously enraptured by her partner.

Meredith took a deep breath, trying to keep the anger from her face, from her eyes. "Captain," she said with a giggle. "How . . . surprising to see you again."

"I'm pleased to see you've recuperated from the illness that kept you from dinner last night."

"Ah la, just something in the air, I think. Hopefully, it will be gone soon."

The corners of his eyes crinkled, and for a moment she wondered whether she was being too clever. There was something all too intelligent in those cold emotionless eyes.

"Perhaps it will, Miss Seaton," he replied courteously. He looked at Gil curiously, and she suddenly realized her lapse in manners.

"Our neighbor, Gil MacIntosh. Quinn Devereux, our banker's brother." The last was said with a disdain that was unmistakable.

Gil shook hands but looked at her with a question in his eyes. "Mr. Devereux," she explained further, "is a gambler."

Quinn bowed low, his mouth twitching. "I also own the *Lucky Lady*, Mr. MacIntosh, and I'm looking for shipping contracts in Vicksburg. I would like the opportunity to talk to you about it."

"Of course," Gil said easily. "Come by tomorrow and we can discuss it."

"I'll do that." He turned back to Meredith, his smile mocking. "Thank you, Miss Seaton."

Meredith merely lowered her head in acknowledgment, hiding her dismay. If he received her brother's business, and Gil's, dear Lord, he would be around all the time.

The dance was soon over, and Meredith accompanied Gil to the overflowing table, guiding him well away from the man she was quickly believing was her nemesis.

Her appetite completely gone, she nonetheless filled her plate. Nibbling would give her something to do, and hopefully take her mind from the altogether too handsome Quinn Devereux.

But Gil wouldn't permit it, peppering her with questions about the guest. "How well do you know him?" he asked.

"Well enough not to trust him," she said acidly, hoping that she might spoil Captain Devereux's plans to do business in this area. "He has the most frightful reputation in New Orleans . . . he just isn't received. My brother was put in the most difficult position when Brett Devereux passed his invitation on to his black sheep brother. I just can't understan' what Brett was thinkin'.''

Gil's eyes went around the room to the striking man in black. He was leaning attentively over another young lady. "He certainly seems to have a way with the ladies."

Meredith clenched her teeth together. "Handsome is as handsome does, Sister Esther told me. I personally see nothing attractive about him." *Lie*, she told herself.

"Would you like to dance again?" Gil asked.

Her eyes went around the floor, and she saw Captain Devereux dancing, moving gracefully across the floor with another very pretty girl in his arms.

"Yes," she said with a kind of ache inside.

When the music finally stopped, she smiled brightly at Gil and saw Devereux's sardonic gaze once more on her. Damn the man. She looked her worst, was dancing her worst, and certainly had been discourteous at her worst, and still he was making his way over to her.

"I wonder," he said when he reached her and Gil, "if I might have the honor of this dance?"

Anger, dark and hurting, flooded her. All he wanted, she suspected, was Daphne, and she didn't understand why the thought was so excruciating. "I don't dance with gamblers," she said rudely, loud enough for those around to hear.

His face flushed with the insult, and his eyes turned icy. He bowed elaborately. "I certainly would be the last to lure you from your very admirable God-fearing ways," he said mockingly.

"You would be the last to achieve it," she replied acidly, not caring that her words carried.

"Perhaps," he said tauntingly, and then turned to Gil MacIntosh. "Tomorrow?"

Gil looked curiously from Meredith to Devereux. Her actions were odd, he thought. He had never seen her take such an open dislike to anyone before. Still, he had already said he would see the man, and he could not break his word.

But he decided he would ask Robert Seaton more about him before committing to any business arrangement. He nodded, unhappily seeing Meredith's fixed expression.

When Devereux disappeared through the doors of the ballroom, he turned to Meredith. "Why do you dislike him so?"

"He . . . he tried to take advantage on the trip up here from New Orleans," she said, remembering the hard taste of Devereux's lips.

"The devil you say," Gil said. "Well, I'll hear him out and send him on his way."

"I haven't said anything to Robert."

"Then I won't either, if you wish."

She smiled, and Gil thought how pretty she could be. If only someone would help her with her clothes and hair, he mused. But she had had no mother, and precious little attention from her father and brother.

"Thank you," she said softly before fluttering her fan nervously. "I do think his presence has given me a headache. Would you think me terribly rude if I excused myself?"

"Of course not," Gil said. "I just hope you'll feel better."

Meredith fluttered her eyelashes. When *he's* gone, she thought with frustration. But she just nodded and put her hand on his sleeve affectionately. And then she fled.

She stopped by Daphne's small room off the kitchen, but the girl was not there, and the other house servants were all very busy. She knew she would need help with her buttons. More than anything she wanted the ugly dress off, along with the corset and petticoats and hoops that held her prisoner.

She paused in the hallway leading to the ballroom, and looked for Quinn Devereux, but he was gone. Something started pecking away at her mind. Could Daphne be in danger?

Meredith slipped out the back door. She would check the barn.

• • •

Cam kept his arm around Daphne. She felt so right there. So small and soft and trusting.

He hadn't missed the light in her eyes when they had met in the kitchen. She had been fetching something for her mistress, and he had been ordered by the captain to add his strong back to other servants'. It was a necessary part of the role he played, and he did not resent it.

Daphne's coffee brown eyes, which were so large and so expressive, had told him how much she had missed him. She had nodded eagerly when he whispered for her to meet him later, during the dance, at the barn. He knew the stablehands would be busy tending the horses lined up in front, and there was a small protected shed in the back. He had already scouted it well.

Now, as he tightened his hold on her, he sensed her fear. He knew that fear only too well, and he wondered if Daphne had the courage to escape. Even if Meredith Seaton was the kindest mistress, she was still that—a mistress who had to be obeyed in the smallest and greatest of all matters.

"I was afraid I would never see you again," Daphne said hesitantly.

"Would that ha' mattered?"

"Oh yes," she said innocently, and he smiled slowly. It was a gesture that was coming easier to him these days.

He felt her tremble and wondered why. Had she been mistreated here? He felt every muscle in his body tense.

"Are you all right?" he asked gently.

She nodded.

"And Briarwood?"

She lay in his arms feeling a safety she hadn't felt since that time on the boat. "Like any plantation, I suppose."

"No one's pesterin' you?"

She shook her head, and he felt vast relief. That had been his greatest fear, that the master of the plantation would try to take her to bed. She was so pretty.

"Miz Seaton?" he persisted. "Is she hard?"

"No," Daphne said. "She doesn't use me nearly as much as my other young missus. She gets impatient but never angry. And she looks at me in a strange way sometimes."

"How do you mean strange?"

"I don't know, like she's looking for something."

Cam felt a sudden disquiet. He didn't like the notion of Miz Seaton taking a special interest in Daphne. He knew Quinn was going to try to buy her again. "Do you think you could escape if there were someone to help?"

She turned wide eyes on him. "Who?"

"Jest someone. Would you?"

Daphne hesitated. She had never had much courage. And more than anything else she was afraid of a whipping. She didn't think she could stand that. She recalled the scars on Cam's back and she wondered how anyone could have borne what he had. But ever since she had first met him and talked to him, she had started to think of being free. Of being free with him.

"Would *you* go?" she asked in return. Perhaps if she were with him, she could hold her fear in check.

His great arms, the muscles straining the cheap cotton shirt he wore, tightened around her. How could he tell her no, that he had to stay with Captain Devereux, that he wouldn't be free until they were all free?

"Not right away," he said softly, "but I could make sure you're safe . . . and join you later."

She tensed at his words. Alone. She would be all alone. And yet the idea of freedom had somehow taken root. She hadn't thought about it until she had met Cam, until their conversation on the steamboat. But now she could think of little else.

Daphne hesitated only a moment longer, then nodded.

"Someone will be in touch with you," Cam said. "If you hear the words, 'Freedom's light,' you'll know it's a friend."

"I'm scared."

"I know," he said softly. "But it will be worth it, I promise." He wanted to tell her about the captain's plan to purchase her, that perhaps this would all be unnecessary and that she wouldn't have to follow the Underground Railroad. If only . . .

Why did Miz Seaton want Daphne so badly?

He lowered his lips and kissed her gently, trying not to scare her. He could feel the fear in her, taste its acrid bite on her mouth. He didn't quite understand his overwhelming need to protect her, to touch her in tender ways, to smooth away the trembling that made him ache inside.

He heard Quinn's voice. "Where's that black bastard of mine?" and he felt Daphne flinch in his arms. He put a finger to her mouth, warning her to be quiet. "Stay here until I'm gone," he whispered.

He stood and stepped out of the shadows into the lantern's light. "I'm here, Capt'n. Jest making sure the horses are okay."

"Well, get on to the house. They need help in the kitchen."

"Yessuh," Cam said lazily, and Daphne feared for him, but then the barn door opened and closed. She had started to move when she heard Captain Devereux's voice. He was soothing his horse, and she wondered how someone could treat an animal so gently and a man so cruelly. She hated him. She hated him more than she had ever hated anyone before. She wanted to strike out at him, to kill him, but she had no weapon. Or courage. With desperate angry tears in her eyes, she waited until she heard the door open and close again. Several minutes later, she crept out.

Quinn's dark eyes swept the lawn. Carriages were lined up along the road, their horses' needs being tended to by the Seatons' groomsmen. Chinese lanterns spread flickering light everywhere, and the great house itself was majestic in the moonlight. Music and conversation seemed to burst from the windows and doors, all of which were open to allow the air to circulate. There were couples under several trees, their heads bent close together in intimate conversation, while an occasional trill of laughter added to the symphony of sound.

He surveyed it all, the cynicism in him deploring the extravagance built on slave labor, the loneliness in him envying the carefree banter between courting couples. The party was far from over, but when he had seen Meredith leave, he was afraid she would be looking for Daphne. He had known that Cam was to meet the girl tonight and it would do Cam, and himself, little good to be linked with a slave who would soon, hopefully, escape North.

So he had gone to warn Cam. He had meant to leave with Cam, but his horse had recognized his scent and whinnied for attention. Knowing that Daphne must be waiting in frightened silence, he quickly quieted the horse and left.

He leaned against a great magnolia tree, its leaves still thick and green although the rich white petals were long gone. He couldn't see the Mississippi from here, but he knew it was less than half a mile away. He longed for it now, for its honest complexity. Quinn closed his eyes, relieved for the moment to be free of people, of pretending. Pretense was becoming so much a part of him now that he sometimes wondered if he was becoming the person he feigned to be—a reckless gambler who cared nothing about others. It was a frightening thought. But perhaps the fact that he worried about it made doubtful the possibility.

Quinn opened his eyes, and he saw Meredith Seaton standing beside the house . . . alone. He wondered how long she had been there and whether she had seen Daphne or Cam or himself, for that matter, leave the barn. He couldn't quite see the expression in her eyes, but she was standing stiffly in the atrocious yellow gown. With an unhurried grace, he walked over to her.

"Miss Seaton. I feared you might be ill again." There was the usual baiting amusement in his voice.

In the combined light of the lanterns and the moon, he could see amber flashes in her golden brown eyes. And indignation. A great deal of indignation.

"I came out for a breath of air," she said tightly. "And you, Mr. Devereux? What did you find so fascinatin' all by your little ol' self? I thought you were bein' well entertained inside."

Quinn's mouth turned up in a wry smile. "I'm flattered by your attention, Miss Meredith. It's too much for a poor disreputable gambler like myself." He managed to speak the last word as disdainfully as she had in the ballroom.

Meredith blushed. Damn the man. He always made her seem the fool. And she couldn't fight back, not without exposing more of herself than she wanted him to see. "I look after all our guests, Captain, even the . . . well . . . more undesirable ones." She puckered her lips in distaste and looked unbearably prissy.

His grin spread wider but there was no amusement in his eyes. "How noble, Miss Seaton," he drawled in that brandy-mellow voice of his, which warmed her insides like the real thing. Even knowing what she did, even after seeing him emerge from the barn, followed several seconds later by Daphne, she couldn't control the reactions of her body to him. Her blood felt like liquid fire, her bones seemed to melt, and a deep ache of need blazed inside her, its flames spreading through every part of her.

She lowered her eyelashes so he wouldn't see the need in her eyes. She had trained herself to hide her emotions, but she had never encountered anyone like Quinn Devereux before. "Yes," she finally said defiantly. "It is rather . . . gracious of me, isn't it?" She hoped she sounded as silly and haughty as she intended. Perhaps he would leave her alone.

But he didn't. He stood there like a statue, his eyes searching her face before he replied, "Let's see how gracious." And before she could react, his lips were on hers.

It was an angry punishing kiss, the retribution he had silently promised himself for her earlier public insult. She fought to get free, her hands pummeling a chest whose hard strength seemed totally immune to her efforts.

The kiss deepened, gentling slightly, and the fire between

them flashed. Her hands faltered, and her lips, of their own volition, started to respond to him, to the warm pressure of his mouth, to the sudden unexpected power of the contact. As on the *Lucky Lady*, she was again defenseless, her body, her tongue, her hands succumbing in the most elementary way. Unconsciously her body leaned toward his, fitting itself to the hard lean angles, and her hands crawled upward to his neck, her fingers winding in the thick dark hair. Her tongue took on a life of its own, welcoming his every probe, his every challenge.

Her mind cried no, but her body wouldn't heed the warning. It was too caught up in the exquisite feelings he was creating in her.

He had probably tried to seduce Daphne . . . or even taken her, uncaring, unheeding of her feelings. As he was of hers. He didn't care about her. He only wanted to punish. And he was doing it. Dear Lord, how he was doing it.

She jerked herself free with such force that she stumbled, and his hand went out to steady her. His face, now bare of mockery, was filled instead with bafflement. They stood there in the shadows, in the deep of night, staring at each other, Meredith with hatred that he had ravaged her well-protected defenses, and Quinn with more confusion than ever at the fire in her, at the response that had awakened something fierce inside him. More than anything, he wanted to taste those lips again, feed the hunger in them.

"You . . . you blackguard," she said, wanting badly to say something stronger.

The words broke the spell on Quinn. He leaned against the side of the house and laughed. He put a finger to her chin and lifted it, demanding that she look at him. "I didn't expect so much fire, Miss Seaton."

"Fury is more like it. You take advantage of my home and my brother."

"What else can you expect from a blackguard . . . and gambler?"

His smug tone infuriated her. Her hand balled in an effort to keep from slapping him.

"Don't even try it, Meredith." It was the first time he had called her by just that name, and his mouth lingered over the sound. Grudgingly, she noted that it had never seemed quite as sensuous. To protect herself, she wondered whether he also caressed the names of other women. But of course he did. It was all part of his practiced seduction.

"I did not give you permission to use my name," she said.

He laughed, and once more it didn't touch his now-hard calculating eyes. "Didn't you, Meredith? How could I make such a mistake?"

She straightened. "I want you to leave Briarwood."

"But my business isn't done," he countered smoothly.

"I'll tell my brother—"

"Tell him what? That you returned my kiss? Before you do, I must remind you that I am very good with pistols." His eyes became colder. She always brought out the worst in him, he thought angrily. And tonight, for whatever reason, he couldn't resist goading her even as he wondered why he was wasting his time.

He saw her fingers curl into tight fists, and then without another word she whirled around and fled. A tendril of hair came loose from a tortuously pinned sausage curl, and fell down her back, the soft gold color glinting in the moonlight.

Quinn stood there silently, watching her awkward movements in the ruffled yellow gown and wondering what had happened to his usually faultless taste in women.

C*hapter* 9

QUINN FOUND CAM alone in the servants' quarters, pacing impatiently.

"She'll go," Cam said.

Quinn nodded. He doubted very much now whether Meredith Seaton would sell Daphne, particularly to him. He didn't even think that Meredith would talk to him again.

"Her brother confirms that Daphne belongs to *Miss Seaton*," he said. The emphasis he placed on the last two words surprised Cam. "I think the Parson's our best bet. We'll visit him tomorrow and hope to God he's there."

Cam agreed. "If you don't need me, I'll go see what I can find out 'bout the Seatons, what they do when there's an escape."

Quinn nodded. Some owners posted bounties, which brought every slave hunter out from under the rocks. Others, not wanting trouble, just chalked it up as a business expense.

After Cam left, Quinn undressed himself, his hands lingering over the expensive wool and linen. Fine clothes were one of his indulgences now. He caught the sight of his back in the mirror and winced, as he always did. He hated the scars that crisscrossed his back. They would always be there, branding him a convict. . . .

He was relieved when the guards came to his cell and told him he was being transferred to a prison ship. He was thankful even as they placed irons on his wrists and linked them with those on his ankles.

How naive he had been, he would soon realize. Newgate had been a palace compared to his next lodgings.

Along with others sentenced to transportation, he was put in the Black Maria, a horse-drawn van specially built for prisoners. It was a unique contraption, and if he had not been one of its victims, Quinn's inquisitive mind would have appreciated its ingenuity. He was pushed down a passageway in the middle of the van. There were doors on each side, and one was opened and he was shoved in. He found himself in a tiny cubicle, too small for him to stand or sit. He could do no more than crouch in the dark as he heard other doors open and close. Finally he felt the jolting of the van over cobblestones. His legs seemed to go numb with pain, and despair, which he had managed to keep at bay, descended with all its black poisoned hopelessness. For the first time, he realized his complete helplessness. They could do anything to him, and he was defenseless, utterly powerless.

When the coach finally came to a stop and his door opened, he could barely move, his legs were so cramped and numb. But a blow from a club made what seemed impossible possible. His chains dragging, he and his fellow prisoners emerged into a sunlight that temporarily blinded them until another blow made them stumble forward. As his eyes became accustomed to the light, he realized he was in Portsmouth, and in front of him in numbers too numerous to count were the hulks, not the graceful sailing ships he had taken from America to Europe and then to England, but ugly, patched, pensioned-off warships.

The prisoners were herded to a long boat and made to awkwardly climb the nets to the quarterdeck. Quinn was singled out by a Marine captain and ordered to stand apart from his fellow convicts as their chains were removed. They were then told to undress, and each man was searched intimately, a ritual that was both painful and extremely humiliating. But that was only the beginning. He was bathed in icy water, and then his hair, of which he had always taken pride, was cropped to the scalp and the whiskers, grown long now, shaved carelessly, leaving nicks and cuts over his face. He was then given prison garb: canvas trousers, a rough shirt that scraped his skin, and a gray jacket.

The blacksmith came over to him and after a few words to the Marine captain, he knelt and riveted heavy leg irons on his ankles. When the last bolt was hammered in, the weight on his ankles enabled him to do little but shuffle as he walked. Then he was pushed down a narrow ladder to the hold. Wooden bars enclosed a large area where lanterns showed dozens of men on the floor or in hammocks. He was pushed beyond that, down a narrow corridor, to another barred area, which was little more than a cage, four feet wide and six feet long. A man lay on the floor, and he blinked at the approach of the lanterns.

"Company for you, O'Connell," one of the guards said as he unlocked the door.

"Why, bless ye," the man said, cropped red hair flaming in the light and a broad smile on his face. He seemed not at all intimidated by his surroundings, or the fact that he too wore double leg irons that were chained to the wall.

With a scowl, the guard ignored the good cheer and roughly pushed Quinn inside. He chained Quinn and O'Connell together, then left, taking the lantern with him.

"Ye must be as out of favor as meself," the man said in the darkness. "Terrence O'Connell at yer service." The

comment was wry but there was nothing apologetic or vanquished in it.

"Devereux," Quinn said. "Quinn Devereux." *He knew defeat was heavy in his own voice, but he couldn't help it. Sethwyck had said he would know hell, and God knew he was finding new meaning to the word. His hand went to his cropped head, then to the heavy iron around his ankle, and he wondered if hanging would not have been the better choice.*

He felt a huge hand on his shoulder. "Don't let the bloody bastards get ye down, boyo," *the man's booming voice gentled.* "They can't win if ye don't let them."

Those words and O'Connell's spirit carried Quinn through the next eight years.

Quinn put on a linen nightshirt. In his cabin on the *Lucky Lady*, he slept naked, but he took no chances here. His past was his secret. He didn't want a helpful servant to wander in and see the scars around his ankles. His hands told enough tales with their hard calluses.

He went to the window and looked out. Briarwood was a beautiful place, well-tended and obviously prosperous. Magnolia trees lined the front drive, and huge oaks shaded the house itself. Yet there was an emptiness here, a lack of love that had filled his own boyhood home. This plantation seemed passionless to him.

But, he suspected, there was nothing passionless about Miss Seaton, despite appearances to the contrary. He knew he had not imagined her response to him tonight, the banked fires that had flared so briefly at their kiss.

It didn't matter, though. He would keep away from her. He and Cam would find the Parson, make arrangements for Daphne, and then he would forget this place.

They can't win if ye don't let them.

Quinn went to his bed and lay down, hoping sleep would come quickly.

O'Connell. Teacher. Protector. Savior. *I miss you, my friend. I miss you.*

Meredith brushed her hair with long furious strokes, trying to work out her confusion and frustration.

She had worked hard to become an effective agent for the Underground Railroad. She was finally confident of herself and even felt a certain contentment, though it was tempered by her failure to find Lissa. She was doing something important, and she was doing it well. That, and her painting, had given her a sense of self-worth that her father and brother had once systematically destroyed.

But now her carefully built defenses were crashing like a house of cards, and all because of a kiss. A mocking, meaningless kiss from a blackguard and rogue.

Perhaps, without quite knowing it, she longed for intimate contact. She had not known a day without loneliness since Lissa had been taken away. It must have been her isolation, emotional and physical, that had responded to his kiss. Nothing more. Certainly nothing more.

It still amazed her that anyone could change so much. She bent over and lifted the lid of the trunk in her room. She picked up the lining at the bottom and took out the pictures she had drawn of Devereux. She recalled how he had once ruffled her hair and called her "pretty little Merry."

But "pretty little Merry" was gone now, and so was the kind young man. He had become the most arrogant man she had ever met. And one of the cruelest. That she felt even the slightest attraction for him made her doubt her own self.

If only he were ugly. Or simply plain. No one had a right to be so handsome, so darkly attractive. Especially someone with a black soul. His room was only down the hall, and his proximity sent shivers through her and warmed her blood.

To distract herself, she thought about her brief conversation with Daphne when she had helped Meredith undress. It had been most unrewarding and even less illuminating.

When Meredith had mentioned she had seen Daphne leave the barn, the girl had frozen like a statue.

Almost unconsciously, she had reached over to touch Daphne, but the girl flinched. "Is something wrong?" Meredith had asked. "Did someone hurt you?"

Daphne shook her head. "I jest needed some fresh air. I didn't mean to be gone so long."

Meredith's brow wrinkled in concern. "No one tried . . . to take advantage of you?"

Daphne hung her head. "No, Miss Meredith."

"You would tell me if . . ."

"Yes, ma'am."

"Has Mr. Devereux said anything to you?"

"No, Miss Meredith, I jest needed some air, that's all."

Meredith knew she wouldn't get any more from the girl. She could only try to keep Daphne away from Captain Devereux during his stay at Briarwood, which she hoped fervently wouldn't be long.

"You won't be punished," she said softly. "Not for something someone else does."

Daphne stiffened. "Is there anything else you need, miss?"

Meredith knew she was defeated. She shook her head.

Morning dawned, golden and bright. And she had not slept. Feeling dull-headed and fatigued, Meredith accepted Daphne's silent ministrations, including hot chocolate and fruit, and then a hot bath. She would stay up here in her room all day, if she must. A prisoner once more in her brother's home, in *her* home. But she could not face Devereux again, or listen to his veiled, and not so veiled, mockery without answering in kind.

She stretched and went to the window, her eyes drawn to two riders, one dressed in black and sitting a gold horse, the other on a bay riding a little behind. They were heading toward the main road.

Forever, she prayed. Perhaps he was leaving forever.

She nearly ran down the stairs in her eagerness to find Robert and hopefully learn that Devereux had indeed left for good. She prayed earnestly that such was so.

Robert Seaton was talking with several guests who had remained overnight, and she bit her tongue to keep from blurting out the question, then went in search of Evelyn, who was directing the cooks.

"Has Captain Devereux left?" she asked.

Evelyn's eyes opened wide. "Do you have an interest in him?"

"Only that he leave," Meredith said unwisely. "I don't understand why someone of his . . . nature was invited in the first place."

"Well, he's not leaving, not today. He went over to see Gil MacIntosh and a few other planters. He plans to leave day after tomorrow."

Dismay ran through Meredith. Two more days. But at least she had the next hours to herself. She would go down to the river, and be back well before he returned.

Quinn and Cam kept a fast pace. They planned to go by the MacIntosh plantation and then on to the Parson's. The directions were indelibly written in Quinn's mind, although he had never visited the Parson in his home before. He had met the man in Cincinnati, soon after he'd carried his first illegal cargo.

Quinn remembered him as a plain man whom he had immediately liked and trusted. Which was well, he thought wryly, since the man held both his and Cam's lives in his hand.

But first he must see MacIntosh. The man had been pleasant enough when they had been introduced the previous night, but later he had seen the planter's eyes turn cold as they watched him. Meredith Seaton, he knew, was probably responsible for that.

That was unfortunate but it was his own fault. Damn his

eyes or, more accurately, his *mouth* for not keeping silent. He wanted the shipping contracts. An increase in shipping from this area would, of course, give him a reason for stopping often at Vicksburg, which would be beneficial to the Underground Railroad. But he also wanted to see the *Lucky Lady* prosper. He had come to love the steamboat, although he knew he would probably have to give her up one day. He had already made legal arrangements to transfer the title to Jamison if anything happened to him. He owed the *Lady*, as he often called her, much, for she had helped him rebuild his life and had given him purpose and confidence. In some ways, he considered the boat almost human, deserving the very best care.

And his own quiet need to be successful at something other than cards and intrigue was a challenge. His words to Brett had not been completely false.

From a distance, the MacIntosh mansion appeared larger than Briarwood although it was of the same Greek Revival and Italianate styles. But where Briarwood had columns only at the front, this home was surrounded with them, and a huge porch and galleries wrapped around the entire home. It was breathtaking, he thought, and would be extraordinarily tempting to a young lady. He recalled how Gil MacIntosh had hovered over Meredith Seaton and he felt an odd pang. But why, he wondered, would Gilbert MacIntosh be interested in such a frumpy woman? Her inheritance, perhaps? Could MacIntosh need money? And why in the devil did he, Quinn, care?

Gilbert MacIntosh was in the fields, and Quinn was ushered into an elegant study while Cam stayed outside with the horses. Quinn studied the room, its Italian marble fireplace, crystal chandelier, and shelves of leather-bound books. Beveled stained-glass windows cast a warm glow on the rich handmade furniture. If MacIntosh needed money, there was certainly no evidence of it here.

Quinn didn't have to wait long. MacIntosh, dressed in riding clothes and mud-splattered high boots, appeared in the doorway and Quinn knew he had not been mistaken last night. The man's eyes were icy, his mouth grim.

"Devereux?" There were no pleasantries.

Quinn regarded the planter inquisitively. He was undeniably homely, his face too broad, his hair too red, his skin too pale despite the hours he must spend in the sun. Yet there was a certain integrity about the man that surprised Quinn.

Quinn tried his most disarming grin. "I think I can offer you very advantageous prices to ship your cotton."

"You've wasted your time, Devereux. I'm satisfied with my current arrangements."

"You said last night you would hear me out."

"That was last night," MacIntosh said curtly. "I've had information since that leads me to believe I wouldn't care to associate with you."

Quinn had not expected so frontal an attack. Meredith Seaton had done her work well. But not quite well enough. Robert Seaton had already signed a contract with him. Quinn's smile didn't fade, although the corners of his mouth twisted slightly.

"I'm offering two cents less per pound than what you're paying now," he said, ignoring the other man's insult. "Robert Seaton has just signed a contract with us."

Gil shook his head. "I said I was satisfied with my present arrangements. My butler will show you out."

Quinn felt a brief respect for MacIntosh, and surrendered. "It's your loss, MacIntosh. If you change your mind, you can contact my agent in Vicksburg."

"I won't."

Quinn nodded, and followed the butler, who had suddenly appeared at the door. He didn't know whether to rage at Meredith Seaton. He had lost business, but she had apparently just added to a reputation he had scrupulously tried to build over the past years.

Yet he didn't like her interference. It was another score to settle. One that perhaps the theft of her slave would even. He gave Cam a brief smile as he remounted his horse. One way or another, he was going to get Daphne away. For Cam. And now there was an added reason—revenge.

They rode for several hours before they arrived at the Parson's cabin on the lake. The dogs were barking, and Quinn hoped that meant the Parson was home. But he wasn't. Four dogs came out to meet them, but no figure in a black suit. The cabin was unlocked but empty.

Cam's face fell, and Quinn knew the reason why. They could spend only another day and a half in the area. If they missed this opportunity, he didn't know when they would be back. And Cam would have to tell Daphne that their plans were off.

"We'll wait," he said, taking the chair Meredith had occupied just several days earlier, and straddled it, resting his arms on the back.

Cam paced awhile, then said he would keep watch outside. Quinn nodded, instinctively knowing that Cam wanted to be alone. There were certain things they could share, and some they could not. Quinn knew Cam's worry over Daphne was intensely private.

After a few moments, he rose and looked around the cabin curiously. There was a large worn Bible sitting on the table in the corner. He went over to it and ruffled the pages, glancing only briefly at the words.

Whatever belief he had had in God had deserted him in the prison ship. Nothing that had happened in the next years had changed his mind. Even now, he questioned the existence of a God, any God. If there was one, he wasn't altogether sure he cared for an omnipotent being who allowed cruelty and brutality and slavery. He started to close the Bible when three sheets of heavy paper fell from it.

He leaned down and picked them up, not intending to look, but his eyes caught the strong sure strokes of a face he recognized. He looked at the second. *The Carroll brothers*. The third sheet captured an entirely different subject—a fox whose wary dark eyes stared at him. There was so much life in the animal that Quinn thought it could jump from the paper into the room. But even more intriguing was the familiarity of those bold, impatient strokes.

"Captain Devereux."

He spun around and stared at the Parson, who stood in the doorway with Cam. Unaccountably, he felt guilty standing there with the sketches in his hand.

"Jonathon."

The Parson acknowledged the greeting with a nod, his eyes on the sketches. "This is a surprise."

Quinn wished he didn't quite feel like a small boy with his hand caught in a forbidden pie, but the circuit preacher's eyes didn't do much to relieve that discomfort. The pale blue, while not accusatory, nonetheless demanded answers.

"You know Cam?" Quinn asked, discomfited.

The Parson nodded. "We met once in New Orleans." He waited for Quinn to continue.

"There's a girl we would like you to help."

The Parson raised an eyebrow. "You've come all this way for that?"

"No. We're staying not far from here. Shipping business."

The Parson seemed to stiffen. "Where?"

"The Seaton plantation. Briarwood."

A curtain fell over the Parson's face. He turned away from Quinn and Cam and went to a small cupboard. "Cider?" he asked, his back to them.

"No," Quinn said, a bit puzzled. "We can't stay long. We just wanted to ask for your help. A girl named Daphne at Briarwood. We were hoping you could help her North."

The gaunt man turned to him, his eyes unfathomable. "Does she want to go?"

"Yes." It was Cam who spoke. "I talked to her last night. Gave her the password."

The Parson nodded. "I'll do what I can."

That was, Quinn knew, a great deal. Still he hesitated, his fingers tightening on the sketches he held.

"Where did you get these?"

The Parson reached out his hand for them. "One of our agents . . . in New Orleans. These two are apparently a pair of slave hunters."

Quinn held onto them. "Who sketched them?"

The Parson's light blue eyes caught and held Quinn's midnight blue ones. "You know I can't tell you that."

"I've seen that style before. . . . I have a painting and I think it's the same artist. I've been trying to find more of his work."

The Parson smiled slightly. "I didn't know you were an art lover."

Quinn grinned at the description. "I didn't know either. It's just that there's something about that particular painting."

The Parson knew before he even asked. Something was growing in him . . . a terrible sense of inevitability. "What kind of painting?"

"A rainbow over the Mississippi. There's something haunting about it." His hands fingered the sketches. "Could these be by the same artist?"

The Parson was a man who believed the end justified the means. And the end, now, was freedom. Freedom for many. It had become his obsession, his life. Nothing to him was more important. Not even the truth. He shrugged. "I wouldn't know. They came to me from New Orleans to circulate among the stations. The man who sent them knows I enjoy animals and sent the sketch of the fox along. I didn't ask the source." The hint was strong that Quinn should follow suit.

But Quinn wasn't ready to let go. "These two men were on the *Lucky Lady* a month ago."

"They've been many places, according to our information. May I have the sketches?"

Quinn reluctantly handed them over, his eyes lingering over the drawing of the fox. "It's extraordinary."

"Yes," the Parson said simply. He took them over to the Bible and slipped them back between the pages. He turned to Quinn. "How long will you be at Briarwood?"

"Another day. Robert Seaton's agreed to ship some of his cotton with us. It will give me a good excuse to stop at Vicksburg frequently if you have cargo for me."

"How do you find Briarwood?"

Quinn shrugged. "Like any other plantation."

The Parson felt briefly relieved. "Tell me about this Daphne."

"She was recently purchased in New Orleans by Meredith Seaton, who apparently owns her." He looked over at Cam. "Cam talked to her on the *Lucky Lady* . . . he'll make arrangements for her after Cairo."

So it was Cam who was interested, the Parson thought as he looked at the large black man who stood silently near the door. He knew Cam's story, at least part of it, and he knew that Quinn and Cam together had been uncommonly effective conduits for the Railroad. They deserved this . . . the gift of Daphne . . . and perhaps it would dull Devereux's obvious interest in Briarwood.

"You've tried to buy the girl?"

"Several times. I believe Miss Seaton has taken a dislike to me." The observation was made dryly.

"From what I hear of you, Captain, that must be an unusual dilemma."

"You can't believe everything you hear," Quinn replied. "But I take it money means nothing to Miss Seaton. My brother says she spends it like water. Too bad it doesn't make her more presentable . . . or agreeable."

The Parson choked slightly. "I think it might be wise if you left, Captain. I don't want anyone to see you here."

Quinn nodded and offered his hand. "Thank you. Just get word to us where Daphne is, and we'll take care of her."

The Parson nodded. "Four weeks, no more."

Quinn and Cam opened the door and went to their horses. The Parson watched them mount and ride from the clearing, his mind trying to sort out this latest complication.

It was amazing that his two best, most observant agents were completely fooled by each other. Or were they? They displayed a certain bafflement, some indefinable current, as they talked about each other. And they were already linked in some way by the painting.

He looked up at the sky. Some divine plan? He fervently hoped not. Singularly, they were both very effective. That effectiveness, he sensed, would come to a complete end were they to find out about each other. Neither did anything halfway, and he suspected their hard-earned disguises would be destroyed if they ever came together. There was no place in Quinn Devereux's disguise for tenderness, and none in Meredith's for love.

He felt a tug of guilt. He must work to prevent their union. The Underground Railroad, and their roles in it, was too important. Personal lives came second. They had to.

The Parson, feeling a hundred years old, heard the sharp bark of the fox. He moved slowly toward the barn to feed it as he thought once more about Quinn Devereux and Meredith Seaton. He prayed silently that he was making the right decision.

Chapter 10

THE MATHIS PLANTATION, like Briarwood, sat alongside the Mississippi but it was farther south, not far from Natchez. Like so many other Mississippi plantations, the house was Greek Revival, but rather than white, it was a brownstone color, which blended with the bluff on which it sat. Large meticulously attended gardens surrounded the home.

Meredith had arrived ten days earlier, coming unannounced with Daphne and Aunt Opal. They had been welcomed coolly, but hospitality, even for uninvited guests, was a Mississippi tradition. No one thought of turning them away even if the Mathis family grumbled privately.

William Mathis was a distant cousin, whom Meredith had visited on other occasions. She usually outwore her welcome quickly with outrageous demands and giggly flirtations. Already, gentle hints were being dropped that she continue on to New Orleans where, she had loudly pronounced, she was going to meet with her miserly banker. But first, she had told William Mathis that she just had to stop and visit her very favorite relatives, particularly the oldest son, Beau. Beau had disappeared that day and not returned, much to her public consternation and private amusement. As if she would have any interest in a wastrel like Beau.

She spent much of her time on a bench in the fine gardens, half dabbling at her canvas, half watching Jim, one of the gardeners.

He had captured her attention as soon as she had arrived. There was a pride in his bearing, a resentment simmering in his eyes. She had spoken with him several times, and though he tried, he could not quite conceal his intelligence. Intelligence was not, she knew, a desired quality in slaves. Too often it meant trouble, and those who demonstrated such an unbecoming trait often ended up in the fields until all the spirit was worked or beaten out of them. Therefore it was best to show a blank face to one's masters.

Jim had obviously mastered the skill, she thought as she mixed a horrendous pink, its color ranging somewhere between salmon and fuchsia. She intended to use it for some equally atrocious camellias taking bloated shape on the canvas. While her right hand played at painting, her eyes stayed on the tall, almost midnight black slave who was trimming hedges around the pink and white camellia plants. Camellias, she thought idly, were stubborn plants that seemed to bloom at their own pleasure, not anyone else's. Now, despite a cold winter, rich blossoms clung to their branches, daring a frost.

People were like that, she mused. Some would dare anything while others did the expected, risking nothing.

The slave working diligently in the garden was, she was gambling, like the camellia, not the begonia, which had to be nurtured and nursed along.

Levi Coffin had taught her to identify those slaves who were determined to be free, who would risk all to grow as they wished, not as someone else wished them to. There was something in the bearing and the eyes of certain slaves that proclaimed their longing for freedom, their willingness to sacrifice to achieve it. Meredith had learned to look for, and recognize, that particular quality.

Today was the day, she thought, that she would drop the words and see whether or not he understood them. If he did, all should be easy enough. If not, she would have to take more time, be more careful.

Freedom's light. The words had sped many slaves, perhaps hundreds, on the long dangerous journey to freedom. She had revealed its path to perhaps only twenty, no more, for she had been taught to be careful. But she was proud of that number. She knew of only one who had been caught and brought back, and he had not revealed her involvement. He had not been whipped but had been forced to wear an agonizingly painful and humiliating iron collar around his neck and head for six months. The collar, a frequently used punishment for runaways, was fitted with horns and bells that made it nearly impossible for the slave to sleep any way but sitting and, of course, the bells announced his presence wherever he went. Meredith knew about it because he had tried a second time . . . and had made his way to Canada.

Now all her attention was centered on Jim, and she secretly blessed the slave for this since it took her thoughts away from Quinlan Devereux.

She had not seen the riverboat captain again after the ball. She had returned from the river in the late afternoon the day after and retired to her room where she had stayed, pleading woman's indisposition, until he left. Since she often used such an excuse when she wanted to be alone, no one questioned it. And so he had left, his disturbing presence now only a ghost. But it was a ghost that wouldn't quite disappear and that materialized at the most unwanted times.

Like now.

Meredith looked down at her canvas, wanting to create beauty rather than this poor ragged caricature, a flower without life, without focus, without substance. Sometimes, she felt that way, especially during the past few months.

She stood, her eyes intent on the black man leaning over a bush. She walked over and stooped, her hands caressing the white bloom of a camellia.

Her eyes looked upward. "It's as white," she said slowly, "as freedom's light."

She saw his back stiffen, felt the tension invade his body. "Wouldn't know nothin' 'bout that," he said slowly, but Meredith saw the glimpse of hope in his eyes.

Meredith's hands stayed on the bloom. "It's perfect. You have a special touch. It's a skill appreciated north of here."

The slave's hands faltered slightly. "The massa' won't sell."

Meredith hesitated. This was always the most dangerous step. "There are other roads . . . a railroad, perhaps."

"I heared of lots o' railroads," he replied cautiously.

"This one goes North. It follows the North Star."

There was a silence, a long deliberating silence, and Meredith held her breath.

He slowly nodded.

"Do you wish to take passage?"

"My wife?"

She inclined her head, as if studying the flower. "But no more. Two weeks after I leave. I'll bring you what you need before I go."

Suspicion hung heavy in the air, but Meredith was accustomed to this. She would have been worried, in fact, if it had not been there. "I'll be back tomorrow. But swear you'll wait two weeks."

"Mistress . . . I wait two months iffen I knew it wuz real. . . ." She watched as his fingers tightened against the tools, his knuckles turning white.

"It's real . . . I'll give you names of people to contact, where you can get food and help."

"Why you doing this?" She was often asked the question, and it was almost an accusation. Meredith understood. They both knew he was risking his life.

"I had a sister sold." She had found this the best answer, the most accepted one.

"What that matter to you?" It seemed scarcely a good reason to Jim. Masters often fathered slave bastards, but seldom cared except to appreciate the added wealth they brought them.

"I loved her," Meredith said simply. "And one day I'll find her."

There was so much sincerity and confidence in her voice that Jim believed her. Still, he was uncomfortable. "I'll do what you say," he said, and moved away, his pruning knife flashing among the green leaves.

Meredith packed her paints, feeling the familiar conflicting emotions of fear and exuberance. She had chosen well. She knew it.

In three days, she would leave for New Orleans, and another confrontation with Brett Devereux. Once more she had spent all her yearly stipend; most of it had gone to the Underground Railroad for settlements in Canada, some to the detective hunting for Lissa, and the remainder for her own travel. She would have to submit to his examination again, and to his disapproval. But at least he wasn't odious, like his brother.

And William Mathis and his wife would be pleased at her upcoming departure. Meredith had made a thorough nuisance of herself, rising late and demanding special meals. She had disparaged the young men in the county, except for Beau whom she had simpered over until he escaped. She'd complained about the cold which seeped into her bedroom. She had, in short, made herself thoroughly disagreeable. The Mathis family would be glad to see her go; they would never connect her with Jim's disappearance in a few weeks.

She took one last look at her painting. She grinned. It would make the perfect farewell gift for Beau Mathis.

Despair settled over Daphne like a shroud as she packed Miss Meredith's and Miss Opal's clothes.

Everything seemed so hopeless at the moment. They were

going, she had been told, to New Orleans for an indefinite stay.

She didn't question her sorrow, or how it happened to attack her after so many years of acceptance of her position. Cam had opened a door and let light in, and now it was closing again.

But despite the darkness of her thoughts, her hands never stopped moving. She had learned long ago to separate her mind from her hands.

Just weeks ago she had been so happy. After the fear-filled visit in the barn with the large but gentle man, she had allowed hope to build. Despite his own position, he had had such confidence that she could escape. It had been so strong, so unshakable, that Daphne had been filled with a courage and elation of her own. Somehow, she knew she would be free, and so would he. The thought had filled her with a joy she had never known.

And then Miss Meredith had announced suddenly they would be leaving in two days' time, and all her hopes went tumbling to the ground. The old feelings of helplessness returned in double measure. How could she have ever believed she could escape? Could be free? Why had she trusted Cam's confidence when he hadn't been able to free himself?

It had been a dream, nothing but a foolish dream. A tear trickled down her cheek and landed on the silk gown she was folding. The material was lovely, but the dress itself, with its flounces, had little appeal. Yet she wondered how such cloth would feel against her skin.

Disliking herself for such frivolous thoughts, she carefully packed the gown in one of the two trunks Miss Meredith had brought. Her hand touched the paper-wrapped package near the bottom, and she wondered briefly what it was. Sometimes it seemed Miss Meredith had secrets of her own.

• • •

On the afternoon before she left the Mathis plantation, Meredith went once more to the camellia garden, praying she would find Jim there. He was there as usual.

In a pocket in her dress was a plainly wrapped package containing a small compass, a knife, and twenty dollars. Kneeling to look at a camellia, she gave him the locations of two stations in Mississippi that would then direct him to the next station, and on and on. Food would be buried in a pouch underneath the largest visible tree in the event the station master was gone. She bade him repeat the names and the directions until she felt he had them firmly in his mind.

"Travel only at night," she warned. "If you leave the river, follow the North Star. If you doubt anyone, wait for them to mention 'freedom's light.'"

He stuffed the small package in the waist of his pants. "Bless you," he said awkwardly.

"Good luck," she whispered. "I hope to hear soon that you've made it."

He swallowed, unable to say anything more. He was being given a chance that he thought might never come.

"Remember—wait at least two weeks." With that last warning, she was gone.

He didn't turn to look after her. He didn't have to. Whether or not he succeeded, he would never forget her, never forget one feature of her face.

Jim's left hand went to the bulge at his waist and then returned to the pruning knife. He would be just about finished with the pruning in two weeks.

Meredith had always liked New Orleans. She had sent word ahead to Brett Devereux to engage rooms at a small respectable hotel on Chartres Street for herself, Opal, and Daphne, and upon docking, she engaged a carriage to take them the short distance to the hotel.

She had been relieved to find the *Lucky Lady* gone from the landing. Relieved and yet strangely disappointed.

Meredith planned to do some shopping. It was part of her pattern, that and the quest for more money from her trustee. She would purchase another dress, not that she needed or wanted one. She took no pleasure in purchasing the monstrosities, although she did derive a certain satisfaction in defying her dressmaker whose advice she never took.

And painting materials! She needed painting supplies, canvas and additional oils, even a new sketchpad. And, when she was able to slip away from Aunt Opal, she would visit Elias and give him the painting by "M. Sabre" that she intended to send North. Perhaps she would put a tiny bit of sleeping powder in Aunt Opal's chocolate tomorrow night. And Daphne? Perhaps an errand?

Yet Meredith was reluctant to send the girl out at night. She was too pretty, and mulattoes were often considered fair game. She wished, in fact, that she hadn't brought Daphne, but she didn't quite trust her brother.

The carriage rolled through the streets toward the hotel, and Meredith stopped worrying as the sights of the French and Spanish architecture came into view. Her artist's eye loved anything beautiful, and New Orleans personified the word with its wrought-iron balconies and widow's walks and lush private gardens. The handsome homes basked beneath canopies of live oaks and were framed by palms, azaleas, bougainvilleas, banana trees, and other tropical plants. But even more interesting to her was the city's personality, a rakish arrogance that taunted and defied her best efforts to capture it on canvas.

Like Captain Devereux.

Since his visit to Briarwood, she had tried to sketch him again. Perhaps if she could capture his image, his essence, she would no longer be so strangely discomfited. But although she felt she had captured the boy correctly, she had never been satisfied with her depiction of the man. The mouth was elusive. But mostly, it was the eyes, eyes that gave the impression of blankness, though something inside her knew this wasn't so. She felt those eyes worked at being inscrutable, which meant there was a great deal to betray. But then she smiled at her own whimsy and wondered why she couldn't just accept the obvious, why she always had to probe beyond the facade.

Obviously, there was very little to Devereux. Very little good, at least.

The carriage pulled up to a small but very respectable hotel, and a tall dignified servant approached them from the entrance, his mouth smiling widely. "Miz Seaton, we've been lookin' fo' you."

In minutes, they were installed in two of the best rooms, and Meredith had ordered a meal sent up to them. Opal was tired, and Meredith had to prepare for her meeting with Brett in the morning. She knew he was going to be troublesome, but she needed additional funds to continue the detective's search for Lissa, and the Underground Railroad was always in need of funds—for clothing, for horse and buggy rental in Ohio, steamboat fare across the border, for new starts in Canada, and occasionally for those conductors who took pay for their risks.

She could see Brett's frowning face now and hear the same lecture. "Your grandfather—"

Meredith's mind once more wandered disobediently to Quinn. How could two brothers be so different? Why did she even care? She wondered over it as she finally fell off to sleep several hours later.

Brett's office revealed much about his disposition: warm, neat, comfortable, yet very practical.

As she entered, he rose from behind his desk and moved toward her, his voice pleasant but a bit wary. "Meredith. I didn't think I would be seeing you so soon."

Meredith forced a silly smile to her lips. "I find myself," she said, "in need of more of my trust fund."

Brett sat on the corner of his desk. "I seem to remember that you've already drawn more than this year's allotment," he said dryly.

"Fiddlesticks," Meredith said crossly. "There's more money in the fund than I can ever use."

"I doubt it," he replied in the same wry tone. "What now?"

"I'm thinkin' of gettin' engaged and I need some new clothes. There's the most divine new silk at Madame Gereaux's."

Brett's brows knit together. "Engaged?" Fortune hunter, he thought privately. It would have to be a fortune hunter. And then he thought of Quinn. He hadn't seen his brother since he had arranged the invitation to the Seatons'. Please, Lord, no.

She fluttered her eyelashes at him. "So you see how important it is I have suitable clothes."

"May I ask the name of this fortunate man?" he said quietly.

"Why, our neighbor, Mr. MacIntosh, of course."

Brett slowly released the breath he had been holding in his throat. The way she had been spending money, God knew, she should have enough clothes to last her a lifetime. However, relief softened his usual reluctance. He sighed heavily.

"Regardless of what you may believe, Meredith, your money is not inexhaustible. I wish you would use a little restraint. . . ."

"Oh horsefeathers, Brett. What else is there to do with money if not spend it?"

Brett winced. With a slight frown, he looked at his visitor. He had not enjoyed inheriting this particular duty from his father, acting, he often believed, as keeper for an irresponsible and silly child. They went through this same discussion at least three or four times a year, and still huge bills for clothing came from Cincinnati and other places. In addition, he had to listen to the constant harping for personal funds.

"Your grandfather," he started, knowing he had repeated the same words many times, "wanted to protect you—"

"And I'm mos' grateful," she interrupted with a secret smile at his predictability. "But you must see I need a new wardrobe . . . an' I need money for Christmas gifts an', well, I just know you understand.''

"I understand only too well," he said. His smile didn't quite cover the sarcasm that had crept into his voice, and Meredith, for the first time, felt a resemblance between the Devereux brothers.

"Then you'll transfer the funds?" The question was asked with a smile that she hoped looked tentative. She knew she would get the money. She always did as long as her demands weren't completely outrageous, and she had purposely refrained from doing that. But she had to complain in such a way that he didn't suspect her. It wouldn't do for the flighty Meredith Seaton to be reasonable.

"How much?" he asked with resignation.

"Oh," she said, "I have this little list . . . but I just remembered my paintin' materials. I do need some money for those too." She took a package from under her arm. "I even brought you a present, my latest work."

She smiled as he took it graciously, but gingerly. She had given him paintings before and had expressed disappointment that he never displayed them in his office. He had always replied that he preferred them at home. In a closet, she thought with amusement. "So you see," she rattled on, "I just must have at least five hundred dollars."

"Three hundred, and no more this year," he bargained.

Meredith allowed her face to fall while silently she calculated her expenses. One hundred to the detective, one hundred for the Railroad, ten for her art supplies. Her lodging and riverboat fare would take much of the rest.

"But—"

"That's all, Meredith," he said with a voice she thought he must also use with naughty children. "I have a responsibility to your grandfather."

She pouted slightly, then urged him to open her present. It was one of her least objectionable landscapes, a painting of the Mississippi near Briarwood. There was nothing good about it, but neither was it quite the horror some were.

He looked at it briefly, complimented her on it, then put it on his desk. "Now tell me about this young man. . . ."

When Meredith finally escaped, a bank draft in hand, she hurried down the stairs to where a hired carriage waited. She had been able to avoid Opal, who had slept late this morning, and Daphne, whom she had put to work sewing a rip in one of her dresses.

If she hurried, she would have time to visit the detective. The sun hit her eyes as she hurried out of the dark bank, and she didn't see a loose sheet of paper on the front steps. When her boot heel hit the paper, it slid, taking her foot with it, and she lost her balance. Her body spun forward, and she threw out her hands to soften her landing, but suddenly strong arms grabbed her and her body was steadied.

She didn't have to look up. The warm tingling of her skin where confident fingers held her told her all she needed to know. She closed her eyes, even as she wondered how she knew.

Captain Quinn Devereux!

C*hapter 11*

HOW LIGHT SHE WAS. So much lighter than he had expected. Perhaps, Quinn thought, it had been the bows and flounces and layers that had made her look gawky.

But there was nothing gawky about the slim form he was holding now. Even under the heavy cloak she wore, he could feel the soft curves.

Reluctantly, he released her.

Quinn waited for her eyes to open, for she had shut them tightly, and he wondered briefly if she would faint. He somehow doubted it. He regarded her lazily as her eyes flickered open, and he saw a momentary flare of golden fire. It was gone almost immediately.

"Why, Miss Seaton, how delightful to be of service," he drawled ironically, his hand very properly remaining on her elbow. "I did not expect to see you here in New Orleans. A most pleasant surprise."

"For you, perhaps," she answered ungraciously, not a little abashed at her body's reaction to him. Her elbow felt on fire. It was a most humiliating encounter, and she did not appreciate his smirk.

"Now, Meredith," he started. "Ah, but you have not given me permission to call you Meredith despite all our . . . many interesting moments together. My pardon, Miss Seaton."

Any gratitude she may have had quickly fled. He was as insufferable, as arrogant, as bullying as ever. She gave him her haughtiest look, then moved her eyes slowly down to where his hand still touched her elbow. "If you would release me?"

"But I would hate to see you faint now. I might not be as quick next time."

"I never faint," she retorted before thinking. She only wanted to get away from him. Damn it, but his face was even more handsome than she remembered. She couldn't keep from looking at him—and noticing the devilment that danced in his eyes.

"You don't?" he said with a raised eyebrow. "I seem to remember any number of occasions when you were indisposed."

"There are many reasons for indisposition," she snapped back. "For example, the company one is forced to keep."

He grinned wickedly. "I can always help you back down to the ground, if you so regret accepting my assistance."

Meredith knew she was behaving badly, as well as stepping out of her role. If only his eyes didn't probe so deeply, if only the words from his tongue didn't sting so painfully . . .

She forced a smile to her face. "I do thank you," she said, bending her head so he wouldn't see the lie in her eyes. She would much prefer to have landed on her backside, injured dignity or not, than endure this charade.

"May I help you to your carriage then?" The voice was soft and suddenly surprisingly gentle.

The change in tone, the unexpectedness of it, sent bolts of lightning through Meredith. The tension, the electricity, had always been there between them, although she'd fought against recognizing it. Now, as she lifted her eyes, there was no doubt of it. His presence, his touch, affected her as nothing else had in her life.

Confused, she stepped away and almost fell again. His arm once more went around her waist, and she felt the enormous strength behind it.

"I think I'd better see you to your lodgings," he said with only a touch of irony, for he too was feeling strange sensations, a craving as dark and deep as the coal pit he had once labored in.

"Just to the carriage," Meredith managed to say. Even to her, her voice seemed drugged.

"If you wish," he said, surprised at the mildness in his own voice. The craving was growing, even as his mind kept telling him he was a fool. The biggest damn fool in the South.

His hand stayed beneath her elbow as they walked toward the carriage. He was close enough that she could smell the barest scent of musk and spices mixed with soap and leather, an aroma that was pure sorcery. She didn't want to let it go. She didn't want to let *him* go.

But when they reached the carriage, she did. Her pursed mouth and the artificial brightness of her words had nothing to do with the loss she felt as he handed her carefully inside.

"Where are you staying?" he asked.

"A hotel on Chartres."

"Will someone be there to assist you?" He was amazed at his concern. It was ridiculous. She had told him any number of times she wanted nothing to do with him. And he really wanted nothing to do with her. Dowdy, awkward, rude—she was all of these, yet there was something else too, something he didn't understand. And it bothered him. God damn, but it chafed at him.

"Aunt Opal and Daphne."

"Daphne?"

Whatever softness he had created in Meredith in the past few moments hardened. So that was where his interest continued to lie. Some vulnerable part of herself started aching. Badly.

She ignored his question. "My thanks again, Captain," she said, her chin climbing into the air.

"I'll call on you to make sure you've had no ill effects."

"There is no need." Her tone was sharper than she had intended, and he looked startled.

"Ah, but there is, pretty lady." Quinn wasn't quite sure what had happened, but she had certainly frozen over more thoroughly than a shallow pool in Minnesota in January.

"You don't understand, Captain," she said tightly. "I don't wish my reputation tarnished. I do appreciate your help, but you need trouble yourself no further."

She was spared a retort for, at her nod, the driver snapped the horses into a fast pace.

Quinn watched the carriage disappear around the corner, a small smile lurking in his eyes. He had again felt that strange incomprehensible fire that always blazed between them, and knew that she did too. He damn well didn't understand why it was eating at him, but it was, and he knew eventually he would satisfy both his hunger and curiosity. Perhaps once he'd had more than a brief whiff, his appetite would find it poor fare indeed.

With that comforting thought settled, another more disquieting one took its place: Daphne. She had said Daphne was with her. Damn. He and Cam had been waiting daily to hear that Daphne had made it North, and now she was here in New Orleans.

He released a long stream of curses that would have made Terrence O'Connell proud.

Meredith directed the carriage driver to a less than respectable quarter of New Orleans. She pulled the hood of her cloak over her hair as she stepped down from the carriage and entered a doorway.

The office she was seeking was on the second floor. She

knocked but no one answered and she leaned against the wall, frustrated, discouraged, and altogether disgusted with herself. She was still there several minutes later when she heard the heavy tread of steps. Her heart sped for a moment. It seemed that Quinn Devereux turned up every place she went, and she would not have been startled to see him here now.

But it wasn't he, and she sighed with relief as she watched the detective she had hired move swiftly toward her. He had come highly recommended by Elias, although she had precious little to show for more than two years and two thousand dollars.

"Miss Seaton," he said. "I'm glad you came today. I might have some news for you."

Meredith held her breath. She had heard those words before. She trusted Bill Milligan now only because Elias did.

He unlocked the door and waited until she entered the dingy office.

"I'm checking out the latest information, but I think she might be in Kentucky."

"A slave?"

He nodded. "I traced the sale of a girl named Lissa, a light-colored female, to a horseman in Lexington six years ago. She was sold again, and the records were lost, but I think I have a lead. I have someone checking now to see if she's still there."

"How long . . . ?"

"Several weeks, maybe more."

Her hands tightened on the small bag she carried. "Perhaps I should—"

"You should do nothing unless you want to spoil any chance we might have in getting her free," he said curtly.

"However much it costs . . ."

"I know, Miss Seaton. And after two years I want to find her as much as you. I don't like failure."

She saw the determination on his face and some of her confidence returned. He was a burly man, a former police-man, and she sensed he could be very dangerous. He had no strong feelings on slavery one way or another, but he was immensely loyal to those who employed him, and that included both Elias and herself. Elias had used him years ago to expose a slave hunter who kidnapped free blacks in the North and enslaved them by swearing they were escaped fugitives.

"I'll do as you say," Meredith said finally, but Milligan noted the reluctance in her voice.

"I'll contact you when I hear more," he said. "Elias can get word to you." He never contacted her directly. He knew little about her and he didn't want to know more. His job was merely to find the girl Lissa, and he understood that Meredith would then try to purchase her freedom. He suspected both Meredith and the Quaker, Elias, were involved in the Underground Railroad, and he had dropped several broad hints to Elias whenever he learned of an impending police raid, but he did not know their involvement as a fact, and he kept it that way.

As Meredith emerged from the building, she felt a mixture of elation and apprehension. Perhaps after all these years, she was finally reaching the one goal that had eluded her. Yet she was desperately afraid to get her hopes too high. She had been disappointed too many times.

What would Lissa be like now? It had been nearly fourteen years since they had become separated. What had her friend and sister suffered? Meredith shivered, and the cause was not the damp cold wind blowing off the Mississippi.

The carriage returned her to the hotel, and Opal, florid and indignant, was waiting. "Respectable women," she pronounced, "do not wander the streets of New Orleans alone."

"I just went to see Brett Devereux," Meredith explained soothingly. "I didn't want to wake you."

Mollified slightly, Opal gave one last attempt at chaperonage. "I really don't think . . ."

But Meredith suggested attending a play that night, and Opal's disapproval quickly turned to delight. Meredith knew such an outing would tire Opal considerably and allow Meredith to slip out later to see Elias. She wanted to tell him about

Jim, the slave at the Mathis plantation, and alert the Railroad to be waiting for him, and she also wished to share the possible good news about Lissa. Elias seemed to be the only one who cared. In the meantime, she and Opal would go shopping. It was expected.

But it would be a very long afternoon.

When Quinn returned to the *Lucky Lady* Cam was gone. It was just as well, he thought. He needed time alone, time to sort through things. His mind was jumbled.

It had been a disastrous day, starting with his confrontation with Meredith Seaton. It had not improved with his meeting with Brett.

Meredith had unsettled him in a way he had not been in years. He had thought himself content with his life. He was doing something he felt was important. At the same time, he was exercising his restless appetite for adventure and tweaking the nose of those who kept others in captivity. He had thought it sufficient to have Cam as his only friend, but now he wondered if Cam's obsession with Daphne wasn't a reflection of a need and loneliness he himself was feeling all too often. Was he being unfair to Cam? To himself?

He convinced himself that Meredith Seaton did not interest him, only that he longed for a woman he could love and be loved by. It scared the bloody fury out of him that even Miss Seaton was beginning to look good to his usually impeccable eyes. Was he really getting that desperate?

His brief visit with Brett had not helped the state of his heart. He had seen the wistful regret in his brother's eyes as once more he refused a visit to Brett's home, and the approbation when he deposited the results of his rather successful card games from the last trip.

Day by day it was becoming more important to him that Brett understand he wasn't merely a wastrel, that someone other than Cam accept him for what he truly was. He ached with the need, though he didn't quite understand why it had grown so strong. He had always been able to submerge this feeling before, to convince himself it wasn't important. A momentary aberration, nothing more. But now it was eating at him like a cancer.

The only relief he had felt during his brief visit to his brother had come when he'd seen the painting lying on Brett's desk. He had picked it up, glancing at it idly, his mind only vaguely paying attention. It was very poorly done, the colors gloomy with hovering clouds looking more like gunny sacks than anything else.

"Your taste has deteriorated, brother," he commented.

Brett smiled wryly. "A present, I'm afraid."

"From your worst enemy?"

Brett grinned. "From my worst client."

Quinn's hands stilled. "Don't tell me . . . ?"

"Miss Seaton. She was here for more money. This, I assume, was a bribe of sorts."

"She really didn't want the money, then," Quinn said with laughter in his eyes.

Brett's grin grew wider, although he was ashamed of himself for doing so. It *was* a gift. "She meant well," he said.

Quinn looked at the painting again, this time with a closer eye. He remembered that the aunt had said something about Meredith's hobby, mentioning it almost apologetically. Now he knew why. But for some reason, he continued to stare at it. The name "Seaton" was scrawled in the right-hand corner. Nothing about the painting was quite right, almost as if . . .

He shook his head at the thought that came and went as quickly as a summer storm. Yet something in his mind continued to nag at him.

"When are you leaving again?" Brett's words brought him back to the conversation.

"Tomorrow afternoon."

"You're quite sure you won't come for dinner tonight?"

"I wish I could," he'd said, and there was a soft note of yearning in his voice. "But I have a business meeting."

"Quinn . . . ?"

Quinn turned and looked at his brother, at the wistful expression on his face.

"The children keep asking for you."

"Next time, Brett. Next time. I promise."

"I'll hold you to it," Brett replied. He went over and held his hand out to his brother, taking it with a warmth that both hurt and pleased Quinn.

He had nodded and left. Now he wondered where in the hell Cam was.

He needed something to take his mind from thoughts he found both destructive and unproductive.

Quinn went to his cabin, seeking refuge from his confused emotions. He felt like the turbulent Mississippi in the painting that adorned the wall and wished, for a moment, that he had something of the tranquility of the rainbow.

Perhaps it was time to consider the future. He and Cam would probably be discovered sooner or later, and he needed to develop an escape plan. And then what? The future seemed to stretch emptily and endlessly before him.

More for the activity than anything else, he changed his clothes, exchanging his black suit for a loose flowing linen shirt and more comfortable black trousers. The mirror caught the ribboned scars on his back, and he imagined the horror Miss Seaton, or any other woman, would feel at seeing them. His hands clenched as he remembered the pain of the lash. . . .

He tried to remember O'Connell's words as they stripped his shirt from him and tied his arms securely around the mast.

"Don't let the bloody bastards git ye down. Think o' the meadow, lad, o' the bright sky. Fix yer eyes and yer mind on that, and don't let it go."

He tried to do that, but the first slash of the skin was like fire running through his body, and the second was like a red hot poker pressed against it. He knew his body jerked, and he bit his lips to keep from screaming, until his throat choked with blood.

The lash tore into his shoulder, and he felt the skin ripping

*through the previous cuts. Even his bare chest was covered
with splattered blood now, and his eyes swam with red mist as
he struggled to keep his voice inside him.*

*Keep your mind on the meadow, on the sky, he told
himself. But how could he when his body was fiery agony,
and each additional slash added to a torment he had never
known could exist, and never known a body could endure?*

*He screamed, and the scream echoed in his ears. But it
wasn't an echo. It was another scream, and another . . .*

"Capt'n?"

Quinn shook his head to rid it of the memory.

"Cam." He opened the door.

Cam looked at him in concern. The captain's face was
white, his mouth tense, his eyes bleak.

"Somethin' wrong?"

"I saw Miss Seaton this morning. Daphne's with her."

Cam's face fell, and his hand stilled on the knob of the
door. He had been expecting word any day that Daphne was
safe in Illinois.

"It's just a matter of a few more weeks," Quinn said.

"It's gonna be harder every day for her to run," Cam said
quietly.

"I know," Quinn replied. Slavery, any form of captivity,
had a way of wearing a person down, of sapping courage,
particularly courage that was but a bud. He often thought
there was no greater bravery or gallantry than that of escaping
slaves, of men and women who knew nothing of freedom,
who had had no experience with it, yet were willing to risk
everything for it.

"Perhaps," he said thoughtfully, "perhaps we can help
her from here. Perhaps Elias . . ."

"And she could travel with us." Cam's voice was explosive
with a feeling that Quinn had never seen in him before.

"Why not?" He grinned.

"How?"

"Elias. I was going to see him tonight, anyway. I received a message that he expects a new shipment. I'll ask him then."

Cam's face relaxed, his lips broadening into a smile as he thought about Daphne. It would be a hard journey in the bowels of the steamboat, but he would be able to see her, to reassure her. He would make sure she was safe and situated happily. Eventually . . . well, eventually, perhaps he could even court her.

He didn't know why she meant so much to him. Perhaps, he mused, it was the innocence she still had, the innocence that he had never had. Or even that reservoir of courage he had sensed in her. He only knew he wanted to protect her, to give her the world.

And then . . . ?

As long as he remained with Captain Devereux, there was no safety for him. And yet, he knew he couldn't leave the captain or the *Lucky Lady*. They had given him a reason to live, had returned his heart and soul to him, had made him feel his worth as a human being and, after thirty years of being considered little but a beast, that was very much indeed. Each escaped slave was a victory that raised his self-esteem.

He could not give Daphne a secure life, not if he continued with the Underground Railroad, and how could he do anything else? How could he not help his own people?

He stared out at the levee, at the bales of cotton waiting for loading, at the dark bodies lifting and stacking under white overseers. He quietly figured the number of bent and tired bodies that had been required to bring the cotton here, from the preparing of earth to final harvest to hauling. He remembered the way every bone and muscle in his body ached and burned and suffered after fourteen straight hours in the field.

Daphne. He would see her to freedom and an unfettered

life in Canada. And that, he realized now, excluded him. He could never give up his work. With a pain that had no physical cause, but was perhaps even more debilitating, he turned and went below deck to prepare the secret space between the walls.

Chapter 12

SHIVERING IN the cold, a heavily cloaked Meredith clutched her wrapped painting and slipped through the streets of a darkened New Orleans.

Elias Sprague's warehouse was on Canal Street, not far from where she was staying, but it seemed a hundred miles away. Coming to him was very dangerous. If the connection between them was ever discovered, she knew it would be disastrous for both of them. Yet there was no other way.

Her blond hair was twisted into a knot and well-hidden under the hood of her cloak. The dark gray of the material blended into the night. She was thankful there was very little moonlight, and that the back of Elias's warehouse was not lit by the gas lamps that adorned so many other parts of New Orleans.

She welcomed the need for concentration. It was a relief to think only of her safety and of those dependent on her—not of Quinn. She pulled the hood tighter around her face as she watched the warehouse for several moments, allowing her eyes to adjust to the darkness. She should be tired. It had been a long day, but instead she was filled with the kind of tension that kept all her senses alert.

When she approached the warehouse, she hesitated and searched the windows for a particular light. It was there, positioned in the third window to the left, a lamp burning brightly. It was a signal that all was safe. Elias Sprague may not know she was coming, but he often had unexpected visitors, and the lamp was his beacon.

Meredith quickly moved to a side entrance, knocked lightly, and after several seconds was admitted by a small man with a ready smile.

"Meredith, how good to see thee."

"I saw the light," Meredith replied. "Are you expecting a shipment?"

He nodded.

"I'll be quick, then," she said, not wanting to see the newcomers or them to see her. The less anyone knew, the better.

"I wish thee could spend more time with us, but I understand," he said. "What can I do for thee?"

"There's a slave, Jim, who will be escaping from the Mathis plantation near Natchez. Can you alert the stations to be looking for him?"

"It will be done," he said quietly without question.

"And I have this." She unwrapped her painting and waited nervously as he looked at it. Meredith was always uncertain about the quality of her work. She liked it, but that didn't mean that anyone else would. The fact that she never saw anyone's pleasure, that she could never reveal this side of herself, always hurt. Although she often chided herself for wanting something as inconsequential as praise or approval, the need was there, deep inside her.

He took the painting to a gas lamp and studied it, his face wreathing into a smile. "I think it's the best thing thee has done. It's very powerful."

"You will send it North?"

"Yes, M. Sabre," he said. "In fact, there's a boat here now expecting my shipment. I'll send it along."

"The proceeds go to the Railroad."

"The last one brought two hundred dollars," he said. "Our agent said there is one particular buyer who's very insistent on purchasing all of Sabre's paintings. I think he will like this very much."

Meredith felt a surge of warm satisfaction. She hated to give the paintings up, but it was good to know that someone appreciated them.

"Thank you," she said. "And I wanted you to know, the detective thinks he might have located Lissa."

His smile grew broader. He knew how much Meredith had wanted to find her half sister. "I will pray for thy success," he said.

She reached out and touched his hand. "Thank you. I'd better go before your other visitors arrive."

His hands tightened around the painting. "*I* thank thee . . . and the joy thee creates with thy work. When will thee be back?"

"Probably four months." She grinned impishly. "I'm afraid my trustee will have a stroke if I return any sooner." The smile disappeared. "Be careful, Elias. I'll keep in touch through the Parson."

"God go with thee," Elias said, and saw her to the door. He watched as she once more lowered the hood over her face and reached out to touch him in farewell. He saw the momentary loneliness on her face, a reluctance to leave, but they both knew she must. She finally lowered her eyes and turned, moving toward the lush garden that hid the back of the warehouse from the street.

Meredith heard a whisper, the soft sound of footsteps on hard earth, and she slid behind some trees. Her eyes had once more adjusted to the dark and she could see a small group of hesitant figures, led by an obviously more confident one, make their way to the door she had left seconds ago. When the last man entered the warehouse, she turned to leave.

She heard a rustle behind her and started to whirl around. But she was too late. She felt an arm around her, and another over her mouth. She struggled violently against her attacker until she felt a sudden sharp pain at the side of her head, and everything went black.

Quinn, as usual, approached his Quaker contact carefully, although he had business reasons to meet with him. Elias Sprague was a merchant and often shipped goods on the *Lucky Lady*. Still, caution had become second nature to him.

He moved into the shadows when he saw dark figures near the warehouse. His fugitive cargo, he suspected. They would be fed and sheltered in a secret room in the warehouse and sometime in the morning placed in crates and carried to his boat. They would know, of course, that they were on a steamboat, but not which one. The only person they would see was Cam, and no one would mention the *Lucky Lady*. It was safer that way, particularly now that there were rumors up and down the river that a steamboat was involved in the Railroad.

Quinn relaxed against the tree, planning to wait there until Elias had time to secure the fugitives in the hidden room. Perhaps it would be possible to secret Daphne with this shipment, although arrangements would have to be rushed. He disliked haste; it usually meant carelessness and errors, but he knew how important this had become to Cam . . . almost like a personal crusade.

But how would he get Daphne away? He could try to lure Meredith Seaton out in the morning. But after their meeting at the bank, he doubted that even his best behavior would move her. And, God only knew, he had a hard time maintaining any semblance of good manners with her. She seemed to unleash the devil in him every time they met. It was a situation that baffled him, especially since he had also sensed her own battle between attraction and aversion to him. Unfortunately, it was the latter that usually won. He smiled wryly. A premonition told him he hadn't seen the last of her, not by any means. He didn't know whether it was expectation or dismay that accompanied that odd knowledge.

He saw a movement in the garden and edged closer, trying to identify the figure, even as he was aware that the last of the silent shadowy figures had entered the warehouse.

Bloody damn, he thought. Someone was spying on the warehouse! How much had they seen? Enough to convict Elias, that was obvious, and probably doom the poor souls who had just entered.

He looked around, seeking other furtive bodies lurking among the trees, but there were none, so the individual wasn't the police. Slave hunter? Or merely a bounty hunter looking for the large rewards offered for escaping slaves?

Quinn's oath expanded into a flood of profanity. There was only one way to keep Elias safe now, and that was violence, though he knew Elias, with his strong Quaker beliefs, would never tolerate that, not even for his own safety. He, Quinn, would have to take matters into his own hand.

He moved silently forward, each step carefully taken to avoid rustling a leaf or a bush. He couldn't tell much about his quarry's figure for it was wrapped in a voluminous cloak.

Stealthily, he reached the spy. One of his arms snaked around the watcher's midsection and his hand covered the mouth. The figure, slighter than Quinn had imagined, struggled violently, and he clipped the side of his captive's head. The body relaxed in his arms, and he caught the form as it crumpled to the ground.

He swore once more. As he lifted the body, the cloak fell open and he saw the dress. He went rigid. His hand uncovered the hair and he saw the gold in the darkness. Something in his gut constricted. From the first glance at the dress, he had instinctively known who it was. Damn it, he knew.

What in the hell was the spoiled Miss Seaton doing on the grounds of an abolitionist in the early hours of the morning? He had always wondered if there wasn't more to her than she allowed to be seen. But this? His mind ran over possibilities, all of them apparently preposterous.

She could not be a member of the Underground Railroad. If she was, he surely would have been told when he had visited the Parson. The Parson would have known. Bloody hell, he would have to have known.

And his brother, who was not easily fooled by anyone, was convinced that little Miss Meredith cared only about money and her own pleasures.

Money.

Nothing else fit. She had to be doing it for the reward. Possibly because Brett wouldn't give her everything she wanted.

But that still didn't feel right. But then nothing felt right.

He thought about taking her inside, but he reminded himself that the Quaker's own unshakable and uncompromising ethics would forbid him from taking any action. The merchant would go to jail first. And the entire Underground Railroad would suffer an irreplaceable loss.

Quinn wondered briefly whether his own stomach or conscience could tolerate harming a woman, even one guilty of the actions he now suspected. He knew neither would, no matter what she was, or what she had done. But he was not above holding her prisoner for a short time. Or even scaring her witless.

Witless. Damn it. He had once thought her witless. He was hastily revising that opinion, and he realized suddenly he had been doing so for some time. Slowly.

He had no good choices. It was likely that either he or Elias would have to be sacrificed. And Elias was, by far, more valuable. Quinn had few illusions about himself. He did what he did because he enjoyed the danger, the adventure, the satisfaction of thieving from a class he despised.

Elias, on the other hand, was a truly good man, one who deserved better than prison, one, Quinn suspected, who would not survive there long.

He made his decision quickly. He would risk revealing himself to Meredith Seaton and find out what she knew. He could then warn the merchant in time for the Quaker to escape North while he, Quinn, kept Meredith Seaton prisoner until they reached Illinois. When Elias was safe, he and Cam would release her and make their own escape.

Otherwise, Elias and this shipment could well be taken today.

But it would mean the end of everything Quinn had built, had worked toward. Damn it. Damn her.

His mind decided, he placed her on the ground. He took his belt from around his waist and strapped her hands together, then gagged her with a piece of cloth he tore from her petticoat. He knelt down and picked her up, then he strode quickly down the darkened street to where his horse waited.

With the exception of one watchman, the deck of the *Lucky Lady* was clear. Quinn, without looking at his watch, surmised it must be about 3:00 A.M., late enough that most of the crew was asleep.

He looked down at his burden. She was still unconscious, which worried him. When he had struck the figure, he had thought it a man, and he had not been overly gentle. Quinn cuddled her as he slid from the horse, one hand holding her head close to his heart, almost in a loving gesture. The gag was thoroughly hidden by his large hand.

Quinn managed a conspiratorial smile for the watchman. "A bit too much wine for her." He grinned. "Can you bring the horse aboard and tell Cam to come to my room? I have some tasks for him."

"Aye, sir," the watchman said, only too aware of who owned the boat.

Quinn carried Meredith to his cabin and laid her on his bed. He quickly lit the gas lamp and returned to her side, removing the hood from her head, his hand gently exploring the bruise on the side of her face.

She looked vulnerable. She wore none of the heavy powder, and her skin was soft and luminous in the flickering light, except for the great purpling on one cheek. Her hair, for once without the tight curls that had never suited her, was pulled back simply, revealing an oval face that now seemed perfection itself. Long dark lashes shuttered those dark brown eyes that he had never been able to penetrate.

What did they hide?

Don't be a fool, he told himself. Remember another woman who had seemed so damned vulnerable, whose plotting cost you eight years of life. Women were all the same—traitorous. And this one, he suspected, was even more so than most. She certainly wasn't what she appeared to be. And that was damning in itself.

He removed the gag and undid the belt that bound her hands awkwardly, then replaced it with a strip he tore from the sheet. He did the same with her ankles, noting with a jaundiced yet appreciative eye how very lovely they were before forcing himself to continue. With another piece of cloth, he linked her ankles with her wrists so she could move only slightly.

Satisfied that she was immobile, yet not too uncomfortable, he set about trying to bring her back to consciousness. There was water in a pitcher, and he poured some into the bowl next to it. Quinn took a clean towel and dampened it, returning to the side of the bed where he sat and wiping her face, hoping she would wake. She was beginning to worry him although her breathing was easy.

The cold water apparently was the needed stimulant. Slowly, very slowly, the eyelashes lifted, and she moved slightly as if to shake the pain she must have been feeling. The eyes finally opened completely, and Quinn watched as, obviously bewildered, they found the strange ceiling and then moved until they saw him, and widened with shock.

She tried to move, and Quinn saw her eyes flash first with panic, then anger, as she found her hands and ankles thoroughly bound. She tried to move her wrists, and the cloth linking them to her ankles pulled up her dress until a good portion of her pantalets showed. She stopped immediately, a flush creeping up her face.

Quinn's hand hovered near her face in case she screamed, but it became immediately evident that she, for some reason of her own, had decided against it. Still, although her movements quieted, her eyes spat angry flames at him. A number of emotions flitted across them—fear, anger, humiliation— and then, quite intriguingly, they all disappeared, and he found the same blankness, the same vacuousness he had seen in them before.

She was marvelous at the game, and he felt a certain admiration flow through him. Quite obviously, she had weighed her situation and decided to let him make the next move.

Almost gratefully, he heard Cam's distinctive knock on the door.

He leaned over Meredith, his finger on her chin, forcing her to look at him. "You *will* be silent."

The gold flecks in her eyes flashed rebelliously.

"I could gag you," he said. "Believe me, it would hurt you more than it would me." There was a cold menace in his voice that made the threat a promise.

She bit her lip and nodded. He could tell that she was bitterly resentful that she was being forced to obey him. She was having a difficult time hiding her anger, which, at the moment, amused him.

Quinn stalked to the door, prepared to pounce back instantly if she uttered the slightest sound. He opened it, gave her one last searching look, and stepped outside, closing the door behind him.

Cam looked as if he had very little sleep. His eyes were

red, and there were lines around his mouth. He looked at Quinn curiously. "Capt'n?"

"Miss Seaton is inside," Quinn announced quietly.

Cam's eyes widened. He had not missed the bristling hostility in the Seaton woman whenever she was in Quinn's presence.

Quinn grinned, understanding. "It's not exactly voluntary," he explained. "She's trussed up like a Christmas turkey."

Cam waited patiently, knowing more information would be forthcoming and that he had been summoned for a reason.

"I found her at Elias's warehouse, snooping. She saw the new shipment entering there."

Cam's large hands balled. "A spy, then?"

Quinn shrugged. "I can't think of another explanation."

"And Friend Sprague?"

"I didn't stop to ask him. You know how he feels about violence."

The words hung in the air with all the implications.

"What are you goin' do?" Cam asked finally.

"I don't know," Quinn said with the first hesitancy Cam had ever seen in him. "First I have to find out exactly what she's up to, and why."

"Daphne?"

"This complicates the hell out of everything, doesn't it?" Quinn said. "Go get her. She should be at the hotel." He hesitated, then continued. "If anyone asks, you can say you have a message for Miss Seaton but, for God's sakes, try to avoid everyone." He shook his head slowly. "Be very careful, Cam. This might be the end of the *Lucky Lady*'s role in the Underground. I don't want it to be the end of you too."

"I'll be back by dawn," Cam promised.

"Before bringing her on board, leave her in the shadows and get me. I'll distract the watchman while you take her to the cargo deck."

Cam nodded, then turned quickly on his heels and left.

Quinn remained outside the room, his hand on the doorknob. He felt sick with failure, with the prospective loss of everything he had worked for. Damn Meredith Seaton to hell and back.

His jaw set angrily, he reentered and found her eyes on him. She was still, but he knew from the mess the bed was in that she had tried frantically to free herself in those few minutes he was gone. And then what would she have tried doing? His eyes went around the room, resting on a pistol that lay on top of his desk. He knew, from the way she averted her eyes too quickly, that she had seen it.

"Bloodthirsty as well as a snoop," he said conversationally. But there was a warning in his voice. "Now tell me why you were in such an odd part of town in the wee hours of the morning." It was an order, not a question.

"It's none of your business," she retorted.

"I'm making it my business, Miss Seaton."

"You have no right to do this."

"You're absolutely right," he agreed amiably. "Unfortunately you're in no position to complain."

Meredith disliked his sudden friendliness much more than the menacing hostility of a few minutes earlier. It was much more intimidating for some reason. "Your brother—"

"I think my brother would be aghast at both of us, Meredith," he interrupted silkily. "I doubt if he would think much of your midnight forays, not to mention trespassing and snooping. He might cut your allowance. Of course, I might do something far more . . . extreme."

"I wasn't—"

"Ah, but you were, my dear Meredith. And don't tell me we're not familiar enough to use first names, not after you boarded my boat in my arms and made such a charming disarray of my bed."

Horrified at the suggestiveness of his remark, she could only stare at him.

His voice hardened. "What were you doing there?"

"Where?"

"Come, Meredith, this loss of memory is becoming too

convenient." His gloved hand touched her chin, forcing her to look straight into his eyes. "Don't play any more games with me."

"I don't know what you mean."

"I think you do. But we will start from the beginning. Why were you hiding in the trees well after midnight?"

Meredith fought to turn her eyes from his, but they were locked there, just as securely as her arms were bound together. Despite the calm tone of his voice, the seeming mildness of his questions, his eyes, those dark blue eyes, were furious. Furious and magnetic. "I . . . I couldn't sleep and went for a walk and . . . I was lost. I saw the light and thought I would ask directions."

He grinned sardonically, amusement joining the anger in his eyes. "Surely you can do better than that, sweet Meredith."

Surely she *could* do better than that, Meredith thought sourly, but right now a better explanation eluded her. She was tired and sore, and her head hurt. Her thoughts were as jumbled as the interior of a child's toy box. She decided to attack, instead. "What right do you—a blackguard, a gambler, an . . . an abductor of women—have to interrogate me? I demand you let me go." She tried to sit up, to maintain some dignity, but her damned skirt rode up again, and she saw his eyes go to her ankles. He smiled lecherously.

"Why don't you yell for help?" he taunted. Her not doing so puzzled him.

"Because," she retorted, "you would probably hit me again."

He had no reply. No matter what he thought she was, he couldn't completely suppress the flash of guilt for having already struck her. The purple bruise on her face seemed more severe than before, and he winced, noting the grim satisfaction in her eyes as he did so.

She was, he told himself, a consummate actress. He moved closer and saw her involuntarily flinch. "Damn," he said, "but you're going to tell me what I want to know or . . ."

"Or what?" This time she was the one who taunted. She was now certain he wouldn't physically hurt her, not again, and the knowledge showed in her face.

Quinn saw some of her fear fade, and he cursed himself for showing even a smidgen of remorse. But there was another way . . . a way other than violence to torment her. Pleasure.

He had sensed her reluctant response to him before, had felt her passion in their few kisses, and recalled her frantic escapes. This time there would be no escape.

He stood and walked over to a bureau and, knowing her eyes were following every move, took a knife from a drawer and returned to her side. He leaned down over her, the steel blade shining in the lamplight. Although her eyes never left the blade, she didn't flinch, and once again, he secretly applauded her.

Quinn slowly cut the cloak away from her. Then very deliberately he laid the knife on a table and took off his gloves. It no longer mattered that she saw his hands, knew they were not those of a gentleman. His left hand moved sensuously across the bodice of her modest dress. Even through the barrier of material, she felt the fire of his touch. It seeped in through the cloth, through the skin, until it reached the core of her, taunting, teasing, arousing.

"No," she whispered.

"Ah yes, love." He was practically purring. Like a cat. A jungle cat. A very, very dangerous sensuous animal. "I've been wanting to do this since we became . . . reacquainted on my boat."

She squirmed frantically, which served only to drag her dress up to her thighs. He reached down and ran his fingers along the length of her legs, caressing and inciting until he could feel her tremble under the slightest pressure. He marveled at the passion he sensed in her, at the glowing embers that needed only the slightest fuel, the merest provocation, to burst into roaring flames. His hands moved farther up her legs, encountering her pantalets, which he shoved up. Kneading, massaging her flesh, he moved nearer to her private place. Her movements became even more frantic as she moaned. He could feel the reaction of her body, the way it strained toward him and heated under his touch. But as he continued, he felt his own body responding and wondered if his punishment was not equal to, even greater than, hers.

"You bastard," she spit out in anguish.

"What language for a lady," Quinn said smoothly, trying to smother the growing ache in himself, to hide his own agonizing need. His hands continued to move with seductive sweetness, with an expertise that had always won him whichever lady he wanted. He had often used his hands to give pleasure, to simulate affection, for he had never been able to give his heart. Not since Morgana.

She shuddered and bit her lips. He could see a drop of blood trickle from one. "Please . . ."

"Why were you on Canal Street?"

"Damn you to hell."

He leaned down and licked the drop of blood from her mouth, then nuzzled her lips with a tenderness she would have treasured if she hadn't known he was doing it for nefarious purposes.

She bit him.

He cursed, tasting his own blood as well as hers. His hands left her leg and went to his lips, touching the cut, feeling the blood flow from it.

Quinn looked down at her. There was no victory on her face. If anything, there was a slight expression of guilt and regret. And intense scrutiny.

How had he ever thought her simpleminded?

As he gazed into chocolate-brown eyes that were as complex and mysterious as the Mississippi itself, he felt his whole body tense with craving. A craving to continue his exploration of her body, to awaken that passion so evident under the carefully composed veneer. He ached to tear it away and discover the real Meredith Seaton.

But he knew he would get no further now. His own

emotions, which he had fought for years to conceal, were too close to the surface. He needed time to reconstruct his barriers, to cool the need within him.

Quinn slowly rose and tore two more strips from the tangled sheet. With one, he tied her already-bound feet to the end of his bed, and looped the other around her wrists, securing them to a bedpost. When he was through, she could barely move.

Reluctantly, he tore a third piece and gagged her, disregarding the plea in her eyes.

"I have to leave for a short while," he said. "I'll have the same questions when I return. And I *will* have them answered. One way or another. You have about an hour to consider your options. Or lack of them."

She lowered those incredible lashes, and once more he thought how vulnerable she looked.

As vulnerable as a cottonmouth snake, he told himself.

Still, he liked himself a good deal less when he left than when he had risen twenty hours earlier.

He hoped like hell that Cam was having better luck than he was.

Meredith opened her eyes when she heard him move away. She saw him kill the flame in the gas lamp, plunging the room into darkness. The draperies had already been closed when she first woke from unconsciousness.

She saw just the barest outline of his stiff back at the door, and heard it opening and closing, a key then grating in the lock.

It was then that total despair enveloped her.

The gag chafed her mouth, momentarily making her panic. If only he knew he did not need it. She had no desire to scream or sound an alarm. This was the last place on earth she wanted to be found.

She tried to move her hands, to wriggle free, which, she knew now, was her only escape. But although the cloth did not bite into her skin, it was, nonetheless, snug and secure, and the more she moved, the tighter the bonds seemed to become. Captain Devereux was not the careless man he sometimes pretended to be.

Dear God, what did he want? And why had he been at the warehouse? What did he know?

Was he working with the Carroll brothers? Why else would he have invited them to sup with him?

There were those missing years no one would talk about, years when he had completely disappeared. She had heard the speculation, the whispers, but no one seemed to really know anything. Could he have been involved with the illegal slave trade even back then? Was that how he had made his fortune? For she knew he was very rich. Her brother had made that clear when she had protested the shipping arrangement between them. Surely Quinn Devereux had not acquired his wealth through gambling. No one was that good.

But even as the terrible possibility ran through her mind, she felt the lingering effects of his hands on her skin, the tormenting unfulfillment of something he had started. . . .

There was a burning, deep in the core of her, as she recalled those insidious hands, the slow seduction of them, the mixture of tenderness and barely restrained violence that was so incredibly, surprisingly alluring.

She remembered the very hardness of them, which had startled her. She expected soft hands since he had always kept them gloved, but they had been callused, the skin rough. Even that had been intriguingly sensual for some reason.

What did he want? What would he do with her?

The questions kept coming back, like the beat of a voodoo drum. Frightening yet hypnotic.

How long before he would return? Once more her hands sought freedom, and once more she failed.

That he had so easily used her body against her was more frightening than any torture he could have devised. She was disgusted with herself, yet she had learned in those few minutes that she was powerless against him, against his touch. She hated him for that. She hated him for the intimate invasion, for showing her how weak she was.

. Levi had warned her about many things, but never about this.

Still, no matter what Devereux did, she would tell him nothing. Nothing.

Chapter 13

CAM EYED the exclusive hotel from its small but verdant garden.

All the windows were dark and, he surmised, all the residents sound asleep at this early morning hour.

He had already been here once just hours before. After Captain Devereux had told him of his meeting with Miss Seaton, he had walked by and stopped to talk with a man tending the garden.

"S'pose there might be sum work for me here?" he had asked the man.

The man looked at him in surprise. "You free?"

Cam nodded.

There was a longing in the man's eyes as he shook his head. "Jest slaves here."

"Looks like a mighty fine place."

"No better hotel in Noo O'leans," the servant replied with some pride.

"You stay here?"

The man nodded toward the stable. "Quarters ov'r there."

Cam sighed. "Mighty hard findin' a job. An' a place to stay."

"Why doan you go North?"

"Got me a woman here."

The man grinned conspiratorially.

"Fac' is," Cam continued, "she's wi' a plantation nor' of here and stayed here once wi' her mistress. She say they need help."

The man nodded vigorously. "Tha' right, but they won't hire no freeman."

Cam looked desolate. His eyes went to the house. "Where you think my woman stayed?"

His source nodded toward the third floor of the hotel. "Guests' servants stay up there. Roastin' in the summer; freezin' in the winter."

"I reckon there's sum there now."

"Jest one I know of. Purty li't' thing."

Cam hitched up his britches. "I bes' be gittin' along. Try to fin' a place to stay."

The man nodded and went back to his work in the garden.

Now Cam wondered how he could get to the third floor. There were vines on one side of the building, but he didn't think they would take his weight.

There would be a backstairs for servants. Probably the female house-slaves were kept in the rear near the kitchen and the servant stairs. How long before they would be up? How much time did he have?

Not enough time to stand here and wonder, he thought disgustedly. If only the door wasn't locked.

He found the backdoor and tried the knob. It turned, and he said one of the few prayers he'd uttered in his life. His mutilated foot usually dragged, and he was careful to lift it high enough so that it wouldn't make the usual shuffling noise. But the effort took both concentration and care, which slowed him.

He lit a match and went past two closed doors until he came to a staircase. Cam mounted it carefully. God knew how he would explain his presence here if discovered. By the time he reached the second landing, the match had burned down to his fingers, and he winced with pain. He lit another and climbed the next flight. At the top he had to bend his head because the ceiling was low, several inches less than his own well over six-feet height.

There were three doors. He hoped the gardener had been correct when he had said only one woman was here. He tried the first, and it opened with a creak. The austere room, with only a cot for a bed and hooks for clothes, was empty. The second one was not.

He saw the slight figure on the cot, covered with a rough blanket, and knew instantly that it was Daphne. The match flame reached his fingers again, and he blew it out. In the dark, he walked carefully to her, kneeling beside her bed, and placing his hand over her mouth.

She sprang up almost immediately, her eyes wide with panic until she heard his gentle deep voice. "Daphne . . . shh."

Daphne nodded, and he released her mouth, but put a hand on her shoulder. "We're going. Can you dress without light?"

She clutched his hand desperately, wanting his reassuring touch. She felt dazed for a moment, trying to comprehend the enormity of his being here, of what he was suggesting. Her body trembled with both fear and a new heady anticipation. But she was able to nod once more.

He turned his back, looking out the window at the moon, which had just emerged from behind some clouds. It was only a quarter moon, but it seemed brighter than usual. A beacon, he thought. A promise. He felt her touch on his arm, and her hand was steadier. He smiled to himself, wishing she could see his face and take courage.

Cam lit a third match and turned to her. She was wearing a cloak that looked heavy and warm. He nodded with approval and gave her his hand.

Her small fingers wrapped around his hand trustingly, and he had never felt quite as good. Quite as strong. He started down the steps, heard a board creak and stopped, listening intently to determine whether anyone else might have heard it. When only silence met his ears, he continued, taking care to lift his damaged ankle, to guide her so she wouldn't stumble. When they reached the main landing, they slipped out the door and across the dark garden. He looked up. The moon had disappeared again, and the sky was filling with clouds. It would start raining soon. He could smell it.

Cam pulled Daphne closer to him, limping rapidly down the street, partially carrying her along. At the end of the street, he looked back. The hotel was still dark; the street clear.

His hand touched her cheek with tenderness and reassurance, and she gazed at him adoringly.

"How?"

"Later," he whispered. He put his arm around her shoulders, and rushed her forward. He wished they could move faster. He had thought about bringing a horse, but it would make them seem more suspicious if they were stopped. So he clung to the shadows, going down one street and then another and another until he saw the levees and the *Lucky Lady*. He looked for the watchman but didn't see him. Instead, there was a familiar dark figure standing at the gangplank, his legs lazily crossed and his arms resting on a crate.

Daphne hung back, and Cam leaned over and whispered, "It's all right."

"But he's . . ."

"I know," Cam said softly. He looked at Devereux, who was nodding for them to come aboard. His hand tightened on Daphne's small one as if to say "trust me."

But still she tried to stop him. Cam swooped her up in his arms as easily as if she were a feather. He didn't understand why Captain Devereux was meeting them openly, but he had stopped questioning his friend a long time ago. Quinn Devereux never did anything without good reason.

Cam grinned suddenly at Daphne, pleased that the captain was, in effect, giving him permission to tell her everything. Or almost everything. "We can trust him," he said. "He told me where to find you and suggested I come for you."

Daphne's eyes grew wider. Her hand tightened on his shoulder. "It's a trick."

"No," he said simply, and she knew she couldn't question him further, couldn't tell him that she didn't quite believe him.

Cam saw the doubt in her eyes. He wanted to tell her that Quinn Devereux was a conductor with the Underground Railroad, but he couldn't. Not yet.

She shivered as he carried her aboard, across the gangplank. She didn't look at his master, as if by not seeing him he would no longer be there. There was no greeting between the two men, or exchange of words, but she could tell when they passed the captain by the sudden tension in Cam's body. They ducked through a door and he put her down. He took a lantern and lit it, then led her down into a great black space on the lower deck where most of the cargo was stored.

He moved between bales and barrels, guiding her with assurance to the back wall. He touched a panel and, as if by magic, part of the wall slid open. The pressure on her hand urged her to enter and, as she did, the lantern showed a narrow passage running inside the wall. There were pallets and blankets, a barrel, and a few boxes. She looked up at him in puzzlement.

"Can you stay here on your own . . . just for a few hours?" Cam said, his eyes demanding her assent.

Daphne thought of the lonely darkness. The room was like a coffin. But then she thought of other places she had stayed, and not by choice, particularly the odorous slave jail in New Orleans. At least this place smelled clean. And freedom lay at the end of the journey. She had never been able to hold that thought before. Not to be sold. Not to be used. The idea was too fine, too achingly wonderful to contain within herself. She laughed for the first time since she had been sold from her plantation home. She laughed with tension, with joy, with anticipation. For she knew she could bear anything now to be free. Anything at all.

Cam heard the exhilaration in her voice and recognized it. He had heard it before when other fugitives had found their hope. "There's food in the boxes, water in the barrel, but you can't have any light," he said gently. "There's too much danger o' fire."

She understood what he was telling her. This place would be black and empty, but her hand merely squeezed his in assent.

"I'll stay wi' you awhile," he said. "There will be others tomorrow."

"Others?"

"Fugitives. Goin' North."

"It's true, then? Truly true?"

His solemn lips broke into a smile. "Truly true," he agreed. "You will be safe here."

She wanted to ask more about his master, about Captain Devereux, but when she tried, he merely shrugged and his arms went around her, holding her, comforting her, reassuring her.

Cam, feeling the too-thin body under his hands, wanted to do more, but he felt she was still too uncertain, too needful. He wanted her, but he wanted to be sure that she wanted him, that she wasn't just grateful or scared or lonely. With his scars and his limp, and his dubious future, he had little to offer her.

His warmth and succor, his quiet encouragement, were what she needed most now. She rejoiced in it, savored it, held it closely to her heart. She had never known there was such gentleness on this earth, and she knew it was that quality, more than anything else, that had given her courage this night, that would continue to give her courage no matter what happened.

For now she knew there was a God. That there was goodness, and hope, and . . . love.

* * *

Quinn watched the dawn break. The ominous clouds, which had been so threatening earlier, sprinkled a few soft drops and then rushed away as if on some urgent mission. Light came creeping through the blackness slowly, in misty gray drabness before fading into a soft pink, then gold. Bright flashes touched the dirty brown of the Mississippi and made it, for a few brief moments, luminous and shining.

The river went about its business, its currents carrying flotsam down the center, and he knew there must have been a storm someplace farther north. Idly he wondered where. He shook his head in dismay at himself. He had tried to think of anything to divert his mind from the problem at hand.

He had to face it, damn it. Questions had to be asked, decisions made.

The boat was coming alive now. Stewards were cleaning the rooms, parlors, and dining rooms in preparation for passengers. More cargo would soon be loaded. He had not seen Cam since his friend took Daphne below several hours ago. Quinn knew he should alert him, before more cargo was moved. He was beginning to learn again exactly how disconcerting a woman could be.

He thought about Meredith in his cabin. Tied and helpless. Perhaps she would be more cooperative now.

But then such tactics had never worked with him. They had only stiffened his resistance. O'Connell had taught him how to use brutality against itself, how to conquer the complete feeling of helplessness when subjected to the whims and cruelty of the lowest of his keepers. He had learned to husband his feelings, to hide his hate, to endure the unendurable to achieve an end result—escape.

His stomach plummeted as he remembered exactly how painful that helplessness had been, and he also recalled the expression on Meredith Seaton's face as he had fastened the gag. Defiance had been there, but so had fear, the panic of a trapped animal.

Don't make the error of sympathy, he told himself. But it

didn't work. He did feel sympathy, and something more, and it scared him as little in his violent life had.

The dawn had spread across the entire eastern sky. He could delay no longer. As he looked at the steps leading down to the cargo deck, Cam appeared, his harsh features more tranquil than Quinn had ever seen them. Quinn wondered if his own would ever mirror that look.

"She all right?"

"She's fine. That little girl has more courage than I thought."

"The others should arrive soon. Watch out for them, Cam. I'm going to my cabin."

"Need any help, Capt'n?"

The edges around Quinn's eyes crinkled. "I need a lot of help, Cam, but for the moment stay here and take care of the shipment."

"What are you goin' do?"

Quinn shrugged. He wished to hell he knew.

Cam grinned. "Wildcat by the tail?"

For the first time since night, Quinn relaxed slightly. "I think you could say that."

"When do we leave?"

"Noon. No later. Particularly now that we have a guest."

"You're goin' to keep her then?"

"I don't see any other choice, Cam."

"You know whatever you decide, I'm with you."

"I know, Cam," Quinn said softly. "I know." He turned and moved swiftly toward the stairs to the upper deck. And his cabin.

Meredith watched the first light seep into the cabin. She had stopped struggling. It was futile. Instead she studied her surroundings. Perhaps it would tell her something about the enigmatic man who seemed to have so many conflicting faces.

The cabin was a comfortable one, with rich wine-colored

draperies and shelves and shelves of books. She was surprised at their number. Reading was not a habit she associated with gamblers and rogues. She wished she could make out the titles. You could tell much, she knew, from what a person read.

The bed on which she lay was large and comfortable, the sheets smelling of soap and spices, a smell she remembered well and which was indelibly associated with him. It had hovered in her mind far too long after their last meeting.

She twisted around until she faced the back wall and saw the painting that dominated it. Even in the dim light, she knew immediately it was a rainbow. In shock, she recognized it as her own. Her rainbow!

Elias had said someone had been asking for her paintings. Could it have been Devereux? Had that been how he'd found her? Had he been tracking her? If so, he was far more dangerous than she had first thought. And far more devious.

When she heard footsteps and the sound of a key turning in the lock, she twisted again until she was as he had left her. But she didn't close her eyes, nor would she try to hide her thoughts from him. Those tactics simply hadn't worked earlier. She decided to challenge him directly.

Meredith watched as the tall lean figure entered and went to one wall, pulling the draperies apart, letting the sun pour in and fill the room. She sensed the reluctant hesitancy in his steps with surprise.

And then he was there, above her, seeming much taller. He had taken off his coat and he stood there silently in a linen shirt open at the neck, tight black trousers hugging muscular legs, and polished soft-leather black boots that came almost to his knees. There was so much power in that body, so much strength. She had sensed it before, but never in so formidable a way.

Her eyes moved slowly upward, to a face that was now slightly shadowed with new beard. All derision was gone from his eyes. Instead, there was something like regret, and that worried her more than threats or mockery or torment.

She could understand those, cope with them, ignore them, tolerate them. She didn't understand this expression, or the quiet thoughtfulness of his gaze.

His eyes broke the contact and with lithe grace he picked up a chair and placed it near the bed. He folded his long tall body into it, and she wondered once more at the leisurely elegance of his movements. He looked unhurried but again she sensed the tension in him, the silent watchfulness that made something in her react so strongly to him. After bearing his scrutiny for several seconds, she felt her own tension clawing at the walls of her body. She couldn't believe how much she craved his touch again, the feeling of his fingers against her face. . . .

She was desperately afraid that those wayward feelings were evident in her eyes, for she could not move her gaze away from him. Dear God, why did he affect her so? She should know only fear, loathing, caution.

Meredith saw his mouth soften, as though he could read her mind, and he leaned down and untied the cloth from her mouth. She took several deep breaths of air, partly because of need, partly to regain her composure.

He cut the bonds around her ankles, then her wrists, and his fingers were unexpectedly gentle. His mouth was set but not in a hostile gesture. Only a throbbing muscle in his cheek gave real evidence of tension.

She stretched like a cat after a nap in the afternoon sun, playing for time, praying for inspiration. She felt rather than saw his intent, searching, intrusive eyes on her and she could not disobey their silent command. Her eyes climbed slowly to his, meeting them, challenging them. A sudden fierce force streaked between them with the same wild splendor as heat lightning on a summer's night. It paralyzed both of them.

"Who are you, Meredith Seaton," Quinn finally asked, his deep voice soft and compelling. "What are you?"

She rubbed her wrists slowly before answering, as if they pained her. She had already discovered he was discomfited by the thought of hurting her. She decided she would use that interesting weakness to her advantage.

"You know who I am," she said breathlessly, but her voice caught, and he heard the strain in it. "And I could ask you the same questions."

His mouth quirked up on one side, and the cleft in his chin seemed to deepen. His eyes, those dark blue remote eyes, suddenly looked as if they had been sprinkled with light. She had never met anyone so magnetic, so mesmerizing, anyone who could turn charm on and off as easily as opening and closing a door.

"Ah, but I asked you first, Meredith, and I, at the moment, have the upper hand."

Meredith didn't miss the wry note in his voice as he said "at the moment." He grew more and more puzzling by the second.

Once more, she hesitated. Her eyes traveled around the cabin and again found the painting. The sun, lying low in the east, hit it directly through the window, and she could almost see the water moving.

"That's an interesting painting," she observed, changing the subject. She didn't think he knew about her own painting. She had never mentioned it to him and she was sure her brother wouldn't have drawn attention to her efforts. She was equally sure his brother would have discreetly disposed of her gifts.

He turned away from her and stared at the painting as if it were new to him. The signature, M. Sabre, was in the right-hand corner, exactly where Meredith's had been on the painting she had given Brett. Now he knew why something had nagged at him in Brett's office. The scrawl of the names was similar. There was something else similar, but he couldn't quite find it. He shook his head. It couldn't be. It just couldn't. The same hand couldn't have produced this painting and the monstrosity in Brett's office. Coincidence in the scrawl, in the name. That was all. Still, his curiosity was pricked. "You surprise me, Meredith," he probed. "I didn't realize you were interested in art."

"Nor you," she retorted. "I rather imagined you would have framed a deck of cards . . . or a roll of bills."

"Even blackguards and gamblers have an appreciation for something well done," he replied with the half smile that so charmed her. "Call it a whim, Meredith." Each time he said her name, the old taunting quality came back into his voice, and she hated it.

But even the half smile disappeared and once more his eyes bored into her. "The art appreciation discussion is over. You're avoiding my question."

"I don't remember it," she said in her old Meredith-the-simpleminded tone. "I'm thirsty. The gag hurt me."

Amusement flickered in his eyes for a moment, then fled. "It won't work, Meredith. Not anymore. Although I must say, you're very good at acting the simpleton. Even my brother believes it, and he's usually very astute."

But he went to a table where a pitcher and glass sat and poured her some water, then set the pitcher next to the bed. He sat, crossing his legs indolently as he watched her sip carefully . . . and slowly. More slowly, he knew, than necessary. A raised eyebrow finally signaled his impatience.

Meredith knew she couldn't delay any longer. "I don't know what you mean," she said, "although no gentleman would call a lady simpleminded." The last word was said with great dignity.

Quinn couldn't help it. He leaned back in the chair and laughed, a full-throated hearty laugh that filled the room and resounded in Meredith's heart. It was, quite simply, the most pleasant laugh she had ever heard, even if it was directed at her. She tried to keep her own mouth from twitching. Her response *had* sounded incredibly stupid, but then she had trained herself for years to say stupid things.

Even as he laughed, his eyes remained cool and watchful, and she became painfully aware that none of her defenses were working with him, that he saw through the facade she had so carefully built. Still, the habit was strong. "I don't know why you're laughing," she said, pouting.

His laugh faded into a chuckle until he realized that she had very astutely changed the subject again.

He leaned back lazily in the chair, stretching his long legs and placing them on the bed next to her. "Very clever, Meredith, but you're not leaving this room until you answer every one of my questions. And to my total satisfaction. I don't mind waiting. You look very fetching." His hand went out and pushed an errant curl away from her face. "I think you have no idea how much."

Meredith felt the flush rise on her face. To her knowledge, she had never blushed before she met Quinn Devereux. It was just anger, she comforted herself. Only anger.

"You can't keep me here forever."

"No?" It was menacingly said, a promise implied in the tone.

"No," she blustered. "I'll scream."

"No," he replied. "For some odd reason, I don't think you will."

She opened her mouth in threat, all the time knowing she could no more scream than he could let her. She could never explain her presence in his cabin at this hour in the morning. Still, she thought, the threat might convince him to let her go.

His reaction was immediate. His lips silenced her.

He meant only to quiet her, but the meeting of their lips quickly became something else. In the past hour, both of them had wanted this, although they stubbornly refused to recognize it.

They knew it now.

With a deep sigh, she surrendered to the irresistible, and her lips responded with all the longing, all the need that had been building inside like a rumbling volcano about to erupt. They were both like two thirst-crazed people sighting a spring. Running, stumbling toward life-giving salvation.

His hands tangled in her hair, relishing its silky richness as his mouth searched and found a response. He felt her body tremble under his hands, and her mouth open to him, inviting, enticing. He moved quickly to the bed and took her in his arms, feeling the incredible softness of every curve, exulting in her surrender, delighting in the unrestrained reaction of her body to his.

Their tongues melded together, meeting in a slow sensuous waltz, languorously at first, but then catching a rhythm that grew in intensity and speed. They moved incautiously, frantically, flaming the new sensations each stirred in the other. When Meredith thought she could bear no more, his mouth gentled suddenly, and the kiss became something fine and wondrous.

Meredith was startled by his gentleness. The evidence that he had leashed his own desires was obvious in the throbbing of the muscles in his cheek, and it affected her as nothing else could. His tongue, which had earlier ravished and plundered, now seemed contrite, tenderly teasing the places he had previously aroused, sending her on new waves of exquisite flight until she knew nothing except she had to have more of him.

Her arms went around him, drawing him closer. She had never known she could feel this way, so . . . wanton, so . . . shameless. Yet she felt no shame, only a sense of rightness, of being where she belonged. It was so confusing, so utterly impossible, but she was helpless against the rampaging feelings. She could merely move along with the flood of exquisite sensations.

"Meredith . . . pretty Meredith," he whispered in her ear. She heard her name as if from a distance. It sounded like music the way he drew it out, the way his soft warm baritone voice caressed it.

Her heart thumped so loudly she knew he could hear it, and her hands pressed tighter against him, her fingers touching his neck, playing the same teasing games as he did. She felt his body go taut as if struck, and then his lips were on her throat, licking and nuzzling until she thought she would go mad.

She felt his hands reach behind her, find the buttons to her dress and release them one by one. As her dress loosened, his mouth moved from the nape of her neck downwards, trailing hot paths until she thought she could bear no more.

"Merry," he whispered now. "Merry."

The name was like a cold blast of air, a splash of freezing water. The name was associated with so many memories of Lissa. Lissa was the only one who called her Merry. Lissa and the Parson.

She was betraying both of them right now.

He was the enemy. And she could help no one as long as he held her captive, either with bonds or with kisses that deadened her conscience and her good sense.

Her gaze found the water pitcher, and without letting herself think, without letting herself feel, she reached out her right hand as her left hand continued to play with his neck. Feeling as desolate, as empty, as miserable as she ever had in her life, she swung it against his head.

*C*hapter 14

QUINN SAW the quick movement and tried to move away, but he was too late.

Meredith heard the sickening thud as the pitcher hit the side of his head, splashing water over both of them. He dropped heavily across her with a groan.

She struggled to push him off her, trying at the same time to banish the even heavier burden of guilt she felt as he lay there silent.

She had done it for a good cause, she told herself.

Friend Elias would say there was never a good reason for violence, although she thought the Parson would approve. The Parson often contended the end justified the means. If, she amended truthfully to herself, the means weren't too extreme.

He lay there so still, so very still.

Go, she told herself.

What if you hit him harder than you thought? The possibility was like a blow to her stomach.

She stared at the crumpled form. He was facing her, a wet lock of black hair falling over his forehead, which still dripped with water. Without those magnetic eyes piercing her, he looked uncharacteristically restful, that seemingly endless energy quieted. Then she saw blood seeping from a wound at the side of his head. What if she really had hurt him badly? she thought.

It was no more than what he did to you, another part of her said. But that justification did not help now. She had seen the blood and she felt chilled to the bone with sudden fear. She couldn't leave him here like this and walk away, not knowing how badly he was hurt. She kneeled beside the bed, seeking to hear his soft breathing, relaxing only slightly when she did.

She took a piece of the torn cloth he had used to bind her and wiped the water from his face, then the blood, knowing she was a fool for not escaping when she could. The regular breathing told her he would be all right, that it would probably be only seconds before he woke. Yet she could not resist one last touch, her finger softly touching the cleft in his chin.

Her hand jerked back when she heard a sudden rap on the door, and the cloth fell from her hand. The knock came again, and she felt nailed to the floor. "Go away," she prayed, hoping the absolute silence in the cabin would turn away the visitor. With horror, she saw the knob of the door turn and the door open.

From her position on the floor, the black man seemed enormous as he looked within, then entered, closing the door behind him.

Meredith looked frantically at the pistol still on the table.

He saw it too and, without a word, walked over, picked it up and tucked it in his trousers before moving over to the bed and leaning down over his master. As Meredith had done earlier, he put his head close to Quinn's mouth, listening for his breathing, his dark harsh features closed and unreadable.

Meredith had never known such fear in her life. And it

was mystifying to realize it wasn't for herself. It was for the unconscious man. She had seen the slave's back, the limp, the flashes of rebellion. Now he had a gun. She unconsciously reached out her hand in supplication.

Cam straightened up, his eyes taking in the entire scene, including her position and the bloody cloth on the floor. At least the captain seemed all right. He looked down at the broken pieces of pottery on the floor, at the drops of water on the captain, on the woman and the bed, and a smile started at the corner of his mouth. It appeared Quinn Devereux had met his match.

The slight smile was enough to bring Meredith to her senses. She suddenly, instinctively, sensed the black slave was no danger to the man on the bed. She scrambled up, her eyes fixed on the door.

"No," the black man said simply, and Meredith turned and stared at him, amazed that a slave would say such a word to a white woman.

"I'll pay you . . . enough that you can buy your freedom. Just let me go."

"I'm sorry, Miss Seaton," he said, and she stared at him in shock. There was nothing now of the servile slave she had seen before. His words were as well pronounced as his master's, his eyes as determined, his stance as proud. There was even a semblance of the same arrogance.

Meredith felt as if she were in a dream, a wildly absurd nightmare. None of this could be happening. None of it made sense. "But why? You don't have to be afraid. . . . I'll help you—"

His eyes bored into hers, and they were suddenly as secretive and mysterious as Devereux's had been. But there was no mistaking his intent. He bent down and uprighted the chair, which had fallen moments earlier, placing it in a corner of the room near the bed. "Sit there, Miss Seaton." His voice hardened as she hesitated. "Please." But it was no request and she knew it. It was an order.

Meredith looked at the door once more. "Let me leave," she whispered.

"I can't do that."

"Are you afraid to let me go?"

"No," he said again with a simplicity that belied the enormity of implications behind that single word. She wanted him to say more, but it was obvious he was not going to accommodate her. In any way. There was a surprising air of authority about him, and it didn't go with being a slave. Her fear battled with fascination. Nothing was as it appeared.

She looked wistfully at the door.

"No, Miss Seaton," he repeated regretfully, but the regret did not extend to eyes that moved to the chair and commanded her to do what he ordered.

She sat.

He nodded, as if her obedience had never been a question, then knelt next to Devereux, picking up the cloth she had dropped. Meredith watched with astonishment as huge hands gently finished the job of wiping the still-running blood from Devereux's wound. The face of the slave, or whatever he was, was inscrutable but the care he provided was not. He cared about the man he was doctoring. And cared deeply.

She bit her lip as she saw Captain Devereux stir and groan. She wasn't quite sure how he would retaliate, but retaliate he would. She did not doubt it for a moment.

"Capt'n?" The black man's voice was surprisingly soft.

"Cam?" There was a hesitation, a confusion in Devereux's voice that Meredith had never heard before. "What . . . in the devil . . . ?"

"It seems you were hit with a water pitcher."

Another sound came from the figure on the bed as he moved, and the groan became a long stream of Irish curses. Meredith winced, then flushed and looked away as Cam's eyes found her. His usually sullen mouth curved into a slight smile.

"You have an audience, Capt'n," he said in that same

quiet voice that had ordered her to the chair with such authority.

Quinn sat up suddenly, groaning again. "She's still here?"

Cam nodded his head toward the corner behind him.

The sudden move made Quinn's head spin, and he went still for a moment, trying to stop the ringing in his ears. His clothes were damp from the spilled water, his head hurt infernally, and he tasted the sour flavor of disgust at his own stupid carelessness.

It was the second time in his life he had allowed a woman to make a fool of him. With so much at stake, he had allowed his physical needs to outweigh every lesson he had so painfully learned. His eyes narrowed now, his facial muscles tensing as he turned slowly and looked at the figure in the chair.

There was apprehension in her face, but also defiance. Her chin went up with stubborn mutinous pride, and he heard Cam's rare chuckle.

He turned back to Cam, the question on his face. He was too chagrined at himself to voice the words.

"She was kneeling beside you when I came in. She dropped a cloth with blood on it. I think she might have had second thoughts about embarking you on a long dark journey." Cam grinned at the startled pained look on Quinn's face.

"What time is it?" Quinn's question was sharp.

"Another two hours before we leave."

"The cargo?"

"Loaded."

"At least that's something," Quinn replied bitterly.

Cam shrugged. "What are you going to do?"

"Get some answers. Leave us alone, Cam."

"You sure you'll be safe?" The question was dryly impudent.

Meredith heard the exchange with both dread and wonder. The black man's tone was anything but that of a slave to a master. It was challenging and impertinent and even teasing. Almost as if they were friends. And equals.

"No," the riverboat captain replied in the same affectionate tone. There was even the barest touch of sheepish amusement in it, although the captain's eyes, as they fastened on her, were chilling. Her hand trembled slightly in her lap.

She tried to think of something else, anything else. What kind of relationship was there between these two men? She forced her mind back to that first dinner with Quinn Devereux when he had intimated all too clearly that he had caused Cam's injuries.

But did he actually say so? Remember, Meredith, she told herself. It could be important. And then she did. She remembered every word of the conversation.

"And you're risking taking him up North?" one of the slave hunters had questioned him.

"... he tried to run once. He won't do it again," came Devereux's answer.

And she had assumed . . . what he had wanted them all to assume, she realized suddenly.

Barely aware now that Devereux was painfully walking with Cam to the door, she looked again at her painting on the wall. Dear Lord, she thought. It couldn't be. The Parson would have said something. He would have told her.

She knew there was someone on the river who transported slaves, but there were hundreds of boats plying the Mississippi. The odds against it being the *Lucky Lady* were ridiculously high.

But why else would he be so concerned about finding her near Elias's warehouse? Unless, as she suspected before, he was in league with slave hunters. And if so, how to explain his easy relationship with the huge black man who, all of a sudden, had dropped the slave dialect and spoken as well as both of them?

It was as if a decision had been made between the man called Cam and Captain Devereux, one that conceded it no longer mattered that they maintain a pretense in front of her.

The implication was a chilling one. No one knew she was here. No one at all. They could easily kill her and dump her in the Mississippi in the dark of night. She suddenly shivered as the door closed and was locked, the key dropped in Devereux's pocket.

She watched, her eyes never leaving him as he ignored her and went to the mirror and investigated the wound on his face. It was still bleeding slightly.

Meredith felt her stomach turn over. The cut looked deep, and guilty anguish replaced part, if not all, of her apprehension. She had never so much as bothered a bug if she could help it; she certainly had never inflicted bodily harm on anyone before, except, she reluctantly admitted to herself, for the slap she had given him weeks earlier on this very same steamboat.

What was it about him that inspired her to such uncharacteristic violence?

Self-preservation, she told herself. Freedom for numbers of people. But now as she looked at the gash at the side of his head, neither reason comforted her.

She started to rise, meaning to go to him, to try to help in some way, but his voice, hard and grim, stopped her. "Sit back down and stay there, Miss Seaton." It startled her for she didn't know he had even been looking at her. She winced at the formal address. So they were back to that. It boded no good. She sank obediently back into the chair.

"I just thought I could help," she said.

"Ha," he said ruefully. "I'd rather have a wildcat help me. It would be safer and not nearly so treacherous, I think." There was, oddly enough, a strained, even wounded, note in his voice.

The remark cut her to the quick. She considered herself devious in her Underground activities but never treacherous. The anguish dug deeper in her marrow. "I'm sorry," she said, and there was no mistaking the sincere misery behind the words.

But he was thinking of Morgana, and what a fine actress

she'd been. "Sorry about hitting me or getting caught doing it?" His voice was weighted with cynicism.

"Both," she blurted out honestly.

The frank answer astonished him. He turned slightly and fastened those hard, startlingly dark blue eyes on her. The corner of his mouth started to turn up in a grin and this time, she noted with shock, the corners around his eyes crinkled and the cleft in his chin seemed to deepen once more. Lord save her, she had never seen a more devastatingly handsome face. Her hands clutched the chair.

"Candor at last," he drawled lazily, his compelling eyes pulling back layer after layer of the protective covering she had perfected. "Am I going to have more of it?"

She could only stare at him, mesmerized. She had been able to withstand his mocking smile, his empty grin, but this was something else again. She felt as if she were a snake being hypnotized by an Indian charmer, able only to sway back and forth to the music he was playing . . . to the deep powerful richness of his voice and the spell of his magnetic eyes.

But neither was he immune to the currents in the room, she knew. Even as his smile invited a reply, a muscle jerked in his cheek and, if he were experiencing anything near the rush of emotions she was, Meredith knew he was exercising enormous control. His eyes were still wary, though. She wondered briefly whether they ever joined in his smile. And if not, why?

"I *am* sorry," she finally repeated defensively, unable to withstand the tension humming between them. "I've never hit anyone before, but you—" She stopped suddenly, afraid of saying too much.

But he wasn't going to let it go. "I what, Meredith? Was in the wrong place at the wrong time?" he probed. "As you were at the warehouse?"

She ignored the question. "You were holding me prisoner!" she accused. "I had a right to try to escape."

He leaned against a wall, looking deceptively relaxed. As

relaxed as the panther he so reminded her of, Meredith thought.

"I'll give you that, Meredith," he said slowly, his voice even but his eyes were still very cold, so cold she wanted to shiver. She suspected he meant them to be intimidating, that he knew very well their impact, and she wouldn't give him the satisfaction. "We'll call it even," he continued easily. "I hit you, although I didn't know then who you were. You returned the . . . what should we term it . . . nefarious act. In rather good measure, I would say," he added ironically as his hand once more went to the cut. He winced as he touched the purpling area around it.

Meredith started to rise, ready to take immediate advantage of his forgiving words but stopped as he shook his head slowly, deliberately.

"We'll put that piece of business behind us, but we have more. Much more," he said softly, his voice loaded with menace. "Now sit down." The words were like a pistol shot, sharp and deadly.

Meredith sank back into the chair.

"No more games, Meredith. My patience has come to an end." He padded toward her, all lean strength and power and barely leashed violence. "What were you doing at that warehouse?"

Meredith was still puzzling over the clues and had not stopped adding bits and pieces, not the least of which was his obvious concern about the warehouse. Part of her now admitted that he could be a member of the Underground Railroad. But she wasn't sure, and secrecy and caution had been deeply ingrained in her. She decided to tell part of the truth.

"My sister . . . I'm trying to find my sister. Someone told me Elias Sprague might be able to help me," she said suddenly, watching his eyes narrow.

"You don't have a sister," he retorted with disgust. More games, more lies.

Meredith hesitated at the glowering look on his face. All traces of that devastating smile were gone; there was only cold, curious hostility. But she had to try. "Think back," she said. "Remember when you visited Briarwood so many years ago?"

He had remembered, but she'd claimed to have forgotten. Still another lie. He was making a list, and it was getting very long. "Yes," he replied cautiously.

"There was a girl named Lissa, Alma's daughter. She was two years younger than I. You built that swing for us."

His brow furrowed as he searched his memory. "Alma's daughter?" He had scavenged in the kitchen several times and had charmed Alma into saving food for him during that four-day visit. He had not liked Robert Seaton and had avoided formal meals when he could. He remembered Alma, and now he remembered the child. She had been younger than Meredith and very shy. Perhaps that was why he hadn't immediately recalled her. He had seen little of her except when he had built the swing, and given her some pushes. "Alma's daughter?" he said again.

Meredith nodded. "And my father's."

Quinn was silent, watching every expression move across her face. The vapid look was gone from the eyes, and there was real torment there. She was a good actress, but he didn't think she was that good. Something in him started to believe. He reached for an armless chair and pulled it up, straddling it comfortably, his arms resting on its back. But his eyes never left her.

"And?" Despite a growing sympathy, there was still skepticism in his voice.

"I took care of her," Meredith said slowly, painfully. "I loved her. I taught her to read." She looked up at Quinn. "You met my father then. He . . . he . . . was not very . . . easy. I don't think he knew what love was. He was a cold, even cruel man. I was lonely, and Lissa . . . well, I could love Lissa, and she loved me back." Her voice faltered, and she lowered her head.

Meredith didn't know why she was telling him so much. She had never told anyone the whole story before. Not anyone. The hurt had been too strong, the rejection too absolute. It had really never gone away, although she had learned, achingly, to live with it.

Drat him. She had needed to explain, but she was giving more than she intended. She was afraid to look at him, to gauge his reaction. She felt the tears gather in the back of her eyes, but she had learned long ago how to hold them at bay. She concentrated on doing that now. She could show no weakness to him. She didn't know why, but it was terribly important.

Quinn felt as if he had been kicked in the gut. And he had a feeling there was another blow coming. He believed her. No one, not even she, could pretend the depth of emotion he heard in her words. Almost involuntarily, he reached out a hand to her shoulder, unspoken comfort evident in the gesture.

"What happened?"

"Not long after you left, Father thought I was too close to Lissa. He sold her. She was six years old." The bitterness came pouring out. "She was six years old, and they put a chain on her ankle and took her away from her mother, and her home . . . and me. All because I loved her." The agony in her voice was sharp and vivid and real. "Because I loved her," she whispered again, and this time a rare tear escaped and wandered forlornly down a cheek now white with intense feeling. "It was my fault. It was all my fault." In all her life, she had never admitted that guilt before, although she had bottled it tightly in her heart. But now the contents came spilling out.

Quinn felt his heart crack at her pain, at the guilt she had been obviously carrying for so many years. He knew the burden of guilt. Christ, how he knew the burden of guilt! Terrence O'Connell would be alive today were it not for him. He closed his eyes against the memory, then opened them slowly.

The tears were gone from her eyes, those very few tears, and the very scarcity of them hinted at feelings too deep to release in such a way. But the pain was there. Stark and desperate. He wanted to touch her. Good God, how he wanted to touch her.

"Why did you think Mr. Sprague could help you?" he asked, not wanting to question but to comfort. Yet there were things he must know. And she was still hiding something. He could see it in her eyes, in the way they wouldn't meet his fully.

"I hired a detective," she said, again telling only part of the truth. "He seemed to think Mr. Sprague might know something. He did not say why."

"Why not go in the daytime?"

"My family is very opposed to my search for Lissa. They think I've forgotten about it."

"Why is it so important that your brother doesn't know? You have money of your own. I assume you can spend it as you like."

"My brother would do anything to keep me away from her. You see, Lissa and I resemble each other. He's terribly afraid if she's found, everyone will know she's father's . . . bastard."

Quinn shrugged. "It's not uncommon. I'd say a good number of planters in Mississippi have slave offspring." He knew his tone sounded casual, even callous, but he felt he would discover more that way. And he wasn't ready to reveal his own secrets.

"Not . . . bastards that look so much like the daughter. I'm afraid that if Robert finds out, he will somehow make sure I never find her."

Her face had regained its normal color, but her body was taut as a bowstring.

Quinn heard the whistle of the boat, and the gay music of the band. The *Lucky Lady* would be leaving any moment. He had to make a decision about her. Now.

But he couldn't. For a man used to making decisions, he was frustratingly unable to do so now. He believed her. As far as her story went. But there was much, much more to

Meredith Seaton, and she intrigued him as no problem he had ever encountered. She was a puzzle he had to unravel.

Quinn looked at her and saw the question in her eyes. She also knew the boat was ready to leave.

He shook his head. "I don't think so, Meredith."

At least they were back to her given name, Meredith thought. So why wouldn't he allow her to go? What was *he* afraid of? "I've told you everything."

"Tell me more about Lissa . . . and the detective you've hired."

"But the boat . . . my aunt . . ."

"You've already been gone the entire night and morning. I doubt if a few more hours can do much more . . . damage to your reputation." It was a deliberately baiting statement.

She nibbled on her lips, a gesture surprisingly endearing to Quinn. There was still the shadow of pain in her eyes, a curious vulnerability, and he ached to take her in his arms. It scared him how much. Remember, he told himself, what happened the last time you made that mistake. His head, for God's sake, still ached like hell.

Meredith felt his eyes bore into her. She wished she could read his expression, but it was much as it had been the first time they met on the *Lucky Lady*: closed tightly against any invasion. It was unforgiving, unapproachable, unsympathetic. It was . . . totally empty of any emotion.

"May I have some water?" she asked.

His smile was that of a cat who had trapped a mouse. "You've used it all on my head, Meredith. And I'm not going to leave you alone, not unless you want to be gagged and tied again."

She looked at him hopelessly. "Please. Please let me go."

He shook his head slowly. "You've changed in the past few hours, Meredith. More, may I say, than a little. I want to know how and why and for what reasons. Lissa is a good story, but not the whole one, I don't think."

"What about you?" she suddenly attacked. "What were you doing at the warehouse in the middle of the night?"

"I do business with Mr. Sprague. Legitimate business, Meredith."

"After midnight?"

He shrugged. "Whenever I have a mind to. But we are not discussing me. We are discussing the simple Miss Seaton who turns out not to be so simple after all." His hand reached out and touched a curl that had fallen over her shoulder. "You do a terrible injustice to yourself, Meredith. You are really quite beautiful, you know, with your hair down and that fire in your eyes."

Her stomach lurched at his tone. The compliment, if it could be called such, considering the implacable inquisition of his eyes, had been coldly, analytically, said. And every time he said her name, he made it a mockery. As if he were playing with her, and nastily enjoying every second of it.

She was tired of it. Her jaw set. "I'll have you arrested for kidnapping but if you—"

"If I what, Miss Meredith?" His voice was silky.

"Just let me go. I'll forget all about it."

"But I won't, Meredith. Not the way you look right now, nor the way you looked, and felt, just before you decided to crack my head. You could have just said no."

"Would it have done any good?" she asked bitterly.

"I don't know," he said. "You didn't try. I seem to remember you being most cooperative, even perhaps eager."

"Damn you," she spat out, her eyes flashing fire, her chin high. Until she realized she had been baited, that she had so completely stepped out of the vapid Miss Seaton role that she could never return. She saw him grin as he realized she understood what had happened.

"Why the masquerade?" he said. This time his voice was gentle, inviting confidences, and seductively intimate.

"I told you," she said desperately.

"It won't work, darlin'," he said. "I'll give you the benefit of the doubt. There is a Lissa. But that's not sufficient reason for all this . . . playactin'." The soft drawl was exaggerated but deadly serious. "No beautiful woman purposely makes herself unattractive . . . not unless there are damned good reasons.''

"I'm not beautiful," she protested, truly believing it. No one had ever called her beautiful.

Quinn heard the conviction in her words and he felt what was becoming annoyingly familiar sympathy. He didn't want to like her. He didn't want to be touched by her. Yet something in him ached for her. She truly didn't know how lovely she was. Because she had hidden that strong quiet beauty for so long, because she had allowed no one to get close enough to see it. He had thought he was alone, but how much more alone she must be if everything she said was true, if the things she'd left unsaid were distinct possibilities. At least he had had his father and brothers for many years. He had had Terrence. He had had Cam. He was beginning to doubt that Miss Meredith Seaton had ever had anyone. Except perhaps the missing Lissa.

He couldn't help himself this time. His hand went up to her cheek, softly touching it with infinite tenderness. His fingers explored her face, seeking to know her thoughts, her very soul. He brushed away a curl that had fallen over her left eye, his hand capturing the silky strands and holding them like newly found treasure.

Her eyes widened at the unexpected touch, at the gentleness of his fingers, at the immediate reaction they caused in the core of her body. The remoteness was still there in his face, but his eyes . . .

Dear Lord, his eyes were like the foaming ocean, deep and mysterious. They invited her to come to him, to surrender to him, to give herself to him.

To betray herself.

And she was helpless against them. Her fingers went up to that devilishly handsome face that made her forget everything she should remember. She touched the cleft in his chin, as she had wanted to since they met, and she watched with fascination as his mouth widened, the ends turning upward in the most charming smile she had ever seen.

The most charming, and challenging. For the challenge was most definitely there. Direct. Sensuous. Compelling.

And then she had no more time to think because his mouth was moving toward her, his lips reaching down for hers.

They touched, gently at first, then fiercely. The alarm inside her clanged, but she was no longer listening. She could only hear her heart, and it was greedy for what he was offering: a warmth so long denied her, a sweetness that turned her blood to honey, a need that made her body hum and tingle and come alive in the most wondrous ways.

His tongue moved inside her mouth, caressing and loving, awakening each sensitive nerve, igniting a chain reaction of exquisite sensations.

Quinn tried to move closer but it was impossible the way they were sitting. Not wanting to break the tenuous bond with words, he took her hand and gently but insistently urged her over to the bed.

She resisted for a fleeting moment of time, but surrender came quickly. She could no more fight him now than she could stop breathing. Closing her eyes, wondering if she was walking into disaster, but no longer caring, no longer able to think straight, Meredith Seaton gave herself into his hands.

Chapter 15

QUINN KNEW he was being a damned fool. His mind kept telling him that, but his heart didn't listen.

He wanted her. He needed her. Christ, how he needed her.

Perhaps because she needed him, too, he thought. It had been obvious in her kiss, in her touch, in the wonder in her eyes. But he didn't, couldn't, go beyond that thought. He only knew that this moment was right. For whatever reasons, it was right.

She interested and attracted him as no other woman ever had. There was an explosive quality between them, that had always been between them even when he'd thought she was everything he disliked, even when she'd looked like a dressmaker's worst nightmare. He had never known anything like this excitement before, this current that flowed between them with the unpredictability of a thunderstorm.

As they sat together on the bed, she looked up at him, and

he wondered how he'd ever thought her unattractive. Her dark brown eyes were alive with emotion, with a wistfulness that reached into him and stole a piece of his soul.

Her light brown hair, so like wisps of gold in the sun, was silk to his touch. Her face was striking, full of character. The lips were full, the chin determined, the eyes wide and deep, the cheekbones high and exquisitely sculptured. His hard callused hand traced every feature. He expected questions, but none came. Instead she leaned into his touch, seeking the rough strength.

Quinn's hand hesitated at the discolored bruise he had put there. He touched it lightly, wishing he could make it disappear.

As if forgiving him, she slid into his arms as if she belonged there, as if God had made them to hold her. He ran his hands up and down her arms, enjoying the feel of her skin against his fingers, relishing the way she snuggled deeper into his embrace.

He felt the boat move and knew they were leaving New Orleans. She stiffened for a moment, and he knew she, too, was reacting to the movement. Any decision had been taken away from them: his to let her go, hers to stay without any additional protestations. He felt her body relax and saw her head turn upward to look at him with lovely searching eyes, and his arms tightened compulsively around her.

There was no fear in her face, no hesitancy. It was as if she had made a silent decision and was at peace with it. Her hand reached out and took his right one, turning it palm-up, studying it. He allowed her to trace a line across his palm, although he didn't like how much it could tell about him. Without his gloves he felt vulnerable, naked. Despite his best attempts, the leatherlike calluses remained from years of hard physical labor on road gangs, in quarries, and, toward the last, the coal mines. They were not the hands of a gambler— or of a gentleman. He saw the puzzlement in her face, but she kept the questions unasked. Perhaps because she had so many secrets of her own. This regard for privacy was, he thought with only a trace of cynicism, a quality unique in a woman, at least those he had known. It served to fuel his rapidly growing respect and fascination.

Gently, he took his hand away and brushed a lock of her hair back. The gesture was both gentle and sensuous as his hand hesitated near her ear, then touched it lightly, tentatively, as a child might reach out to touch a butterfly.

The air between them was pregnant with questions unasked and unanswered and yet neither was ready to shatter a peace that astounded them both with its quiet intensity. For the moment, there was a rare understanding, a silent communication between them that neither wished the other harm. There was something magical between them and it would disappear if either questioned it too far.

Meredith relaxed in his arms, her hands playing with the downy hair on his arms. His sleeves were rolled up, revealing arms the color of oak, deeply tanned and hard with muscle. There was so much strength in them. She had always sensed it in him, and felt it when he had kept her from falling that day at Brett's bank. Now she watched the muscles straining against the skin, felt the tautness of a superbly disciplined body.

No questions, she told herself, or he might disappear in a puff of smoke. Or he might start asking some himself, again. And she didn't want to lie to him, not anymore. She wanted to look up at his magnificent turbulent eyes and feel their warmth, not their mockery.

She wondered how anyone could feel this way, so tense and so eager and so alive. It was as if she had just awakened from a long sleep to find a world made of spun gold and silver and all the lovely colors of her beloved rainbows.

Meredith pushed away the nagging doubts; the distrust and suspicion. He was the young man who was once kind to her, who wiped away tears and built a swing. He was strength. He was comfort.

Yet there was a fragility about these moments. Like a crystal glass teetering on the edge of a table.

Perhaps he felt it too, that tenuousness, for as his hands

lightly massaged her arms she sensed that he was restraining himself. Every touch seemed a test of his control, and he, like she, was painfully holding back, afraid of what might happen if he did not. They were both waiting.

Waiting for what?

Perhaps, Meredith thought, for the trust that would make it perfect, that would drive away the private demons that, even now, made them wary of each other.

She looked beyond him to the light streaming through the window. Perhaps several words, words that only a few people knew, would tell her what she wanted to know. But still she hesitated. At the moment, she was afraid to know, afraid that she was wrong, that she would be betraying all she believed in, that he was nothing more than what she once thought.

Her hand ran along a muscle on his lower arm and felt his body tense. She wanted to lean down and kiss the back of that hand, to nibble the rich brown skin until he trembled as she was doing.

Meredith shivered. She had never felt this way before. She had never really been kissed before, except by him, had never felt a man's touch in this lazy erotic way.

Her hand dug into his arm, and she felt him lean back against the wall of the cabin, pulling her firmly to him. One hand took her chin and guided it toward his face. "You are a pretty lady, Meredith, and an intriguin' one," he said in that low drawl that made all her senses sing with an excitement she still didn't understand.

But he didn't give her any more time to analyze it, for his lips captured hers as a small groan rumbled from his throat. She could not stop one of her own as she hungered for a closer union of their bodies. She felt the bunching of his muscles against his clothes and the barely contained passion that warmed her clear through to her soul.

The questions in her mind, the reasoning of her brain, all disappeared as the fire between them ignited once more, this time with more appetite and greed and fury. He smothered her mouth, his tongue darting inside with voracious, searching need.

It was a need matched. Meredith had never known a kiss could have such power, could melt her down to her bones. An elemental force was between them now . . . as primitive and potent as the ocean pounding against cliffs or a tornado ripping trees from the ground. And as impossible to contain.

Her hands glided up his chest, feeling every knotted muscle under the shirt, touching the smoothness of his skin as the cloth separated at the neck. Shamelessly, she proceeded, fascinated with every facet of his lean taut body, intrigued at the way her own body responded when she touched him. Sensations, like whispers of a growing wind, rushed with increasing power through her veins, reaching into every extremity, and then pounding against the confines of the shell of flesh.

His mouth moved from her lips, and his tongue trailed fire upward until it reached the area around her eyes. It played against her skin with teasing gentleness, the gentleness that had once surprised her but did no more. She lifted her eyes and looked into his dark blue ones, and saw his own vulnerable puzzlement.

Her hands went farther back, to the nape of his neck and started downward, wanting to feel more of him, but he winced and drew back. No woman had touched him there in twelve years.

"You don't know what you're doin', Meredith." His voice was half groan, half plea, the drawl even more pronounced.

Amusement danced in her eyes. "I think, perhaps," she said slowly, even tauntingly, "I do."

But she didn't, and he knew it. She was undoubtedly a virgin. That had been obvious from her puzzled and often frightened responses to his earlier kisses. For a woman of such Machiavellian traits, she was surprisingly innocent in many ways. There was a kind of . . . wanton shyness about her. He knew those were contradictory terms, and he hadn't thought the combination possible. But he knew now it was.

Her hands explored with a hesitancy that both soothed and aroused, while her eyes were like those of a startled deer, curious and fearful. He wanted her. He wanted her more than he had ever wanted anything in his life, yet he couldn't have her.

He should stop now, stop until the puzzle was solved, the riddle answered. He was astonished at the intensity of his own feelings, of the aching longing he had for her, even though a certain wariness persisted in the back of his mind.

Perhaps she was nothing like Morgana. Or perhaps she was an even better actress. How could he even think about risking his neck, his freedom, again for a woman?

But quite traitorously, his hand moved up and down her back, causing her to tremble once more, and his lips went to the nape of her neck, which he nuzzled, feeling every movement of her body as it reacted to his hands, to his mouth. He wished bitterly his own body wasn't reacting in the same fundamental, undisciplined way.

When a soft purr came from her throat, his mouth moved from the back of her neck to her lips. He claimed them urgently, with hunger and demand, with questions and accusations all unsaid, but there. They might as well have been spoken because her mind, all but senseless now, knew them. His kisses were punishment, and she meted out some of her own, her lips nibbling his, her tongue reaching into his mouth and spreading the same fire that was consuming her. And then his body was stretched taut against hers, and she could feel the swell of his manhood even through their clothes, could feel her own body's response to it. It was a madness...an astounding, unbelievable lunacy.

Yet despite both their reservations, their suspicions, their best intentions, there was no longer any way they could hold back. If anything, the lure of forbidden fruit had made it impossible to stop, and there was nothing on earth now that could hinder the inevitable.

Quinn knew it even as he fought against surrender. But his body wouldn't obey. His emotions wouldn't obey. His hands wouldn't obey as they went to the back of her dress and finished the job of unfastening the buttons. One hand played with her back, fingers running over her skin with breeze-light teasing while the other, with her help, tugged her dress and chemise from her body. He looked then, his dark gaze finding the elation, the wondrous expectation in her eyes, even as she shrank the slightest bit from the intensity of his eyes. Christ, but she was contradictory.

His hand gentled against her bare skin as he looked at her openly, at the beauty she had always kept well hidden. She had a lovely body, slender but well formed with breasts that held an invitation of their own. He leaned down, his tongue teasing the nipples into hard red buds, luring her body into new dimensions of yearning, of frantic hunger.

Meredith felt every nuance of that hunger. She knew it wasn't all physical desire. There was also a fierce need to enter that mysterious world he inhabited, to share the thoughts and feelings he protected so well, to uncover his cryptic past. For only then did she believe she would really know him. And she wanted to know him. She wanted to cross the chasm that separated them in so many ways, not just in this one thing. Not just in the fire they fanned in each other, not just in this fury to touch, to stir, to arouse, to sing the same sensuous song. Not just . . .

Her hands slid into his shirt again, and she felt an almost imperceptible withdrawal, a warning that exploration would not be tolerated even as he probed every part of her body, slowly and carefully, as if memorizing it for some future time. Her eyes went up to his, and there was regret and even a kind of sorrow there, a certain despair that made her heart constrict painfully. She wanted to whisper reassurances to him, to soothe the raw agony that flickered briefly in his eyes, but it was gone so quickly she thought she might have imagined it. But she didn't imagine the impact that impression made on her heart, swelling it until she thought it might burst.

Then his mouth was nuzzling her ear, and she knew little

but the wild beating of her heart, and the raging current of her blood. Having been silently warned about not touching his back, her hands went instead to his neck, burying themselves in now tousled black hair that curved around her fingers like down. She felt his fevered breathing against her neck and wondered at her own quickened breath.

"Quinlan," she whispered, saying his name to him for the first time since they had met as adults. Her voice quivered slightly, and his mouth smiled against her neck.

"Quinn," he corrected softly.

"Quinn," she amended obediently. And there was a smile in her voice because it sounded so right for him. It had a mystical, musical quality to it, yet also a fine strength.

He moved away from her, and she watched as he peeled off his boots, then his trousers. She wished he would also discard his shirt. She wanted to see the whole of him. Instead, he went back to her side and, as the skin of his leg touched her skin, she no longer cared. Nearly bursting with bittersweet agony, she brought him against her . . . until her breasts touched his hard chest, and his throbbing manhood stroked the most private part of her. He stayed there a moment, letting her feel him, allowing the blazes in the very core of her body to rage out of control. And then he moved back slightly, his hand sliding between her legs, massaging and caressing, each subtle loving movement bringing forth the most miraculous sensations. He shifted his weight and looked into her face, his eyes glittering with blue fire.

"Are you sure?" he rasped out, his body suspended above hers. "Are you sure, Meredith?"

Meredith wasn't sure at all, but her body was—and her soul. She nodded, unable to speak, for she was afraid she would say things she shouldn't. Things like love. Love had never been mentioned between them, nor had affection. Her eyes closed with a fierce hurt. She wanted words of love, or promise, or devotion, and she understood in some way that this man would never give them.

But she couldn't stop now. At this moment she needed

him more than she had ever needed anything in her life. She was on fire, and only he could extinguish the flames. She felt his warmth as he slowly entered her, his mouth lowering to shower kisses on her face. There was a quick sharp pain, and she couldn't stop a small cry of surprise. She felt him hesitate, but her hands urged him on although her mouth could not because it was covered by his. He moved unhurriedly within her, and she could feel the taut control of his body, see the throb of a muscle on his cheek.

But with her first cry of rapture, her first compulsive motions in reaction to the growing pleasure inside her, he moved faster, rhythmically, each time thrusting deeper and feeling her own warm moisture embrace him and ask for more. Suddenly Quinn felt a glorious conflagration, a soaring splendor that eclipsed all previous sensation, all previous knowledge. Vibrant fury and honeyed sweetness mixed together and spun wildly until her cry of profound pleasure and his own groan of exquisite satisfaction registered and whirled him back to a troubled present.

Still indelibly, incredibly joined, they stared at each other, their bodies quivering with the afterglow of making love, with the enormity of what had just happened between them.

Stricken by what he had done, by his complete lack of control, Quinn's hand went to her mouth, which trembled slightly as her eyes questioned him. With every ounce of discipline he had ever built, had ever learned, he reconstructed his defenses and retreated behind them. His mouth quirked up in that curious way of his. "I wonder who is whose prisoner," he said dryly, his blue eyes glittering like shards of crystal.

The words could have meant anything. It was the eyes that destroyed her, that struck deep inside her, more painful than any sword. She had wanted reassurance, words of love, of tenderness. Warmth. Even a drop of warmth.

Meredith swallowed. I will not cry, she told herself although she wanted to do just that. She turned her face away, not wanting him to see the wound he had just inflicted.

Quinn flinched from the obvious pain in her face, in the way she turned from him, breaking away from him, from the union of their bodies. He swallowed words he wanted to say, afraid they would betray his own depth of feeling. He was afraid of it. He was afraid for himself, but mostly for her. He had been a Jonah to everyone who had ever cared for him. Yet he couldn't resist touching her, caressing her arm.

"Merry, what are we doin' to each other?" It was more a groan than a question, and he expected no answer. He knew his drawl had deepened, a sure sign of his internal conflict. He was glad no one recognized it but him. His hand went to an unruly gold curl settling on Meredith's back.

Quinn held it for a moment, treasuring it, but then he dropped it quite suddenly. He unwound himself from the bed, going to his armoire, and extracting one of his silk shirts. He handed it to her knowing he would not get anywhere with her sitting naked on his bed. He leaned down and picked up his trousers, slipping into them quickly before she could realize how she was affecting him again.

Meredith stared at the shirt, then her dress. She knew she could not put on the latter with her hands still trembling. She took the shirt and slowly slipped her arms into the sleeves. Despite its obviously newly laundered condition, it still smelled of him. Like the sheet.

She buttoned the shirt carefully, trying to regain her poise, her disdain for him. She should hate him more than ever, but she couldn't. And she hated herself for it, despised herself. He obviously didn't care about her. His eyes had shown that only too clearly. He cared only about using her, only about extracting information from her, and he had used the cruelest possible way to do it. She decided to tell him no more, although minutes earlier she had nearly made the opposite decision.

She watched as he stood there, his eyes as remote as ever, the curve of his mouth telling her nothing. It was as if what had happened had happened only to her. It did not seem to affect him in any way. She felt barren inside. Barren and dead. She wanted to do something, to say something to get a reaction. "You're a bastard," she attacked, her eyes going to a splotch of blood on the sheet.

"Aye," he admitted dryly, his eyes going to the same spot, a muscle twitching in his cheek. "And you, pretty Merry, are an impostor, a very lovely impostor. You might be many things, but lightheaded and simple you most definitely are not."

"Don't call me Merry." The words, derived from hurt so deep she didn't know how it could be borne, were spit out.

Quinn looked at her in surprise.

"No one calls me that but Lissa and . . ."

"And who?" Quinn asked the question quietly.

She stopped. Her face closed. She had been ready to say the Parson.

"Who, Meredith?" Christ, he wanted to know. He wanted to know who else she had allowed into her life. The sudden jealousy was almost more than he could stand.

"Who?" he repeated softly.

Meredith looked up. His eyes were not cold now, but blazing, compelling an answer.

His hand went around her arm, and she knew he wouldn't release her until she replied. And she had to get away before he saw the tears gathering in the back of her eyes.

"A . . . a minister . . . a parson I know."

Quinn closed his eyes as the words penetrated. He knew now. He should have known sooner. Maybe he had, but he just hadn't been ready to accept it. He released her arm and went to the painting, studying it closer. Now he knew what had nagged him. It had been partly the signature, similar to the one on the canvas in Brett's office, but it had also been that particular bend in the river. He had seen it at Briarwood, but he had seen so many bends in the river that his mind had not isolated it until she mentioned the Parson . . . and he remembered the sketch of the fox.

Damn the man and his games to hell. He should have said something, damn him.

Meredith Seaton was M. Sabre. Meredith Seaton had been at Elias's warehouse because she was with the Underground Railroad. She knew the Parson because she was an agent. And her half sister Lissa was the reason. Meredith hadn't faked her anguish earlier when she had talked of a half sister.

He felt the budding of elation inside. No wonder they had been so attracted to each other from the first moment they'd met. They had more than one bond between them. Admiration for her swelled in him. She had played the fool's role well, and it must have been a devilishly lonely game. He, at least, had Cam.

But the elation was soon overcome by self-loathing. In kidnapping her, he had done irreparable harm to her and to her masquerade. And yet she had given herself to him with a sweetness and passion he had never believed existed. And he had returned that gift with cruelty.

Quinn turned back to her, to where she was sitting huddled against the cabin wall in a shirt that dwarfed her. She looked like a desolate lost child, yet he knew she was neither. The Underground Railroad used neither fools nor children in the network. Meredith Seaton must be uncommonly bright and courageous.

Bloody hell, but he had misused her. The knowledge kept his eyes colder than he intended, his mouth grim. Terrible, pounding guilt racked him. And he hid that guilt behind the facade he had perfected.

When he took several steps toward her, she moved even closer to the wall. He noticed there were sparks of anger in her eyes as well as accusation. Furious defiance became evident in every stiffening bone of her body. He smiled slightly, his face taking on the crooked wry expression that was indecipherable. She was extraordinary. Really extraordinary.

He sat down and took her hand, holding it tight enough that she could not pull away from him although she tried. "That painting," he said, nodding to the rainbow on the wall, "was bought at a shop in Cincinnati." He watched as her eyes widened with apprehension. "It was," he continued in the same even tone, "a station of a certain railroad." He felt her fingers tense in his.

"I've been trying to locate that painter," he continued as if there had been no reaction, "because his work is quite ... exceptional." Meredith's face turned white, and if he had any doubts, they were gone now. "I wanted to find him to get more of his work and to tell him how very good he is. I'm telling you that now, Meredith."

Meredith stared at him. There was an intensity in his face she could not fathom.

"I don't know what you're talking about."

"I saw a sketch of a fox in a certain Parson's cabin. He is a friend," Quinn said, his voice searching now, wanting to hear her confirm everything.

Meredith stared at him, at eyes no longer shuttered but sharing knowledge ... and a regret that bit straight through her.

"As is Elias Sprague," he continued softly. Her back was still stiff, her eyes still wary, and her hand still seeking release. "Damn it, Meredith," he said, feeling more than a little pain that she didn't trust him. His hand tightened on her wrist, demanding agreement.

If he had taken her in his arms, if he had said the words she longed to hear, she would have flung herself toward him with joy. But he did none of those things, and she knew with a certainty that he had made love to her only to discover what he wanted to know, not because of any feelings for her. It was, she realized, why he was remorseful now. Guilt, not love, had put the softness in his voice.

She suddenly hated him.

"I don't know what you're talking about," she said coolly. "I do paint, but I don't know any ... who did you say it was? M. what?" Before he could answer, she continued on. "And I want to return to New Orleans. You can let me off at

Natchez. I'll say I've been kidnapped and I escaped. I wouldn't want to see your brother disgraced.''

"Merry—"

"Meredith, damn you," she said with no little fury. "You have what you wanted." She would let him guess whether it was his assumption about her identity or her body she meant. "And you will let me go or I will make a scene neither you nor anyone else will forget." The terrible stabbing anguish, the deep aching rejection that she had experienced once before, boiled into an anger so deep she was shaking. She had felt empty before, but never like this. Never like a shell with its core ripped out and exposed.

And that was what he had done. He had exposed her need, her weakness, her vulnerability. No one had been able to do that before. No one.

"Meredith," he tried again, seeing some of the pain writhing inside her, knowing he was responsible. He remembered how curtly he had left her after making love to her—no, after they had made love to each other—and he could have driven a stake into his own heart. He swallowed, seeing how her eyes had changed from shining curiosity to bitter distrust. He was still holding one of her hands, and his other one went to her face, trying without words to apologize, but she was having none of it. She only looked at him with something akin to loathing.

She jerked her hand away from him. "Just go away," she said. "Please." It was the defeat in the last word that nearly unraveled him. He had kept his emotions bottled up for so long he didn't know how to uncork the bottle, how to express any but the most superficial of feelings. From the look in her eyes, he suspected any attempt to soothe her would be rejected. She would accept nothing. The distrust in her eyes was too strong. She felt used, and he knew that feeling, knew it only too well. He felt a complete helplessness, but still made a move toward her until she shrank back from him.

He swallowed against the hard lump forming in his throat and he knew he had to leave, had to give her time, give himself time. Quinn slowly nodded and walked quietly to the door. He unlocked the door and left almost soundlessly.

Meredith saw that he didn't take the key with him. He had no reason now to lock the door. He knew who she was, at least in part, and he also understood she was of no danger to him, to whatever it was he had to hide. Only now did she remember that she had told him much, if not everything, and he had told nothing. Nothing at all.

The nagging doubts returned. Who was he? What was he? And why couldn't she resist him? For she had learned tonight that she could not. What else would she eventually tell him? What danger might she put others in?

But that was not all of it. Even if he was, as he had suggested, a member of the Underground Railroad, he had used her. It was only too obvious that he did not have the slightest feelings for her. She closed her eyes in pain. When he had touched her, she had believed otherwise. For one glorious moment she had believed that he really cared.

Fool! As much a fool as she so often pretended to be. She knew then she had to get away from him. No matter who he was. No matter what he was. She had been terribly shameless with him, and even encouraged him, but then she had deluded herself that he wanted her too. Wanted her for herself, not for what he could seduce out of her mouth.

For the first time in nearly fifteen years, she cried. Cried as if her heart had shattered. And it had.

Chapter 16

QUINN HESITATED outside the door, not wanting to leave but believing it was the best thing to do at the moment. He was almost as bewildered as she and he needed to sort out his thoughts. Damn, but he needed to do the impossible.

Meredith had touched a part of him he never thought could be touched again. Yet his life had no place for someone like her.

He lived from day to day with risk, never knowing what was beyond the next bend. Until now, he had never wanted to know. Life had a way of playing tricks on the best prepared plans, and though he would take responsibility for his own life—and for those he helped—he could not sacrifice another human being. Too many people had already been hurt by him.

Cam was different. Cam knew the risks as well as he, and he had an anger as great as his own, and a need as deep to channel it. To do otherwise was to die in another way. But Meredith? How could he endanger her?

And himself? He doubted whether he still had the ability to get close to another person. There was even a barrier between him and Cam, as closely as they were pulled together by common purpose and common danger. Part of it, he knew, was because Cam probably could never entirely trust a white man. But part of it was also due to himself. He didn't think he could ever again risk the pain he had felt when Terrence died. Even recalling the memory was like stripping skin from body, exposing raw red wounds that were as agonizing now as they were five years ago.

He looked at the lock and felt for the key in his pocket, then realized he'd left it behind. He couldn't force himself to return, not without being prepared to offer Meredith more than he dared. Besides, where would she go? They were on the river now, and would be until they reached Natchez the next day.

Christ, what a mess he had made of the whole matter. What a complete, disastrous mess. He thought about Meredith hunched against the wall and he wanted so badly to go to her. And do what? Tell her about his life? That he was a murderer? An escaped convict who was wanted in England? That there was no future because of the past? He looked down at his callused hands in self-loathing. If only she knew how they came to be that way . . .

With dragging steps, he climbed up to the pilot house, which stood alone like a watchful sentinel over the restless and often treacherous river. Jamison greeted him with his usual smile, which was little more than a twist of tightly pressed lips.

"Mr. Devereux," he acknowledged. Despite the number of times Quinn had asked him to use his given name, Jamison refused. It was not the correct thing to do with one's employer.

"Do you have any of those cheroots left?" Quinn asked. He had given Jamison a box of the finest cigars from Cuba, and the man hoarded them as if they were gold.

"Aye, sir," Jamison said with a certain reluctance. He hated to part with one of the treasures.

"I'll replace it, Mr. Jamison," Quinn said with a slight, crooked smile. Since Jamison refused to call him Quinn, he refused to be any less formal.

"That's not necessary, sir," Jamison said, but his eyes warmed a bit. He went to a wooden box and almost reverently took out a long thin cigar wrapped in chocolate-brown leaf and cut square at both ends.

Quinn took it and bit down hard on the end, chewing with a vengeance not entirely necessary. "When will we be in Natchez?" he asked, after the steamboat pilot lit it.

"Just after dawn," Jamison said.

Quinn nodded and turned to leave.

"Mr. Devereux?"

"Mr. Jamison?" Quinn spun around, one eyebrow raised inquisitively.

"I've been hearing that there are questions being asked about the *Lady*." He said the last with a caress. Quinn had often thought his boat was Jamison's one and only love.

"What kind of questions?" Quinn's voice was lazy, unconcerned.

"About our cargo. Our stops. Anything suspicious."

"Do you know who was asking them?"

"Brothers. Name of Carroll. They've been with us several times."

Quinn stiffened slightly. He did not like undue curiosity. Nor did he like Jamison getting involved. Jamison did not know about the secret compartment, nor about any of the illegal cargo, although Quinn knew he must have suspicions. Jamison was not a stupid man, but he was a discreet one, who minded his own business and who was, Quinn knew, immensely loyal. Quinn nodded once in acknowledgment of the information and left the cabin, pausing on the upper deck.

Dusk was falling, and the sky was turning vivid shades of crimson and vermilion in the west. He looked down at the men below, scurrying to light the oil lamps that adorned the decks. In minutes, the boat would be a fairy-tale land of flickering lights and crystal, echoing with laughter and conversation and music.

And one deck below, in a cabin once his sanctuary and now his hell, was a young woman whose eyes haunted him.

He despised himself more than he ever had before. When he had left, her eyes were those of a wounded fawn, baffled by a cruelty it couldn't comprehend.

Quinn had never thought he could feel anything for a woman again. Not after Morgana's treachery. And yet from the very beginning, Meredith Seaton had stirred something strong and vulnerable and even tender in him. He had not understood why until today, when he fully comprehended the extent of her courage and intelligence.

He leaned over the railing and chuckled ruefully. Even he had been duped, and that was not easily done. He was usually too wary, too instinctive of danger.

But even faced with his accusation, Meredith had revealed little. She was wise enough not to deny; she had simply ignored his assumptions, leaving that insidious cloud of doubt. And she had continued that tactic even after he had . . .

Had what? Made love to her. Taken her maidenhood, and then left her coldly without a word of tenderness. His hands clenched the railing. He had excused himself then because of his suspicions. But he knew he was wrong. He'd been fighting his own demons, the fear of trusting, of giving part of himself again, the fear of loving again, or having someone love him. It had always led to disaster. People died around him. He didn't think he could bear another death. Especially hers.

What was she thinking now? Was she hating him? How could she not? He had destroyed everything for her, including the life she had created just as surely and carefully as he had his own. He couldn't stop the groan of intense pain that started in his heart and stuck in his throat, finally expelling it like the moan of a soul lost in hell.

He wasn't sure how long he stood there, wondering how he could right things. But finally he made his way back to Meredith. Merry. He didn't know why he wanted to call her that. He had seldom seen any but the solemn side of her except the few times she had teased him in her role of foolish Meredith. He smiled as he remembered that dinner party the first night she was aboard the steamboat, and she had so neatly excluded him from the ranks of gentlemen. It had proved a prophetic barb.

Yet there had been a certain delight, an obvious joy in the drawing of the fox, a mischievous touch that he suspected lurked deep inside her, along with that passion she had gifted him with, and which he had seemed so casually to toss aside.

Quinn knew such thoughts were doing him—and Meredith Seaton—little good. Somehow he had to find a way to mitigate the damage to her life. His footsteps heavy, as if the old chains were still binding him, he returned to his cabin.

He was surprised to find the door still unlocked. For some reason, he had expected her to turn the key, or bar the doorway with a chair or table from the inside. Quinn's hand hesitated before turning the knob, a certain premonition making his fingers tremble. Finally he opened it and stepped inside.

The cabin was dark, lit only slightly by the flickering flames of a lamp hanging outside on the deck. The curtains were open. The bed, with the sheets still tousled and stained, was empty.

But there was no sign of Meredith.

Meredith coughed and stumbled out of the water. She was almost frozen, and every movement was a supreme effort. Her breath came in short desperate gasps and her legs seemed nothing more than stiff boards. Rigid fingers untied the oilcloth she had found in Devereux's trunk, and she took out a towel wrapped, for extra protection, around her dress and cloak. The towel, thank God, was dry.

She'd survived the whole terrifying episode: the initial shock of the cold water; the several seconds of paralysis until stark terror set her arms moving.

Desperation had forced her to leave the boat. The same desperation drove her to fight the cold and current. Both acts were based on pure survival. She knew Quinn Devereux's effect on her, and she didn't think she could bear to see him again, or see the mocking smile and remote eyes. It had been obvious when he left and didn't return that he had cared nothing for her, less than nothing. For the first time in a long time, she had offered something of herself to another person, and it had been taken, used and discarded as if it were nothing but an old unwanted shoe. The hurt was worse than anything she had ever known. She bent over in silent agony, her hands digging into the hard earth as if to seize some comfort from it.

It was nearly full night; only a last slash of red at the horizon remained. She finally straightened from her tortured position and took stock of where she was. She had emerged from the river into a damp swampy area inhabited, she knew, by inhospitable creatures. But then, she thought, any one of them would be less dangerous than the one she had left on board the steamboat.

Shivering in the cool night, Meredith rid herself of the soaking shirt and trousers she had stolen from the cabin, and put on her dress and cloak. She should be warm enough to survive the night there. In the morning, in the sunlight, she would try to flag down one of the many boats on the river. She would claim she was kidnapped and brought upriver to be sold, and that she escaped. Her reputation would be in tatters but that didn't matter. Nothing mattered at the moment but escaping those cold emotionless eyes of Quinn Devereux.

The *Lucky Lady* was gone, the twinkling lights faded from the dark brown of the Mississippi. They were replaced by stars in the sky, sparkling diamonds on a midnight-blue cloth. The trees rustled slightly in the wind, and water splashed against the banks. Everything was as it should be, as it was yesterday and would be tomorrow. Everything but her. In the past hours, she had discovered a part of herself she never knew existed, but she had lost another part: the core of her. Her heart.

Meredith hadn't thought she had any tears left, but one found its way out of an eye and wandered down her face. She thought about brushing it away, but it was joined by another. And another.

She had always been alone—but never had she been this alone.

Shivering against a centuries-old oak tree, Meredith made a vow to herself. Never, never again would she risk her heart. And God help Quinn Devereux if she ever saw him again.

Meredith had more trouble than she had envisioned in trying to flag down a boat the next morning. Standing in the cool wind that swept the river, she shivered as four vessels, including a large riverboat, ignored her frantic waving. She was finally rescued by a small packet heading north and carrying cotton. It was operated by a family of redheads, including a father and mother and their eight children, one a son her own age. Their name was McClury, and they were kindness itself when they heard her tale of being snatched off the streets of New Orleans, wrapped in a blanket and taken upriver for an unmentionable and obviously loathsome purpose.

"Oh, my poor dear," Mrs. McClury said, her face wrinkling in concern.

"You have nothing more to worry on," said Dennis McClury, a red-faced man who obviously drank too much but who looked on each of his family members with an affection that made Meredith ache with envy. "We'll see you safe to the law."

Meredith sobbed out her thanks. No pretense was needed. She had started to believe no boat would venture the shallows to help her until this packet, unpainted and cluttered, had arrived. She had been cold, hungry, and dirty, and her spirit, momentarily at least, crushed. Both her cloak and her dress, which was torn during her abduction from Elias's warehouse and during her stay in Devereux's cabin, were stained from the night in the woods.

There had been suspicious looks from the family at first, but those soon disappeared as they saw the tattered but fine cloth of her dress and heard her speech. The McClurys listened raptly to her story.

"I was feeling ill, you see," Meredith said pitiably, not needing to act much at all, "and I couldn't get the windows opened so I dressed and went down to the porch for some fresh air. I don't know what time it was. I was just standing there, when—" She stopped and shuddered.

"Ah, dearie, you just stop and take your time. Ain't no hurry," Mrs. McClury said kindly.

Meredith knew she looked trembly. She felt trembly. But not for the reasons the McClurys believed. She was testing her story now, for it would be one she would have to tell over and over again.

"I heard a noise," she continued bravely, "but before I could turn, someone threw a blanket over me. I thought I would die. I couldn't breathe." She took a couple of swallows of air as she looked at the intent faces around her. She was not protecting Quinn Devereux, she told herself. She was protecting herself and the Underground Railroad.

She didn't have to lie when she told them how terrible it was when her hands and feet were tied, how she didn't know what was going to happen to her. "And then," she said, "I heard them say they planned to sell me . . . to sell me to some . . ."

Meredith obviously couldn't go on, and Mrs. McClury put big comforting arms around her and crooned soothing words. They needed to be told no more. They were only grateful they could help.

Later, Mary McClury, taking a look at Meredith's ruined dress, offered a clean one of her own and, although it was much too large, Meredith accepted. She wanted no reminder of the night and day she'd spent with Devereux. She could not bear to think of him as Quinn, because that was too intimate, too hurtful. She now bundled her pain with the dress and threw it over the side of the boat, hoping that somehow its disposal would remove some of her memories. The McClurys had readily agreed to take her to Natchez where she could contact friends.

The oldest son was particularly thoughtful, bringing her a huge plate of food she could barely look at, much less eat, although for his sake she nibbled at it. They then offered her the elder McClurys' tiny cabin to rest.

But, once there, she wondered whether she would ever really rest again, or whether Devereux would continue to haunt her with icy detached eyes or contemptuous mocking ones. She didn't know which were worse.

Meredith realized now that he was, indeed, with the Underground Railroad, but the knowledge that once would have delighted her heart and brought them close was now only more wounding. She didn't want to share the same cause with him, the same friends, the same acquaintances. She wished to hate him completely and fully for the complete blackguard she wanted him to be. He must be involved for the money. She knew some conductors were paid for their efforts by escaped slaves in Canada who now sought to free relatives and friends.

How he had fooled her with his pretend gentleness! How he had lured her with eyes of false passion! Even after he had left his cabin so abruptly, she had waited for him to return. Waited for what seemed hours. Waited for him to come and kiss her and make her feel wanted. And then she couldn't wait any longer. She couldn't bear any more rejection. She hated herself for running, for not standing up to him, for not showing an indifference of her own. But it was too late now. She could only hope never to see him again.

When they reached Natchez, the McClurys insisted on accompanying her to the sheriff's office where she told her tale. She had gone over it so many times in her mind that it came easily now.

"I was feeling ill, you see," she started, and the sheriff, who quickly ascertained she was a relative of William Mathis of Natchez, was the soul of discretion and sympathy. He very gently asked for descriptions of the kidnappers, and she gave him some very imaginative ones.

"One was huge," she said. "And shaggy. Like a brown bear. The other one was thin with broken teeth and a terrible odor." She then burst into tears and swooned, leaving the sheriff panicked and yelling for help. Any other time, she might have enjoyed the deception. She had long ago discovered within herself an appreciation for the ridiculous, and she often took delight in pricking the pompous and authoritarian. But now her tears were not pretend, and all she wanted was to get away by herself, to someplace safe from a tall enigmatic gambler.

Inwardly she stiffened her spirit, but outwardly, when William Mathis arrived at the request of the sheriff, she was swooning once more.

Two days later, Aunt Opal arrived and made arrangements for their return to Briarwood. She had another piece of bad news.

Daphne had disappeared.

The captain acted like a dead man. Cam had never seen him this way before. As they had searched the boat for Meredith, his face took on a bleak expression. His movements had become stiff, and his eyes had looked empty.

When they reached Natchez, Quinn wanted to take his horse and ride back, oblivious to the fact that he had no idea when and where Meredith Seaton had left the *Lucky Lady*. Even if he had, Cam was afraid there would be nothing to find. Few women could swim, and fewer still could combat the strong currents of the Mississippi.

But still the captain had insisted. "She's too damned stubborn to die," he said over and over again. "She might be out there alone ... cold. ..."

Cam shook his head sadly. He had been taken aback when the captain had brought the young woman to his cabin. But when the captain said she also was a member of the Underground Railroad, she had seemed a good match. Cam didn't know what exactly had happened in that cabin, but it had had a profound impact on the one man Cam had come to think of as unassailable.

He was anything but that at the moment. If they weren't on the open deck, Cam would have put his hand on the man's shoulder, but as it was he had to maintain his sullen expression, his defiant stance. "Remember," he said softly, "we have fifteen people below dependin' on you."

"I have to go back."

"I would have to go with you," Cam said. "No one would believe you'd allow me North on my own. Who is going to know about those people between the walls? Who will take care of them?"

"I can make up the time ... catch another boat, a faster one."

"You'd never make it, Capt'n."

Quinn stared out at the foaming water. Fifteen lives against one. And that one life was probably already forfeit.

Because of him. Solely because of him.

For the second time in his life, he was a murderer.

He turned around and looked at Cam, hell in his eyes. "We'll go on," he said in an emotionless voice, but Cam saw the pulse throb in his throat, and he knew Quinn Devereux was hurting.

There was nothing he could do. Not even sympathy would be welcome now. Everything about the captain said he wished to be left alone.

With heavy steps, Cam moved away, leaving Quinn staring with unseeing eyes at the wake of the *Lucky Lady*.

Chapter 17

CINCINNATI LOOKED LIKE a welcoming friend.

Meredith's soul was sore, and she needed a friend. She needed Sally Grimes—Sally Bailey now. And Sally's grandparents, the Meriweathers. And Levi. Perhaps Levi most of all. She needed a renewal of purpose, for she had never been quite so hollow inside.

The last two weeks had been the worst she had ever spent. Worse even than that first month at school. Daphne had disappeared mysteriously, and there was no word of Lissa. Even the Parson was gone. And at Briarwood, there was no peace, only explanations and more explanations. Recriminations. Scoldings. Censure.

She was used to it all, but never from so many people at the same time and never when she was feeling so lost.

Bitter and confused, she had ridden one day to the Parson's, but he was not there, nor was his dog, which meant that he was traveling. She was angry with him, angry that he had not told her about Devereux. She had briefly considered the possibility that he hadn't known about Captain Devereux's connection with the Railroad, but dismissed it. Jonathon Ketchtower coordinated activities in Mississippi and Louisiana. He knew *all* the stations, *all* the conductors. He should have warned her, and then that day on the *Lucky Lady* wouldn't have happened. She would have been able to quickly explain her presence at Elias's warehouse and been on her way, with no one the wiser.

Whenever she thought of that afternoon, she was flooded with humiliation and festering hurt. And something else, something very unwelcome. Her body now ached for something she knew she would never, could never, have again.

Meredith had hoped time would blur the memories of what had happened in Quinn Devereux's cabin, but it hadn't. It had only sharpened the need, made more precise each recall of the feelings only once experienced and which made life a living torment.

And she worried constantly about Daphne. Robert and Opal had assumed she had escaped and urged Meredith to post a reward. Meredith had steadfastly refused, saying she did not want an obstinate and unwilling servant, and good riddance. But secretly she wondered. She had not thought Daphne determined enough to escape on her own, and she was afraid harm had befallen her. She had written her detective and asked him to inquire discreetly, but she had as yet heard nothing.

It was December now, nearing Christmas, and she had announced her intention to visit the Meriweathers for the holiday. There had been no protestations from her brother; he hoped the talk would leave with her. And she quickly dismissed any suggestion that she take Aunt Opal. Other than locking her up, Robert had no choice but to let her travel unchaperoned.

He also had been heartened by Meredith's renewed interest in their neighbor, Gil MacIntosh. Meredith knew her brother had high hopes that she might announce an engagement upon her return. It would quiet some of the speculation that had continued about her missing two days. News, unfortunately, traveled fast between Natchez and Vicksburg.

Gil, she thought, as the riverboat neared the landing at Cincinnati, had been quite wonderful. He was one of few who had asked no questions, nor offered any censure for putting one's self in a position to be kidnapped. He had simply been there, offering quiet support.

She had wished futilely that she could care for him. She had even allowed him a kiss, hoping that there would be even the tiniest spark, that she could feel with him even a little of what she had felt with Devereux.

But there had been nothing, not the smallest twinge or slightest quickening of the blood. Her legs hadn't trembled, nor had her heart beat faster. She had only wanted the kiss to end.

Yet all those things happened when she only *thought* of Quinn Devereux.

When she'd boarded the *Dixie Belle* in Vicksburg, she'd heard its whistle and thought of the whistle of the *Lucky Lady*. She had felt the boat move and remembered that day when Devereux's steamboat moved as she lay in his arms.

But now she was finally in Cincinnati, and she was sure the city would not hold the same shadows.

She looked out at the crowd gathering as the boat docked. She picked out Sally and Mr. Meriweather. They looked so good to her. So familiar.

The boat nudged up to the landing and was secured. As Meredith made her way to shore, Sally rushed to her, hugging her with enthusiasm, while Mr. Meriweather grasped her hand warmly. When they were in the carriage, Mr. Meriweather examined her face carefully and looked at her with concern.

"Any news of Lissa?"

Meredith shook her head. "The detective believes she's in Kentucky, but he hasn't located her yet. I received a note just days ago. He's checking the records of slave dealers in west Kentucky, and apparently there are a number of them."

Henry Meriweather shook his head. "Too many. And

President Pierce's affection for Southerners is only encouraging the business. Pray God, we can elect a Republican.''

"John Frémont?"

"I hope so. He's captured the imagination of the country for his explorations, and although he's owned slaves, he claims to be antislavery now. I believe he's the only man who has the slightest chance to defeat Buchanan and the Democrats.''

Meredith sat back and listened as he talked about the elections to be held the next year and the Dred Scott case, which was in the courts. Dred Scott was a slave whose master had moved from a slave state to a free one and back again to a slave state. Dred Scott had filed suit, saying that his residence in a free state made him free. The whole country, both proslavery and antislavery factions, was anxiously awaiting the outcome.

It was good to be included in the conversation, to be considered an equal, and not a fool. Even if she had not cultivated her role as a fiddleheaded flirt, she knew she would have been excluded from participating in such topics at most Southern homes. Women were not considered intelligent enough to have opinions. It was an attitude that had always pushed Meredith to a simmering fury, one she had to hide.

"Levi?" she asked. "How is he?"

"As persuasive as ever." Henry chuckled. "The other day he convinced three slave owners to contribute to the welfare of a family of poor people. One of the men asked if they were very poor, and our Levi answered they were the 'poorest of the poor.' Each contributed, not knowing they were donating money to help that same family escape from slavery.''

Meredith smiled. When Levi was collecting funds, he was not beyond a little chicanery himself. But like Elias, a fellow Quaker, he drew the line at violence. "It's better to suffer wrong than to do wrong," he often said. "We should love our enemies.''

She wondered what he would think of Captain Devereux, who obviously had few scruples about violence, if her kidnapping were any indication. She knew Levi disapproved of

Virginian John Fairfield, who warned the slaves he assisted that he would escort only those who would fight and kill, if necessary, to gain freedom. Meredith had often wondered which side she would follow if faced with such a decision.

She wanted to ask Mr. Meriweather about the mysterious riverboat captain, but the necessity of secrecy had been too well drilled into her. So she listened with interest until they reached the Meriweather home.

She looked over at Sally, who was watching her anxiously, and she knew her distraction was obvious. She straightened and smiled at her friend. "And Garrett," she asked about Sally's husband, "how is he prospering?"

Sally beamed happily. Garrett had started a blacksmith shop and livery not long ago and it was doing well, far better than their expectations. "I have news," she announced, clasping Meredith's hands. "We're going to have a baby."

Meredith embraced her friend delightedly. "When?" she asked.

"Six months. You will be the godmother, won't you?"

"Of course," Meredith said, her spirits rising although that ugly sense of aloneness was still there, growing larger as she watched Sally's glowing eyes dance with love. *Is that how it can be?*

I won't do this to myself, she told herself. She forced herself to grin and added, "I would adore being a godmother."

Quinn Devereux's gaze rested on the canvas in the little shop in Cairo. To the shopkeeper, his eyes were as remote as ever. But Elmer Davis would swear he saw the captain swallow hard before he nodded and said, "I'll take it."

From the moment Davis had unwrapped the new painting not more than two weeks earlier, he knew Captain Devereux would want it. There was a certain majesty to it, a pride that radiated through the work-bowed figures in the field. He could almost feel that sun burning into his own back, the hoe in his hand, the aching pain of the standing woman.

Quinn's hands shook slightly as he took the painting. Three weeks. It had been three weeks since Meredith Seaton had disappeared into the dark waters of the Mississippi. He had spent much of that time in drunken oblivion.

But it had done no good, had not blotted out the nightmares in which he saw her face through a dark mist. Sometimes it faded into that of Terrence O'Connell, and he would wake, his face wet with tears, and see Cam, his face creased with worry, looming above him. He would reach for a new bottle, trying to erase the knowledge that he *was* death, that he brought destruction to everyone he cared about: his father and older brother, Terrence and now, Meredith. More than once, he urged Cam to leave him, to go north to Canada with Daphne.

But Cam only regarded him stubbornly, helped him clean up, and told Jamison the captain had a fever.

Which, Quinn admitted, he did. One that wouldn't let him go.

They had reached Cairo five days after Meredith had disappeared. Quinn had sobered enough to oversee the unloading of the fugitives, including Daphne. He and Cam made arrangements for her to stay with a free black family, and though Cam had urged Daphne to go on to Canada, she insisted on staying there where he could visit often. Cam, secretly pleased, didn't argue much.

Quinn had again considered riding back to where Meredith had disappeared, but he knew it would be, as Cam reminded him often enough, an exercise in futility. There was also the danger he would bring himself and everyone connected to him if it was discovered Meredith had been aboard the *Lucky Lady*.

So, mainly for Cam who wanted to spend time with Daphne, the two of them stayed behind while the *Lucky Lady* went on to St. Louis. Quinn engaged rooms at a hotel and frequented Sophie's Parlor to drown his guilt in alcohol. He was only marginally aware that Cam was usually gone during the day, appearing only at night to care for him. Quinn, when he thought at all, supposed his friend was with Daphne, and he was pleased that something fine was happening to Cam.

The *Lucky Lady* returned to Cairo from St. Louis, but Quinn wanted no part of it. He couldn't bear going into his cabin, nor did he want to spend time on the river. From his hotel room, he heard the band playing and the whistle blowing as the boat started its trek south. He cursed both. He closed the window and went to the bed, sitting and burying his head in his hands. When Cam returned that night and saw the captain still there, a nearly empty bottle by his side, he finally lost patience.

"You can't bring her back," Cam said. "You goin' give up everything now, let everyone down?"

Quinn looked at him with haunted eyes. His mind had kept going over that last afternoon with Meredith, had continually seen the light fade from those brown eyes and watched them cloud with misery while he remained unable to express the slightest tenderness. And so he had left her when he should have taken her in his arms and . . .

And what?

Told her that he loved her? He had told Morgana that and she'd betrayed him. He had sworn never to utter those words to another woman. And yet during the hours in the cabin with Meredith Seaton he had felt things he had never felt before in his life. An aching tenderness that had crumbled all his defenses, a sweet passion that had made him feel young and invincible again. From the very first, there had been that curious, rare magnetism between them. Now he knew it was her spirit that had drawn him, the beautiful outrageous spirit that had somehow shone through her masquerade. And he had killed it. Along with the remnants of whatever soul remained in him.

Through bleary and ravaged eyes he looked up at Cam.

Cam, and the Underground Railroad, had saved him years ago. Perhaps they could again. And perhaps there was something he could do for Meredith Seaton. Her half sister! Perhaps there was a way to help her half sister. If Meredith worked for the Underground, it was possible she knew Levi Coffin, and the Quaker might have some knowledge of the missing half-sister she had been seeking. It was, at least, worth a try.

The next day he shaved for the first time in days and then went to the wharves to seek passage on a boat to Cincinnati. He had left his horse on the *Lucky Lady*, knowing that Jamison would see it was well tended. He paid his bill at Sophie's after an uncomfortable encounter with Sarah, the young mulatto who had declared herself in love with Cam. She wanted to know where Cam was. Quinn could only shrug, and her eyes had gone black with anger.

Before he and Cam were to board the *Ohio Star*, Quinn went to Elmer Davis's shop where he found the painting, discovering, ironically, that it had arrived in a shipment from his own boat two weeks earlier. Devastated, he found Cam, and together they boarded the riverboat to Cincinnati. Quinn had to find out about Meredith's half sister, and he knew he had to tell Levi Coffin what had happened, to explain if he could, why one of his agents had disappeared. It would be the most difficult explanation he would ever have to make.

Meredith wished she could share the Meriweathers' Christmas spirit. The house was filled with evergreen and mistletoe, with packages and secrets.

She had always enjoyed spending the holidays here, although she had sometimes felt like an onlooker. As much as the Meriweathers tried to make her feel like a member of the family, and as much as she tried to pretend it was true, there was always an emotionally detached part that proclaimed her otherwise.

She did enjoy a certain freedom in Cincinnati, and could

dress to her own taste. The Meriweathers lived a quiet life, and few, if any, Southerners from her class came to this Ohio city. She had never encountered a Southern acquaintance here, and she stayed away from the one fine hotel any might frequent. She needed this time to reestablish the real Meredith.

Meredith had already purchased and wrapped her own cache of gifts. A book by Frederick Douglass for Mr. Meriweather, scarves she had knitted for Mrs. Meriweather, Sally and her husband and, newly added, a tiny baby blanket for the expected child.

Restless to the point of madness on Christmas Eve, she went to visit Sally at her new home, and then decided to stop at Levi's. She had had little time with him alone, and now she could obtain news of those slaves she had assisted. That, she knew, would be the best possible Christmas present. She had said nothing to him of her encounter with Captain Devereux, knowing that she would have more than a little difficulty explaining exactly what had happened.

Levi was not at the mercantile store, and a clerk told her he had gone to his adjoining home. Meredith decided to visit him there; she had always liked Mrs. Coffin and particularly enjoyed the warm affection between the couple. Mrs. Coffin was a wholehearted supporter of her husband's cause and frequently fed starving fugitives at any time, day or night.

Levi opened the door quickly when she knocked, and she was greeted with a gentle smile. "I'm delighted to see thee," he said. "Will thee not join us for some refreshment?"

Meredith immediately felt better. There was something very soft and comforting about Quaker speech.

She had no more than settled in a kitchen chair and accepted a glass of hot cider when she heard the sound of another knock. Levi and his wife exchanged looks. "It appears our day for visitors," he said with a pleased smile, and went to the door.

Meredith took another sip of cider, but the cup fell from her fingers and shattered on the floor when she heard a deep

masculine voice. "Levi. I dislike calling on you at home
but... there is something..."

A tingle ran down Meredith's spine. She desperately
wanted to crawl under the table as she heard the approaching
steps. Fastening her eyes on a hooked rug on the floor, she
saw the mud-splattered boots first, and her gaze, reluctantly
but uncontrollably, moved upward while the familiar voice
stilled, its timbre echoing in the room. Or was it in her head?

Or worse, her heart.

Levi must have taken Captain Devereux's coat, for the
gambler was standing there in his usual tailored black suit
although it was uncharacteristically dusty and wrinkled. His
dark hair was tousled from the wind and the strong angular
chin was shadowed and in need of shaving. She saw his eyes
register shock; his hand started to reach out, then dropped to
his side, his fist clenching. The muscles at his throat moved
compulsively.

The black man at his side had also gone completely still,
and Levi looked from one person to another, baffled over the
potent storm obviously brewing in his usually peaceful kitchen.

"Captain Devereux," he started, but the captain completely
ignored him, his eyes fixed on the figure sitting as still as any
statue.

Quinn's eyes drank in every detail of her presence. Good
God, but she looked lovely, and it wasn't only because he had
never expected to see her again.

Her hair was down, flowing over a red dress that made the
most of her deep brown eyes. They were as startled as he
knew his must be, and suddenly filled with the golden light
he now equated with strong emotion. Quinn saw the broken
cup, and the hand that was trembling, and he realized her
shock was as great as his own. Years of practice, of hiding
the deepest emotions, deserted him. He felt Cam's hand on
his back and he stiffened. But something inside him cracked,
and he felt the most enormous need to laugh. To laugh from
relief, from joy, from admiration.

He bowed instead, only a ghost of a smile on his lips.

"We do meet at the most . . . unusual times and circumstances," he remarked, much more coolly than he felt.

Her face flushed, and her eyes, which had looked trapped, caught fire and blazed. "I thought you reserved prowling for night," she said nastily.

" 'Tis preferable to swimming at that hour," he replied, the smile growing larger.

"It depends on the choices."

"And how odious they are?"

"Exactly."

Levi broke in. "I assume thee have met."

"Ah, yes," Quinn said. "In fact, I came here to tell you of her demise."

"Her . . . ?" Levi's face, if possible, became even more puzzled.

"She left the *Lucky Lady* last month," Quinn said. "Between stops." He turned back to her, his eyes very dark, very intense. "It was a damn fool thing to do."

The very intensity of his expression left her without a retort. His face was thinner than it had been, his bearing not quite as arrogant despite his challenging, teasing words.

He didn't wait for her to reply, and continued. "But I'm damned glad to see you alive."

Meredith heard the underlying strain in his voice, the concern, even the pain, and it startled her. She had not considered the possibility that he might believe her dead or that he might care. He seemed not to care for much at all. But as she slowly looked up at him, she saw the muscle throb at his throat, the only outward sign, she was beginning to learn, that betrayed deep feeling.

"I swim well," she said merely.

"In the winter, even the strongest swimmer can die in those currents, or of the cold," he said. "I'm sorry you believed it preferable to my presence."

This time she could not mistake the pain in the words, although they were spoken in the same light mocking tone. She realized with sudden insight that they were intended as an apology and self-accusation and, furthermore, that both were rare and excruciatingly difficult for him.

She wanted to reach out to him, to drive away the shadow lurking in that handsome face, to touch the cleft in his chin. She no longer cared what he had done; she only wanted to ease the strain so obvious in his body.

As if he understood, his mouth relaxed slightly and he looked once again at Levi. "Would you tell Miss Seaton that I am one of you and of no danger to her?"

Levi had been studying both of them: the tautness of their bodies, the shock in each face as they saw each other, the flow of energy between them, which, if not wholly visible, was certainly strong and alive and vibrating.

"It's obvious thee know each other," he said dryly, answering his own earlier question, which had been ignored. "Captain Devereux has been with us four years and has become our most successful conductor along the Mississippi line." He turned to Meredith. "And our Meredith joined us when she was but fifteen. Thee did not know . . . ?"

Quinn turned to Levi. "Unfortunately, I only guessed several weeks ago . . . after I found her outside Elias's warehouse and," he hesitated a moment, "kidnapped her."

Levi stared at him with reproach. "Thee knows my feelings on violence."

"Aye," Quinn said. "But I believed there was no choice. When I discovered later that she might be with the Railroad, she disappeared." It was only half the truth, even less than half, and he thought Levi knew it from the piercing look he received from the Quaker. Yet Levi asked no questions, and Quinn was grateful.

Quinn heard the uncomfortable uncertainty in his own voice when he looked at Levi. "May I talk to her alone?"

Meredith started up out of the chair, more in retreat than agreement. "No," she exploded.

Once more, Quinn and Meredith received searching looks from the leader of the Underground Railroad. He saw the anguish in Meredith's eyes and the determination in Quinn

Devereux's. His hand went out to her shoulder. "I think it well that thee listen," he said softly, nodding to his wife and Cam to follow him as he left the room.

"Levi?" she said in one last cry for help, but it was ignored. She felt, more than saw, Captain Devereux approach and gently guide her back into her chair, then take one next to it. She felt her hand being taken by one of his, and her chin being lifted by the strong callused fingers of another. She kept her eyes lowered, not wanting to see the face that had always fascinated her with its strength and secrets.

"Meredith," he said, and his voice, low and compelling, commanded her to look at him.

Her eyes slowly moved upward until they finally met his, and she was instantly lost. For the first time since she had met him, they were unguarded, and she saw not the weeks of pain she had suffered, but years. Years and years of raw lacerating loneliness and something else, something she couldn't define. Despite her resolve to keep away from him, she moved closer, her hand reaching up and touching his face as if to wipe away the horrors she was seeing there.

The tenderness was his undoing. That she could have such a feeling for him after what he had done, after what he had made her do, was incomprehensible to him. "I thought . . . I thought I had killed you," he said in a broken voice, and she suddenly understood his ravaged look as he came into the kitchen, the new shadows in his face.

"I'm sorry," she whispered. "I didn't intend that . . . I just had to . . . get away."

His jaw worked. "From me?"

"From the way you made me feel," she said simply, knowing all the games between them were over. "And I thought . . . that you cared only to find answers to your questions."

"I knew the answers, Meredith. I think I knew them for a long time, but I needed the excuse . . ." His voice trailed off and he closed his eyes as he admitted the truth. He *had* known, somehow he had known. From that first dinner on the

Lucky Lady, something inside him had told him Meredith was different, that she was special. It was why, he knew, he had taken the trouble to fence with her, to tease her, to enrage her. He had never done that before; he had merely used women, and dismissed them. As he had been used and dismissed.

And he had nearly destroyed her because he had not been able to admit to any affection, any love, any emotion other than curiosity. His hand tightened on hers.

"I'm not . . . very good at saying . . ."

His stumbling words, so unlike anything she knew of him, sliced to her heart. She ached for him. She ached for herself. Neither of them had been very good at expressing themselves, except with their bodies. Perhaps that was why they had been so very good together that afternoon.

The remembrance brought back sensations she had felt with him, red-hot sensations that even now were gathering strength inside her. But there was more, so much more. As she looked at his face, which was for the first time vulnerable, she knew it was love that beat so fiercely inside her. She swallowed hard, afraid of herself, more than a little afraid of him, and the stark raw emotions he unleashed in her. She was afraid to love him, afraid of what he would do to that love.

It was as if he read her mind, and he wanted to say he would never hurt her. But he couldn't. As long as he continued with the Underground Railroad, as long as she continued, the danger of loss was there, of death, of imprisonment. And there were his other dark fears.

Desire hovered in the air between them: the need, the longing, the sweet wild craving that had always been there and that had been made stronger by their lovemaking.

He wanted to say he loved her.

She wanted to say she loved him.

Yet years of caution, of hurt, made the actual words impossible for either to voice. But they were real. Very real.

Meredith felt warmth running in honeyed streams throughout her body. Dear God, but she loved him. The realization was both like a knife to her heart and a balm to her soul. He would not be an easy man to love. Yet it was such a fine feeling, so giddily wonderful, to know she could.

He smiled ruefully, fully understanding the battling emotions in her face. He felt them all too well himself. He wanted to laugh. He wanted to cry.

Instead, his hand increased its pressure on hers, and he rose, gently bringing her up with him.

"We have to talk," he said simply, and she could do nothing but nod. If he had asked her to accompany him to hell, she would have done so.

Chapter 18

MEREDITH WOULD never know how he managed it on Christmas Eve, but Quinn found a closed carriage and, with a bill to the driver and an admonition to keep driving, he hustled her inside and took her in his arms.

They had not even said farewell to Levi and the others. Quinn said they would understand. Meredith was not quite so sure, but his magic had once more wrapped her in a cocoon, making her oblivious to anything or anyone else.

It was cool in the carriage and freezing cold outside. Dusk was forming and, from the glass windows, they could see the cozily lit homes decorated with Christmas finery. Wandering groups of carolers filled the air with songs of triumph and joy and hope.

They had always been bittersweet songs for Meredith, striking deep into the part of her that had always longed for family. But now, tucked under the strong arm of Quinn, she relished them, and her heart hummed along with the eager young voices and filled with a quiet but potent exultation of its own.

There was a possessiveness in Quinn's touch, an almost desperate quality that made her look up. His lips brushed hers lightly as if he couldn't quite believe she was here.

His hand traced the curves of her face. She had never looked so delectable, this silly Miss Seaton, who had been a member of the Underground Railroad since she was fifteen, who obviously could swim better than most men, who apparently thought little before plunging into a river and swimming to snake-infested shores, and who could paint with the best of artists. She was all that and more, he thought, as an uncertain smile formed on her face. The look in her eyes seemed to reach inside him and steal what remained of his senses.

"You will never know what damned agony I've been through in the past weeks," he said softly.

"I thought . . ."

He leaned down and kissed her mouth, his hand disentangling her hat from her head and running through the long honey-colored hair. His heart thudded as the kiss deepened, and his tongue entered her mouth with long scalding sweeps. He rejoiced as her own tongue responded, and met his. She was almost shy at first, but soon she was meeting his every thrust with one of her own. He could feel her body quiver with his slightest touch, and knew his own was doing the same.

Could this really be love?

He tore his mouth away and rained kisses up and down her face, then her neck and finally her throat, thinking how fine her skin was, how it tasted like spring flowers. He felt her hand move behind his neck and play with the hair that grew long there, and he loved every light touch. He had dreamed of this over and over again in the past fortnight, and now he groaned as the dream became reality.

He pulled away and stared at her face, at the kiss-swollen mouth and eyes now misty. He had almost destroyed her once. He would not do it again.

"How did you come to be in Cincinnati?" he said finally, when the great ball of sadness cleared his throat.

"A girlhood friend. I've been visiting her and her grand-parents for years."

"Abolitionists?" It was a guess, but little else made sense. Something, or someone, other than her half sister had to have been involved.

She nodded, not sure whether she was relieved at the change of mood. She had been drowning in him, in his magnetism, in the feelings he always created in her, the feelings that disregarded practicality and the good sense she had always held dear.

"The painting was yours?"

She nodded shyly.

He grinned. "I found another. I think it came on the same trip we did, but I didn't know it then. I was bitterly afraid it was your last."

"The fields," she said.

"The fields," he confirmed. "It's buried in one of my trunks. I didn't think I could bear to look at it again. Now . . . perhaps . . ."

Meredith snuggled deeper into his arms. "I'm glad you like my work, particularly the rainbow."

"Hmm," he murmured, his temperature beginning to rise once more. She fit so well, cloak and all, into the planes of his own body. "There was someone else on that boat."

She looked up with puzzlement.

"Daphne, your maid."

Meredith clapped her hands with joy. "I'm so glad. I've been terribly worried about her. I've had . . . friends in New Orleans looking."

Quinn couldn't hold back a chuckle as she grinned and started laughing herself.

"We *have* been at cross-swords, haven't we?" she said with a giggle, but it wasn't the silly giggle he had heard in company. It was delighted and delightful, and full of amusement. "I had been trying to find a way of getting her North without giving myself away."

"Despite the wonderful way she dresses your hair?" he asked teasingly.

"No one else has been able to do it quite that way," she admitted with mirth. "She kept trying, in her quiet way, to do something else. I think she was quite distressed that I insisted on that particular fashion."

He leaned back and laughed. "Perhaps that's one reason I was desperate to get her away from you. I always thought your hair held a great deal of promise." His fingers touched it now. "And I was right."

"How did she escape?" Meredith asked.

"Cam abducted her from the hotel. We'd been trying to find a way to get her North. When you ended up in my . . ."

"Clutches?" she offered.

He ignored her observation. "We thought it best to get her out then. . . . We were afraid it might be the end of the *Lucky Lady*."

"Because of me?" she said with amusement.

He shrugged. "There was always something . . . hidden about you. Brett said you always needed money, and I thought perhaps you might try to . . ."

"Expand my income?" She was bent over then with merriment. "I thought exactly the same about you. When you entertained the slave catchers . . ."

He had the grace to look discomfited. He could scarcely blame her for that. "It suited my purposes," he excused himself.

Meredith sobered. "Why Daphne?"

He misunderstood the sudden change in her. "She wanted her freedom. When I was at Briarwood, Cam and I approached the Parson about her."

Several things were becoming clear to Meredith, but still another suspicion lingered. "And found my sketch of the fox?"

"And of the Carroll brothers."

"And how did the Parson explain that?"

"He said they came from New Orleans."

Meredith's expression turned thoughtful. "He could have told me about you."

"And me you. It would have saved us a lot of trouble."

They looked at each other and smiled again.

"Why do you think he didn't?" Meredith asked.

Quinn shrugged. "Very few know my identity. Most of the slaves we carry don't even know which boat they're on. It's safer that way."

Meredith looked at him doubtfully.

"Or maybe he worried about what might happen if we got together." He looked down at her and gave her that funny little half smile that hid so much. She could almost feel him withdraw from her.

"Don't," she commanded.

"Don't what?" His brows wrinkled together.

"Don't go away again."

He understood what she meant, and he didn't try to deny his purpose, but he touched her cheek longingly. He wanted to keep her with him, yet he knew it was dangerous for her and for the cause they had embraced.

Meredith sensed the battle going on inside him and changed the subject. "Where's Daphne now?"

"Cairo, with some friends. Well hidden, I believe. We didn't know whether . . . your brother might take ownership and come after her." His face closed again at the specter of her imagined death, and she felt the tension in his body as he relived some of his guilt.

"She didn't go to Canada?"

Quinn smiled, this time openly. "She didn't want to be that far from Cam. This way they can see each other occasionally."

"Daphne?" There was surprise in her voice. And then she remembered the time Daphne had come back from the barn and she, Meredith, had blamed Quinn.

"I think I have an apology to make," she said with a hint

of wry humor in her voice. It was strange how, all of a sudden, she felt so natural with him, so comfortable. Especially after hating him so bitterly during the past few weeks. But she had understood, in Levi's kitchen, that he hadn't just used her, that he had suffered just as badly, if not worse, than she.

He raised an eyebrow.

"I thought *you* wanted her. I thought that was why you wanted to buy her."

He leaned back and let out a sound full of astonishment and humor. "So that's why you were so hostile."

"Well, I saw Cam's back, and you indicated at dinner it was you . . ."

"That happened long before I found him. He's as free as you or I now," Quinn said, chuckling. "Was I that convincing?"

Meredith squirmed. "So much so I was afraid he was going to slit your throat that afternoon in your cabin."

"You worried about me," he said, touched by the revelation.

"I don't like violence," she retorted defensively.

"Tell that to the side of my head." He grinned, and she thought how completely charming he was without the mockery, with a true smile on his lips.

"You deserved it," she defended herself.

His smile thinned. "Aye. After, if not before."

Her hand clutched his. "I thought you just . . . wanted information that afternoon."

"Ah, darlin' Meredith, I was scared to death of what I was feeling. I didn't know what to do with it. I had to think. And when you were gone . . ." His voice was suddenly raw and ragged, all the amusement gone from it.

Meredith wanted to find out so much about him, but there was still a wall around him, one that warned about asking too many questions. Yet it felt completely right to be with him. Even as his prisoner weeks ago, she had felt oddly safe until that moment he had left her after making love. And then her own hurt, her own insecurity, had made her do something immensely dangerous.

"Why did you come to Cincinnati?" she asked.

"To tell Levi what happened," he replied slowly. "And to try to find your sister for you."

Her hand tightened on his. She needed no more assurance than that one statement. He understood. He cared. But as the silence grew uncomfortably long, she decided to tease him, to see how far she could get. "All of it?"

"All of what?"

"Were you going to tell him . . . everything?"

He choked. "Everything," he finally admitted.

"And now?"

"I'm delighted I don't have to. The less said, I think, the better, though I think Levi will guess most of it." His arms tightened around her as if he were afraid she would flee again. A laugh started down in his chest, and she could hear the faint rumble of it, like distant thunder. "I think Levi would say there was a plan somewhere, the way we keep smashing into each other."

Meredith stretched her head up to look into gleaming blue eyes. "But whose?" she retorted with a small grin.

"I take it you mean the devil might be responsible," he said wickedly.

The corners of her mouth went up impishly. "I was convinced of it for a long time."

The carriage stopped, and the window between the coachman and passengers opened. Quinn thrust another bill up at the driver, and the wheels started rolling again. Meredith took a look outside. The sky was a soft gentle pink, and the sound of Christmas carols still wafted over the streets.

"He might," she said, referring to the driver, "want to go home for Christmas."

"His family will have a very nice Christmas," Quinn said dryly. "I don't think he's unhappy."

"We can't stay here all night."

"Why not?" he answered. "I can't very well take you to my hotel room."

"We can go to the Meriweathers'."

"There will be people there?"

She nodded. "Many."

He sighed. "Then that won't do at all."

"Everyone will wonder where I . . . we . . . are."

He leaned down and kissed her very satisfactorily, his lips dismissing her concerns. "You have a delectable mouth, Miss Seaton," he said on successful completion.

"Hmm," she murmured, unable to find a suitable reply, considering the way her senses were spinning. She was oblivious to the clipclopping of horses' hooves and the clack of wheels and the lurching of the carriage except when it threw her even closer to him.

There was only one reality, and that was Quinn Devereux and the fact that he had suffered over her and worried over her and, quite obviously, cared for her. Though he didn't say the words she wanted to hear, he was conveying them in different ways, and she knew even that was extraordinary.

For minutes, there were no more words between them. It was enough that they were together.

Quinn felt his chest constrict and buried his fingers in her hair. "I like it loose this way," he said.

"That's one reason I like coming to Cincinnati," she said quietly. "I can be myself. And you—is it safe for you to come here, to visit Levi?"

"That's the advantage of my profession," he said. "Levi is a merchant. So is Elias in New Orleans. Both have shipments going North and South, and my visits are both rare and circumspect. And though Levi is a known abolitionist, he's careful to keep silent his connection with the Underground Railroad."

"Does Brett know?"

Regret crept into his voice. "No. He believes exactly what the rest of the world believes—that I'm a scoundrel, a misfit, and a blackguard."

Her fingers ran up and down his wrist comfortingly.

"And I am much of that," he added warningly.

"I know," she agreed cheerfully.

"Impertinent witch," he observed.

"Arrogant wretch," she returned. "Nothing like the boy who built a swing for me one summer day."

He captured her fingers, which were making little designs on his wrist and sending great rushes of desire throughout him. He brought her hand to his mouth and kissed each finger, then turned the palm up and licked it with insidious insistence. When he was through, he nuzzled her ear.

"I thought you enchanting as a child. It was a terrible disillusionment when I met you on the *Lucky Lady*." He shook his head. "That giggle."

"No more so than I." She grinned. "My knight in shining armor dining with slave catchers. I was appalled."

"And I sat there wondering what had happened to the pretty little girl with the shining eyes." His own were dancing with devilment. "Until you made that barbed remark about gentlemen, and a voice inside started nagging at me."

"You brought out the worst in me."

"I did, didn't I?" he said with no little satisfaction. "I would see those eyes spark, and you'd try so damned hard to cover it up."

The carriage stopped again, and the window opened. It was dark now, and the carolers had gone home, as well as most of the other carriages. Another bill, apparently of significant denomination, went up, and the creaking of wheels continued. "The man's going to be rich," Quinn remarked easily, deflecting the protest he thought was coming.

"Do you know we've been up and down this street twenty times?" she said.

"You've been watching," he accused.

"No. I just know each time I'm going to be thrown against you."

"Not often enough."

"I'll complain to the Cincinnati mayor that the streets are too even."

He nibbled her ear. "Good idea."

"Quinn . . ."

"Say it again."

She obeyed, drawing out the short name seductively, making it sing in the small confines of the carriage. "Quinn."

"I think we'll stay here forever."

"The driver will have something to say about that."

"Not as long as I keep handing him bills."

"The Meriweathers will be worried about me."

There was a long silence. "I don't want to take you back," he said finally.

He didn't have to explain. Here they were in a sheltered place, where nothing could intrude, although questions lurked in the back of Meredith's mind. Who exactly was Quinn Devereux, and why was he involved in the Underground Railroad? What had happened during the years he was away that now he risked everything?

But she didn't require answers, anymore than he did. It was enough that they were together, that he had reentered her life and given it strength and substance and even glory.

Glory. Was that what she felt?

She knew it was seconds later when he kissed her. The wistful yearning of his lips, the quiet searching, caught her soul in a maelstrom, both violent and tender.

It was Quinn who finally drew apart. "Beautiful Meredith, Merry. Merry fits you, love."

"Only because you make it so," she whispered.

He held her tightly. "What do we do now, Merry?" It wasn't so much a question as a groan.

She didn't want to think of it. From the first moment she had met him she sensed he was not a man to be tamed, or tied down, or haltered in any way. And she had her own goal—to find Lissa—and her own small efforts against a system she detested. She suddenly realized why the Parson had said so little. There was no future together for the two of them.

But she would take now. She would take today, and tomorrow, and as much more as she could grab.

Meredith purposely misunderstood him. "I really must get back."

"I know," he said with a sigh. He tapped on the carriage and it stopped, the small window opening and the driver's cold face looking at them inquisitively.

Quinn turned to Meredith. "The address?"

When she gave it, the window closed and the carriage clattered forward at a faster speed. She welcomed the lurching for it thrust them together one last time before the wheels would soon roll to a stop.

The house was glittering with lights, and the front door opened quickly as the carriage pulled up. Meredith watched as Quinn gracefully descended and pressed more bills in the driver's palm and wished him a Merry Christmas. He then held out his hand to her and helped her out, standing with her in the night as the carriage moved away.

She hadn't expected him to do that. She had thought he would protect his gambler's identity. But he stood there patiently, waiting to be introduced, as the Meriweathers, Sally, and her husband gathered around, voicing concern which had obviously plagued them for hours.

"It's my fault," Quinn said with a quick charming smile. "Miss Seaton is an old friend, a client of my brother, and we started talking. . . ."

It left Meredith with little choice but to introduce him, and he was quickly invited inside for Christmas cheer. She was startled when he accepted with alacrity.

She leaned over and whispered, "Cam?"

He merely grinned wickedly. "I think Cam will understand."

"Is this wise?" she questioned.

"No," he answered softly in her ear. "But I haven't been wise since I met you."

And then he turned from her and fastened his charm on the Meriweather family. She had seen him charm Opal and then her brother. Still, she was amazed at how easily he now worked the same magic on her friends. Within minutes, they had invited him to attend church with them, that night, and again to her surprise he accepted.

Sally winked at her approvingly as she tucked her arm under that of her husband.

Of all the strange things that had happened to Meredith since she'd met Quinn, none turned out to be more emotional than standing next to him in church, his dark face lit by flickering candlelight and his strong baritone voice dominating in the singing of centuries-old carols. Sally looked at him in complete delight, as her perfect soprano and his deep resonant voice caused every eye to turn their way.

So much for secrecy and subtlety, Meredith thought. But they were only small warning signals compared to the great joy of standing there with him, her arm tucked in his possessively, and feeling a part of Christmas for the first time in her life. Her heart swelled until she thought it might burst, but a tiny voice kept warning her it wouldn't, couldn't, last.

But it seemed, for the next few days, as if it might. He showed up Christmas morning with a small package. She didn't even wonder how he managed to find something on Christmas. Nothing he did surprised her any longer.

His eyes gleamed as she took the small package and opened it to find an exquisite gold locket. It was by far the finest gift she had ever received, and Meredith clutched it possessively even as she knew she probably should not accept it. It was far too expensive for propriety, but then, she thought, she lived a life of impropriety.

"I have nothing for you," she said sadly.

He grinned down at her. "You gave me the most magnificent present in the world yesterday—just being alive and here."

"But that doesn't count," she argued.

He looked at her worried, distressed face. "I have a solution, then. A sketch of the *Lucky Lady*."

Her eyes brightened. "Done," she agreed.

His own eyes caressed her, the open smile he had never seen before, the face full of animation, and eyes glimmering with golden lights. He made an instant imprudent decision. "I plan to stay a few days."

He didn't think her face could brighten any more, but it did, and he shoved back all the warning voices in his mind. She made him feel so damned good, so damned free.

"Cam . . . ?" The name came easily to her tongue now. He was a friend of Quinn. He was her friend.

His mouth twitched at the corner. "I think he might go on to Cairo."

"Is it safe?"

"Not if he's recognized, but he's very good at slipping in and out of places."

"I'll have a present for him then too," she said delightedly. "Daphne's manumission papers. Levi has an attorney who can handle it tomorrow."

His hand tightened on her arm. It was the best gift Cam and Daphne could have. He knew from his friend how terrified Daphne was of being taken back. It had required a great deal of courage on her part to stay in Illinois. He wanted to lean down and kiss Meredith, but there were several pairs of openly curious eyes in the room.

His approval already showed in his face, and it was enough for Meredith, more than enough. But even as the glow inside her flared brightly, she warned herself to be wary.

Quinn saw the brief shadow in her face and guessed its cause. He was surprised to discover that, rather than being disappointed, he was rather pleased. Wariness, in their world, was a necessary and admirable trait. And there was something about her odd combination of innocence, suspicion, and talent for deception that both excited and fascinated him.

In some ways, he felt like the young man he had been before he'd lost his own innocence in England. For the first time since his arrest, he felt truly alive and hopeful. He grinned, realizing that he was actually courting.

He tried to warn himself to go slowly. She knew nothing about him, about those years in Australia. How would she feel if she knew he was an escaped convict, that he had been chained like a dog and subjected to every humiliation known to man? That he was responsible for his best friend's death?

He had told himself that over and over last night . . . and continued to tell himself this morning when he had pounded at Levi's door and convinced him to open his mercantile so he could select a present. He had told himself that as he looked into Levi's worried eyes, and related just a little of the conversation in the carriage. He had told himself that as he hurriedly dressed and arrived at the Meriweather home at an embarrassingly early hour for dinner. He had told himself that so many times that it was like an echo in his head.

He reminded himself that he somehow always managed to bring disaster to those he loved, that he had vowed not to get too close to anyone again. He would have to bar his heart from loving her, and make her see that caring for him was both unwise and dangerous.

Yet his heart filled with joy every time he thought of her, of the tentative little smile and the wistfulness in her eyes, of the way she held his hand, as if it were made of gold instead of scarred by calluses. Especially the way she touched him, as if he were special and cherished. It had been a very long time since he had felt special. And he liked the feeling. He liked it very much. And, damn his soul, he couldn't fight it. Not anymore.

Quinn looked at the locket in her hand. "May I put it on for you?" he asked.

Her slow smile, still tentative, still a little hesitant, made him ache inside, made his hands tremble slightly as he gathered the golden hair to one side, and fastened the slender chain around her neck. His fingers rested a trifle longer than necessary on her neck and might have stayed there if Sally had not come over to admire the locket.

He stepped back, watching the golden brown hair settle in soft curls around her face and down her back. He remembered how it had felt in his hands when he had made love to her, and his whole body ached with longing. He was relieved when they were called to dinner and she was seated across from him. He was only slightly aware of the fond, amused glances of their dinner companions as he and Meredith spoke to each other silently across the table.

After dinner, Sally asked if Quinn would join her in some carols at the piano. It had been a very long time since he last sang, years until last night, and he was reluctant. He didn't really know why. Perhaps because he equated music with happiness, with his family, with memories smothered by brutality. He had often sung with his family, all of whom had rich voices, but when he had returned home to find two dead, he had avoided it, avoided reminiscences of carefree times.

"Please," Meredith said, noting his hesitation.

He nodded and went over to the piano. Sally sat and arranged some sheet music and gestured for him to sit next to her. Sally was an excellent musician and the soft note of "I Saw Three Ships" wafted through the room. She started singing, her soft pure voice soon joined by Quinn's sure rich baritone. As if they had rehearsed it perfectly, they divided the phrases, joining together in the refrain, the sound of their voices lingering in the room as the song ended.

Sally then played "What Child Is This," and her voice stopped suddenly as Quinn continued the plaintive melody.

Meredith sat transfixed, for there was more emotion in Quinn's voice than she had ever seen in the man. There was pain and compassion and love there. The room was so still that she knew the others were as affected as she was. She was unaware of the tear rolling down her face, that her hands were clasped so tightly they were white. When the song ended, there was no movement, no talk, only complete silence, and through eyes blurred with tears she saw his face twist into the old self-mocking lines, and his voice, without accompaniment, started "God Rest Ye Merry Gentlemen," and was soon joined by the piano and other voices.

He left soon after, pleading another engagement, but Meredith suspected it was something else, that he was embarrassed at exposing something of himself he had kept previously hidden.

Quinn leaned over and, quickly and almost indifferently, kissed her cheek at the door. "I'll call tomorrow," he said. "For Daphne's papers."

She nodded, feeling the strain in him, the tension that radiated from his body. She wanted to ask him to stay, to beg him not to go, but she could not. Something in his guarded look told her not to.

"Tomorrow then," she said.

His grim mouth relaxed slightly. But he merely lowered his head in acknowledgment and strode quickly away.

Sally came up behind her. "He's wonderful," she whispered.

Meredith didn't answer. Dear God, but the sense of loss was overwhelming as he disappeared around a corner. Don't, she told herself. Don't be a fool.

Quinn Devereux, she had learned, was the consummate actor and, after her kidnapping, she did not doubt his ruthlessness. The wary part of her, the part that guarded against hurt, couldn't help but wonder now if the gentler, more vulnerable Captain Devereux was only his latest role.

C*hapter 19*

QUINN HAD experienced many restless nights, but none quite as tormenting as this one.

For a time yesterday, he had felt like a schoolboy courting his first girl. He had completely lowered his guard and revealed feelings he had thought submerged forever.

But it had felt so good to be surrounded by warmth, to be touched gently by eyes that asked little in return. He kept seeing the pleasure in her face as she opened his present, as she looked across the table from him.

But bloody hell, it wouldn't work. It *couldn't*. They would only endanger each other. Unless they both gave up the Underground Railroad. And he doubted she would do that until she found her half sister. He now knew exactly how stubborn she could be.

He had already risked much. Despite his casual words, coming to Cincinnati had been unwise, perhaps dangerous.

But he was no longer the cool calculating outlaw he had been. His stomach was tied in knots, his heart twisted in contorted anguish. He was seeing everything that he had missed. Going without was endurable if you knew nothing else, expected nothing. But once you did, it was pure misery. In the past two days, he'd tasted love and warmth and joy, and he had an appetite for more. No. He had a fierce, uncontrollable craving that was eating away at him. Quinn now understood Cam's preoccupation of the past days, and his obsession with Daphne. He had an obsession of his own now to deal with.

They'd had a drink together last night, he and Cam. More than one, more than two. God knew how many. Cam was celebrating the news about Daphne's manumission; Quinn was seeking comfort. After the last weeks of drunken grief, he should have known there was none in the bottle.

He wanted Meredith. Damn, he wanted her.

He rose slowly the next morning, realizing he had gained nothing from the previous evening other than a headache and a stomach that felt weighed by stones.

Amazed that his hand was steady, Quinn shaved, although very cautiously, all the while searching his face curiously in the mirror. It was the same, yet it was different. A side of his mouth quirked upward at his image. Damn fool. Ever since Morgana, he felt immune from love: infected once, protected always. Like a smallpox vaccination.

Nonetheless, his heart was beating in a quicker fashion than usual, and he could scarcely contain his impatience to see whether Daphne's papers were ready. He couldn't admit to himself that part of the reason for his rather singular eagerness was seeing Meredith. He would obtain Daphne's papers and leave, he promised himself. He made lists of things he needed to do, excuses to keep away from her, all the time knowing he would discard them in a moment if invited to do so.

Sally visited her parents' home early the morning after Christmas. Meredith was busy with her sketch, trying to remember every detail of the *Lucky Lady*: the gingerbread lacing, the lanterns, the great paddlewheel. It was already taking form on her sketchpad.

Sally leaned over and looked. "His boat?"

Meredith nodded, her face turning crimson.

"Tell me everything about him. He's intriguing."

"I wish I could," Meredith said. "I don't know that much myself. Just that he owns the steamboat and that his brother is my trustee."

"He's the most handsome man I've ever met," Sally said dreamily, "except, of course, for Garrett." The last words were added hastily and loyally.

"Hmm," Meredith answered. "Too handsome."

"No one can be too handsome."

Meredith lifted an eyebrow in disagreement.

"He looks at you as though he's passionately in love."

"Looks can be deceiving."

"And you looked as if you were passionately in love with him."

"They can be *very* deceiving."

"Then why are you sketching his boat?"

"A promise. Nothing more."

"I think there's a lot more."

"He's a gambler, Sally."

"All the more fascinating."

"And a rogue."

"I know," Sally said with satisfaction. "He's just what you need."

Meredith tried to look insulted, but it came to no more than a silly grin. "Sally!"

"Besides, he has a wonderful voice. You two can come visit, and we can sing together."

"I can't sing."

"I know that." Sally giggled. "I meant your captain and me."

"And what will Garrett think?"

"He thought we were wonderful last night. Garrett is very

broad-minded. Besides, everyone noticed your captain had no eyes for anyone but you, certainly not for an old married lady like me.''

Sally looked so unlike an old married lady, Meredith had to laugh. Her friend had never looked happier, and never laughed nor teased so much. Marriage had been very good to her. Meredith wondered what marriage would be like with Quinn Devereux. He was so unlike the industrious but amiable Garrett Bailey. She couldn't imagine him being satisfied, or happy, with one place, one person.

"Nonsense," she said, surprised when it came out aloud. She had intended the comment only for herself.

Sally's eyes twinkled. "I'll bet he calls on you as early as he did yesterday."

"Nonsense," Meredith repeated, yet the idea had definite appeal.

As if on cue, an impatient rapping sounded on the door, and Sally grinned. "Nonsense?" She laughed at the blush on Meredith's cheeks, then ran quickly to the door, opening it to find Quinn Devereux, looking as baffled at being there as Meredith was in seeing him. Sally couldn't resist an "I told you so" smile to Meredith before she turned back to Quinn and grinned broadly.

"Mrs. Bailey," he said formally to Sally, "Meredith said she had some errands to run this morning. I thought I might escort her."

"I think that's a fine idea," Sally said. "I have to go out, and we were just wondering how we could amuse Meredith today." She avoided Meredith's glower. "Do come in, Captain. She can be ready in a few minutes. She just needs a cloak, don't you, Meredith?"

"More like a gun," Meredith muttered just within Sally's hearing, making no secret that her intended prey was her friend.

"Oh, and a bonnet, of course," Sally ran on heedlessly. "I'll get them for you." With a wink, she went out of the room, leaving Meredith alone with Quinn.

He couldn't prevent a slight grin of his own at Sally's

obvious matchmaking and Meredith's discomfort. He saw the sketchpad in her hands and moved to her side, studying the lines intently. "That's very good."

Meredith's hands trembled slightly. He always had that effect on her. "It would be better if I could see it again."

He gave her a level stare with unblinking blue eyes. "You can," he said. "Go back with me. We can take the *Ohio Star* to Cairo and wait there for the *Lucky Lady*. The timing should be just about right."

Quinn didn't know where the suggestion had come from. He certainly hadn't considered it earlier. He had intended something quite opposite in fact. He had planned to escort her to the attorney's office for Daphne's papers and then say good-bye and leave. Leave her, Cincinnati, and all the turmoil she created within him. Over a breakfast he couldn't eat this morning, he had decided that course was the only wise one. Yet now he held his breath for her answer.

"Yes," she said simply, quite unable to say anything else. She could barely breathe as she looked up at him. Was Quinn, fresh-shaven and smelling of those enticing spices, even more irresistible this morning, or was it just that he was becoming more important to her? Piece by piece she was fitting together the puzzle that was Quinn, and the more she learned, the more intrigued she became.

She liked his friendship with Cam. She liked his easy charm with her friends. She liked the emotion in that fine voice of his. She liked the gentle way he touched her with his hands and especially with his eyes. She even liked the way he glowered at her because it meant he was as confused as she.

And he was glowering now, as if he couldn't believe her easy assent. "You know what I mean?" he added roughly.

But he no longer intimidated her. She had wondered last night whether she was seeing the real Quinn Devereux, or merely a shadow figure he wanted her to see. Perhaps a part of her still wondered. But she was willing now to take a chance. Not only willing, compelled.

She nodded, watching a quick flash of life in his eyes before he shuttered them once more.

He sighed with something like surrender. "I don't know what in the hell we're doing, Meredith, but I can't seem to do anything about it."

"I know," she said.

The simple affirmation made him grin. He had never met a woman with so little guile. When, he amended silently, she was not playing the role of a ninny.

"It could be dangerous," he warned. "And most assuredly not prudent."

Now she grinned. "Is this the way you conduct all your seductions, by warning the lady off?"

He shrugged, drowning his laughter in his throat. He was beginning to wonder who the seducer actually was. "There haven't been enough to establish a pattern," he replied with roguish modesty.

She gave him a skeptical stare. "The notorious Captain Devereux?" she teased. "I'm disappointed."

"I can always try to improve," he retorted, but his eyes said something entirely different.

Her heart beat at an accelerated rate, and she had to strain for breath. Quinn Devereux was undoubtedly the most wickedly attractive man she had ever known, with that devilish smile on his lips and laugh crinkles around his eyes. Yet, she noticed abruptly, his eyes, so deep a blue they made her ache inside, still didn't smile. It was ... almost as if they were unreachable, a part of someone else, a stranger who stood apart and watched.

She stood, forgetting about the pad in her lap. It fell, and he quickly swooped down and picked it up. "Such carelessness with my present," he admonished her.

"It's your fault," she said. "You have a way of ..."

"Confusing you?"

She nodded.

"Good," he said with satisfaction. "Now let's go see Levi's attorney. I have a most impatient friend."

He waited, not very patiently himself, she noted, as she found her cloak and hat and gloves. When she presented herself, he took her arm.

"How—" she started to ask how they would travel.

"The coachman from the other night," he interrupted, seeing the question in her face. "He learned my name from Levi and presented himself at the hotel early to say he would be at our service. I think he believes me an eccentric millionaire."

"Eccentric, anyway." She giggled.

"Only where you're concerned. Usually, I'm quite practical."

"No gambler is practical."

"Ah, but you're wrong, my proper Miss Seaton. I win far more than I lose, which makes gambling a very practical profession."

"But I've always heard the opposite."

"The opposite is usually true."

"Then how . . ."

They were at the carriage, and the driver took off his hat and bowed from his seat, smiling as if they were old friends. Perhaps they were. They had spent practically all of Christmas Eve together.

Quinn helped her inside, then sat down beside her, smiling at her until she thought she would spin off the confines of the earth. She sought to right herself, struggling to return to a conversation that hopefully would tell her more about him.

But it was a conversation that no longer interested him. Nothing interested him except her proximity. Nothing except the smell of flowers in her hair, the gently shaped bones of her face, the defiant tilt of her chin, the rosy glow in her cheeks. "You're enchanting," he observed with a rueful smile as if he wished she were anything but.

She blushed, and he knew she was unaccustomed to compliments. It was, to him, astounding. And it made him ache for her. She had missed so much, was so unaware of her own beauty. She had tried so hard over the years to disguise it, he reasoned to himself, she had actually come to believe it didn't exist.

His arm went around her. Even through the heavy cloak, he could feel the softness of her body and it brought back images of that afternoon in his cabin. Quinn felt his body tighten, and tiny flames lick its mid-environs.

Levi's mercantile store was only blocks away, and Quinn was both relieved and regretful that they arrived before the heat spread. He helped Meredith out, hoping that his physical reaction to her didn't show.

Levi greeted them with a smile. "I see thee have solved thy differences."

Quinn didn't exactly know how to respond. He and Meredith had solved old differences only to find new complications. So he merely nodded noncommittally before turning a smile on Levi. "Meredith wishes to obtain manumission papers for a former servant. I understand you have an attorney who can handle it."

Levi's smile broadened. "Yes, indeed. Mr. Fletcher. He's just two buildings down. He's handled such matters many times."

"Due to your persuasion, I'm sure," Meredith remarked.

"And others," he said. He turned to Devereux. "How long will thee be staying?"

"A few days, no more," Quinn said. "I have to get back to the *Lucky Lady*. There can be no shipments as long as I'm gone."

"So many owe thee thanks," Levi said gently. "Thee has been as effective as anyone we have."

Quinn shrugged, and Meredith noted the awkward, uncomfortable way he accepted the praise. "We'd best be going, Levi," he said abruptly, obviously not wanting anymore of it. "I'll probably not see you again before I leave."

Levi nodded his head. While one or two business visits

would not be suspicious, it was well that they not be seen together often. "God go with thee."

Quinn had learned years ago not to depend on God, but he merely nodded his acknowledgment, and he and Meredith took their leave and started out toward Lawyer Fletcher.

It had been a most unusual and disconcerting day, Meredith decided later as she snuggled down beneath the warm quilts. At times moody and quiet, at others teasing, Quinn had stayed by her side. Once they had taken care of the manumission papers, Quinn had located Cam, who gifted Meredith with a rare smile when he took the papers and when Quinn said they would meet him in Cairo in ten days. The *Lucky Lady* was due there on January third. Cam would rent a horse and travel on to Cairo so he could spend some time with Daphne.

Throughout the rest of the day, Quinn was the perfect proper gentleman, returning her to the Meriweathers and again taking dinner with them. He spoke easily of politics, and the prospect of war between the North and South.

"You don't think it will really come to that?" Henry Meriweather said.

Quinn shook his head thoughtfully. "Here in the North you have no idea of the depth of feeling about slavery in the South. The regional economy rests on it, of course. But that's only part of it. Every attack on slavery is not only an assault on the planters, but a condemnation of their parents and their grandparents, of a way of life proudly carved from a wilderness. Their heritage. To admit slavery is wrong is to convict their own roots. They become so defensive that nothing can change their mind; they only see the threat to everything they value. Like a cornered bear. It's not ordinarily dangerous but, backed into a corner, it'll strike out mindlessly. The addition of each free state is like another dog rushing for the jugular, threatening extinction, and they will fight back, even knowing they can't win."

"But surely . . ."

"You've been taught, Henry, from childhood that slavery is wrong. They've been taught from childhood that slavery is right. They're not going to change their opinion any more than you are."

"Only a small percentage of Southerners are slave owners," Henry continued to argue.

"Ah, but many others are dependent upon them. The merchants who give credit, the brokers, the shippers, the fishermen. If the great plantations go, so will the towns that service them. Their economic interest is as strong as the slave owners' in maintaining the status quo. And then," he added wryly, "there is the natural resentment of being told by others that they are wrong. Even the poorest farmer who may oppose slavery, resents outside interference."

"You're a Southerner," Henry observed. He had not been told of Quinn's Underground Railroad activities, but the fact that he was friendly with both Meredith and Levi told him where the captain's sympathies must lie.

For the first time during the conversation, Quinn looked uncomfortable. "I was abroad for many years. That . . . influenced my thinking."

Henry's interest was more than whetted. And so was Meredith's. It was the first time she'd heard him mention the years he had been away.

Henry's inquisitive eyes settled on Quinn. "Where were you?"

Any ease in Quinn's features fled, and they became as taut and grim as she had ever seen them. And then slowly, almost by will, they relaxed again, but his eyes were wintry blue, almost frightening with their icy barriers.

"Several places," he said shortly, and even Henry, whose good-natured curiosity was usually unquenchable, was quelled.

Dinner was finished in uncomfortable silence, and Quinn left early, his eyes still remote as he bade her good-bye.

"Damn, if I don't like that man," Henry Meriweather

commented, "even if he doesn't say much. What he does say makes a great deal of sense."

The observation soothed Meredith's spirits. Despite the abrupt leave-taking, she knew he would be back. She had always known he was a complex man, but she was beginning to learn just how complex.

That day started a pattern that continued during the week. It was as if he were two different people, one charming and teasing and gentle, and the other moody and aloof as if regretting the presence of the first. On the third morning, he announced he had booked passage on the *Ohio Star* to Cairo, and awaited her reaction, raising an eyebrow as if expecting her to retreat from his previous invitation and her acceptance.

But that was the last thing she planned to do. And her nod said as much. She didn't know if his return look was resigned or regretful, or merely indifferent. It was still difficult to tell what he was thinking. But she didn't care. She would have a week with him, or more, and that, for now, was enough.

If she'd had any doubts at all of leaving Cincinnati earlier than she'd originally intended, they were quickly dispelled the day before she was to depart. A telegram came to her in care of the Meriweathers. It was from her New Orleans detective.

"Believe Lissa found. Home of Marshall Evans, Murray, Kentucky. Milligan."

Excitement welled in her. Excitement, anticipation, fear, and so much else. She had waited so many years for this. She looked down at the paper in her hand. It was shaking. And then she realized her whole body was shaking. Lissa. At last.

When Quinn arrived that evening, she could barely speak. She merely handed him the telegram. He read it silently. "You want to go after her now." It was a statement, not a question.

"Yes. I must." After all these years, there was no alternative. None at all. So much of her life had been leading up to this moment.

"I'll go with you," he said quietly.

"But . . . you can't. I shouldn't have any problems. I have enough money . . ."

His eyebrows met in a frown as he remembered how Brett kept a close rein on her funds. "Do you?"

Meredith stopped. She had money. A great deal of it, but at the moment it was completely tied up in her trust fund. Brett, she thought, could be talked into releasing enough, but that might take weeks.

She looked up at Quinn, agony clear in her eyes as she shook her head slowly.

"So you see I have to go," he said.

She looked at him with wonder. "You . . . would . . ."

"Of course," he said, a bit hurt that she would even question it. "But perhaps this Evans won't sell?"

"I'll help her escape."

His hand reached out and touched her cheek gently. "You're too involved, Merry. It can be very dangerous when you're personally involved."

"It doesn't matter," she said stubbornly.

"What if she doesn't want to come?"

"She will," Meredith said with certainty.

"You won't wait until we can organize something?"

"I've waited my whole life."

He took her hand. "Go to Cairo with me, first. I have money there. Friends."

"But—"

"We'll figure out something between now and then."

There was so much quiet assurance in his face that she surrendered. A few more days wouldn't matter. Success did. She nodded.

"We'll get her. I promise," he said softly.

The *Ohio Star* was much smaller than the *Lucky Lady*, but it had much the same charm and impeccable service.

Quinn soon discovered their staterooms were on opposite

ends of the same deck. Having arrived early, he stood on deck watching the carriages arrive and the last cargo being stowed.

He watched intently as the Meriweather carriage drew up, and the occupants stepped out. Wryly, he noted that she was overdressed in flounces and bows, her hair curled in those ringlets that did little for the fine bone structure of her face. His fingers ached to take down the pins and run his hands through the delicate strands of hair. He watched as she awkwardly climbed the gangway, totally without the grace he had noted in her the past few days, and he had to admire her acting skill. Only her eyes, as they met his, showed any fire. And they were like amber flames in the gray frigid light of morning.

Quinn stayed away from her throughout the day. He found a poker game in the saloon, settled his lean frame in one of the comfortable upholstered chairs, selected a cheroot from one of the stewards, and sipped an expensive port. Usually, these were enough to make him content, especially when he was winning, which he was this day, but a tornado was building within him, a whirlwind of need.

His attention continued to wander, but he won anyway. The cards simply kept falling his way: a straight; a full house; even a royal flush, the most rare of all hands. His opponents, one by one, departed with disgust and empty pockets.

He finally went to the dining room, eating on one side of the room while he watched Meredith on the other, her eyes staying studiously away from his. Her appetite, he noted with satisfaction, seemed as poor as his own.

The hours crept by. News of his winnings had spread, and he was approached by two other gentlemen for a game. Such luck, they figured, couldn't last. But, to his own amazement, it did. He was several thousand dollars richer when he finally called it a night.

It was after midnight. The air outside was cold and crisp, the sky midnight-black with a bright silvery moon hanging high. There was still music in the saloon, and a few couples strolled along the brightly lit deck, but most of the passengers had retired for the night.

He suspected she was waiting for him. She had made no maidenly protests when he had suggested they book passage together, even before she knew about Lissa, and the implications were explicit in both the offer and the acceptance. Yet he hesitated for he knew this could be no one-night, or one-week, or even one-month dalliance. Meredith Seaton would want forever. The fact that she had still been a virgin was proof. He didn't want to destroy her, as part of him had been destroyed by Morgana's faithlessness.

And then there were the inevitable discoveries she would make.

In themselves, his scars no longer bothered him; he had learned to live with them years ago. What did matter was what they revealed about him. He had guarded against exposure these past years, because explanations were sure to raise suppositions, some of which might come close to the fact that he was an escaped convict and a wanted man in England. It was one of the reasons he never went as far as Canada where he would be back under British law. He could fight extradition here, but he doubted his chances in Canada.

If he made love to Meredith again, he suspected he would no longer be able to hide certain facts from her. She would have to know a great deal, and he wasn't quite sure he was ready for that.

Finally there was Lissa and the possible danger ahead. Perhaps her master would sell her willingly but, if indeed she looked like Meredith, if she had grown to the same beauty, there was a strong possibility the man would not. If they did have to engineer an escape, there would be great danger for them all. He did not mind it for himself, only for the others who would be involved. Too many people had died around him. It was an inescapable fact he lived with.

Yet he couldn't allow Meredith to go alone. She was too anxious. And anxiety often meant taking unnecessary chances.

He had to go and he knew he should stay away from her until then.

But even as he listed the reasons he should not go to her, he knew he could no more keep away than the currents could stop running in the Mississippi.

Slowly, he turned and made his way down the stairs to the staterooms below, to where he knew Meredith was waiting.

Chapter 20

MEREDITH HAD WAITED and waited.

It had been the worst torture possible. All day, she'd seen Quinn but she was not able to talk with him . . . to touch him. The entire week had, in fact, been dreadful.

Quinn was obviously fighting demons of his own. He was so visibly trying to fight the attraction that sparked between them. He always lost and not gracefully.

She knew he would come tonight, just as she knew he would try not to. It cheered her to know he was as helpless as she against whatever force bound them together. She had debated long and hard about what to wear and finally extracted from her trunk a simple white nightdress. In Cincinnati, she had thought about purchasing something more exotic, but while she was willing to don a disguise on behalf of others, she wasn't quite willing to do it for herself. And an exotic nightdress would be just that. She wouldn't feel comfortable in one.

She did know how much he liked her hair, and she had taken it down, brushing it for an hour until it shimmered. She lit two oil lamps, one beside her bed, and took out a book by Charles Dickens.

She couldn't concentrate, however, on the miseries of Oliver Twist. Her thoughts bounded from feverish anxiety over finding Lissa to the enigmatic mystery of Quinn Devereux.

It was extraordinary what she still did not know about him, even after all the hours they had spent together in the past week. She didn't know why he had joined the Underground Railroad. She knew little about his childhood, and none about the years when he was abroad. He spoke of his brother with affection but not attachment, as if he were wary of any. He retreated when questions were asked, or when emotions surfaced.

He seemed unguarded only with Cam. Although he had an easy charm with the Meriweathers, he had fired warning shots, so to speak, when topics became personal. The boundary had even been there with Levi and, she imagined, with his other contacts on the Railroad.

Meredith climbed into bed. The cabin was cold, and the large feather bed was covered with a great down comforter. She snuggled down into its warmth, wishing for a warmth of another kind.

She had left the door unlocked, feeling safe enough in this luxurious section of the boat which catered to the wealthy.

She knew he would wait until he could come undetected. They had been very careful to keep their distance during the day, although every moment had seemed a lifetime. She wanted him so very badly. She wanted to talk about Lissa and talk about him. She wanted him to touch her, to reassure her, to love her.

What if he didn't come at all? As he had not on the *Lucky Lady* that afternoon after they made love. Doubts began to crowd her mind.

She tried to read a few more pages, and her tenuously hopeful spirits dipped even further when Bill Sikes murdered Nancy. An omen? She dropped the book on the floor next to her bed.

Why didn't he come? It must be very late.

Meredith pushed deeper into the bed and closed her eyes. Perhaps she would sleep for a few moments. Perhaps that would pass the time.

It wasn't as difficult as she had thought. During the past weeks she'd had very little sleep, and the gentle hum of the engines was a lullaby, the movement of the ship a cradle. In minutes she was dreaming.

And that was the way Quinn found her.

Her golden hair was strewn over the pillow while great dark lashes covered her eyes. Her slender form barely showed under the huge quilt, and her breathing was soft and easy.

Tenderness wrapped around him like a gentle morning fog. It was disconcerting, at the least, because tenderness, until he'd met Meredith, had been alien to him. But it felt good. Gentle and peaceful and good. It filled the emptiness in him, squeezing out the darkness that had been there so long.

There had been other strong emotions in past years, including a hard fierce grief. There had been rage and hopelessness that events happened that should never have happened, that never *would* have happened had it not been for the shallow indulgence of a lovesick boy. He thoroughly believed that mistake had cost three lives, lives that were the dearest to him.

But as he looked at Meredith, pretty Merry, he knew he could not keep away from her. His need was too strong. Need of his body but, even stronger, the need of his soul and his heart. They were going to do their damndest to be fulfilled, regardless of cost.

Especially as she lay there looking so incredibly vulnerable. And she was that. So softly vulnerable. So softly desirable. And so easily wounded.

It was best if he left now before she woke. But as he started to turn, he saw the covers move slightly and her face turn toward his, her eyes full of sleepy wonder. She raised an arm from the comforter and held it out to him.

Unable to resist the lazy, unconscious sensuality of her

movements, he dimmed the light. He took the few steps to her side and found the proffered hand, his own stroking it as he sat beside her.

"I was waiting for you," Meredith said shyly.

"I had to wait until everyone was asleep," Quinn replied.

"Was that the only reason?" The question was simple but all too intuitive.

He could barely see her eyes, but her voice, although sleepy, was compassionate, as though she understood the conflicts raging inside him.

"No," he answered honestly. "But I don't seem able to do anything about the other reasons." He leaned down and kissed her throat with barely leashed passion.

A sound came from deep within her, a sleepy contented welcoming sound that aroused him more than any word. His mouth moved up to her lips, touching them gently at first and then with growing hunger.

Her mouth met his with awakening longing, and a ravenous yearning of her own. His hands, almost of their own volition, touched her nightdress where the buds of her breasts tautened against the soft material. His hands moved over her body with poignant slowness as if memorizing every curve, every one of her shuddering reactions to his touch.

His eyes met hers, and Meredith marveled at the turmoil in them, at the expressiveness of eyes that were usually so expressionless. They were like storms at sea, boiling with turbulence and a certain majestic splendor. The hard lines of his face appeared deeper with tension. Yet his hands were incredibly gentle as they continued to caress and arouse and love with their own magic.

"Pretty Merry," he whispered, his voice hoarse with feeling. "My lovely Merry."

His words were like a drug to her, a heady aphrodisiac. As if she needed one, she thought ruefully. Her body tingled with anticipation, the need inside growing as his hands continued their loving exploration. The ribbon holding the neck of her nightdress was loosened, and she felt the touch of his hands on her breasts. Just when she thought she would explode with delicious heat, his lips replaced his fingers, and they softly, ever so softly, licked the sensitive skin before reaching the taut nipple of one breast and resting there, his tongue creating a string of fires that ran through her body like lightning.

Her hand entwined itself in his hair and her lips touched his forehead with soft kisses that said what neither of them had been able to say. Love was in every caress, each an expression of a wondrous feeling. Her other hand touched his cheek, feeling the slight roughness of new beard, relishing the intimacy of tracing the tiny lines that arched out from his eyes, wondering what caused them.

But she did not have time to wonder long, for his lips moved up and caught her mouth in a kiss that swept them both into a dizzying, dazzling journey, into worlds Meredith never knew existed, full of color and sunbursts and splendor. She didn't know when or how he stripped off his trousers, but suddenly there was warmth and power reaching into her, plunging deeper and deeper as if seeking the very core of her soul, and then there were spasms . . . each growing in strength until they climaxed in one magnificent blazing explosion.

They clung to each other, savoring the intimacy of sharing such rare pleasure. There was wonderment in their embrace and a certain desperation. Meredith felt it, and she knew that he did too when his mouth closed once more on hers with a kind of bittersweet resignation.

Meredith didn't understand it. But she recognized his quiet hopelessness and, because now whatever hurt him hurt her, she shared the pain wordlessly. Her instinctive knowledge and acceptance flowed between them, causing his arms to tighten even more around her.

She didn't know how long their wordless communication continued before he gently withdrew from her, and pulled her body against his chest, holding her there until she finally heard his breathing soften, and knew he was sleeping.

Meredith didn't move, not wanting to disturb him, reluctant to lose the possessive feel of his arms around her. She thought how warm and sheltering his body was next to hers. With that comforting thought, she too fell asleep.

He was gone when she woke in the morning. The morning sun was filtering through the thick curtains, and she stretched out under the soft comforter. Her body felt thoroughly satisfied, and it tingled every time she remembered how he felt inside her last night.

She wished he were here now so that she could watch his eyes open, and his lips bestow that breath-catching smile that was so rare.

She stretched lazily, recalling every detail of the night. Ruefully, she realized she had learned no more about him than she knew before. Except that he had a deep reservoir of gentleness he'd been hiding only too well.

Meredith sighed, wishing he weren't quite so mysterious and secretive. That he hurt badly from something was obvious. She wanted to reach inside him and extract whatever it was, freeing him from that which clouded his eyes and made him so infernally remote.

She rolled out of bed, flinching as the cool air hit her naked skin. She looked for her nightdress, finding it in a ball at the foot of the bed. She decided to put on her warm dressing gown instead.

When she had finally dressed, twisting her hair into tortured curls, it was noon. Meredith couldn't remember when she had slept so late, and she was hungry. Starved was more like it, for she had eaten little the previous day. She steeled herself for seeing Quinn, seeing him and not running to him, seeing him without betraying either him or herself. It would be the ultimate test of hard-learned discipline.

But when she entered the dining room, it was Quinn who came to her, bowing slightly with the familiar mocking smile with which he had greeted her months ago.

She raised a dark eyebrow in question. Quinn turned to

the steward and said loudly enough that several other passengers could hear, "Miss Seaton is a client of my brother. If you will seat us together..."

He needed to say no more. They were whisked away to a fine table, and Meredith suspected Quinn tipped the steward with the same generosity he had tipped the Cincinnati coachman.

As she slipped into a chair, Quinn regarded her with amusement. She was the old Miss Seaton, her dress clumsy with frills and her hair in great sausage curls that made her fine face look narrow. But her eyes sparked with barely banked fires, even while a frown puckered her mouth.

"It would appear odd," he remarked casually, "if I did not ask my brother's favorite client to dine."

Her eyebrow arched again. "Favorite?"

"Well... perhaps I exaggerate a bit."

"A lot, I believe. I think I'm his nemesis." She tried to keep an impish grin off her face but it didn't quite work, and Quinn's heart skipped several beats. Dear God, he wanted her again. And again. And again. And...

He forced his voice to behave, although he knew a lower part of his body was ignoring similar admonitions. "Along with me," he said dryly. "He still hopes I'll turn to an honest living someday."

There was real regret in his eyes when he uttered the words he had said so lightly and mockingly before, and she longed to lean over and touch him. Instead, she displayed her best simpering smile. "I'm pleased you don't want to appear odd." She meant something else entirely, that she was delighted he had asked her to share this meal with him.

He couldn't help a chuckle. "I think, Meredith, you and I are very odd, an anomaly, if you will."

"Perhaps," she admitted.

"But a very lovely one," he said so quietly that no one could hear.

"Oh how you do go on, Captain," she drawled, but the light in her eyes flamed even brighter, and he knew he had to be careful. He wanted to reach over and kiss her.

This had not been a good idea, he thought. But then she started giggling and talking about people in New Orleans, and the moment passed.

As they started to leave, his hand remained on her arm a second longer than necessary. "Tonight," he whispered.

"Tonight," she agreed.

The second night was like the first, except this time he came with champagne and glasses. He opened the bottle expertly, with the simple grace and ease she had come to expect from him. He poured two glasses and handed one to her.

"A new year," he explained with a quick delighted grin at the startled look on her face. He raised his glass slightly. "To the last year, with all its surprises, and to the new one . . . to the promise of 1856."

Meredith lowered her eyes, wondering at his meaning. He had said nothing about a future together, about love, but then there was no reason he should. They both lived dangerously and had their own personal commitments. And he was restless— an adventurer, a wanderer. She had sensed a shadowed dissatisfaction in him from the beginning. Perhaps not dissatisfaction exactly, but an endless search for something that didn't exist.

She still didn't know why he was involved in helping fugitives slaves, whether it was whim or danger or adventure or real commitment. His conversation at the Meriweathers had revealed little other than insight into both sides of the slavery question.

But his expression was warm now as he looked at her, the restlessness gone, and the corners of his lips crooked in expectation.

She slowly lifted her glass, the shivers along her spine ruining her concentration. But it would never do to let him know how much he meant to her, how much she searched for hope in those last few words. In the past, she had never celebrated the new year; she had never really seen much meaning or happiness in the prospect of a new year. Each year, her only hope, her only wish, had been to find Lissa and, over those years, the hope had dimmed. But all that had changed now. Lissa was only days away, and Quinn, his eyes now alight with blue fire, was bringing something else into her life. Something wild and beautiful. Something she had never expected.

"To promise," she said, and together their hands lifted and they drank slowly, their gazes feasting on each other. But as she looked at him, she saw the shadows that still lingered in the corners of his eyes. It was like a tornado appearing on a previously lovely day, unexpected and dangerous and even terrifying. Meredith felt a deep stabbing pain. It struck deep inside, and she realized it was for what could not last forever. The promise was today, and she could depend on no more. But she would take it and exact every wonderful moment, enshrining each for the future, for when she was alone again.

He dimmed the oil lamp and turned back to her. When his arms reached out for her, she went into them gladly, her heart pounding against her breast and her mind only barely aware that his own was beating rapidly against her face. And then their lips touched, and there was only tonight.

He woke her before he left, his mouth sleepily nuzzling her mouth, her eyes, before he dressed in the dim light. "Good mornin', sleepy love," he drawled, his eyes devouring her tousled hair, the half-opened eyes that regarded him so invitingly that he almost stayed. Instead, his hand cupped her chin. "Tonight, Merry?"

Meredith nodded, not wanting him to leave, but knowing it was the wise thing. She hated being practical. She resented his caution. She tried to smile, but only managed a trembling semblance of one.

There was a bleakness in his eyes as he leaned down and

kissed her, a sweet, regretful, lingering kiss, and then he turned and strode to the door.

The third and fourth nights were much the same. If splendor could ever be the same! They learned, moment by moment, how best to please the other. They talked softly about unimportant things, never about the past or the future, but about the Mississippi and New Orleans and the opening of the West. But talk was just the prelude to joining, to uniting their bodies in sometimes gentle, sometimes fiery love. Each morning, he was gone when Meredith woke, but he came back at night, his eyes loving, his mouth hungry, his body giving.

She withheld the dozens of questions she had, knowing that he would say nothing until he was ready. She basked under his quiet approval that she didn't pry, that she accepted what he was ready to give, and asked no more.

The fifth night, the night before they were to leave the *Ohio Star*, was different. It would be different, Meredith knew, from the moment he stepped inside the cabin. His eyes were dark, unreadable. His mouth was set in grim lines, as if he had made a decision, one he didn't like but was determined to go through with.

The eyes changed a little, intensifying if that were possible, as they studied her sitting cross-legged on the bed with her hair tumbling over her shoulders.

He sat next to her, tipping her chin up until their eyes met. "I love you, Meredith," he said simply. "I didn't want to. I tried not to, but I do."

"Why try not to?" The question was characteristically simple, without guile.

"For many reasons. One is the danger I could bring to you."

"Or I to you," she replied.

"I'm used to danger," he said.

She was silent. She sensed he was going to tell her more, knew that he had to do it his own way.

He leaned against the side of the wall and pulled her

against his chest. "There are so many things you don't know about me, about what I've done."

She moved until she could turn her head and look into his eyes. "I know I love you," she said. It was so trustfully, so sweetly said that he ached all over.

"Don't say that, Meredith. Not now. Not until you know ... more."

"I know you," she said. "I don't care about anything else."

There was a painful silence. He moved her slightly and leaned down and pulled off his boots, and then dark stockings.

"Look, Meredith," he said, his voice now hard as steel. "Look at my ankles."

Warned by his voice, she did as he asked. His ankles were ridged with bands of scar tissue. One of her hands went to the left ankle, touching it softly. "Dear God," she said.

"I'm a convicted murderer, Meredith. A convict. An escaped convict." His voice was tense, harsh. "My back is scarred. From a whip. Like Cam's. It's why I haven't wanted you to touch it. You would have wondered about it."

"But where? How?" Meredith's voice was unsteady as she tried to comprehend his words. They didn't make sense.

"England. I killed the son of a nobleman and was sentenced to transportation for life. I was shipped to Australia where I served on iron gangs with chained convicts who carved out roads, and later in coal mines."

The missing years. The missing years he never discussed. The passionless tone of his voice said so much more than fury or anger could. He sounded almost dead when he spoke. Her eyes went to the deep marks on his ankles, and she suddenly understood a great deal. "Then that's why ..."

"The Underground Railroad? Partly. I can't tolerate seeing a man in chains. Or whipped. I see myself in every one of them. So you see it's not compassion or mercy. It's for my own survival." There was a tone of desperation in his voice, an acute need for her to understand.

She took her fingers from his ankle and found one of his

hands. It was balled in a fist, the sun-browned skin white with the strain of exertion. She bit her lip against the sympathy that wanted to pour out. She knew instinctively he didn't want it, would never want it.

"How did you ... escape?"

"My father and oldest brother never gave up trying to track me down. They spent a fortune doing it, finally hiring an adventurer to help me escape. He bribed some guards and smuggled me aboard an American-bound ship. I'm still wanted in England."

"And here?"

"There were discreet inquiries made in Washington. The matter involved a duel, and American authorities are not prone to hand over an American citizen in such a matter. Canada, however, is a different matter."

"But if it was a duel ... ?"

"Dueling is illegal in England. It's customarily ignored, but I killed the son of a very powerful man. I had to confess to murder to escape hanging ... but he had the last word. He said he would make my life hell, and he did. Eight years of it. I often thought hanging would have been merciful."

"Can he ... do anything now?"

"He's dead," Quinn said flatly. "Otherwise I think he would have tried to bring me back, one way or another. Now I'm not worth the special diplomatic problems to English authorities, although I'm sure they would be delighted to get me back were I to enter their territories. Escaped convicts were not looked upon kindly in Australia. They encouraged others to attempt it."

There was a new note of bitterness in his voice, and she sensed he had not told her the whole story. Not yet. And she couldn't ask; the warning signs were up again. She was still trying to sort out what he had told her, to comprehend the horror of the marks on his ankles, the lash marks he said were on his back. No wonder he was restless. No wonder he guarded his feelings so fiercely. Prison, captivity, for someone as vital, as proud, as Quinn must have been terrible beyond imagination.

Her hand went to his face where rigid muscles strained against his cheek.

"A convict," he said bitterly. "Lower than any animal. We were treated worse than one. An animal has value. Even a slave has value. We had none. The one objective was to strip every vestige of humanity from us. And they did. There's so damned little left, so damned little." He hesitated, his arms touching her so tentatively that she wanted to scream at him. She longed for that arrogant assurance that had enraged her so many times. She didn't know how she could bear the pain of this other man, for it now was equally hers. She waited for him to continue, for more words that she knew were bottled in him.

"Could you really love a convict, a murderer?" The words were said almost indifferently, as if he knew the answer.

"I love *you*," she said in an even voice, made so by immense will. "I will always love you. There's nothing you can tell me, nothing that you can do, that will change that."

"I don't want you to love me," he said roughly. "Don't you understand? I don't want you to. I tried like hell to stay away from you. I thought if I told you—"

"That I would run and hide? Dear Lord, don't you know me better than that . . . now?"

One side of his lips twitched unwillingly. "Perhaps," he admitted, partially to himself. "You don't run from much, do you?"

"I wouldn't exactly say that," she replied with an uncertain smile. "It seems I ran from you several times."

"You should keep running," he warned.

"No. I learned my lesson when I slipped into the Mississippi. I've never been quite as cold . . . or as frightened, except perhaps when I was with you and those cold eyes bore into me."

He arched one of his eyebrows. "They are the same eyes."

"But not so cold," she teased. "Not quite."

"You're changing the subject, damn it. I've never seen anyone quite as adept at it as you."

And she was. She wanted to drive the shadows from his face, the harsh memories from his mind. Part of her wanted to know more, but he had exorcised enough devils this one night. Her hands went to his shirt, and started unbuttoning it.

He wanted to stop her, and then shrugged. He couldn't hide his back from her forever. But it wasn't, he immediately discovered, his back she was interested in. Her tongue was already licking the dark hair on his chest, her hands caressing the back of his neck. With a groan of capitulation, he lowered her gently to the bed.

Hours later, warm and contented with love, they lay on the bed holding hands. Their lovemaking had never been quite as exquisite now that secrets were shared, confidence given and understood. The actual consummation was secondary to the comfort, the quiet joy they took in merely touching, of being truly together without fear or suspicion, without haunting pasts lurking in the shadow. There was a freedom this time in their love, a readiness to say what needed to be said, to whisper love words.

As she did now. "I love you, Quinn."

Only a remnant of his fears remained, nagging in the back of his mind. *People close to me die.* He tried to ignore it. For the first time since he was twenty-three, the sun was shining again. He could not give it up. He leaned over and nuzzled her mouth. "Would you marry me, Meredith?" The words came without intent, exploding from his heart.

She lifted her head and looked up, her eyes wide with surprise. But there was a sudden blazing joy in them too.

"I know you still want to find your sister, but if all goes well . . ." His voice trailed off. "There could be a child, Meredith."

"That's a lovely thought," she said. "I believed I would never have children."

"What about your Mr. MacIntosh?" he teased.

"I gave it a passing thought," she retorted. "Especially after I met you. It seemed the only way to get rid of you."

"That bad?" he asked.

"You were horrid."

"I can still be horrid." He grinned.

She nuzzled his chest some more. "I know," she muttered. "But there are certain other abilities that . . . tend to outweigh some unfortunate character traits."

He chuckled. "Would you like to enumerate them?"

"I like the way you laugh. When you mean it."

"And when I don't?"

She frowned. "It can be quite . . . chilling."

"Good," he said with satisfaction as one of his fingers played with the corner of her mouth. "What other things?"

She nibbled on him. "You taste good."

"Hmmm. I like being tasted."

"And you have an adorable dimple."

He frowned at that. He had never liked that damned dimple, but then she lifted her head and licked it, and he started to reconsider.

When she finished, she looked up. "And then there's that icy stare. You are very good at icy stares."

"Not anymore," he corrected her ruefully as he tried one and failed miserably. Quinn was amazed at himself. He had never felt so relaxed. He delighted in their light bantering, the soft warm companionship of it, the quiet but intense pleasure that flowed between them.

He leaned over and kissed the corners of her eyes in a wondering, disbelieving kind of way. "You didn't answer me," he finally said softly.

"Which particular question?" she whispered back.

"Will you marry me? You keep changing the subject."

"Yes, oh yes," she said slowly.

"Yes, you will marry me or yes, you keep changing the subject?"

"Yes, I will marry you." This time she carefully pronounced each word.

"And you'll tell me more about those things that outweigh my more 'unfortunate traits'?"

She started to do just that, but then his tongue licked the nape of her neck until she could barely stand it. Tremors started rocking her body again.

And Meredith knew she didn't have to say more as their bodies engaged in a very intimate conversation of their own.

Chapter 21

MEREDITH AND QUINN spent the rest of the night making plans. There were occasional interruptions as one started nibbling the other, and retaliation demanded a more substantial type of response.

Quinn couldn't take his eyes off her. He had never expected such acceptance, such unquestioning belief after he told her things he had revealed to few others. Both Brett and Cam knew very little. Brett knew, of course, because he was part of the family's search. And Cam knew about the scars on his body. But Quinn had never been able to speak of those years; the humiliations had been too deep, the misery too profound, the guilt too intense. Even now, remembering, recounting, had been excruciatingly difficult.

But he should have known from her paintings that she had extraordinary instincts about the world about her, and unjudgmental compassion for the beings that inhabited it. In her role as a giddy-headed fool, she had shielded that part of herself so very well. Just as he had shielded himself.

It would be an adventure, prying open each little window to her. He wondered how many more surprises were in store for him. And he wondered how he could bear the separations that would be necessary. She had become so much a part of him, everything that made him whole again, that filled the empty aching places caused by loss and grief and guilt . . . and hate.

The want went so much deeper than his loins. It was in his soul, so very deep in the core of him. His hand traced patterns in her cheek, his eyes watching the happiness blaze in her face. It was good to give joy, to see as he held her the pleasure in her eyes. These feelings were new to him, and so precious.

"It will be exceedingly difficult staying away from you," he said after a long silence.

Her hand tightened on his arm. Even the thought of separation was painful. Yet they had agreed that, for now, it might be necessary.

Quinn realized that Lissa was the first concern. He knew Meredith would never be really happy until she had righted her own past. After Lissa, if things went well, there might still be separations while he found someone to take his place in the Underground Railroad.

Then, perhaps, they could go West. He had long turned his eyes in that direction in the event he were discovered and had to make a run for it.

But uncertainty hung between them. They had been together less than ten days, yet in that time she had become his life. Totally and unconditionally.

And, miraculously, he knew he had become hers. It didn't even have to be said. He marveled at the communication that flowed between them without words. They were like two halves of a whole, finally together after a lifetime of seeking. He shoved aside any other thought, the insidious warning that would never quite go away but sat like a vulture, waiting.

They talked over plans to free Lissa. Murray, Kentucky, was approximately sixty miles from Cairo, according to Quinn, and they would ride there together. Meredith's original thought was simply to approach Mr. Evans and offer a large sum for Lissa, but Quinn had discouraged that. If Meredith went there for the specific purpose of buying Lissa, and if Marshall Evans refused to sell, then a later escape would be traced back to her. Particularly, Quinn said, if the half sisters still resembled each other as much as Meredith believed they would.

It would be far better, he offered instead, if he posed as a horse breeder from Virginia who had been guided to the Evans farm. If Lissa was there, he would find her and make an offer. If it was not accepted, then he would help her escape. They would not leave Murray, he promised, without Meredith's sister. But timing was important. The *Lucky Lady* would be in Cairo in one week on its way North. If all went well, she and Lissa could board the boat and travel upriver to St. Louis together while getting to know each other again. From there, Lissa would be helped to Canada.

There were many holes in the plan. Hell, it wasn't even a plan. There was no time to allow, as he usually did, for every contingency. But it was the best he could devise on short notice, and he knew Meredith was not going to wait. He saw it in the stubborn set of her jaw, in the gleam in her eyes. She had simply waited too long already. If he didn't help her, she would try alone. And she was inexperienced at the kind of stealth and danger presented by physically participating in stealing a slave. It was one thing to give information; quite another to run ahead of dogs.

And once Lissa was free, in Canada or wherever she wished to be . . .

"The Parson," he said. "We will get Jonathon to marry us. It will serve him right for not telling me about you."

"And me about you," she agreed.

"I don't think," Quinn said thoughtfully, "he'll be particularly happy."

"Why?" she demanded.

Quinn shrugged, but he knew why. It would be for all the reasons he had already told himself: the danger to her, the danger to him, the danger to their usefulness to the Underground Railroad. That came first with Jonathon Ketchtower, the Parson. It always had. Quinn suspected the Parson realized Quinn would never allow Meredith to continue if they fell in love. Just as he must have known that marriage would also mean the eventual end of Quinn's involvement. Rogue gamblers didn't have loving wives.

He had been holding Meredith in his arms on the bed, and his arms tightened possessively around her. "I never want to let you go," he said.

"I never want you to," she replied, snuggling deeper into them. "I don't know how I can bear ever being away from you."

He hesitated. There were many things to say, to decide. "I've been thinking," he said slowly, "about going West. How do you think you would like San Francisco?"

"But the Underground Railroad . . . ?"

"Can do without you," he said, his eyes once more growing aloof, distant. "The danger is too great."

"But I can't . . ."

"Have you ever been inside a prison?" he asked, his voice taut now, with none of the softness that had been there most of the night.

She shook her head, a lock falling over her forehead, and he brushed it gently aside. But his eyes blazed, and she knew he was seeing something else.

And he was: the convict women in Australia, whose hair had been shorn, whose eyes had been dulled and faces made despairing. They paraded before him. And now, for this instant, Meredith's face was among them, the lovely features distorted and old and drained. America was not Australia, but prisons were the same. And he didn't think Meredith could survive it. As stubborn and determined and brave as she was, she could never survive, not intact. He certainly had not. Part of him had been destroyed, the innocent part. He had returned a shell without substance. Until now. He shuddered as he thought about her in prison, and tremors ran through his body.

He felt her hand on him, as if to bring him back from wherever he had gone. When he was finally able to look at her, her eyes were anxious, the golden lights barely visible under the mist of gathering tears. And they were, he knew, for him.

"Tell me," she said in an achingly gentle tone. "Tell me what happened those years."

He wondered if he could, if he should, bring the ugliness and despair into her life even for a moment. Yet he had to make her realize what was at stake, what could happen. He had to convince her, before he lost her as he had lost the others.

"The voyage," he said finally, his voice harsh, devoid of emotion, "was as bad as anything you can imagine, and worse. Three months in the bowels of a rotting ship, three months of black hell. I was chained to another man, an Irishman. He kept me alive when I wanted to die, when my back was festering with infection and my stomach was swollen with hunger.

"He kept me alive with the idea of escape. We understood that the convicts would be sold, portioned out, so to speak, to settlers." He laughed bitterly. "The British abolished slavery for the black man, but they were perfectly willing to enslave their own citizens for stealing a loaf of bread, or poaching, or, in many cases, because of their politics.

"But the military had other plans for us, for Terrence and me. While the others went to merchants and farmers, we were kept in chains and sent to a road gang where we worked from sunrise to past sunset. We pulled our own cage, a cage on wheels, where we slept chained to the walls. There was not enough room to turn at night."

Quinn's fingers bunched in a fist as he remembered the tightness, the enforced proximity of sweaty bodies, the helplessness as they were chained each night, the overwhelming loneliness for those things familiar, those things loving, those things clean and sweet.

Meredith was completely still, as if knowing the slightest move and sound would end his retelling. And he needed to; she could tell from the tense controlled monotone of his voice that the pain had been sitting there in him for a very long time and needed release.

"But Terrence never gave up," he continued slowly, "and one day he found a nail in the road. A little thing, a nail, but he worked it and worked it, and finally one night succeeded in loosening the rivets in his ankle irons. Night after night, I worked on mine until they too were loose. The next day, when the guards were inattentive, we escaped." Quinn paused, remembering the elation they had both felt and then the growing certainty of capture as they heard the dogs, and men on horseback, closing in on them. They had had two days of freedom before they were caught.

"When they found us, we were both whipped and then sent to Norfolk Island." No two words could ever have been said with more hopelessness, and Meredith closed her eyes against the terrible emotion in them. Her hand clutched one of his, trying to absorb some of the raw naked anguish.

He took a long tortured breath and forced his lungs to release it, forced his muscles to relax. He could see his own horror reflected in her eyes, and he cursed himself while hoping it would pierce her confidence, the confidence that nothing could happen to her. Quinn held her tight. "The worst thing about prison," he said finally, "is the loneliness, the dark hopelessness, Meredith. It's something I don't ever want you to know."

Meredith felt there was more. Much more than what he was telling her. "How did you escape?"

"Norfolk Island's reputation for brutality shocked even the English," he said. "There were more and more delegations visiting to 'investigate conditions,' and finally orders came to begin closing it down. I didn't know it then, but my father had sent a man to help me escape. Still, no escape was possible from Norfolk. It was unapproachable except by water, and that was constantly guarded. But as Norfolk was drained of prisoners, I was transferred to the coal mines, and my father's agent was finally able to bribe the guards and smuggle me aboard a ship as a sailor."

"And your friend?"

Quinn's body stiffened, and a facial muscle throbbed in his cheek. "He died." Quinn said it so curtly that Meredith winced. Suddenly the wall was back between them, and she did not dare another question.

"I'll be careful," she whispered, trying to dispel some of the despair in his eyes.

His hands ran up and down her arms, and Meredith could feel the barely restrained possessiveness of each stroke. There was an emotionally charged violence in him, a taut awareness that belied the relaxed poise he usually wore like a cloak. She felt the need growing in him, in herself, a need to cast away the still-vivid memories and enduring anguish of the past. She felt his heart beating against her, and she raised her lips, touching his throat softly, feeling his pulse race. When their lips met, it was with hurricane force, growing in fury and screaming for a liberation that only they could give each other.

Afterward, Meredith lay quivering from the intensity of the sensations that had racked her body and the emotions that savaged her heart. She rested against him, once more listening to his heart, which had now slowed and was beating again with a steady evenness. The tension was gone from his body, and his hand wandered over her face with tender awe. There were still shadows in his eyes, and she wondered if they would always be there, but there was also, if not softness, a certain calm she had not seen before.

"You have the most wonderful, mysterious eyes," she said, unashamedly bold.

He smiled at her. "Hmm," he murmured. "I like yours too." And to prove it he started kissing around at the edges of them.

"But yours are so . . . secretive. When we had dinner that first night, I thought they were like a maze, so many false paths and hidden traps."

His smile widened at the description. "Not now, I think," he drawled in the lazy deep voice that always made her bones melt. "They're loving you."

Meredith stared directly into them. "No," she said slowly. "Your mouth does. Your words do. I think your heart does. But your eyes . . . they're still wary."

Quinn drew back, slightly tipping his head inquisitively to one side.

She nodded. "They never laugh when you do," she added.

"Habit, I suppose." He frowned, then a small smile curved his mouth. "It's why I'm such a damned good gambler."

Meredith nodded, but part of her sorrowed and feared. When his eyes smiled, when they laughed with his mouth, she would feel safe. Completely safe. Until then . . .

"You didn't answer my question. Will you go to San Francisco with me?"

"Why San Francisco?"

He frowned. "Canada's not safe. If anyone does find out about us, California is far enough away that I doubt anyone would look there. Most of the Californians hate slavery, and I don't know of any instance where their courts have returned a slave or those accused of helping one. It's a new state, Meredith, young and free and vigorous." There was a certain excitement in his face that crowded out the darkness that had been there moments earlier.

"And Lissa can meet us there."

"Umm," he said, not wishing to share any of his misgivings. She had not seen Lissa in nearly fifteen years. Perhaps her sister was happy, perhaps she wouldn't want to come. Or perhaps her sister even hated her for what had happened all those years ago. But he did not give voice to his thoughts. "If she wishes. I know how important it is to you."

Her eyes sparkled with anticipation. "I love you," she said.

He dismissed his wayward doubt. "I'll begin making plans then. If all goes well with Lissa, we can get her to Canada, and then I can stop with you in Vicksburg to visit your brother. The Parson can marry us there. It will take several months, no more, for me to settle my affairs and try to find someone to take my place. Perhaps Jamison might." His hand stopped stroking her shoulder and rested there a moment. "Until we leave for California, we will have to be careful not to be seen together."

She grinned suddenly. "I guess I'll just have to go to your brother for more money."

"On the *Lucky Lady*," he agreed.

"And you will have to continue charming Aunt Opal."

He groaned slightly. "And you harassing my brother."

She kissed one of his fingers. "You sound as if you enjoy my tormenting Brett."

"He needs some agitation in his life."

"I don't think he agrees," she said ruefully. "I'm more an anchor around his neck. I always feel guilty when I leave his office, particularly after I give him a gift." She expected him to ask why. She wanted to share her small joke with him.

She felt him shake and heard the deep laughter she loved so much. "I saw one of your gifts."

Meredith, her eyes twinkling, swung around. "You didn't say anything."

"Perhaps I wanted to forget it," he teased. "Right after I bumped into you outside the bank, I visited Brett in his office. Your painting was still on his desk." His hand caressed her hair, running his fingers through the strands.

"Ah, that one," she said, impishly pouting. "You didn't like it?"

"I was...a little intrigued by it. Particularly the signature."

She sat up quickly, suddenly alert. "What do you mean?"

"The name, of course, is different, but the signature showed a certain...similarity to that of M. Sabre."

"Dear God," she whispered.

He put a finger to her mouth, running it along her lips. "Don't worry," he said. "I doubt if anyone else would ever see paintings by both M. Seaton and M. Sabre...and fewer still would see any similarity. It was just that I had a particular interest in both. And even then I didn't put it all together at first." He chuckled approvingly. "You can really produce a damned dismal painting when you try."

She ignored the questionable flattery, interested instead in an earlier sentence. "You had an interest in M. Seaton?" she questioned doubtfully.

"From the very beginning," he added. "There was something about her that—"

"Irritated?"

"Fascinated," he corrected. "Though I had a devil of a time trying to figure out why."

"I hope so," Meredith said. "I would hate to think all my efforts were in vain. It takes hours to do my hair."

"I remember," he said slowly, "when I went out on deck of the *Lucky Lady* after a card game, and there was a woman whose hair glinted in the early mornin' sun. I thought I had never seen anything quite as lovely as that figure with her hair blowing in the wind and flanked by a rainbow."

She flushed. "I didn't think anyone was up."

"I couldn't figure who she was. Her face was turned away, and all I saw was that hair and I thought it must be spun gold. I went over the passenger list, and the only possibility..."

"Was me?" she guessed delightedly. She liked the idea of his confusion.

He was silent a moment. "How did you get involved in the Underground Railroad?"

"Gradually. My father... didn't want me home during school vacations, and I started going to Cincinnati with Sally. The Meriweathers were abolitionists and I began reading accounts of slaves who had escaped. Then one Christmas, a group of fugitives needed help, and... for the first time in my life I felt needed. There was a mother whose baby had died on the way. There was so much grief in her face as she clutched the child to her, but triumph too. 'She dead,' she told me. 'But she free.' It wasn't until then, I think, that I realized how tragic slavery was."

Meredith hesitated a moment, then continued slowly. "I knew how I felt when Lissa was taken away, the loss I felt. And I suddenly realized that I had grieved over *my* loss. Mine. I couldn't really understand hers. But I started to comprehend a little that Christmas. I know I can never really understand how it is to have no freedom at all." She looked at his dark turbulent eyes. *He* knew. And because she loved him so, she now knew better the agony of it. "I know I can't even imagine the horror of being bought and sold, of being used and discarded without a thought. But I saw that woman's pain, and her belief that her child was better dead than alive as a slave, and I knew I couldn't stand by and watch, not any longer."

She watched him carefully, wanting so badly for him to understand. "I can do so little. Just encouragement here and there, a little money, a map, a name. It's not much, nothing to equal your efforts."

"Ah, Meredith," he said. "It's a great deal. Every escape is a victory, every fugitive who survives to tell his story is another step closer to abolition. I just hate the danger you're in."

She stared up at him. "The danger to me is slight. But you're actually transporting them." Her throat went dry as she thought of what could happen to him, what had happened to others. She had heard of many who were in prison, and some who had died there. And Cam? She didn't even want to think of that. She had learned in the past few days how much he meant to Quinn.

"I'm very careful, love," he said.

"But why do you continue?" she said. She now knew the full cost to him if he were caught. After what he had already gone through, more time in prison would be much worse for him than anyone else, and there was always the possibility that an angry government would send him back to England. Involvement must require enormous courage on his part.

"Don't misjudge me, Meredith," he warned softly as if he knew exactly what she was thinking. "Don't think I'm something I'm not." Quinn hesitated. "When I returned to Louisiana, I was so full of hate I came damned close to destroying myself.

"And then I found Cam and, in so many ways, he was a mirror image of that hate and rage. We simply found an outlet for it. Every fugitive we assist is a strike back, a blow against systems that brutalize in the name of profit, and law, even religion." He hesitated, his hand caressing her arm. "I don't do it for noble reasons," he said tightly. "It isn't altruism, it's revenge, plain and simple. I've enjoyed tweaking noses, but I won't risk you."

Meredith knew he was warning her, telling her not to expect that knight in shining armor she had confessed she once thought him to be. Perhaps he even believed his own stated reasons. But she didn't. There was too much gentleness in him. It spoke of caring, of a deep compassion for others, although he sought to hide it under arrogance and surface indifference. Even now, even when he had asked her to marry him, he still maintained barriers between them. Caution was so embedded in him, self-protection so much a part of who he was that she wondered if he would ever be wholly hers. She swallowed, knowing she would take whatever he chose to give her, whatever he was able to give her.

She felt his hands tense, and she reached one of hers to

his back, touching the scars. Her fingers ran over them, and she felt him stiffen again.

He looked in her face and saw the grief there, the tears that hovered in her eyes. Tears for him. And for a moment he regretted telling her what he had. Thank God, he hadn't told her the full story, the bitter finish that he knew would stay with him forever. He would not make her bear that also.

He wiped a tear away. "There's no need, love," he said. "It's over, and now I have you." To distract her, he started licking the nape of her neck, and soon he had distracted himself too. With new urgency, his hand moved along her body, claiming it as his own. His need, the deep desperate need of his heart, made his kiss rougher than usual. "I love you," he murmured.

"And I love you," she whispered. "Always and forever."

"And you'll go with me?"

"Anywhere," she replied softly. "Anywhere."

Cam and Daphne walked among the small cluster of huts that housed many of the free men and women of color in Cairo. Most of the men worked on the docks, transporting cargo from boats using the Mississippi to those plying the Ohio River and vice versa. The women worked mostly as maids for the merchant families. It was a poor area, but the residents, only too conscious of their cherished free status, kept both their homes and tidy little gardens in good repair.

It had taken Cam three days of hard riding to reach Cairo. He had purchased a strong, albeit inglorious-looking horse in Cincinnati and had followed the line of the river, avoiding the towns and settlements along the way. He had traveled alone before, and he and Quinn had worked out a plan if he were stopped. It was crucial to Quinn's safety that Cam be known as his slave. If Cam were to be caught or stopped, he would play the runaway fugitive, begging not to be taken back for the reward. The reward was the key. Both Cam and Quinn knew it unlikely anyone would hurt property that carried a substantial bounty.

But Cam didn't mean to be stopped. He had learned much during his years with Quinn, including the ability to play many roles, both humble slave, which was the most difficult, and confident freeman. When he and Quinn traveled North, Cam sometimes spoke to small private groups about his experiences. The recitals were difficult. They would always be difficult. But, he knew, they were important. The story had to be told. Although books like *Uncle Tom's Cabin* fueled antislavery opinion, the South continued to portray the institution as benign, even compassionate. Only those who had escaped could relate the true reality and degradation of slavery.

He enjoyed the ride, hard as it was. It gave him time to think. And he relished the freedom, both of his body and thoughts. When he was a slave, he had hated the sun for it was his enemy, as was the cold wind sweeping off the river. But now, protected by a plain but warm coat, he enjoyed the taste of both. He was still filled with the wonder of it, of the ability to go where he wished, when he wished. It gave him immense pleasure that he carried papers, sewn into his suit, that would give Daphne that same gift.

When he had reached Cairo, he extracted the papers from their secret place and went immediately to the home sheltering Daphne. When he asked her to go for a walk, she agreed readily.

There was still a fragility about her, but Cam had uncovered a strength that seemed to be growing daily. Her smile, which had once been so rare, came easier now. It had greeted him and widened by the time they reached a private wooded place along the river. When they stopped, he handed her the papers, and she looked at them blankly. They looked official, but she couldn't read.

When he explained what they were, she stared at the documents with disbelief. He recalled his own confusion when the captain had done the same with him. "It's real," he said softly.

Daphne clutched the document to her, her eyes searching his, barely believing the unlikely, the impossible.

"But how . . . ?"

"Miss Meredith," he said with a small chuckle. "The capt'n ran into her in Cincinnati and bought your freedom." He had wanted to tell her the truth, that Meredith Seaton was a member of the Underground Railroad and had planned to free Daphne herself, but the captain had convinced him otherwise. It was safer for Miss Seaton if her own role was known by only a few.

"It's true then," she whispered. "It's really true."

He nodded, watching her as she continued to hug the papers to her chest, still unable to comprehend the full majesty of what had happened.

Free!

Free from the constant fear of being taken back, of the soul-robbing horror of the slave jails and auction, of white men reaching for her and telling her to open her mouth so they could study her teeth as they would a horse, free of the humiliation of being herded through the streets like an animal.

Wild, giddy feelings—gratitude, admiration, love, most of all, love—rushed like great storm clouds through her, and the tears came faster, washing away the bitterness and terror. Her waist was grabbed by two huge hands, and with bubbling joy, she felt herself lifted and swung around in circles until she laughed delightedly. She heard his deep laughter join hers, and together they spun, the sound of freedom echoing through the street and drifting up into the sky.

Chapter 22

WHEN THE *OHIO STAR* reached Cairo, Quinn quickly found Cam at the home where Daphne was staying. He grinned as he watched Cam's gaze follow the ex-slave wherever she went. And the smile grew broader as he noticed that Daphne's eyes followed him right back.

When she first saw Quinn, she approached him shyly, but she didn't duck her head as she had before. She looked him straight in the eye and held out her hand. "Thank you," she said simply. "I will always bless you."

Quinn looked up at Cam, and his friend shrugged, the dark eyes twinkling as if to say "what did you expect?"

Quinn wanted to lay the gratitude where it belonged—with Meredith—but he knew that, for the moment, it was safer to hide the truth.

When Daphne had said her thanks, she retreated, still a

little in awe of the white riverboat captain who had helped her. Quinn looked at Cam. "A walk?"

Cam nodded, and they moved swiftly through the neighborhood. The black man's eyes fixed curiously on Quinn. There was something different about him, an ease that hadn't been there before.

"You have an interestin' week?"

"You could say so," Quinn replied with the curious crooked grin that said little. "How would you like to be a witness to a wedding?"

"I would like that fine, Capt'n. Any particular lady in mind?"

The side of Quinn's mouth lifted even higher. "Go to hell, Cam."

There was a brief silence as they walked companionably. "What about you, Cam? And Daphne?"

The expression on Cam's face was grim. "She's already had too much fear in her life. I don't want her worried about me too."

"I thought about that . . . with Meredith," Quinn said softly. "But, damn it, there's something right about it. And there's something right about you and Daphne too."

"Maybe," Cam said slowly.

"Meredith believes she's located her sister in Murray, Kentucky, about a hard day's ride from here. I'm going with her. We're going to try to buy her, but if we can't, I promised to help her sister escape . . . if she wishes."

"When do we leave?" Cam's face was impassive.

"You stay here with Daphne."

"No, Capt'n," Cam said simply. "You may need me."

Quinn didn't argue but merely nodded his head. It would do no good to try to dissuade Cam. Quinn knew that determined tone of voice. And Cam could be of help. Quinn had no idea what to expect of Meredith's half sister, and perhaps Cam's presence would be reassuring to her. He didn't even want to think that the detective might have identified the wrong person. Meredith would be devastated. There was so much hope in her, so much anticipation.

"We'll leave just after dawn tomorrow," he said. "I have some things to do this afternoon: letters to give to Sophie, the purchase of horses. And the bank. We might need a great deal of cash."

Cam raised an eyebrow questioningly.

"We can't use our names, either of us. If this Evans does sell, it will have to be a cash transaction," Quinn said. "Thank God, I have over ten thousand dollars in an account here and don't have to wire Brett."

Cam looked startled. "You taking it all?"

Quinn nodded.

"That's a lot of money to carry."

"I know," Quinn said. "But it might take a lot, and if anything goes wrong, we need the money to escape."

"Where?" Cam knew Quinn had avoided Canada, that there was a problem there, although he didn't know exactly what.

"West. San Francisco. I've been thinking about it for some time. Even if things do go well with Meredith's sister, we plan to go there in a few months. I don't want her in any more danger. I would like you and Daphne to come with us."

Cam looked stunned. The Underground Railroad had become part of his life. Every man and woman he helped, every slave he assisted to freedom, had helped him piece back together his own dignity. "The *Lucky Lady* . . ."

Quinn turned to him, his mouth grim. "There's been questions about the boat. I have a feeling we've run this hand almost to the limit."

"But the Railroad . . ."

"We can still help out West. Provide employment for those who escape, continue sending funds. I don't know anything about farming or ranching, but I do know gambling and entertainment. I've been thinking about building a hotel in San Francisco. The West is the future of this country. And neither the damned slave catchers nor the Fugitive Slave Act have much influence there.''

"But it's still the law."

"Perhaps it is, but from everything I've heard, the Californians are damned independent and don't like slavery a whit. And who in the hell is going that far for one man accused of violating a law that's hated?''

"Two men," Cam corrected, and Quinn knew Cam had just decided to go with him.

"Two men and a woman," he amended.

"And if there's war, Capt'n?''

Quinn's frown deepened. "I doubt it will affect California much. It's too far away.''

"And you?''

"Damn if I know. I want peace. Dear God, I want some peace.'' His voice was ragged with emotion.

"The captain of the *Lucky Lady*?'' Cam's voice was half searching, half doubtful. He had never seen this side of the captain before. He had assumed for a very long time that Quinn Devereux enjoyed the games he played, but perhaps, like him, they had been only a diversion, a neat white bandage over wounds that hadn't completely healed.

"Most especially the captain of the *Lucky Lady*," Quinn replied dryly.

They came to a stop outside Miss Sophie's Parlor, and Quinn hesitated. "I need to talk to her. Do you want to go with me?''

Cam studied him. "Where's Miss Meredith?''

"Still on the *Ohio Star*. It's docked here overnight, and I thought she would be more comfortable there rather than a hotel.'' He didn't add that it would also be more respectable, but he knew it was. Meredith was a frequent traveler on the riverboats and no one thought much of it, but to stay in a hotel alone was something else. And at the moment appearances were important.

In the morning, the captain of the *Ohio Star* would believe she was simply transferring to one of the Mississippi boats. Quinn had already arranged for her trunk to be picked up and stored. Within a week he hoped to have her on the *Lucky Lady*, with no one the wiser about the missing days.

Quinn saw the slightly amused look on Cam's face and understood the intent of his question. "That's not why I'm here."

Cam smiled slowly. "I'll wait then."

Quinn gave him a sour glare, and they climbed the steps, Cam obediently several steps behind.

Quinn asked for an audience with Sophie, and almost immediately he was ushered into a private office.

"Quinn," Sophie said delightedly. "You look much better than the last time I saw you. There's actually some life in those eyes."

"The dead was not so dead," he replied cryptically, a wry smile on his lips.

Sophie remembered some of the drunken rambling of two weeks earlier. Quinn had said "murderer" several times over when she had tried to put him to bed. There had also been something about a lady but he had mentioned no names. Even drunk, Quinn Devereux had been discreet. "I'm glad," she said simply.

"I need your help."

"Anything," she said simply.

"Cam and I are going after a slave in Kentucky. It's a long story why, but there could be trouble. I have some letters I want to leave with you, and a package for my brother. If anything happens to me, I want you to see that Jamison gets them. One letter clears him from any involvement in the Underground Railroad and leaves ownership of the *Lucky Lady* to him. The other goes to my brother, along with the package."

Sophie nodded. She had learned a long time ago not to ask for explanations from Quinn.

"Anything else?"

"If a woman who calls herself Merry ever comes here, do everything you can to help her."

"Does she know about me?"

"No. Not yet. But she's associated with Levi. I'm going to give her this address in case there's trouble."

"I think I'm envious," she said.

"Now Sophie, you know you never mix with the customers," he teased.

Sophie was surprised at his grin, at how attractive it was. He had smiled before, but it had always been tinged with mockery and a certain remoteness, never real warmth. "Now you might have been an exception," she laughed. "You never gave me a chance."

The corners of his eyes creased. "I never thought I had one," he said with a charm that made her head spin and blood run faster.

"I would like to see this lady who is so adept at miracles. Rising from the dead. Taming our infamous captain."

He was suddenly serious. "I hope you don't, Sophie."

She understood. His "Merry" wouldn't come here unless there was trouble. "I wish you and your lady Godspeed."

Quinn leaned over and kissed her cheek. "You'll take care of the letters?"

"Of course," she reassured him. "Would you like a drink before you go?"

"Is there any left after my last visit?" he queried lightly.

"Not much," she retorted, "but for special friends . . ."

"Some other time, Sophie."

She nodded, a trace of wistfulness in her eyes. He was, she knew, saying good-bye. She liked him. She liked him very much indeed. And she would miss him. But as he turned and left, part of her was pleased to observe that some of the grim cynicism had left his face and his step was lighter.

Cam sat in the kitchen and talked to one of the cooks while he ate hot bread. He knew everyone in the establishment and felt comfortable with all of them. It was certain that they were aware of Sophie's involvement in aiding fugitives.

There were quiet knocks in early morning hours at the servants' entrance—knocks of poorly dressed and fearful figures. If slave hunters came searching, a new woman might suddenly appear among the ladies, and if she seemed nervous, it was explained that she was fresh to this oldest of all professions. If the newcomer was a man, he was quickly employed as a stablehand. And sometimes people seemed to disappear completely, as if by magic. Only very few, including Cam, knew there was a secret passage from the basement of the building to a small hidden room in the stable.

Although no one was told of these occurrences when they first came to work at Sophie's Parlor, each new employee gradually sensed what was going on, but by then, their loyalty to Sophie and to each other was usually complete. Sophie chose her girls and servants very, very carefully. She cared about her employees, and they cared about her. And they took a certain satisfaction in the quiet conspiracy.

So Cam felt it unnecessary to pretend when he came here. He had always enjoyed his occasional visits, at least until lately when Sarah had started to look at him with wistful eyes that said she wanted more from him than he could give.

Before he met Daphne, he had harbored no desire for permanent attachment. Like the captain, he had carried so much bitterness, so much hate, that he believed there was room for nothing else in his life. And then that hate had been slowly replaced by a fervor to help those who, like himself, had been helpless for so long.

"Cam." Sarah's voice was soft and inviting, and Cam straightened up quickly. He had hoped she was upstairs, that his presence would go unnoticed. He had stayed only because he had wanted to walk back with the captain, because he had more to say to him, even something to ask.

He turned toward the door where Sarah was standing nervously. Sarah had been too pretty for decent work; no woman would hire a maid who was bound to attract the males of the family. She had been unable to find work and finally ended up at Sophie's. Cam knew she had found it not altogether disagreeable, even enjoyable. And Cam had liked her, had thoroughly enjoyed his brief times with her, but there had never been anything more between them, even less when she had turned possessive and hinted at marriage months earlier. He had not returned, not until today.

"Cam." She spoke again, and held out her hand to him. To refuse her would be to humiliate her, and Cam didn't want to do that. He hesitated, then stood and went to her.

"Let's go upstairs, Cam," she said softly. "It's been so long."

He nodded, knowing it was time to talk, time to tell her he wouldn't be back. He followed her up the steps, along a hallway lined with rooms to one he recognized. When they were inside, she turned to him and stood up on tiptoes, raising her lips to be kissed.

Cam put his large hands on her shoulders and shook his head slowly. "I won't be coming back, Sarah," he said.

Her eyes narrowed, but the practiced soft smile remained on her lips. "I . . . didn't make you happy?"

"You made me happy," he said with a smile of remembrance, "but . . . I might marry soon."

Sarah went stock still. "But I thought . . ."

He watched the dismay in her eyes turn to fury. He had not expected it. She had always been passionate, even moody, but there had also been a wistfulness in her manner that he had read as gentleness. There was nothing gentle in her eyes now. There was, instead, a veritable storm, and he knew with sudden sickening certainty that he had misjudged her. He tried to remember everything he had ever said to her, but knew there had never been any promise. He never made promises.

"You can't," she said, the certainty in her voice making him wary.

"Sarah," he said. "I never promised . . ."

"But you did," she cried. "You did with your eyes and your body and—"

"No, girl," he said softly.

"I was just a . . . whore to you?"

Cam didn't know how to answer. Because she was right. That was how he thought of her; that was what she was. He had liked her, had sympathized with her when she had said she intended to start her own respectable business, yet there was a sensuousness about Sarah, a sexual aura that had told him she was not here altogether against her will.

He tried to lie gently. "No, Sarah." But it did no good. Cam saw the eyes widen with realization, then anger. And something else. Cam didn't know what it was, but it worried him. There was something frightening about it.

He heard his name being called and recognized the captain's voice. "I must go," he said. He took some bills from a pocket in his well-worn trousers and set them on a bureau. "I'm sorry," he said, meaning it. He closed the door softly as he left.

But worry nagged at him as he met the captain in the foyer. And the captain recognized it.

"Something wrong?" Quinn asked the question quietly, his brows knitted together at Cam's frown.

"I don't know. Sarah . . . was . . ." He shrugged. "I don't know. She was acting strangely."

"Sophie told me weeks ago she hoped to marry you."

"Damned if I know why. I never said anything."

"She'll get over it."

Cam wasn't so sure. The captain hadn't seen her eyes. But there was nothing he could do about it now. And he had other concerns.

When the captain had confided in him about his proposed marriage to Meredith Seaton, he had reassessed his own position with Daphne. If the captain was willing to risk it, then why not he?

But still the uncertainty was there. Everything was new to Daphne, and she should have time to adjust to it, to know what she really wanted. He didn't want her out of gratitude. He was only too aware of his sometimes mixed reactions to his own benefactor. He didn't think he could stand her coming to him out of obligation.

He felt, rather than saw, the captain's eyes on him, studying him, appraising him in that curiously detached way.

"Don't wait, Cam," he urged with a small smile. "We may not have that much time."

Cam shrugged. Damn, but the man could read his mind. "Perhaps the next trip," he said. "She needs time to get used to the idea of being free to make choices."

"Choices," Quinn said, tasting the word. "I wonder if we ever really make them ourselves." His tone was thoughtful and even a little melancholy, and Cam darted a quick look at him. Despite the smile on Captain Devereux's lips when he had mentioned his plan to marry Meredith, there was still something wary about him, almost as though he expected disaster of some kind. The suspicion lurked in the back of the captain's eyes, like some shadowy presence.

"It seems you've made one," Cam observed.

"It does seem that way," Quinn answered enigmatically. The statement ended the conversation, but Cam noticed a certain tension in Captain Devereux's body, and in the glint in the dark blue eyes before the familiar curtain shielded their emotions.

Sarah stared at the door as it closed quietly, signaling the end to every dream she'd ever had.

Freedom had meant nothing but misery to her. She had been safe and secure with Mr. and Mrs. Hitchcock. When they had moved to Cairo from Kentucky, they had brought her with them. Although technically a slave, she had always been treated as a member of the household. She was taught to read the only book allowed in the house: the Bible. And she was taught to write by copying scriptures.

But then Mrs. Hitchcock sickened and died, and Mr. Hitchcock, who had loved his wife dearly, seemed to lose his will to live and succumbed just six months later to a fever.

Sarah was freed in his will. She also inherited everything, but it was very little. He had left Kentucky because his business there had failed. His new business in Cairo had been no more successful. There were only debts.

Sarah was fifteen. Suddenly and for the first time in her life she had no place to go, and no one to care for her. Freedom became a curse. She tried to find a position, but she had no references and she had seen the quick dismissal in women's eyes as they ran over her figure and face. Finally, in desperation, she went to Miss Sophie's, although it took every ounce of her courage to do so. Mr. Hitchcock had been a God-fearing man who insisted on the highest morals and held out the specter of hell for those who deviated from The Path.

But hunger and cold were powerful forces, and she finally, bitterly, ventured to a place where she knew her face and body would not be disadvantages. To her surprise, the proprietress had turned out to be very kind, very sympathetic. When Miss Sophie learned Sarah's age, she had merely asked whether she would like to be a maid. Sarah quickly accepted.

Over the next three years, Sarah battled internally with herself, with Mr. Hitchcock's teachings and with her growing fascination for the women who worked at Miss Sophie's. They were all kind to her, and she noticed that many went on to make respectable marriages. All of them, it seemed, had had some kind of tragedy in their lives, whether it was abandonment as a child, or some horrible abuse. But her mind kept telling her they were evil, and her living and working here was punishment for . . . admiring them.

When she was eighteen, one of the customers took a fancy to her. He kept coming back offering a great deal of money if Sarah would go upstairs with him. Sophie had said it was her decision.

The money was a fortune to Sarah. Enough to go away and start a respectable business, and she finally agreed. The man, knowing she was a virgin, had been both gentle and passionate, and Sarah discovered she had a craving for something other than survival. Once aroused, her appetite became insatiable. And she decided that it was time to join the other girls.

But all the time, a part of her brain was remembering Mr. Hitchcock and his vision of hell. She kept telling herself that she would do as others at Miss Sophie's did: find a man to marry. Then Cam started visiting, and she fixed in her heart that he was the one who would take her from sin. Once married, she was sure that the devil in her would go away, that God would forgive her. Cam was a wonderful lover, and she wouldn't need anyone else; the constant, painful appetite in her would go away.

She awaited each of his visits with anticipation and she planned for them. She always wore her prettiest negligee. Painfully, she forced herself to rein in her own desire and take her time in arousing him, in giving him pleasure while she ached inside for him to take her quickly and roughly. She played the wronged victim to the hilt, her eyes filling with tears as she told him about being alone and fearful in a world of uncertainty and terror.

And she did feel terror, only not for the reasons she gave him. The terror was in her soul. Day by day, she was being ripped apart by the war being waged between her body and her mind. Her body seemed to have an endless need for gratification, while her mind told her it was wrong and she would go to hell for it.

She came to believe that Cam was her only hope for salvation. And now he was gone. He thought of her as nothing but a whore. The anger in her, anger that had been directed for so long at herself, swirled in her head. And as it became more powerful, the fury sought vengeance. Cam had made her feel important, had given her hope, and now he was discarding her. It was he who was evil, and she had to punish him.

But how? How could she do anything to someone as strong as he?

He always came with another man, a white man named

Devereux, and she had heard whispers about him, that he was in some way involved in helping fugitives escape. Sophie was too, she knew, but she wasn't prepared to hurt Sophie, who had always been kind to her. It was Cam who needed punishment. The fact that Cam was helping fugitive slaves meant nothing to her. She told herself she had been happier as a slave; there had been someone to care about her, to take care of her, and tell her what to do. It was when she was free that the devil had taken over.

Her fists clenched, she resolved that Cam would pay for his betrayal. She would find a way to expose him. And he would suffer as she was suffering.

Chapter 23

MEREDITH WATCHED Quinn walk from a carriage to the gang-plank below, just as she knew he had watched her board in Cincinnati a week before, or was it a lifetime.

It was very early, just after dawn, and only she and several of the officers were on deck. She'd awakened early from a restless sleep, eager to see him, eager for this day.

She questioned whether she would ever get used to his striking handsomeness: the thick midnight-black hair and the fine evening-blue eyes framed by black brows and lashes. He wore his usual black clothes; that alone made him stand out in a crowd of more gaily dressed travelers.

Meredith wondered how her heart could bear the weight of the happiness she felt when she thought of him, or saw him.

Or bear the loneliness of being without him. She'd had a

taste of that last night, and she'd tossed and turned, remembering the quiet bliss of drifting off to sleep in his arms.

There would be other such nights alone. There would have to be—for his safety and for her own.

So she memorized his every feature as he strode toward the boat and then her eyes turned slightly toward Cam, who was at his side. The confident man she had seen in Levi's kitchen no longer held his shoulders straight, but slumped as he dragged a foot. The black man's eyes, which she knew could be as wary as his companion's, were turned now toward the ground, no longer challenging as they had been in Cincinnati. For the first time, she thought how difficult it must be for him, for such a proud man to act so servile. But then they were all playing difficult roles, although she imagined hers the easiest. She recalled seeing the regret in Quinn's eyes as he spoke of Brett's disappointment over his gambling. She'd never regretted her family's disapproval and, although she sometimes chafed at being unable to speak her mind, she compensated through tactless Meredith's wont to sting pomposity with outwardly innocent remarks.

How much longer?

It would be wonderful to give up that role. But she had hidden behind it so long, she sometimes wondered where the real Meredith started. Still it would be a fine thing to paint whatever she wanted. She shivered with delight when she thought of all the glorious opportunities in the West. She had seen paintings of majestic mountains, and the golden hills of California, and she longed to paint them herself. That Quinn, and hopefully Lissa, would be at her side was a prospect too splendid for belief.

She had tried not to think too much about Lissa. After so many years, the thought of seeing her again, of reversing what had happened, was too fragile to dwell upon. She could not let herself think that Lissa would not remember her, or would not want to come with her, or had been irreparably injured in body or soul. Nor could she consider that anything might happen to Quinn in helping her.

Meredith looked down at the portmanteau she carried. As according to plan, it carried two fresh dresses and two sets of undergarments, including corsets. There was also soap, hairbrush, and hairpins. Quinn had said he would supply additional clothes but had not mentioned exactly what. Her trunk with her other clothes had been picked up earlier.

She watched as Quinn approached the captain of the *Ohio Star*, said a few words that apparently amused the officer as they both looked at her. Then he was by her side, his eyes shuttered and his mouth in the remote amused half-smile that he presented to most of the world.

He nodded to Cam, who took her portmanteau. Then holding her arm lightly, Quinn guided her from the boat to an open buggy. Cam put the bag on the seat beside her and leaped up next to the driver. Slowly they moved from the wharf. Quinn was quiet, too quiet. He said nothing even though she knew the driver couldn't hear them.

Her hand touched his briefly, and he seemed to flinch away before he turned to her. She saw how troubled his eyes were.

"Would you consider staying?" Quinn finally asked. "There are friends here, and I swear I'll bring her back."

She shook her head slowly. "Lissa's my sister," she said. "I've waited too long." Meredith hesitated. "And she may not come with you."

"Have you thought she might not come with you either?" Quinn said softly.

She nodded slowly. "Yes, but I have to go with you."

He knew it. He wondered why he bothered to ask. But he'd had a strange feeling last night and it was still there this morning. Something was wrong, and he didn't know what. His hand went to his waist where he wore the money belt.

The buggy was now moving quickly away from town. They turned south at a fork, then turned again onto a narrow rutted path. When the vehicle stopped after what seemed like hours, they were in a small clearing near a tumbledown shack. Four horses, one without a saddle, were tied to nearby trees.

Quinn took her portmanteau, along with another on the buggy floor, and passed them to Cam. After helping her down from the seat, he extended a hand to the driver, and Meredith knew the man must be a contact with the Underground Railroad. She watched as the buggy disappeared back along the road.

Quinn put an arm around her shoulder and led her inside. The cabin was surprisingly well kept, and she realized it must be one of the stations for the Railroad. Quinn opened one of the portmanteaus, extracting a shirt and breeches of rough wool and handing them to her. "We'll get less attention if they think you're a boy," he said. "From now on, you're my groom."

She looked at the clothes with hesitation. The only other time she had worn male clothes was when she had stolen his much too large ones and escaped from the *Lucky Lady*. Even then, she had felt a little decadent in doing so. But she quickly saw the wisdom of such a masquerade and she knew she could ride faster and longer without a sidesaddle.

Quinn helped her with her buttons, his hand lingering only a moment on her bare shoulder. There was no time to play the ardent lover; they had to reach Murray by nightfall. But still his body reacted to the sight of her undressing, to the soft ivory of her skin. As she finished pulling on the loose trousers and started to take the shirt, he stopped her and took a piece of linen from the satchel and quickly tied it around her breasts. When she put on the shirt and looked down, she saw little that would identify her as anything but a boy.

"My hair?" she asked.

He gave her that troubling little half-smile and took out two jars from the portmanteau. "Spread this on your hands and face," he said, giving her one. As she did what he asked, he removed the pins from her hair, which he then smeared with a black glob from the other jar.

In minutes, her wrists and hands were a dark walnut color. Her now-black tresses were quickly braided and twisted into a knot and pinned at the top of her head. A floppy, low-brimmed hat was then set securely on her head.

She watched as he surveyed his creation. "Cam," he called out, and almost immediately the man appeared. He looked startled, then a wide grin spread across his face, and he nodded.

"He'll do."

Meredith wondered if they would ever reach their destination. She was a good rider but she had never ridden quite as long at one time. Her body was also used to a sidesaddle, and she was utilizing long-dormant muscles. Her backside hurt, her legs ached with pure agony, and her hands were blistered.

She was also cold. She had left her fur-lined cloak, along with her dresses, in the cabin, and she had only a roughly woven coat to replace it.

The first hours had been wonderful. She had enjoyed the freedom of breeches and the feel of the horse between her legs. It was far better than the awkward perch of the sidesaddle. She enjoyed riding next to Quinn, watching him master his horse easily.

She could barely keep from gazing at him. After she had changed clothes, she had been surprised to see him do the same. The tailored black clothes came off as she watched, and he donned buckskin trousers that fit like a second skin, a linen shirt, and an exquisitely tailored tan riding jacket. He looked up at her, and a smile arced his mouth as he saw her expression. "Do I pass as a Virginia horseman?"

She nodded, unable to speak as she surveyed the change in him, and she suddenly realized that the severely cut black clothes had made him seem remote and dangerous. They had placed him apart from others and, she realized now, it had been done very consciously.

Now he looked...approachable. More than approachable, dear Lord. Absolutely irresistible. He looked almost a different man. After he had darkened her hair, he did the same with his own, erasing the white around his face, the one distinctive feature most people would remember. A thatch of his usually tamed hair fell over his forehead, adding to the impression of a thoroughly likable Southern gentleman rather than a cold-eyed mocking gambler. Even his smile was different.

It had been all she could do to keep from going to him and running her hands over his face. As she stared at him, his smile faded, and he held his hand out to her. "We must go," he said. "We're already late."

Now she guessed they had been riding nearly six hours without a pause. Since he had assisted her into the saddle, he had been quiet and withdrawn, although his eyes often swept over her with intensity.

At one point, she knew he'd noticed she was drooping. "I'm sorry, Meredith," he said. "We don't have time to stop. I want to get there just before dinner. He won't have much choice but to invite me to stay."

"I'm fine." With supreme effort, she straightened her back.

He smiled, a heart-catching prideful smile, and Meredith's breath caught in her throat.

"Is it wise," she said hesitantly, not wanting to lose that sudden emotional contact, "for me to go in with you?"

"You said Lissa was very light." Quinn smiled. "And you are very dark at the moment. Even if you have similar features, I doubt anyone will notice them. You just stay with Cam. He'll tell everyone you don't speak."

She nodded. With every hoofbeat, she was getting closer to Lissa. Closer to the goal toward which she had worked so many years. Her hands tightened on the reins, and her horse sidestepped in protest. She looked over at Quinn and saw his eyes, understanding and sympathetic, and she thought how wonderful it was that she seemed to love him more and more every minute.

Cam was riding directly behind them and, as if he knew

they needed to be alone, he spurred his horse and galloped on ahead.

"I love you," she said, unable to help herself.

Quinn's mouth turned up at one corner. "Even if I ride you to death?"

"*Because* you're riding me to death," she admitted, knowing that he was doing this for her.

"We'll get her, love," he said, his eyes roving over her. She saw a spark of desire in them and wondered, since she knew she looked anything but seductive at the moment.

"You're blushing," he accused.

"How did you know," she retorted since her skin was far too dark to reveal any such color.

"I'm beginning to know you, Merry, love," he teased, wanting to take her mind from the soreness he knew she must be feeling, and from Lissa. "I can tell by the way you lower those eyes of yours. I'm damned glad at the moment they're not blue."

"I'm sure you would have found a way to solve that problem too."

"Probably," he admitted, "but it would be a bit odd to have a blind groom."

She laughed. "With your reputation, Captain, I don't think anything would be considered odd."

"Ah, but I'm not me today," he said. "I'm a perfectly respectable horse buyer with an eye for beauty."

She looked at him skeptically. "I've heard the good Captain Devereux also has a very wide-ranging eye for such things."

"Rumor, love. A rumor I did my best to foster."

"And no truth whatsoever?"

"Well," he admitted lightly, "perhaps a little. But not after I met a golden-haired girl with the most fetching golden brown eyes."

"Who you thought was a ninny," she accused.

"But an interesting ninny."

"And you were a fascinating scoundrel."

"Incredible, isn't it?" he said, and now his mouth was laughing. "One of these days I would like to sit down with Brett and . . ." Suddenly his face closed again, because he wondered if he would ever get a chance to tell his brother everything. Brett would probably disapprove of his activities, since the banker was the very soul of rectitude, and most people in the South considered what he was doing outright theft. But part of Brett, Quinn thought, would be pleased to know that he wasn't a complete wastrel.

He sometimes wondered why he found it so damned important to have Brett's approval. But deep inside he knew. His family had risked so much for him, had spent so much of their fortune. His father and brother had even died waiting for him to return. He didn't want Brett to believe it had been all wasted. Quinn owed him that much at least.

Meredith saw the curtain slide over his face again. She knew there were still things he had not told her, events that still weighed heavily on him and apparently were too painful to talk about. It hurt her to the core, but she wasn't sure whether the hurt was for him or herself. She understood, though, for there were still things she had not told him, things that ran too deep inside herself, like the day Lissa had been taken away.

They stopped briefly at a stream where they watered and rested the horses, and went over the plan one final time.

Then they were riding again, and the sun was on its downward spiral. They stopped at a farm, asked directions, and continued. The sun was just beginning to dip beyond the trees when they arrived at their destination.

Meredith reined her horse behind Quinn, alongside Cam. She pulled her hat down so it shaded much of her face, and she kept her eyes to the ground. When Quinn dismounted in front of the house, both she and Cam stayed well in the shadows.

A servant had evidently noticed their arrival, for the door opened and a tall husky man appeared. His clothes—those of a gentleman—told Meredith that he must be Marshall Evans.

Meredith watched as he and Quinn talked. Quinn was at an angle and she could see half of his face. She saw the smile and she knew his plan had worked. This far, anyway. He said a few more words, and Meredith saw the Kentuckian nod his head. Quinn turned toward Cam and strode quickly to him, totally ignoring her. "You'll stay in the stable with the horses," he said curtly. "Rub them down carefully."

Meredith had to fight to keep her grin to herself, as she heard Cam's resentful murmur. "Yes, Massa."

Quinn liked Marshall Evans. He didn't want to, but he couldn't help it. There was something about the man's ready hospitality and enthusiasm about horses that was contagious.

He had been warmly welcomed as soon as he mentioned the name of a banker in Cairo who, he said, had recommended Mr. Evans's stock. As soon as Quinn had mentioned he would travel on to Murray for a room, he was quickly dissuaded.

"Not too many horsemen around," Marshall said. "Most of them are in central Kentucky. It'll be a delight to talk horses for a change. How did you happen to come this way?"

"I went to New Orleans, came by riverboat to Cairo where I bought the horse that you've kindly allowed in your stable. I'll be going through Louisville on the way back, but then I heard you might have some excellent stock."

"I do," Marshall said. "You will stay then?"

Quinn nodded. "Gratefully."

"Good. I'll just tell my housekeeper."

Quinn's eyes never changed when the housekeeper appeared almost immediately. Meredith's information was correct. He could never mistake those features. The resemblance between the two women was remarkable. If he hadn't been prepared, if he hadn't remembered the small girl from so very long ago and how much, even then, the two girls had resembled each other; he was sure his face would have given him away.

There were differences of course. Lissa's hair was dark,

and her eyes a deeper brown. Her skin was duskier but not by much. She could easily pass for white.

But there were other differences. There was a mischief in Meredith that was not apparent in this solemn slim woman. Instead, there was a rare dignity to her, made even more unusual by the fact that Quinn knew she could be no more than twenty-two. She seemed ageless in her poise. His eyes went to his host, and he saw something in the man's face that was much stronger than a man's regard for a servant.

"Lissa," Marshall said, "this is Cal Davis from Virginia. He will be staying with us tonight. Show him to one of the guest rooms, and have another plate set for supper."

The housekeeper smiled, and Quinn felt warmed. He didn't know whether it was caused by her resemblance to Meredith or by Lissa all on her own. He did realize, however, that Marshall Evans also felt it, and his hopes for buying Meredith's sister plummeted.

He followed Lissa up the stairs to the room, and stood at the doorway, watching her sure, quick movements.

"I'll have some water sent to you," she said pleasantly, and started to leave.

Quinn's hand detained her. "You look very much like someone I know," he said softly. "A Meredith Seaton."

He watched carefully as she jerked away from his grasp. And then the words seemed to penetrate and something clouded the brown eyes, reminding him of Meredith. They lacked her sister's golden lights but they held just as much feeling.

She stood still, her shoulders straightening the way Meredith's did. There was, apparently, the same raw courage in this woman. But she said nothing, merely looked at him warily.

"She's been trying to find you," he added quietly. "For years."

Still, she said nothing, merely listening.

"Do you remember her?" God, he wanted an answer. Any answer.

"She's alive?"

The question surprised Quinn. "Yes. Why do you ask?"

She closed her eyes, remembering that day, which was burned into her mind. She had tried to forget it. But it had haunted her for years. She still dreamed about it, about being dragged away from her mother and calling for "'Miss Merry." She had seen Miss Merry at the window and then watched as she fell, the scream echoing in the hot summer air and later in so many dreams. But the wagon carrying her had not even stopped.

Lissa looked up at the stranger. His face was uncommonly understanding, and she felt an immediate trust that surprised her. "I saw her fall," she said slowly. "She screamed for me, and then she fell from a window. She was trying to come after me, I think. I thought she was killed."

The hold on her arm tightened. Meredith had not told him that part of the story. "She always remembered her promise to you, that she would take care of you."

"I don't need taking care of," Lissa said unemotionally.

"No," he agreed. "Are you happy here?"

She shrugged. "Mr. Evans is kind."

"Meredith would like to buy your freedom."

Lissa smiled, a smile full of quiet sadness and knowledge. "He would never sell."

"He loves you," Quinn said. It was not a question but a statement.

She nodded.

"And you?"

"I don't have the choice of loving or not loving."

"You do now," Quinn replied, his voice low.

Her eyes widened. "What do you mean?"

"Meredith is in the stable now. We can help you escape. Tonight."

But only the first words caught her attention. "In the stable?"

He nodded.

"But how? Why?"

"She's stubborn," Quinn said, his mouth turning up in a smile. "She swore years ago she would find you, and she's been trying to do just that ever since."

"And you? Why are you here, Mr.—"

"Davis. For the moment, anyway. I'm here because of her, and you and I met years ago. When I built a swing."

Lissa narrowed her eyes, trying to remember, but she didn't. She remembered little before that day she was taken away. Those events—being taken away from her mother, Miss Merry's fall—had darkened the better days before them. She shook her head.

"No matter," he said. "You were very young, and very shy."

"That doesn't tell me why you're here."

Quinn was surprised at the perfection of her speech. Meredith had told him she had started teaching Lissa how to read. That education must have continued, which was unusual. Education was forbidden most slaves.

"Doesn't it?" he replied softly.

"Are you married to her?" she asked bluntly.

"No, but soon, I hope."

Her mouth softened, as did the rich dark brown of her eyes and he saw a hint of the golden light that he'd thought was Meredith's alone. "I'm glad," she said.

"Can you go see her?"

"Oh, yes. Mr. Evans places no restrictions on me."

"Have you thought about leaving?"

She looked at him as if he'd stepped from another world. "Where would I go, Mr. . . . Davis? What would I do? I have no one."

"You do now."

"Mr. Evans has been good to me . . . as was his mother before she died."

"Just see her, Lissa. Please."

"Yes," she said. "I would like that. Perhaps after dinner if you can keep Mr. Evans occupied."

"Where?"

"The moon is full tonight. There's a small pond, about a quarter of a mile to the north of the house. It's well sheltered by trees, and there shouldn't be anyone there at night."

Quinn nodded.

"I have to go now," she said. "I supervise dinner."

"I'll go see to my horses," Quinn said.

Without smiling, Lissa nodded slightly in response. "When you return, I'll have hot water sent to you. Is there anything else you require?"

"I think not," he said slowly. "It's incredible how much you look like her."

"Do I?" she said curiously. "I don't remember."

He smiled slowly, just one corner of his mouth turning up. "She does," he said.

Lissa's hand tightened on the doorknob before she nodded and left, closing the door softly behind her, leaving Quinn to stare after her. He hadn't known what to expect, but certainly not this quiet maturity, the solemnity, the surety of manner. It bespoke many things, including a certain security in the past years. He recalled the look in Marshall Evans's eyes when he had gazed at Lissa, and Lissa's calm statement that "Mr. Evans has been good to me."

Did she want to leave? And would Meredith accept it if she didn't?

Hell, nothing was turning out as he'd expected. He swore softly to himself, then made his way to the stable to tell Meredith of the meeting place and to retrieve his saddlebags. He would tell her nothing of the conversation, but let her discover the situation.

Meredith found the pond easily and sat on the trunk of a fallen tree. Cam was someplace behind her, keeping watch. The past hours had gone impossibly slowly.

She heard the crackle of dead leaves and looked up. A slender figure in a cloak came toward her, looking anxiously around. The figure stepped backward as she evidently saw the servant boy, not the woman she was expecting. Meredith stood up and reached out a hand. "Lissa," she said softly.

"Miss Merry?" The voice was low and disbelieving, and Meredith grinned and stepped forward, taking the cloaked figure in her arms.

"Lissa," she said, years of wistfulness in her voice. She could say no more. Her breath caught in her throat, and her heart thumped so loudly Meredith was afraid it could be heard in the house beyond the pond.

By common consent, but without words, they stepped back and looked at each other, Meredith holding on to Lissa's hands. "You . . . look"—she started to laugh—"just like me."

Lissa's face, visible in the moonlight, relaxed slightly. She even smiled when she saw the dark face and floppy hat. "I do?"

There was a quizzical amusement in the voice that delighted Meredith. "Well, perhaps not at the moment," she replied wickedly. But then the laughter fled, and she touched her sister's face as if she couldn't believe Lissa was there. "I've been trying to find you for so long. Are you all right? Are you . . . ?" Meredith didn't know what to ask. The woman in front of her, two years younger than she, looked safe and composed, even contented.

Lissa smiled slowly. "I'm fine."

"What . . . happened? After."

"I was fortunate," Lissa said. "Mr. Evans's mother bought me, and she was very kind. Her husband had died, and Mar . . . Mr. Evans was gone a great deal. I think she was lonely. She loved books and when she discovered I could read a small bit she continued teaching me. She died two years ago, and I became the housekeeper."

There was something about the way she had started to say Marshall that troubled Meredith, and Lissa saw the expression. "Mr. Evans has also been very kind. . . ."

"But—"

"It's not what you think," Lissa said as she saw growing

anger in Meredith's face. "He never married and I think he was lonely too. He never forced me."

Meredith understood. Lissa was Marshall Evans's mistress. "Do you love him?"

Lissa hesitated. "I don't know. Perhaps. It's hard to know when there's never been anything else. It just seemed . . . inevitable, and I was lonely."

"Has he ever offered you your freedom?"

Lissa's face was startled. She had never even thought of such a thing. As she had told the gentleman earlier, she had no place else to go. And she was not unhappy. She shrugged now.

"Come with us," Meredith said suddenly.

"Where?"

"Canada . . . but just for a few months. Then Quinn and I will be going West. Come with us."

"I don't know," Lissa said softly.

"Do you want to stay? As a slave. If anything happens to him . . ."

A coldness seeped into Lissa. It had been a long time since she had really thought of herself as a slave. She often dined with Marshall Evans unless there was company. She shared his bed, although she noted he was very careful not to get her with child. Now she thought of both of these things. She would never be more to him than a black mistress. She would never have children, children who would be anything but bastards, even if he did allow her to have a baby. And she wanted children. She wanted them very badly. Marshall loved her, she knew that from his gentleness, his frequent kindnesses, but not enough to defy the society he lived in.

"I haven't thought of myself that way," she said slowly. "But that's what I am, isn't it, Miss Merry?" she said, reverting back to the childhood name.

"Just Merry," Meredith corrected. The sudden sadness in Lissa's eyes stabbed her like a knife. "Come with us, Lissa."

"I have to think about it," Lissa said. "I don't know." Her eyes found Meredith. "He won't sell me."

"You can escape. I've been . . . working with the Underground Railroad. We can get you to Canada."

"It's dangerous. I know it's dangerous. I . . . why should you . . . ?"

"I've been doing it for years, Lissa."

"But why?"

Meredith just looked at her, and Lissa suddenly knew why. It was because of her. Emotion, poignant and intense, lodged in her throat. She had never known, never realized, that someone cared this much, that anyone could. Her hand reached out and took Meredith's, and they clung to each other, as if they were children again.

"Come with us," Meredith said again, in a soft crooning voice that was almost irresistible. But everything was happening too fast for Lissa. She was not unhappy, at least she hadn't been until tonight. And there was Marshall Evans. She did care for him. More than a little.

"I have to think," she repeated.

"We can stay only one day," Meredith said. "If you decide to go, we'll leave tomorrow night."

"But how?"

"Does your . . . does Marshall Evans drink?"

Lissa nodded.

"Then Quinn will see to everything."

"Quinn?"

Meredith smiled, the dark skin around her eyes crinkling. Lissa hugged her. "He seems . . . very nice."

"Sometimes," Meredith agreed. "He can be very aggravating at others." But her voice was soft with love, and the words were clearly said with teasing mischief.

Lissa felt a lump in her throat. It was so very obvious how much the mysterious Virginian and Meredith were in love. She had thought she loved Marshall, at least cared about him, but now all the doubts that had been in her heart flamed. She would never be his equal, never be considered as a mother to his children. She was someone to hide from visitors, whose existence was denied at times. Still he did love her. She had to find out how much before making a decision.

She turned her eyes away from Meredith. "I'll give you an answer tomorrow." Suddenly, everything became too much. There had been too much emotion, too much offered, too much to ponder. "I have to go," she said, then turned around and fled, never looking back. She just barely heard Meredith's parting words.

"Tomorrow. I'll meet you here tomorrow evening."

"Tomorrow." The word echoed in Lissa's mind as she went into Marshall's room that night. "Tomorrow."

When she had returned, she'd checked on him and the visitor, making sure they had enough brandy. She had tried not to look at the tall dark-haired man with the easy smile but wary eyes, tried to avoid the question she knew was in his mind. And she knew he noticed when Marshall gave her a small nod as he told her nothing else was needed this evening.

An hour later, Marshall Evans came into his bedroom and kissed her, his hands playing affectionately with her neck. "I missed you at dinner," he said.

"You seemed well occupied."

"But not as well as I'd have liked."

"Is he buying some horses?"

"Perhaps. He's going to look over the stock tomorrow." His hand moved to a more intimate place, and he sensed suddenly a hesitancy in her.

"Is there something wrong, Lissa?"

She sat on the bed and looked at Marshall. "I . . . I have to ask you a question."

His hand stroked her. "What, Lissa?"

"Will you free me?"

He put his arm around her. "What's brought this on?"

"I just wondered."

He paused, completely surprised. He often forgot that she

was a slave. That he owned her. His hand went up to her hair. "Why? Aren't you happy?"

He waited for her to say yes, his hands tightening in her hair as the silence continued. "Aren't you?" he said again.

"I just wondered," Lissa finally replied. "Almost all your other workers are free."

"It just happened that way," Marshall said slowly, wishing this conversation had never started. "I need skilled people to work with the horses."

"But not in your bed?" Her voice was bitter as it never had been before, and he looked startled.

"I love you, Lissa. You know that."

"Then free me."

"Will you stay?"

She was silent.

"Will you?"

"I don't know."

"Then I can't," he whispered. "I can't let you go."

Any doubt Lissa had vanished. She *did* care for him. She couldn't help caring for him after the years they'd lived together. But she couldn't stay with someone who would keep her by force, who would keep her a slave. If he had said he would free her, she would have remained. She would even have given up hopes of having children. But now she could not.

She looked at him sadly, and let him pull her down in bed, knowing that it would be the last time.

Chapter 24

LISSA HOVERED outside the library. Nearly twenty-four hours had passed since she had made her decision, and there was no hesitation in her, only a growing elation.

The night before she'd realized she had submerged her own hopes and dreams under a facade of contentment. She had done so, because she had not thought she had a choice.

But now she let herself think of the future.

And children.

Even if she never had any of her own, she could teach. She could love.

Miss Merry. Merry. She seemed to have come out of a mist. A glowing faraway mist to offer a kingdom.

It still seemed a dream. But when she woke up that morning after a fitful sleep, the Virginian was still at the house, and the slightly built groom around the barn.

Marshall was the same affable man she had known. He seemed to have completely dismissed their conversation from last night. It had no importance to him. For a moment she hated him. But the feeling quickly fled. He could not change any more than he could control her feelings, her needs. He considered himself a good man, a kind man, and he was that, in many ways. But he didn't understand, could never understand what he had done to her the night before.

He was genuinely delighted that their guest decided to stay another day, and Lissa knew she should feel some guilt at the deception. But a door had opened, and once she had decided to pass through it, there was no going back.

The day passed slowly. Marshall and Mr. Davis spent much of it riding the farm and talking horseflesh. After dinner, they settled in the library, a new bottle of brandy between them.

It had been arranged that Lissa would call Marshall, ask a question about the household so the stranger could slip something into Marshall's glass. She had been assured that it would result only in a deep sleep.

It should be working now. Any minute.

She heard the door open, and the tall lean Virginian emerged. "He's asleep," the man said. "I'll carry him upstairs. Is everyone else asleep?"

Lissa nodded.

"Are you ready?"

Lissa nodded once more. She had laid one extra dress on a piece of cloth and rolled it up. She wanted nothing else from this place.

The man whom Merry had called Quinn nodded approvingly, his dark eyes gleaming in the candlelight. Lissa thought fleetingly how confident he seemed. She felt very safe in putting herself in his hands. He radiated power and control and assurance.

Merry was very lucky. Very, very lucky.

•   •   •

Meredith was thinking the same thing minutes later as she watched Quinn's deft movements. He and Cam quickly saddled their horses while she stood nearby, her arm reassuringly wound around Lissa's.

One of the grooms, who slept in the stable, was lying in a corner, drugged from the whiskey bottle offered earlier by Cam.

Using a minimum of words, Quinn helped Meredith onto her saddle, and then Lissa. Cam took the reins of his mount and cautiously led it out the stable door. It was after two in the morning, and the farm was totally quiet. Cam nodded to those inside, and Quinn leaped to the back of his unsaddled horse, eyeing the tack room enviously. He had stolen enough tonight, though, and could justify only the one theft to himself, not the other.

Even then, it was not exactly theft. He had left five thousand dollars in his room, a sum which would more than cover Lissa's monetary value. He hoped that Marshall Evans would think he wanted Lissa for himself; he had certainly ogled her enough during the day and had even offered a good price, only to meet the refusal he expected.

Quinn hoped to hell that Evans wouldn't be able to trace them. The only possible lead was the banker in Cairo; Quinn had needed the name to gain acceptance. The man, however, was not one of Quinn's bankers. Quinn knew of him only by reputation. He had never met the banker and doubted if the banker had ever seen him. He prayed that that dead end would discourage Evans.

He didn't believe there were any other leads. Without the white streaks in his hair, the Virginian would not be readily identified as being the same person as the riverboat captain. His clothes and manner had been far different from those he usually sported. And he'd heard enough accents at the gambling tables to assume the less distinctive drawl of Virginia. Quinn was depending on Evans looking toward that direction.

But he was taking no chances. He turned east, rather than

north, until they reached a creek. Once there, he lay pepper along the banks where they entered the water, and again a hundred yards down where they emerged briefly. He hoped the confused dogs would not go back to the water. They continued down the creek for several miles, and only then turned north.

Of them all, Lissa had the most difficulty and they had to slow their pace to hers. She had never ridden before and she was terrified of the horse. Quinn finally dismounted and helped her down, then handed her to Cam, who placed her in front of him in the saddle.

They stopped at midmorning to rest, and Quinn knew word was probably already spreading. The disappearance of a slave called for immediate community action since time was essential in bringing one back. Nearly every slave holder participated because one successful escape would lead to others, particularly this close to the border. Quinn couldn't depend on the fact that Evans was misled as to purpose and destination.

While the others rested, Quinn scouted the area and heard hoofbeats. He hurried back, and they retreated farther into the woods. Quinn decided to stay there until nightfall.

Meredith sat with Lissa, and Quinn felt the awkwardness between them. He wondered whether Lissa regretted her decision. If she were taken back now, her situation would worsen tremendously.

He smiled reassuringly at both and then leaned down and offered his hand to Meredith, who quickly looked at Lissa.

"Go with him," Lissa said, smiling faintly. "I'm tired."

"Try to get some sleep," Quinn said. "We'll leave again just after dusk. It's going to be a long ride."

Meredith rose, swinging up gracefully with the strength of his hand, and they walked hand in hand past Cam, who was holding his pistol that he had kept in his saddlebags. The two men exchanged nods, and Meredith and Quinn moved outside the small clearing, through a jumble of underbrush and briers.

But Meredith didn't care about the scratches or the rough uneven ground. She was with Quinn, really with him for the first time in two days.

"Thank you," she said.

"Don't thank me yet," he warned.

"Oh, but I do. And I wonder if you'd be willing to kiss this thoroughly repugnant-looking groom."

"You could never be repugnant."

"Never?" she asked wickedly, recalling some of her more unflattering hair fashions.

"Never," he repeated, grinning down at her, remembering.

"You must be in love."

"I must, indeed," he agreed. "For I think I've never seen anything quite as lovely as you at this moment."

"You're mad."

"Completely," he assured her, his hand circling her waist as his lips reached down and kissed hers hungrily. It had only been several days and already it seemed a lifetime had passed since mouths had touched and spoken to each other silently. Danger heightened their already enormous need for each other. Heightened and stimulated and spiced.

His arm tightened around her. "It's cold," he said as he looked at the ground.

"Is it?" she retorted teasingly.

"Now that you mention it . . ."

"In fact, it's getting very warm."

"Very," he admitted, already taking off his jacket and laying it on the ground. His arms went around her again, and both would have sworn it was a sweltering July day.

They started riding again at dusk, staying away from the roads, traveling slowly in the thick woods. Lissa was back alone on her horse, her shoulders hunched with weariness but her eyes bright whenever they rested on Meredith, who stayed next to her.

Quinn was often gone, moving quickly around them. He was there and then he wasn't. He would suddenly appear and they would rein in their horses and remain still until he disappeared again and returned, giving them the signal to continue.

Cam stayed by their side, his face impassive, his hand never far from the pistol that he now kept in his belt. When daybreak came again, they stopped, although Meredith recognized Quinn's impatience. The *Lucky Lady* should be nearing Cairo, but Lissa was exhausted and Meredith could tell by Quinn's expression that he was sighting more and more patrols. It had started to drizzle, and Quinn dared not light a fire. He and Cam tried to make a shelter out of branches, covering it with a blanket taken from the back of one of the horses.

Quinn disappeared into the woods, and Meredith went after him, finding him leaning against a tree. "What's wrong?"

He looked at her. "Marshall's already posted a reward, a huge one. I heard some men on the road talking about it. That's why there's so damned many of them."

"They didn't believe you were headed toward Virginia?"

"I don't know. They might be covering every damned road, just in case."

"Is it wise to go back to Cairo then?"

He sighed. "We don't have much choice now. I don't know the Underground stations in this area, or even if there are any. We could go straight north into Illinois, but that's exactly where they will be looking. With the reward, every slave hunter and sheriff in both states will be looking for us, and I don't think Lissa can last much longer on horseback. The *Lucky Lady* is still the best bet. We have a hidden panel in back of the boat, large enough for all of us if necessary."

She took his hand, feeling his tension, knowing it was more for her and Lissa than himself, and she loved him for it. He was taking so many chances for her.

"I love you," she said, tightening her hold on him. But he didn't respond as he usually did. Instead, he took his hand away from her and placed it under her chin, forcing her to look up at him. "If anything happens, love, promise me something."

"What?" she asked suspiciously, sure he was going to tell her to leave him. She was prepared to do almost anything but that.

"There's a woman in Cairo." He felt her stiffen, and he smiled at the instinctive action. "If anything goes wrong, you and Lissa go to her. Tell her it's Merry, and she'll help you."

"The Underground Railroad?"

"Yes," he said. "But . . . you have to know it's . . . well . . . it's a . . . sporting house."

He didn't know what reaction to expect from her, but it was definitely not the one he got.

Her mouth widened into a broad grin at his obvious awkwardness. The rogue. The gambler. The notorious womanizer. Even in the drizzle, she could see his discomfort, and some horrid mischief-maker inside her enjoyed it. "I always wanted to see one," she confided.

"Meredith!"

It was a bellow of outrage, and Meredith couldn't stop the laughter from bubbling out, her eyes sparking with rascality. She thoroughly enjoyed his shock, especially as it erased the worry lines from his face. His indignation seemed so out of character, but a very, very typical masculine reaction. She'd just never associated him with most males.

Their eyes rested on each other, and then he grinned, too, shaking his head ruefully. "I never quite know what to expect from you."

"Frustrating, isn't it?" she remarked lightly, thinking the same thing of him.

"Extremely," he agreed. "But . . . challenging."

Their mouths agreed as he bent down and kissed her, before they turned back.

• • •

They reached the cabin on the third day, five days after they had ridden out. Everything was as they had left it. All of them relished the shelter, for it was raining hard now. But they still couldn't risk lighting a fire. Instead, they changed into other clothes, wrapping blankets around themselves for warmth.

Quinn fetched water from the nearby river and washed the color from his hair. The rain had already partly removed it; the rest was scrubbed out. It was a theatrical substance, easily removed, that Sophie always kept available. Quinn then changed into his black clothes.

"I'm going to see whether the *Lady* is there yet," he told Meredith. "Cam will stay with you tonight. In the morning, a buggy will come for you with your trunk in it. There are widow's weeds and a veil for Lissa in my portmanteau. They are your size and should fit."

Meredith nodded. They had agreed that Lissa would masquerade as Meredith's bereaved cousin who was returning to Minnesota to attend a brother's funeral. Kinship was necessary because of the similarity of appearance between the two women, yet Quinn hoped that Lissa could remain hidden under the bonnet and veil.

Meredith walked to the door with Quinn. He turned abruptly to speak briefly with Cam. "If the *Lucky Lady* is in, and I'm not standing on the top deck tomorrow at nine A.M., don't come aboard. It means trouble. Go to Sophie's. I'll meet you there."

Cam nodded.

Quinn leaned down and kissed Meredith. It was meant as a light good-bye, but it deepened into something else altogether, a hungry desperate urgency. He finally forced himself to break away, staring at her as he moved back. Her hat was gone, and the long black braid had fallen over her shoulder. Her skin was still dark from the coloring, and she looked utterly beautiful, her golden brown eyes misty with love, her lips red and swollen from his kiss, her hand slightly outstretched as if to keep him from going.

"I love you," he whispered and spun around to where the horses were tied. He took the saddled horse that Cam had been riding, and without a backward look spurred the animal into a trot.

Sarah had awaited her opportunity. She found it as she passed a stable on the way to the mercantile store where she planned to buy some thread. Two men were standing there, burly, rough-looking men, who were quizzing the proprietor. One held a paper in his hand. "We're looking for a runaway," he said. "Possibly with a tall white man and a large black man."

The storekeeper's eyes were hostile as he shook his head. "No one like that around here."

"There's a reward . . . anyone gives us information, we'll share it."

"I said I ain't seen anyone like that." The owner turned abruptly and went back into the barn, leaving the two men outside.

"Damn," said one. "We've been all over this town. Mebbe we were wrong. Mebbe they went toward Ohio."

"I don't think so," the other said. "The trail was too obvious. And there's something about that description . . ."

"A Virginian?"

"I got a feelin', John. That damned boat, the *Lucky Lady*, came in today."

The other man shrugged. "So what? We only made fools of ourselves when we asked the sheriff to search it that time."

"But the description . . ."

"It didn't say nothin' about white streaks, and Devereux's hair sure as hell is noticeable."

"Still . . ."

"Hell, John, give it up. You're just still mad 'cause he took you at poker."

But John only regarded his brother stubbornly before looking around. He saw a mulatto wench staring at him and his eyes stopped moving. There was something in her face, something that compelled him to move over to her.

"You know anything, girl, about a young, light runaway?"

Sarah stood rooted to the ground. This was the chance to bring retribution down on Cam. A big black man, the slave hunter had said. And a white man. It had to be Cam and Captain Devereux. And she suddenly realized a way of telling without involving Miss Sophie.

"I might know somethin'," she said slyly.

One of the men jingled coins in his picket. "Five dollars," he said.

"A man . . . he was drunk and told me he worked with the Underground Railroad, said he stole any number of slaves away."

"Who . . . ?"

Sarah looked toward the wharf. "He came from one of the riverboats. Said his captain was in it too."

The man looked at her suspiciously. "Why you telling us this, girl?"

"He didn't pay me," she said spitefully.

It was the perfect answer. The two men looked at each other. "When did you see him last?"

"Five days ago."

John Carroll looked at his brother, Ted. "The *Lucky Lady* wasn't here then. And that was two days before the girl disappeared."

Ted's mouth stretched into a wide grin. He took several coins from his pocket and handed them to Sarah. "Here, girl," he said.

The two men turned toward the wharf, leaving Sarah standing there, five dollars clutched in her hand. She looked at the coins, and her head spun. She started to feel dizzy; words moved around in her head like flotsam in the river. "You're a good girl, Sarah," she heard a faraway voice say.

Then the words changed to something else. "Thirty pieces of silver," Mr. Hitchcock said plainly. "Thirty pieces of silver."

Sarah opened her hand and stared at the coins. *"Thirty pieces of silver, and Judas betrayed his Lord."* The dead Mr. Hitchcock's voice came clearly over and over again. She threw the coins down as if they burned her hand.

Thirty pieces of silver. She stared at the gold mixing with the dust of the road. What had she done?

He deserved it, she told herself. He had let her think . . . Cam was a thief. He should be punished. As she should be punished for her wickedness.

Thirty pieces of silver.

The words echoed in her mind, and she started running to escape them. *"You're a good girl, Sarah."* She was. She had been. And she would be again.

Thirty pieces of silver. "No," she screamed, running even harder, never seeing the carriage coming down the street. She stumbled and fell, hearing noise all around her. There was thunder in her ears, then scarlet all around, like flames from hell. And finally blackness.

The *Lucky Lady* was safely at the wharf. Quinn slowly released his breath; the timing couldn't have been better. Usually the boat remained overnight because there was much activity here, and he could see the feverish bustling as barrels and crates were transferred from boat to land. Meredith and Lissa could board early in the morning, before many others were astir.

He strode easily up the gangplank and found Jamison. The Scot looked up at him dourly. "Thought you might be dead. You've been gone long enough."

Quinn smiled and shrugged. "It was Christmas, Mr. Jamison."

"Since when did you care for that nonsense?"

"I'm trying to change my ways."

Jamison raised a dubious eyebrow.

Quinn ignored it. "Do you have a stateroom available?"

"Aye."

"Miss Seaton will be boarding with a recently bereaved cousin."

"The Miss Seaton who was kidnapped?"

"You heard about it?"

"Every damn soul up and down the river heard about it. Thought we got rid of river pirates a long time ago. Is the lass all right?"

Quinn closed his eyes a moment to keep from smiling. "She seems well recuperated," he said mildly.

"Poor lass. We'll take good care of her."

"Good," Quinn said, nearly choking on the word. It was one of the few times his pilot had shown human emotion, and probably it never was less needed. "Anything unusual happening?"

Jamison looked at him. "Unusual?"

"Any more questions being asked about the *Lucky Lady*."

"Not that I've heard," Jamison replied with a frown. "Just the usual check. There was a runaway not far from here, and the boats were searched more thoroughly, but of course they didn't find anything."

Quinn looked out over the town. It was still drizzling, and the river was rough. The sky, already gray, was darkening even more, and he knew nightfall was only minutes away. He had one remaining errand: to arrange for a buggy to bring Meredith and Lissa into town in the morning. If there was a second search Lissa's "widowhood" would protect her from much questioning. According to everything he'd heard, the authorities were searching for a white man and a mulatto woman. There should be no suspicions of two bereaved white women and a well-known local black resident.

Going to his cabin, Quinn hoped he could get everything done before he dropped from exhaustion.

• • •

He awoke to pain. Jabbing, throbbing pain that started in his arms and stretched down into his back. Sharp, tingling pain at the base of his throat.

Quinn's sleep had been so deep, it took him several minutes to realize what had happened. By then the pain had intensified. His eyes opened slowly as his mind struggled to comprehend.

The room was dark, but his tired eyes could make out shadows. One large form had a knife against his throat; the other was binding his arms behind him. When he tried to speak, the knife pressed tighter against his throat; he felt a trickle of wetness run down it.

"No loud noises, Devereux," a voice commanded, "or this knife goes deeper. Much deeper."

Quinn stilled, playing for time. "What do you want?"

"The girl from the Evans plantation," one of the voices said, and Quinn recognized it. One of the Carroll brothers.

"I don't know what you're talking about," Quinn whispered.

The knife cut a long line along Quinn's throat, and he could feel the trickle increase to a flow. He closed his eyes. The pain didn't bother him. God knew he had suffered much worse and survived. That was his ace. He was reputed to be a coward because he wouldn't race, wouldn't duel with those who called him a cheat when they lost. But he had discovered long ago that his tolerance for pain was immense; he had simply learned how to shut it out. But the Carrolls didn't know that.

"For God's sake, stop," Quinn said, forcing panic in his voice.

"Where is the girl?"

"I don't know. You have to believe me."

"Then where's that big darky who's always with you?"

"He better damn well be working," Quinn said.

"He ain't on the boat."

Alarm ran through Quinn. This had something to do with Cam, and the Carrolls obviously knew a little. But what? And how did they find it? "Is that what you want?" he said.

"Take him, the worthless no-good bastard. Never been worth the money I paid for him."

"Is that why you let him go whoring?" The question was dangerously soft, full of insinuation.

Quinn's heart went cold. Daphne. Had something happened to Daphne?

"I don't let him do nothing," Quinn replied.

The knife carved into his chest. "That's not what a pretty little black whore says. She said your man bragged you and he was with the Underground Railroad, and that he refused to pay her for services used."

"Is that what this is all about? You damned fools. You believe a whore?" Quinn's mind quickly ran over possibilities. It couldn't be Daphne. Then who? And then he remembered Cam telling him about Sarah. "She was acting strangely," he'd said. Christ. Not only he and Cam were in danger now, but Sophie as well. And Meredith, damn it. Meredith and Lissa. Thank God, he had told Cam not to board in the morning if he wasn't on deck.

"I believe this one," John Carroll said. "We knew there was someone running slaves on the river, and I had a feeling about you."

"Your feeling was wrong," Quinn protested indignantly.

"You like games, do you?" John Carroll mocked. "I don't mind them myself." The knife cut again and, for the Carrolls' benefit, Quinn winced and moaned.

"I'll have the sheriff on you," he groaned.

"Oh, the sheriff will be here all right. He's out looking, like everyone else, but I left a note on his door. And I want that little bird before he gets here. Do you understand, Mr. Devereux?"

"I told you I know nothing. . . . If that black bastard was involved in anything, he did it on his own." One of the Carrolls laughed, and once more the knife dug deeper.

Quinn took a deep breath, and faked unconsciousness.

•   •   •

Cam had a bad feeling. A very bad feeling. And what made it worse was that he had never felt anything like this before.

He and the captain had been in dangerous situations several times, yet this dread crawling along his spine was unfamiliar. Therefore, he was of a mind to pay attention to it.

He was sitting just inside the door of the shack. He'd insisted that the two women use the cots. Cam had no intention of resting, not tonight. He wanted to stay awake, to make sure he would hear any noise. He'd prowled outside the shack several times, but there had been no sign of man or beast other than their own tired mounts.

Perhaps, he tried to tell himself, it was the waiting. He had never liked the waiting.

Cam rose again and quietly unlatched the door. Outside the sky was dark and forbidding. He was cold, very cold, and not because of the weather. He heard a noise behind him, and the door opened. A moment later Meredith stood beside him.

"Something's bothering you, isn't it?" she asked quietly.

He shrugged. Cam had come to admire Meredith in the past few days. She never complained, never asked for special considerations. She had endured the first day's long ride, and the cold miseries of the following days without comment. And he liked the way she and the captain looked at each other, and touched each other. Some of that iron hardness, the remote aloneness, had faded from the captain's eyes.

"What is it, Cam?"

"I don't know," he said honestly. "It's just a feelin'."

"You want to go to him."

He turned around, surprised at her instinct. "The capt'n asked me to stay with you."

"We're safe enough here," she said. "Quinn said he would send the buggy in the morning."

The uneasiness in Cam deepened. "You have a gun?"

She nodded.

He hesitated.

"Go," she said.

He finally nodded. "I should be back no later than midmorning. Ask the buggy driver to wait until then. If I don't show up, go to Sophie's. Wait for us there. They won't be looking for two women."

Meredith reluctantly assented. She wanted to go, but she had Lissa to worry about, and they really didn't know that anything was wrong. Just the same, Cam's restlessness scared her. From what she had seen of him, he didn't alarm easily.

She watched him saddle one of the horses huddled under the trees. He mounted awkwardly, and looked back at her for a moment. Then he disappeared among the leaves.

WATER SPLASHED in his face, and Quinn couldn't help sputtering.

He wondered what time it was. Time was a commodity that was running out, he feared.

If the sheriff did appear and he was held, Marshall Evans would surely identify him despite the changes in his hair color. He was profoundly grateful that he had told Cam not to board if he did not see Quinn on deck. The three of them—Cam, Meredith, and Lissa—would be safe. Cam would ensure that.

Quinn blinked his eyes, feigning confusion. There had to be a way for him to escape! He thought of Newgate again, and Norfolk Island in Australia. Christ, he didn't know if he could survive prison again. At least, this time no one else would get hurt. There was some satisfaction in that.

"He's awake," he heard one brother say, and the front of

his wet shirt was bunched in a fist as he was pulled to a sitting position. Another groan escaped his throat, this one not altogether voluntary as agony arced through his back.

Quinn tried to think, tried to concentrate. Without Lissa, they had no evidence except Marshall Evans's testimony that he had used another name, and that Lissa had disappeared the same time he did. He could make up some story that would probably soothe a divided Illinois jury if not a proslave Kentucky one.

If only he could goad or trick the Carrolls into untying him.

His eyes adjusted once more to the dark. The Carrolls were careful to keep the room black. They wanted no alarm, no rescue from Quinn's friends. Quinn wondered again what time it was, how long before dawn.

Suddenly, out of the gloom, a fist struck his face, and pain shot across his strained back. He grunted.

"Once more," John said pleasantly. "Where's the gal? She's all we want. Perhaps we can even make a deal. If you're carrying fugitives for money, you can continue to pick them up, and we can collect them from you and split the rewards." Quinn could imagine the man's eyes narrow speculatively. "Is that why you're doing it? The money? If so, we can all make a fortune before anyone's the wiser."

Quinn let his head fall. "I tell you I don't know anything about a girl."

John shook his head sadly. "Now why don't I believe you?"

Quinn tried a sneer. "You think any goddamned fugitive slaves have a penny? You think I'd risk my neck without so much as a coin? You think I would risk it, even with gold?"

"Now that is a puzzle," John replied. "I've been trying to figure that one out. I heard you won't fight. Won't even race the *Lucky Lady*. So why don't you tell us, or mebbe I should try the knife again."

Quinn watched the curve of steel in the air and drew back as much as John Carroll's hold on him allowed. He couldn't help flinching. He could smell his own blood now and feel the rivulets still running from previous cuts. His skin stung in a dozen places, but the knife cuts weren't nearly as painful as the whip lashes had been.

He blocked out the present and thought about that whip now, slicing through open skin and tearing muscles. He saw Terrence suffer another hundred strokes for the third straight morning, his back already infected. That was the day Terrence died. As he had been dragged to the post because he could no longer walk, he'd turned to Quinn and whispered the words that had gotten them both through seven years. *Don't ever let the bloody bastards get ye down*. How readily the words came back, and the image of Terrence O'Connell with that devil-be-damned smile, although that day it was only a ghost. Yet it had been there to the end. Even as he lay dying, he had mocked the guards with it. Terrence had been a true ironman. And he, too, would be.

Quinn forced a smile on his own face now. "Damn it, I'd tell you if I knew anything. If that damned slave of mine is involved, I'd be the first to see him hang. I might anyway, him getting me into this."

"Then where is he?"

"He should be down in the cargo deck, where he sleeps."

"He ain't there. He ain't anyplace on this boat."

"Then I'll pay you to find him."

"Him instead of the girl," John mused. "Now that's an interesting proposition."

"Kind of like a bribe," Ted, the brother who had lingered in the background, replied.

"Is that what it is?" John said, like a cat playing with a mouse.

"Hell, no," Quinn denied. "I just want him back."

"Mebbe we can get both him and the girl," Ted said hopefully.

"And mebbe we're being played for fools," John answered. "Like we were several months ago."

Quinn silently cursed himself as he dropped his head

wearily. He'd used poor judgment that long-ago evening, inviting the Carrolls for supper and then relieving them of all their money. But something within him had wanted to teach them a lesson, to tweak their noses. He was certainly paying for that error now.

He started to lift his head when he noticed the door behind the Carrolls open very slightly. His hands behind him curled into frustrated balls. Cam. It had to be Cam. The Carrolls must have broken the lock to enter his cabin. They had to be damned good to do it without waking him, but they would have been unable to lock it again.

And Cam was the only man who would ever enter his cabin without warning. That Cam knew something was wrong was evident by the fact that he did not knock. A trickle of sweat ran down Quinn's back despite the cold chill that had lodged there. Damn Cam to hell. Why hadn't he done what he was told? Quinn's entire body tightened with foreboding. But still, he had to do what little he could to help.

Quinn groaned suddenly, falling against the wall. As one of the Carrolls started to grab his shirt again, his feet went out, hitting the man in the chest and sending him against his brother. Then Cam was there, his fists catching the second man in the chest and face and sending him crashing to the floor. The first Carroll recovered quickly, his hand darting for the knife, which had fallen to the floor at Quinn's kick.

Cam's foot caught Ted Carroll's wrist and pressed down on it unmercifully. Quinn heard the crack of bones and Carroll's scream just before Cam's hand smashed the man's mouth, knocking him unconscious. Cam then checked the other man, making sure he too was unconscious. As the head rolled, Cam's teeth flashed with satisfaction before he picked up the knife and quickly cut Quinn's bonds.

The sudden release sent a cramp through Quinn's body, momentarily making it useless, and he gritted his teeth against the debilitating pain. His hands were numb, his wrists bloody, and when he stood he had to spend a moment trying to get feeling back into his limbs. He looked down at the

Carrolls and knew it was only a matter of time before half of Kentucky and Illinois were after him.

He looked at Cam. "I thought I told you to stay with Meredith and Lissa."

Cam shrugged. "I had a feelin' you were in trouble."

"Meredith?"

"I told her to wait at the cabin until midmorning. If I wasn't back by then, they were to go on to Sophie's and go through the Underground route."

Quinn winced as he took a step, shrugging aside Cam's hand. Even though Cam had probably saved him from a prison term, he couldn't stop the anger boiling in him. It wasn't an anger he understood, for he and Cam had long had a partnership in which neither was dominant, and Cam was under no obligation to follow his orders. Yet Cam's sudden appearance made his skin crawl with some terrible premonition, and his mind kept flashing back to Terrence and the sound of the whip cracking against his back. He shook his head to rid it of images he couldn't control. "Let's get the hell out of here," he said roughly.

Quinn gave one last look at the two fallen men and went to the door, opening it quietly. "They said they sent for the sheriff," Quinn said. "I think we can expect him at any time."

"Should we tie them up?"

"No time," Quinn said.

Cam nodded, following Quinn as he darted out and made his way to the main cargo deck. As they started for the gangplank, they heard the sound of horses and saw five men approach the *Lucky Lady*. Quinn and Cam ducked behind crates and made for the back of the boat.

"There they are!"

Quinn heard the shout and looked up. One of the Carrolls was on the top deck, looking down, his gun pointed at them. On the wharf more men were gathering.

"We have to go into the water," he said to Cam, who quickly nodded. They ran along the deck, their speed increasing as they heard the sounds of pursuers around them, now on both their own deck and above.

There was the sound of a pistol shot, and Quinn felt it speed by him, striking a lantern and spilling oil. He and Cam kept running. There was another shot, like the crack of a whip, and Quinn felt Cam falter, then heard his brief cry. He grabbed Cam and together they went off the side of the *Lucky Lady*, hitting the freezing water as another shout went up. They went down, the water trying to tear them apart, but Quinn wouldn't let go as he struggled against the current. They finally came up, and Cam was a dead weight in his arms. Gasping for breath, Quinn looked around and discovered they had already been swept beyond the lights of the riverboat. He could see flames on the deck, and increasingly small figures turn their attention from him to fight the blaze. If the fire spread, not only the riverboat would be destroyed but much of the wharf also.

Quinn felt regret for the *Lucky Lady*. But he realized that the fire would give them valuable time to escape. He took one last look. There was still a figure on the top deck, his gun extended as his gaze swept the dark shadows of the river. If no one else came after them, Quinn knew the Carrolls would.

"Cam," he whispered, but there was no answer. Cam's body was motionless except for the movements caused by the river. How badly was he hurt? Deep chilling despair filled him. Not again. Dear Christ, not again. Death followed him like a shadow, falling on everyone he cared about. The echo of that last shot reverberated in his ears, like the sound of the whip had for so many years.

His body was freezing in the icy water, but his heart pounded as loudly and harshly as a hammer against iron. His arm tightened around Cam and he allowed the current to take them farther downstream, his legs moving in steady strokes to keep them above water and heading slowly toward shore. He thought about praying but disregarded it. Prayer had never helped him before. Never helped those he loved. Terrence, who died under the lash for attacking a guard who was beating Quinn. His father and older brother, who died because they wouldn't leave New Orleans during an epidemic, because they were anxiously awaiting word of him. And now Cam. All of them destroyed trying to help him.

He yelled out against the night, against the river, against darkness, only the cry died in the roar of the river. His legs started to stiffen with cold, and his body once more cramped with fatigue and pain. He thought about letting go, letting the water take him, before he killed anyone else, before he killed Meredith too.

Just then the figure in his arms stirred and moaned softly, and Quinn struggled toward shore. He could no longer see the *Lucky Lady*, nor, thank God, any more flames. Yet he knew that even if the flames had been doused, attention would remain on the boat for a long time. There would be too much danger of a spark igniting again. He and Cam had a chance.

Quinn moved slowly toward the bank, every movement a supreme effort. God, he was tired. His strength was gone, and only determination drove him on, determination that Cam wouldn't die because of him.

At last his feet found bottom and he dragged Cam to the bank. He turned Cam over so he faced the ground, and water flowed from his mouth as he choked and sputtered. Then Quinn pulled Cam farther inland until they were well under the cover of the trees. Only then did Quinn sink down beside his friend. Cam groaned, and Quinn knew he was still alive.

But for how long?

With fury so deep and so strong that it rejuvenated a body drained of all strength, he leaned over Cam and swore, his every word an anguished cry in the night, a tortured moan that tore from his throat. "Damn you, Cam, damn you. Why did you come? Why?" And he fell over Cam's form, tears mixing with the muddy river water that dripped from his face.

The harsh breathing of the man next to him startled Quinn into action.

Quinn cursed the darkness as he tried to find the extent of Cam's injury. He heard the rasping attempts to breathe, felt the movement of Cam's chest as he gasped for air. Quinn finally found a rip in Cam's trousers, both front and back. The bullet had gone through his thigh, and Quinn worried that it might have shattered the bone. The impact of Cam's hitting the water might have also caused a head injury. Quinn had been prepared; Cam, hurt by the bullet, had not.

Drizzle fell from the skies. Shivers ran through Quinn's body, and he felt the icy skin of Cam.

"Don't die on me," he whispered. "Don't you dare die on me."

The cold, he knew, was deadly. He had to find them some shelter, some warmth.

How far were they from the shack where he had left Meredith?

It was downriver from Cairo, and they had been carried perhaps a mile by the current. Not nearly close enough. He had to find shelter now, or they both would die. Already he was feeling the drowsiness that came with extreme cold, and he had to fight to keep awake. To give into it, as he wanted to, would mean death.

He looked around. He saw only trees, no sign of light, no indication of any farmer or fisherman. But his eyes caught a path on the ground. A path led somewhere.

He stood and moved along the path. His toe caught a root, sending him sprawling. As he pitched forward, his hand landed on something hard and curved—and hidden by branches.

His fingers skimmed over the find, and he knew instantly it was a rowboat. Because of fugitive slaves, there was a law along the Mississippi that all boats had to be secured. The owner of this one apparently hid his, for as Quinn tossed aside its camouflage, he could find no chain tying it to a tree. He did discover a length of rope attached to one end of the boat, and a paddle and an oilcloth nearby. His luck was changing.

Dragging the boat to the bank, he moved through the trees, mindless of the branches scratching his arms, and the cold eating into him. He only had to carry Cam back to the river; the boat would carry them to the shack.

He put the boat into the water and tied it to a tree. Shivering, he returned to Cam with the oilcloth in hand. The first sign of light was in the sky, but it was a dismal shade of gray, not the bright glimmering of a fresh day. Still, it would help him find the curve in the river that was near the cabin.

Quinn reached Cam and gently shook him. "Cam?"

"Capt'n." The voice was weak but audible, and Quinn sighed with relief.

"Can you sit?"

Cam's mouth tightened as he struggled to sit, and his body shook and wavered as he sought to stay upright. Quinn wrapped the oilcloth around him. "I found a boat. Can you make it to the bank?"

Spasms ran through the large man's body, but he nodded. Quinn held out a hand to him and felt a sudden warmth as their fingers clenched together. Strength, born of desperation and resolve, pulled Cam to his feet, although he looked as if he would fall any second. He tried to stand on his wounded leg but it gave way, and Quinn grabbed him.

Once again, they tried to move, Cam using Quinn as a crutch. The good leg, the one Cam used for balance, was the one wounded, and now both legs were crippled. Cam's stomach was queasy from too much river water, and his head spun. Even with the oilcloth, he was freezing; every part of his body convulsed with shivers. Only thoughts of Daphne kept him going.

Pretty little Daphne who looked at him so worshipfully. No one had looked at him like that before. No one had made him weep, or laugh with love. He tried to take his mind from the present misery, the physical agony of moving, and instead remember the day on the bank when he had whirled her around, and she had laughed so delightedly. He tried to hear that laughter now rather than the steady drumming of rain on leaves, rain on ground, rain on the oilcloth. He stumbled and felt Quinn's strong arm. His eyes swung over and met his companion's. Challenging eyes that wouldn't let him stop.

Cam wanted to close his eyes, he wanted to stop, but he knew he could not. If he stopped, he would never rise again. One foot moved, and then another as pain ran down his leg like runaway fire. Finally they were at the riverbank. Cam leaned against a tree while Quinn untied the boat. Holding on to the rope with one hand, Quinn stretched out the other to Cam. Cam somehow took the few steps toward Quinn and dropped inside. The boat swayed and tipped, and he feared he would go back into the dark cold water. But it steadied and he lay down at one end, unable to do anything to help Quinn except try to keep the boat still by keeping himself still.

The boat rocked once again as Quinn stepped in, and then it was caught by the current. Quinn took the oars in his hand, and, steadily, they made their way down the fog-shrouded river.

Chapter 26

THE BUGGY CAME at daybreak. The driver, the same dark
taciturn man who had brought them here several days ago,
frowned when Meredith told him that Quinn and Cam were
gone, and that they should wait here until midmorning. He
had heard nothing, no alarm, he said, before he'd left Cairo
just two hours earlier.

The driver gave his name as Butler and, during the tense
hours that they waited together, said that he had been born
free in Kentucky and had come to Cairo ten years earlier. He
had worked at a livery stable until he earned enough money
to buy first one horse, then another, and finally a buggy. Now
he hired out his buggy. He had often been used by Captain
Quinn to help fugitives and sometimes he donated his services to those who couldn't pay. He had built a false front in
the buggy, an area large enough for two people to hide,
although not comfortably.

Meredith had told him earlier that Cam said they were to go to Sophie's if neither he nor Quinn appeared. The driver accepted the instructions without comment, but his manner became distinctly nervous.

But no more nervous than Meredith's. She tried to hide her fear from both Lissa and the man called Butler, but apprehension weighed her soul like a ship's anchor. Every minute that passed meant Quinn was in trouble. Otherwise, Cam would be back by now, and they would be on their way to the *Lucky Lady*.

Something had happened. She had sensed Cam's own distress before he had left. And it had taken root in her and grown like a cancer, gnawing at the very essence of her heart and soul. Dawn had come and gone, its gloom a portent of disaster. She had wanted it to clear, wanted the sun to emerge from the boiling clouds and spread life and hope over the river. But the sky continued to foam with clouds, great bloated blobs of puce and purple riding across the horizon.

Where is he? Dear God, where is he?

She wanted to go after him, to fling herself on a horse and ride at a gallop to Cairo, but she had been trained too well. She knew a rash action could destroy them all. Although it went against her grit, against the pounding terror building in her heart, she forced herself to wait. She had promised. She paced the cabin and then, disregarding the chilled rain, she put on her cloak and went outside. She walked down to the usually placid stream, now swollen and racing, and followed it to the river. She could see only a portion of it, for it was shrouded with fog. It seemed endless, like an empty lonely infinity. Before long she felt a presence beside her, and she turned to see Lissa. Her sister's eyes were sad and her arms were held out in comfort.

Meredith moved into them. They held each other, years falling away until they were frightened children again, and it was the two of them against the world. For the first time since they had left Marshall Evans's plantation, Meredith felt something of the old bond that had been between them as children, the old desperate need for love and understanding and belonging. Meredith was tired of being alone, tired of fighting by herself, and now, more than ever, she needed someone to tell her that everything would be all right, that Quinn would return to her. She and Lissa clasped each other, tears mixing with tears, fears with fears, uncertainty with uncertainty. But there was a certain strength, too, and hope. Meredith felt both flooding back into her, and she looked out over the river again, hearing the waves slapping against the bank.

Then she heard another sound, and tipped her head, trying to identify it. A boat moving through water. She silently motioned Lissa to the protection of a tree. Surely there would not be patrols in this kind of weather. The river was dangerous now, its current fierce with rainwater, visibility completely gone. Not even the most diligent searchers would risk the Mississippi in this weather.

Meredith saw the curve of the rowboat first. It was jerking back and forth, as if trying to escape the conflicting tugs of the current and the oars. Then she saw the oar as it came up, shakily, as if the one handling it was barely in control. The mist had settled around this person, but she could see another form slumped over. Then the boat swung toward the stream, again jerking back and forth as if it were all the rower could do to just keep it moving. One oar dropped, and the second figure seemed to bend forward, as if he could no longer manage one more sweep of the oars, one more tiny effort to bring the boat safely in.

Without knowing why, Meredith scrambled down. She would be endangering them all if the boat's occupants were enemies, yet something compelled her to go to them. The boat was bumping against the shore, right where the stream emptied into the river, and Meredith slid down the mudbank and grabbed the front of the boat, just as it seemed to be slipping back into the river. She pulled the boat's rope, and realized other hands were now helping her. Lissa's. Together they tugged the boat upstream, both of them slipping repeatedly into the water until they found a bank they could climb. Lissa wrapped the rope around a tree while Meredith looked in the boat. There were two men, both of them slumped over. She touched the first and felt the icy black skin. She didn't have to look at the face to know it was Cam. She moved quickly to the second man. Quinn! He wore only black trousers and a once-white shirt now cut in a dozen places. His breathing was harsh and his skin as cold as Cam's.

"Go get Mr. Butler," she told Lissa. "Tell him Captain Quinn and Cam are here. Bring blankets. As many as possible."

Meredith touched Quinn's face, and his eyes fluttered open for a second, then closed again. She took off her cape—at least the top of it was dry—and put it over his shoulders. Cam, she noted, had an oilcloth wrapped around him. Quinn's hands were still clutching the oars, and she gently pulled them away, rubbing them to try to restore warmth. Dear God, but he was cold. And then she saw the cuts on his chest, ugly slashes where the shirt parted. Her hands kept working on his hands; they were deathly white and still, when usually they were so strong and sure.

It seemed like a lifetime before she heard voices and saw Mr. Butler appear with Lissa. He took one look at the two men and issued quick orders. "I'll take the larger one. You two try to take Captain Quinn."

All three pulled Cam from the boat, and then Quinn. Butler raised Quinn to his feet and placed the captain's arms around the women, watching as they staggered under his weight before moving slowly forward. He then leaned down over Cam, trying to wake him. He slapped Cam's face twice, and finally Cam's eyes moved slightly and focused accusingly on his rescuer.

"You have to help me," Butler said to Cam, and he saw some awareness spark in the dark eyes. When he reached down, the help was there. The huge black man awkwardly rose with his help and, leaning on him, stumbled toward the cabin where warmth and safety waited.

Strengthened by desperation, Meredith and Lissa got Quinn inside the cabin. They laid him down on one of the beds, and Meredith, terribly aware of the way his whole body shivered, quickly started to undress him, wincing as she saw the many bruises and cuts on his body. She was grateful none of them were bleeding for she had no bandages, no medicine. She carefully and gently wrapped him in blankets provided by Lissa. "Start a fire," she told Lissa.

Wordlessly, Lissa nodded. She knew, as Meredith knew, a fire was dangerous but they had no choice. Both Quinn and Cam could die of exposure if they weren't warmed quickly.

The door slammed open again, and the carriage owner and Cam staggered into the room, shaking water over the floor. Cam was helped to the other bed, and Butler, as Meredith had done, quickly stripped Cam of his soddened clothes, rubbing his legs and arms and layering blankets over him.

Meredith could hear the spit and crackle of logs catching fire, and willed the flames to hurry. Quinn was so cold. His lips were blue, his dark hair icy. The tremors continued, and his eyes remained closed, as if he had used every ounce of strength to bring the boat to them. Her hands felt the cuts under the blanket and she winced with the number of them. He obviously had been tortured.

"This man's been shot," Mr. Butler said of Cam, and she reluctantly left Quinn to go to his friend. She saw the bullet holes at the front and back of the leg.

"You go back over to Mr. Quinn," Lissa said, still uneasy with using Quinn's given name. "I can take care of this one." She gently steered Meredith back to Quinn's side and knelt beside Cam, her fingers gently probing around the wound.

Meredith didn't know how long she stayed next to Quinn, massaging his hands, his legs and arms, reaching down to kiss the cold lips and finally flinging herself next to him, to give him her heat, her strength, her life.

He moved restlessly, his eyes opening and yet they were blank. "Terrence," he cried. "Terrence." His fingers bunched in tight fists and he struck out, hitting her. "Not again," he screamed. "Not again."

Her hands moved along his skin, trying to soothe, to comfort, yet he kept striking out. "The bastards," he screamed. "It was me, not him, not Terrence. Kill *me*, damn you. Kill *me*."

There was such torment in his voice that Meredith couldn't keep shivers of her own from traveling up and down her spine. She caught his flailing hands and held them tight, kissing each finger, and then the palms of his hands. But her comfort went unacknowledged. Instead, Quinn's mouth twisted in despair, and his eyes looked as if they had seen every horror in hell. "No," he screamed, and the noise echoed through the small cabin, the terrible denial behind the word hovering in the air.

"Quinn," she whispered, trying to break through the terror trapping him. "It's all right, Quinn. Cam's all right. We're safe, love."

"Safe?" Somehow, he had heard the word. "No one's safe around me. No one. Meredith. Merry. Pretty brave Merry. I'll kill her too." The words faded into a sob, and Meredith thought she had never heard such defeated anguish in a voice. Her heart shattered, pierced by the thousand shards of agony in his voice, in his life and his world. How well he had protected her from them. How well he had protected himself from her.

She looked up at Lissa and saw the unspoken helpless sympathy in her sister's eyes.

Meredith looked back at Quinn's glazed eyes, at the lines around his eyes and mouth, at the lips twisted with grief, and thought of the cool arrogant man with whom she'd first matched wits. She wondered whether she had ever really known him at all. She leaned down and kissed him, and put her head next to his cheek, wanting to share some of his pain, to absorb it so he wouldn't bear it alone. Slowly, he quieted, his hands stilling, his dark blue eyes losing that faraway look as dark lashes slowly, ever so slowly, once again curtained all the emotions he had so ably hidden all these years. Still she stroked his arms, unable to relinquish this brief hold on him.

"I love you," she whispered, knowing the words had a desperate quality. "I love you." And her own tears mixed with the tears that ran from the corner of one of his eyes.

By afternoon, it was obvious that Quinn was recovering. It was equally obvious that Cam was not.

Quinn had finally fallen into a deep healthy sleep, and the shivers that racked his body gradually receded. But Cam had become feverish and the wounds on his leg discolored.

Mr. Butler shook his head as Cam tossed restlessly, his body dripping sweat. Whenever Lissa wiped the perspiration from his body, he would start shivering again.

They kept him wrapped in blankets. Once the two men were warmed, and their clothes dried, it was deemed too dangerous to keep the fire going. It was, in fact, terribly perilous to stay where they were. Search parties would be combing the riverbanks before long, even in this weather.

As Quinn slept, Meredith, Lissa, and Butler discussed their options. Meredith felt Lissa and Cam were in the greatest danger. Between racking spasms, Cam had told them a little of what had happened. Meredith knew, that if captured, he would die for attacking white men. Only God knew what would happen to Lissa.

And Quinn? Meredith was sick inside with apprehension. Not only would he go to prison, but he would have to live with more guilt. And he was already consumed with it. She hadn't known that until now. She didn't know why or how, but she had seen the force of it, and it terrified her.

And she'd thought she knew him.

She leaned down and ran her hand along his cheek. Dear God, but she loved him. Her finger hovered at the lines around his eyes and moved slowly to the hair, crusty with dried muddy river water. She remembered that open friendly smile when he was a young man, and later that crooked sardonic grin when she met him again on the *Lucky Lady*. She couldn't even start to imagine all that had happened in between those two periods of time, or what additional secrets he withheld from her.

He looked so . . . vulnerable now. So tired. Fatigue had erased all the protective devices under which he hid so much of what was inside. But the raw naked pain, the loss of hope were visible now.

Something twisted and squirmed inside her, something as frightening as the specters that haunted him. The last words he had uttered—*I'll kill her too* . . . If he believed that, if he truly believed that, he would leave her. And if Cam died . . .

She heard a groan from the other bed and looked up.

"We must get him to a doctor," Butler said.

"But how?" Meredith's question was full of bitter despair. "All Cairo will be looking for them. And Lissa."

"The false front in the buggy. It will be tight, because both are big men, but I think we can get them in there. You and Miss Lissa can do as you'd planned, wear the widow's weeds. There's a small church where I can take you until nightfall when you can rejoin them at Miss Sophie's. She has ways of hiding people, but I can't take two widows there."

"I won't leave him," Meredith said, fearing that if she did she would never see him again.

"I can't take a widow to Miss Sophie's," Butler said stubbornly.

"Isn't there a backway?"

The man nodded slowly.

"If we're stopped, you can say you're taking us to the

hotel. You can then go to the back of . . . Miss Sophie's. It's raining. No one will notice us in dark clothes."

Butler thought about it. He didn't particularly like the idea of taking two women, obviously ladies, to Miss Sophie's. But it was clear that Meredith Seaton was going to get her way— one way or another.

He finally nodded and looked toward the two injured men. "We've got to get them up."

Meredith hated to wake Quinn but knew it was necessary. Her hand went to his shoulder and she shook him gently, watching as his eyes fluttered open, dazed at first from heavy sleep, then widening as he started to remember. He sat up abruptly. "Cam?"

"He's ill. Mr. Butler says we have to get him to Cairo, to a doctor."

Quinn's eyes went around the cabin and fastened on the figure on the other cot. He wrapped a blanket around his naked body and stood, moving quickly to Cam. His hand felt Cam's forehead, and he winced at the heat, his mouth tightening. He knelt beside the other man. "Cam?"

Cam's eyes opened, and he tried to smile but it was more a grimace.

"We have to go. Can you make it?"

Cam nodded.

"We'll get you a doctor. You'll be all right." There was a fierceness to Quinn's words. A quiet desperation.

Cam closed his eyes, as if the mere effort of nodding his head were too much.

Quinn dressed, slowly and painfully, in the buckskin trousers and shirt he had worn at Marshall Evans's plantation. He then helped Butler dress Cam. Butler and Quinn wrapped several blankets around Cam and half carried, half dragged him out to the buggy while Lissa and Meredith changed into the mourning clothes. When they were through, they went out to find Quinn squirming next to Cam into the tight space at the floor of the buggy. He barely fit.

As Butler placed a board over the opening, Meredith

recoiled, already feeling, in her mind, the bouncing of the buggy along the jutted road they would be taking. It would be nothing less than agony for both injured men.

Butler helped her and Lissa into the back of the buggy and spoke softly to the two horses. The carriage lurched over the muddy road, as rain continued to pelt the top of the rocking vehicle. Thinking of Quinn in the small box up front, Meredith was only slightly aware that Lissa had taken her black-gloved hand and was holding it tightly.

Quinn wondered how he could bear the tight closed space. It reminded him of the journey to Australia, of the endless black hours with only Terrence's gallows humor to remind him he was alive. His confinement now was as terrifying as the nightmares he'd endured the past few hours.

The discomfort was minor. It was the darkness and walls crowding around him that nearly paralyzed him. He heard Cam's rasping breath and tightened his hold on him. "Fight, Cam," he whispered. "For Daphne."

He felt the heat from Cam's body even through the blankets. Bloody hell. The anger, the rage that he had subdued these past years flared anew. And the grief. The deadening soul-wrenching grief. He thought of Meredith, part of him recalling the tender touch of her hand, the infinite gentleness of her fingers, the sweetness of her tears.

Why did he cause so much suffering? So much pain?

He'd had so much hope. He had almost believed his curse had ended, that he and Meredith could find that elusive rainbow he had been seeking, that he no longer brought death and destruction to everyone he touched.

All he had to do to know differently was to touch Cam, to listen to him try to breathe, to hear the low moan when the buggy stuck in the mud and lurched free with a hard jolt.

The only right thing to do now was to leave Meredith. She had Lissa. She would no longer be alone. She was strong and lovely and courageous, and she would find someone to marry, someone who wouldn't hurt her, someone who could protect her.

Something inside him started to crumble, to fall in so many pieces it could never be put back together. Terrible bitter loneliness took its place. He had said he would never allow anyone to get close to him again. He had betrayed that vow, and Cam was dying for it.

Another kind of darkness closed around him, sealing off emotions, his heart.

C*hapter 27*

THE HIDING PLACE at Sophie's was ingenious.

Meredith had been taken by tunnel to the small room beneath the stable. She could hear the hooves of restless horses above her.

There were two entrances, she was told. One was a trapdoor under the feet of one of the most spirited horses. Meredith now knew of the other.

Upon arrival at the backdoor of a large frame building, she had asked for Miss Sophie, giving the name of "Merry." In seconds she and Lissa had been whisked down to the wine cellar and eyed curiously by a tall striking-looking woman.

Meredith had told her that Quinn and Cam would soon be in the stable, and the woman instructed her and Lissa to stay where they were while she saw to the two men. She had been gone what seemed a very long time before reappearing, her mouth grim.

With few words, she explained that Cam and Quinn were safe in a secret room beneath the stable and that she had sent for a doctor who sometimes worked with the Underground Railroad.

"I want to go to Quinn," Meredith said.

"He believes you and Lissa will be better off upstairs." Sophie didn't say that Quinn ordered Meredith away from the room. Instead, she turned to Lissa carefully. "I have some dye I can use to make your hair red."

Meredith ignored the last comment. "I want to see him."

Sophie turned all her attention back to Meredith, studying her closely. The girl's jaw jutted forward, the eyes unyielding. Merry, whoever she was, wouldn't give up easily, and perhaps she was what Quinn needed. Sophie had never seen Quinn as he had been minutes earlier. He was even worse, if that was possible, than the time just before Christmas. He had been angry then. Now, he was more like a walking dead man. She slowly nodded.

"All right. But the other one goes with me. We need to do something about that hair."

Meredith looked at Lissa, who nodded and stood back.

Sophie went to a wall lined with wine casks. She leaned over and touched a place on the bottom of one of the casks, and it swung slowly away from the wall. Sophie touched another spot on the wall, and immediately a part of the wall opened, revealing a tunnel fortified by walls of wood.

Meredith was handed a candle and, after looking at Lissa for a minute, stooped and walked through the tunnel until she reached another wall, seemingly of solid brick. As she had been told, she pressed against the third brick on the left from the bottom, and part of the wall opened. She found herself in a small room with several cots, a stack of blankets, and a small table holding a pitcher and several cups.

Light came from three oil lamps, two on hooks protruding

from the wall, and the third on the table next to the cot.

Meredith looked again, finally finding Quinn. He was standing, leaning against the one dark corner of the room as if afraid of the light.

Meredith knew he had seen her. She heard his swift intake of breath.

"What are you doing here?" he said, his voice as cold as she had ever heard it.

"Cam?"

Quinn shrugged. "Sophie's sent for a doctor."

Meredith moved slowly to him. His eyes were unfathomable, all the light gone from them. The deep blue was almost black in the shadows.

He broke the silence. "Where's Lissa? Shouldn't you be with her?"

"Sophie's making her a redhead."

"I'm sorry you had to come here, to Sophie's," he said, his voice totally indifferent, as if he were a stranger.

"I'm not. Sophie's very nice."

"It's no place for a lady."

"I haven't been that in a long time."

His eyes sparked, then died. "Go away, Meredith."

"I won't make it that easy for you."

"I don't know what you mean."

"Don't you?"

He turned away from her and walked over to Cam, gazing down at him bleakly. Cam had lost consciousness shortly after they arrived. Something inside Quinn despaired at seeing a man that large in such a weak state.

"What about Daphne?" Meredith's question was unexpected, and Quinn turned around slowly, raising an eyebrow in question.

Meredith faced him directly, unyieldingly. "Don't you think she has a right to know?"

"To watch him die?"

"Damn you, Quinn, he isn't going to die."

"You know something no one else knows?"

"He's strong, Quinn."

"It just takes a strong man longer to die." His voice was flat, devoid of emotion.

"What happened to Terrence, Quinn?"

He looked at her this time.

"You mentioned him on the boat, and yesterday, when you were unconscious, you kept calling his name," she persisted.

"You don't want to know, Meredith. Believe me."

"You asked me to marry you!" Desperation made her plead.

"It was a bad idea."

"You think you're going to get rid of me that easily?"

"I'll see you and Lissa to Canada. Then I'll be going on alone."

"What happened to Terrence?" Terrence was the remaining piece of the puzzle. The most important piece. She knew that now.

He stared at her through those damned protective eyes. "Terrence is none of your business."

"Don't do this," she said, her voice breaking.

Raw pain flickered through his eyes before he hid it again and looked away.

The dismissal was absolute. Meredith knew with sick certainty she wouldn't get any further now. But he had conceded to take them to Canada. She would change his mind on the way. She had to.

Just then the door to the room opened, and a young man stepped through, a bag in his hand. He quickly looked around the room, then went to Cam. "What happened?" he asked tersely.

Quinn left Meredith and walked to his side. "A bullet wound, and then he was in the water for a long time. I'm afraid he might have pneumonia."

The man nodded, then focused all his concentration on the unconscious man as Quinn stood by helplessly.

Finally, he looked up at Quinn. "I think I can control the infection in his leg, but his lungs . . ."

Quinn's face didn't change at all as he heard what he had expected to hear. "Is there anything I can do?"

"Pray," the doctor said wearily. "Just pray."

And Meredith did, all the prayers she had learned at the convent. She prayed for all of them, for Quinn as much as Cam because she feared he would die if Cam did. Perhaps not in body, but in soul. She knew she prayed alone. Quinn remained at Cam's side as the doctor worked. It was, Meredith thought, as if she no longer existed for him. But as she had told him earlier, he wasn't going to get rid of her easily.

Sometime later, Meredith heard the door open once more and Sophie stood there, her eyes questioning as they went from Quinn to Cam to the doctor to Meredith. Then she nodded to Meredith to follow her out the door where they stood hunched over in the tunnel.

"No change with Cam?"

"No," Meredith said in a low aching voice.

"And Quinn?"

Meredith shook her head and there was a silence, one that Meredith appreciated. She didn't think she could stand platitudes at the moment. Or reassurances. "How long have you known him?" she asked suddenly.

"I don't know if anyone really knows him," Sophie said. "I met him four years ago when someone who was supposed to pick up a shipment didn't appear. He had been given my name as an alternative."

Meredith looked up, her face creased with despair. "He asked me to marry him."

"And . . ."

"And now he just wants to hide again . . . like he's been hiding . . . from feeling anything."

"But you won't let him." Sophie's voice was so sure that Meredith couldn't stop a whisper of a smile.

"If Cam dies..."

"Dr. Smythe won't let him die. He takes death as a personal insult."

"Why do you...?"

It was a question she had wanted to ask since she and Lissa appeared at the backdoor. Meredith had been amazed at how efficiently they had been handled. Orders had been quickly given and immediately obeyed as she and Lissa had been whisked downstairs. It was clear that unexpected visitors were not unusual.

Sophie shrugged. It was obvious she wasn't going to answer the obvious question, why she was involved in the Underground Railroad.

Meredith knew she had no right to ask, to persist. So she went to another question. "Is there any news?"

"The town's being turned upside down by bounty hunters and the sheriff's men. They've closed every road, and they're searching every boat. They even came searching here, but a bottle of good whiskey dulled their efforts."

Meredith's eyes widened. "Lissa?"

"They didn't get that far," Sophie said with amusement. "And she's a redhead now. No one would recognize her from the broadsides they showed me."

"The *Lucky Lady*?"

"Damaged some, but fixable," Sophie said. After an extensive search, she related, the boat had been allowed to leave for New Orleans, and repairs. Jamison had convinced the law that he knew nothing of the captain's nefarious activities.

"Aren't we dangerous to you?" Meredith finally asked Sophie.

Sophie shrugged. "No one will ever find the secret room. And you, are you making any headway with our stubborn captain?"

"He doesn't want me," Meredith stated frankly.

"Oh, I think he does. Give him time," Sophie advised softly before turning away so Meredith couldn't see the doubt in her own face.

But time didn't seem to help. Cam wavered between life and death for several days. She and Lissa nursed him when the doctor wasn't there. Meredith knew that Quinn had refused to let the doctor tend his own injuries, and she had insisted that she do it herself. He allowed it indifferently, never flinching as alcohol cleaned the cuts around his throat and chest. His eyes were clear and cold, and his mouth set in the arrogant half-smile she had seen on his face months earlier. She had learned to distrust that smile.

His manner was as distant as if he inhabited another world and looked upon the residents of this one with bemusement. Only once, when Meredith turned suddenly, did she see the raw agony in his eyes before he was able to push it back somewhere in his soul.

He appeared relaxed, his body folding easily in a corner of the room. But Meredith knew his background well enough now to realize what hell it must be for him to be confined in the small room. It was a measure of his enormous self-discipline that he did not prowl it like a caged animal.

The tension, however, was palpable. She could feel it sizzling in the room, alive and dangerous and begging to be released.

Meredith thought about ways to bring down the walls he had so securely reconstructed around himself. Blowing a trumpet, she noted wryly, would not be a wise move at this point. So she plotted an entire military campaign, complete with retreat, advances, and flanking movements.

The retreat maneuver started when she seemed to accept his decision.

"I'm going back," she announced one morning.

"Back where?" Quinn narrowed his eyes.

"To Vicksburg. I'm going to keep working with the Underground Railroad."

"To hell you are!"

She shrugged. "You said you're going on alone. If you're going your own way, then I'm going mine. I might even marry Gil. No one would suspect *his* wife."

"What about Lissa?" The question sounded strangled.

"Oh, I'll go with you to Canada and see her settled with enough money to keep her comfortable. Then I'm going back home."

"Bloody hell you are!"

Time for the flanking movement. "You've already said that," she observed tranquilly. "You have to do what you have to do. Well, so do I. I never should have agreed to go West with you. People need me."

I need you. The words hovered unspoken in his mind. He was leaning against the wall, his hands pressed behind him. His fingers dug into the rough wood as he sought to restrain perilous words from spurting out, like lava from an exploding volcano.

"It's too dangerous now," he said, forcing calm reason into his voice.

"Why? No one's seen me. They've only seen a black groom. No one can connect me with Lissa's escape; no one knows she's my sister, and the Meriweathers will say I've been with them or visited other friends."

She was right, damn it. They had been bloody careful about protecting her. Too bloody careful, he realized now. He couldn't stand the thought of her going back into danger. She had been lucky thus far. He knew luck eventually ran out. He had only to turn toward Cam for evidence.

He looked down at Cam's restless tossing figure. "Isn't this enough?"

"Nothing is ever enough if you want something . . . really want it."

"You don't know what you're talking about," Quinn said roughly, angrily.

"Then tell me," she challenged, now attacking. "Tell me why you're so afraid to live."

"All right," he retorted fiercely. "You want to hear. I'll tell you. You asked about Terrence. I'll tell you about Terrence. He was the best friend I ever had. He never gave up. Never. We would escape someday, he was sure. And he made me sure of it.

"But there was a guard who developed a particular dislike for me. God knew it was easy for him to express it. There were rules against everything. Talking between prisoners. A look deemed disrespectful, a moment's pause in cutting trees or hauling logs. The British had some rather creative punishments, including a pit filled with water. They would lower you into it and leave you there for days. If you went to sleep, you drowned. After one stay there, I was weak and stumbled as we were hauling logs. The guard started beating me with a club, and Terrence went after him. He accidentally killed the man.

"It didn't matter that it was accidental. Terrence was accused of murder and sentenced to die. They whipped him to death. Every morning for three days, they dragged him to the post while all of us were forced to watch. Every morning they gave him one hundred lashes and dragged him into a dark cell where his wounds festered, only to be opened the next morning. He died on the third day."

"Dear God," Meredith whispered.

"I decided then, sweet Meredith," he said cruelly, "that there was no God."

"Oh, Quinn . . ." It was all she could manage at the moment. The horror was too great, the hell in his eyes too vivid.

"But you haven't heard it all, Meredith," he continued tonelessly. "I wanted to die then, but something, perhaps it was Terrence's last words, wouldn't let me. I lived for him, to escape as he had planned all those years. And I did, with the help of my family who had sent a detective to find me. He had sent a letter back saying that he had located me, and would soon be able to help me escape. My father and oldest brother stayed in New Orleans, even after a smallpox epidemic broke out. They sent Brett upriver. But they wanted to be there to welcome me home, and they caught the sickness. They both died a week before I arrived in New Orleans. Like Terrence, they died for me. Like Cam almost did.'' He allowed the words to soak in, to penetrate every pore of her body, every corner of her soul.

He looked at her stricken face and ached to hold her, but the telling had frozen him. His mouth curled on one side. "I won't let you be my next victim, Meredith."

"And I'm not already?" she asked softly. "You've already taken my heart. There's little left in this body without it."

Her words were like a dagger to his heart. His hand started to reach out, then dropped hopelessly. "I'll not risk it," he said simply.

"Damn you," she said suddenly, and the emphatic tone of her voice made his eyes return to hers. "You have no right," she said, "to make decisions for others."

"I have every bloody right," he roared, all his rage and despair bottled up in the words.

"You're a bloody ass," she said unexpectedly, unconsciously taking on his own oath. She groped for the panel in the wall, not wanting him to see the tears that were beginning to form in her eyes. She stepped through the opening, then slammed the door behind her, leaving him staring at the wall in stunned amazement.

"You *are* a bloody ass," came a croaking sound from the cot where Cam lay, and Quinn spun around to see Cam trying to rise, his body, for the first time in days, free of sweat.

"Don't interfere, Cam," Quinn warned, although his voice was not quite as cold as he would have wished. He was, in fact, damned pleased to see the impertinence in Cam's eyes.

"Daphne?"

"I didn't . . . think we should tell her until we knew . . ."

"She had the right, Capt'n." A long exhausted sigh came from deep within him. "You can't protect everybody, not when they don't want to be protected."

"You . . . heard."

"Enough. I made my own decision, Capt'n, to come after you. You didn't. In fact, you ordered me not to."

Quinn's eyes hardened. "Not very good at following instructions, are you?"

"No. Don't suppose I ever will be. That's part of bein' free. That's what you gave me. Don't complain about it now."

"Damn your hide."

"Don't let her go, Capt'n."

The plea surprised Quinn. They had always kept out of each other's personal lives. He looked at Cam, and something in him lightened. Cam would live. Perhaps, just perhaps, the curse was broken. But he recalled Terrence's broken body again. If anything happened to Meredith . . .

Cam saw the hope flare in Quinn's eyes, then die. He turned over, and closed his own eyes, but not before he had the last words. "Damn fool."

Daphne came that afternoon.

Meredith opened the door to the room, and Daphne emerged from the tunnel to go to Cam's side. Quinn, sitting at a small table, a book in his hand, turned away from the reunited lovers. His jaw set and a muscle worked determinedly in his cheek.

But Meredith watched Cam and Daphne with unashamed longing.

Daphne knelt beside Cam, her small slender form delicate beside his large one, and as their hands met, Meredith thought she had never seen anything quite as tender, as loving. She wondered that so much love could be expressed with only a touch, a look.

Meredith's heart was already aching, but she felt a new stab of sharp agonizing pain when she looked over at Quinn. With a set face, he studied a spider making a web in a corner.

She went over to him, placing a hand on the sleeve of a clean white shirt Sophie had found for him. "Come out to the tunnel with me," she said.

He started to refuse.

"Please, Quinn. Give them some privacy."

Quinn turned and looked at the two. They were oblivious to anyone else, but he knew he had to leave, for his own sake if not theirs. Being near the couple in love was too damned painful to bear. He nodded, following Meredith out the paneled door, closing it slightly, but leaving enough light so that they could see.

"Quinn." The word was part love song, part plea.

It was too much for Quinn. With a groan, he bent his head, his lips ravaging hers in savage hunger and desperation.

Her lips opened to his, as rapacious as his own. Her whole body strained toward his in a frantic effort to convince him they belonged together. As Cam and Daphne belonged together. They had strength together, not weakness.

Her heart was pounding as never before, and her tongue reached into his mouth, seducing him until she could hear the moan start low in his throat, and feel the heat of his manhood as his body became taut against hers.

His lips, his hungry eager lips, moved from her mouth to her neck, then up her cheek. Like burning firebrands, they left trails of flame along their path until Meredith thought she would be consumed in their racing fury.

Then his arms were around her, holding her tightly against him as if his life depended on the sureness of his embrace. "Dear God, Meredith," he whispered. And where his lips had been rough and angry, they now turned sweet and wistful as they explored once more every curve of her face and neck. Meredith could feel him tremble, and her soul and body ached with need as she felt the war within him.

She looked up to eyes churning with ferocious desire.

"I'm not going to let you go," she whispered. "I won't ever let you go."

His eyes closed, and there was another moan, this time not of lust, but of pure animal pain. He jerked her away from his embrace and whirled around, disappearing back into the secret room, leaving her stunned and alone in the dark tunnel.

Chapter 28

DAPHNE STAYED by Cam's side for the next two days, which made the small room immensely suffocating for Quinn. Love and tenderness were palpable, filling the room until there seemed no escape for him. Sweet and gentle words were whispered softly, yet he could hear every one, and each was like a nail being pounded into his heart.

He brooded. Although he was happy for Cam and vastly relieved at his recovery, it was all he could do to see a kiss exchanged and not smash everything within reach. Every once in a while, he caught himself holding his hands tightly together so he wouldn't do just that.

Meredith had not returned to the room since she left two days earlier, and everything in him ached for even a brief glimpse of her. He saw Daphne and Cam clutch each other's hands, and his soul yearned to touch a lock of golden hair, or soft cheeks, or a kiss-swollen mouth.

He took to pacing the small room, wishing heartily that he could leave, but he had already put Sophie in too much danger. His face was well known in Cairo, and now there was a large reward for his capture, according to Sophie.

Quinn thought he had learned to curb his impatience, his restlessness, in prison. But he now realized that the discipline he'd exercised during his last years in Australia had not come from self-will but complete and utter exhaustion. They had been worked close to death. Now he wished for the pickax he had once so hated. He itched for anything to grab, other than images of Meredith. Beautiful Meredith.

Sophie had supplied him with books, but his eyes couldn't, wouldn't, concentrate on the print. How could they, when every moment he waited for the panel of the wall to open, to look up and see her standing there?

How could he spend the rest of his life without her? Only when he'd met Meredith had he realized how empty his life had been, how he had deadened all his emotions, how black and white and without color everything had been. She had made the world alive again, alive and vibrant and beautiful, and now, in this room, the colors were once more fading.

A day later, the doctor declared Cam strong enough to move, and plans were made. Cairo, according to Sophie, was locked up tight. Patrols, both official and unofficial, were on every road. Every boat, no matter how small, was searched ruthlessly.

The rewards of five thousand dollars, posted by Marshall Evans for both Lissa and Quinn, and a smaller amount for Cam, drove the stakes high, and bounty hunters from several states had come to the small river town.

Quinn intended to see Lissa and Meredith safe in Canada before he headed West. He worried that his presence would endanger them further, but he could no more leave without knowing they were far from harm than he could cut off his right leg. He had to take the two women there himself. He wouldn't admit that perhaps it was more than assurance he needed, that he couldn't yet bear to leave Meredith. Instead he told himself that he simply owed it to her to see that Lissa was free at last. He had given his word.

Slowly, he pieced together a plan. He told Sophie about his other Cairo Underground contact—Davis, the cabinetmaker who had sold him Meredith's paintings. Quinn outlined specifically what was required and gave her a detailed sketch for Davis. His scheme was, he believed, the only way to leave Cairo.

And he haltingly asked about Meredith. The words popped from his mouth without conscious thought; against, in fact, such thought.

Sophie peered at him with disgust. "She looks about as bad as you do," she observed bitingly, not adding that she had been the one to advise Meredith to stay away. Absence, she had told Meredith, sometimes does wondrous things, like make a man realize exactly how much he might miss the woman he loves. After looking at Quinn's haggard face, Sophie decided her ploy was working well enough. She even felt a tug of sympathy for the stubborn gambler, whose usually detached arrogance was, at the moment, lying in tatters on the dirt floor.

"If Davis can finish in time," he said after a moment of digesting her comment, "we will leave day after tomorrow. Can you make arrangements for passage?"

"Of course," she said, shuddering. "But are you sure you want to do this? It'll be even worse than the buggy."

He grinned suddenly, the old Quinn Devereux smile, full of mockery and black devilish charm. "From your face, I think you believe I'll deserve every minute of it."

"Ah, you read me well, Captain," she said, affection in her voice. "But then I never thought you a fool." She paused, before adding, "Nor a coward at heart."

He stiffened, the smile fading from his face. "Don't interfere, Sophie," he said curtly. "You don't know anything about it."

"But I do," she said, and saw a muscle throb angrily in his cheek. "She didn't tell me," Sophie said. "She didn't have to."

"Then . . ."

"We are a little alike, you and I," Sophie said. "We keep running from people, from attachments. I know why I do it. I think I know why you do. At least some of the reasons." She paused again. "You say it's for her sake, but I don't think it is. It's for your own. Otherwise you would let her make her own choice."

Sophie started to walk away, then turned back. "I've adapted to loneliness, Quinn, but you don't have to. Meredith loves you. And you love her. Don't ruin her life because of some noble idea you have of saving her from yourself. Because it's not noble, it's only selfish and cowardly."

She left the room, leaving Quinn standing in stunned silence.

"She's right," Cam agreed, his voice a low rumble.

Quinn spun around, glaring. "You almost died because of me."

"You also made sure I stayed alive," Cam said calmly. "It couldn't have been easy holding on to me in that river."

"It's not over yet." The retort was full of anger, but Quinn immediately regretted it as he saw Daphne's face pale.

"And when will it be?" Cam asked softly. "You can't take responsibility for everyone, forever."

Quinn's mouth tightened. "I'm not doing that, damn it."

"Aren't you?" Cam whispered softly. "I went after you for myself, not you. I heard what you told Meredith. I suspect that your friend also acted for himself. You can't control other people. And you damn well can't order what's right for them."

Quinn glared at him. Every one of his goddamned friends, including a madam and the man he thought as hardened as himself, had turned into preachers.

Bemused and thoughtful, he returned to his book. He had been reading it for two days and he still hadn't got beyond the first paragraph. He doubted he would progress much further today.

The coffins arrived late the next day. The buggy carrying them came inside the stable, and the doors of the building were locked. After the horse was taken from the stall with the trapdoor, Quinn climbed up to inspect the two wooden boxes.

Mr. Davis's fine craftsmanship was not readily evident. There were decided splits in the wood, cleverly designed to allow a sufficient flow of air. But only the closest inspection would indicate they were not the result of clumsy work.

The coffins were also a bit larger than usual, but few would notice that. The extra room was for several bladders of water and some biscuits. There would be precious little space for movement.

Remembering the panic he had felt in Butler's small buggy compartment, Quinn looked uneasily at the coffin. This trip would be worse, much worse, for he would be alone. But there was no help for it.

Sophie had made shipping arrangements for the coffins, the grieving family, and a maid with a packet-owner who was active in the Underground Railroad. Once past the inspections, they would be dropped off at a small farming community where the local minister was a member of the Underground. From there they would be directed from one station to another through Indiana to Oberlin, Ohio, and then across Lake Erie to Canada.

Satisfied that everything was in order, Quinn lowered himself to the secret room, closing the door after him. He knew straw would be thrown over the stable floor and the horse installed once more. In minutes, there would be nothing to indicate the haven beneath.

Quinn now told Cam of the plan; he'd been hesitant to do so until all the requirements had been taken care of. Once out of Cairo, he said, Cam and Daphne might wish to separate from the others. Although there was a small reward for Cam, it wasn't enough to keep bounty hunters on his trail. Authorities apparently believed that Cam was only following Quinn's orders, and Quinn was the one they really wanted.

"No," Cam said flatly. "We go with you."

Quinn turned to Daphne, and she nodded, her fingers tightly braided through Cam's.

Quinn nodded curtly. He still couldn't shake the belief that he was bad luck. But he also knew that he couldn't dissuade Cam, not if Cam was determined.

When the door to the secret room opened that night, Meredith appeared, laden with food. Lissa followed, her eyes cautiously moving from Quinn to Meredith and back again. But Quinn's glance went quickly to Meredith. Her eyes were a little too bright, her mouth a little too anxious, and Quinn's insides twisted. The journey to freedom would be very dangerous, and he wanted to soothe her, to take her in his arms and hold her closely. When he saw her swallow with uncertainty, he took the tray from her hands and placed it on the table. Then he held out his arms and she walked into them.

Home. This was home, Meredith thought as she closed her eyes and reveled in the feeling of belonging, of protection, of love. Home was wherever Quinn was, wherever he opened his arms and heart and welcomed her inside. She would not worry about tomorrow. Tomorrow would work itself out.

They had a quiet thoughtful meal. Lissa felt a little like an outsider, but Meredith had insisted that she eat with them. Lissa was one of them. They would be together for the next several weeks, and this was the beginning, the first step of many. But when they had finished, Meredith's sister quickly excused herself, pleading exhaustion.

Quinn watched her leave. Sophie had dyed Lissa's hair to an auburn color, and Lissa and Meredith looked more like sisters than ever. Lissa was a beautiful woman, poised, but with a haunting poignant quality that made a man want to protect her. Meredith, on the other hand, was stubbornly determined and reckless, her golden eyes challenging and direct, her mouth sometimes teasing, sometimes inviting.

But he didn't draw back when she leaned into him, her hands running up and down one of his arms triggering all the urges and sensations he'd been trying so hard to contain. He thought of the coffin overhead and tomorrow, but that only aggravated his need.

There was, however, no privacy with Cam and Daphne in the same room, and he was half relieved, half agonized. Quinn didn't know how long Meredith stayed in his arms but finally her breathing became soft and relaxed and he knew she had fallen asleep. He lowered Meredith on the cot and lay next to her, enclosing her in his arms possessively, and he knew Cam had done the same with Daphne. For the moment, it was enough.

For tonight, it was everything.

Quinn wondered if there could ever be an experience as soul-searing as hearing the lid of your own coffin nailed shut.

He had tried to prepare his mind, but he kept remembering the other tight places he had been in: the hold of the ship, the waterpit at Norfolk, all the torturous confining places.

Each strike of the hammer was another memory, and he had to force himself not to pound at the lid and demand to be released. This was the only way out of Cairo, he kept telling himself. There was no other option.

He had learned, through Sophie's spy system, that searchers were routinely opening crates and barrels. He was gambling that superstition and fear would prevent them from doing the same with coffins. He also hoped that no one would suspect two grieving sisters, one of whom was blond and the other redheaded. Lissa had said that Marshall Evans was unaware that she had relatives, and Meredith had been disguised beyond recognition at the Evans farm.

The plan was as foolproof as he could make it. But still he touched the pistol that Sophie had given him. Cam had a similar one in his grasp.

But bloody hell, the next hours were going to be misery.

The hammering stopped, and he now felt completely encased although he knew he could probably break free. Most of the nails were only heads glued to the wood. Only six, just enough to prevent the coffin from accidentally falling apart, kept the lid on.

He felt the coffin being lifted and settled on the buggy that would take them to the docks. He jiggled and lurched with each movement of the seemingly endless ride. The buggy finally came to a stop, and he braced himself as the coffin was lifted again, this time by hands obviously unaware of its living contents. He tried to steady himself, but he felt battered by the time the coffin was laid down once more. Still he felt a certain satisfaction, knowing he was finally on the boat. He heard voices, rough angry voices, and then there was silence.

Quinn tried to calm his fiercely beating heart. Close your eyes, he told himself, for to keep them open was to see darkness he couldn't control. By closing them, oddly enough, he felt he did have some control. He waited for the nightmares to close in on him—but they didn't. Instead he saw Meredith: as a child happily soaring toward the sky on his swing, and then as a giggly woman with the hideous hair on the *Lucky Lady*. There was Meredith framed by the rainbow, and Meredith's suspicious but passion-filled eyes when they first kissed. And then there was Meredith aboard the *Ohio Star*, her gold hair flowing over the pillow and her arms raised up to him.

He felt movement again—the boat was leaving the docks. They had made it!

Quinn smiled to himself. He had known Meredith would convince everyone that their elaborate charade was real. She could do anything, be anyone. Ninny, lady, groom, artist, widow. Lover.

Lover.

How good she had felt in his arms last night. How very, very good. And right. The images kept flitting through his mind, eclipsing the dark ones that had been with him so long. With something close to astonishment, he discovered that the bright happy memories had washed his mind of the bitter ones.

"They've had to slip by you," Ted Carroll blustered angrily.

The sheriff looked at the Carroll brothers with distinct unfriendliness. He'd had just about enough of them, of their damned demands and threats.

"I've done my duty, damn it," he said. "I've searched every last bundle that's gone through Cairo, and it's been a waste of time. I'm not going to hold up any more river traffic on your account."

"It's your job to catch runaways and thieves."

"And I've done my best. They probably drowned in the river. You said you thought one of them was injured."

"Then where's the girl?"

The sheriff shrugged. "I'll be damned if I'm going to spend any more time helping you get blood money."

Ted Carroll, his right hand swathed in bandages, looked at one of the deputies. "You sure you searched everything?"

The sheriff turned toward his men. They nodded. One of them added for emphasis, "Every damned bag and box 'cepting some coffins."

"Coffins?" the sheriff repeated.

"Well, the widow said her husband and father died of fever. I sure as hell wasn't going to open those damn things. There's been cholera downriver."

"Widow? What did she look like?" Ted Carroll asked.

"Nothing like your description. Blond, she was. And her sister was redheaded."

"Where were they going?"

"They said a small landing 'bout fifty miles from here, then up to Indianapolis for burial."

"You fool," John Carroll said. "You ever hear of taking a body all that way for burial?"

The deputy drew himself up tall. "If it were my daddy or wife, I sure would."

The sheriff gave the deputy a disgusted look. "And I suppose the widow was pretty."

The deputy's sheepish expression answered the question. But still he protested. "She didn't look nothin' like you said. The description said black hair."

"You ever heard of dye?" John Carroll asked.

"But they wuz sisters," the man defended himself. "You didn't say nothin' 'bout sisters."

"The women could be with the Underground Railroad," Ted Carroll wondered aloud. "The girl and Devereux could have been in the coffins."

"You're just reaching for straws," the sheriff said. "Now git the hell out of here."

The Carrolls looked at each other. They were uncanny at ferreting out runaways. They both had a sixth sense about them, and now they knew how their quarry had fled. And where.

John nodded wordlessly to Ted, and they left the sheriff's office, heading toward the stable. "I'll bet my last dollar they're headed for Canada," Ted said.

"Lake Erie!"

"And Oberlin, I'd wager. It's a hotbed of damned slave lovers."

"If we can ambush them . . ."

Ted looked down at his hand. "The reward for Devereux is dead or alive."

"And then there's the woman."

"Ten thousand dollars." Ted grinned. "No split either."

"And goddamned satisfaction," John added.

They nearly ran to the livery stable for their horses.

•   •   •

Quinn was bumped and bruised as his coffin was moved, heaved, and bounced. He didn't know how long he had been entombed in the damned thing when a tool wedged in a crack and the lid was pried open. He sat up, his eyes slowly adjusting to the light, and saw Cam doing the same in the coffin next to him. The three women—Meredith and Lissa, both still dressed in black, and Daphne in servant's clothes—were looking on anxiously.

A man in black stood over him, a smile on his weathered face. "I've been doing the Lord's work nearly thirty years but this is the first time I've raised the dead," he said with a chuckle.

Quinn tried to move, but his legs were cramped. Meredith leaned over and started rubbing them, and Daphne did the same for Cam. Within minutes, Quinn's limbs were feeling alive again, more than alive, as splinters of heat ran up and down where Meredith's fingers touched.

"I don't like to rush you," the man in black said, "but I think it would be wise for you to be on your way as quickly as possible. We've already heard about the search in Cairo, and inquiries have been made here. My son will take you to the next station."

Quinn nodded. "Thank you."

"It's I who should be thanking you. A message arrived from Cairo yesterday from the Underground Railroad telling me to expect you. I've heard whispers about the man on the river, and what fine work you've done."

Quinn flushed. "No more than others." He felt distinctly awkward under praise he didn't want or feel he deserved.

The preacher merely nodded. Quinn looked around. They were behind a small church, amid a clump of trees next to a small cemetery. The coffins, he expected, would be buried there. Once he stood, the preacher ushered them into a house adjoining the church, and led them to a table loaded with food. "While I summon my son, please eat."

Quinn needed no urging. Although he'd had both food

and water in the coffin, he'd taken neither, afraid of a subsequent bodily function.

Within an hour, the preacher reappeared with a young man of seventeen or eighteen. Each member of the fleeing party was given a pack containing two blankets, biscuits, cheese, dried beef, and a canteen. Quinn, who had borrowed money from Sophie after discovering his own cash had been destroyed in the river, asked about horses. The minister shook his head. There was only his own mount, which he needed for calls, and no one else in the vicinity had extra animals. The purchase of five horses would also be suspicious, he said. Perhaps as they traveled north they could purchase one at a time. Quinn winced. It had been a long time since he'd traveled far on foot. But then he looked at Meredith, and decided the longer journey would be worth it. He would be with her. Until Canada.

By the end of the third day, they all had blisters on their feet. They had passed from one conductor to another, from one hidden place to the next. The sheriff in Cairo had evidently telegraphed descriptions of Quinn, Lissa, and Cam throughout several states, and their guides said they were being sought by both law officers and bounty hunters. They traveled mostly by night, sleeping during the day. One day was spent resting in the woods but they were sheltered on the other two occasions at stations of the Underground Railroad. In one home, they were led up to an attic; in the other, to a strawstack that hid a shelter walled up with rails. On the fourth day, they were able to buy two horses, and the women rode, Meredith and Lissa on one mount, and Daphne on the other.

The trek to Oberlin was nearly four hundred miles, and when they rested, Meredith was often too tired to do more than collapse in Quinn's arms. Quinn would hold her tight, pushing back wayward curls that escaped from the long braid she had started to wear. It was, she said, the only way to keep her hair out of her face and out of the briers and twigs.

Each day, she looked more beautiful to Quinn, although

her black dress and cloak were dingy and torn. Each day, as they started again, her back was straight and her chin up, her eyes bright with adventure and warm with love, and he wondered how he ever thought her plain. Or how he could let her go.

Meredith didn't want the journey to end. As tired and sore as her body was, she relished each day's respite when Quinn pulled her into his arms—even though she knew he did it reluctantly, even bitterly because he could not control himself into doing otherwise.

Although his eyes settled on her with pride and approval, she knew he had not changed his mind about their future.

Since Cam's recent injury, Quinn had held part of himself back. The wall she had always sensed in him until that last night aboard the *Ohio Star* had been reconstructed and even fortified. Every once in a while, when he didn't realize her eyes were on him, she saw a terrible sadness in his face and she knew he still intended to leave her. For her sake.

It was such a terrible irony, she thought. He didn't realize he would be killing her in quite a different way than would a gun or knife or any other instrument of death. A broken body was no worse than a shattered heart.

She would convince him of that. She must!

Tomorrow or the next day, or the next.

She must!

Chapter 29

JOHN AND TED CARROLL rode into Oberlin and took a room in a boardinghouse overlooking the main street. They told the proprietor they were heading west, and had stopped to get some rest before continuing.

Oberlin, they knew, was a hotbed of abolitionists. They had heard all the stories. How, when a fugitive slave was seized just outside the town, hundreds of its citizens had followed him and his captors, and freed him. The whole town was, in effect, a station of the Underground Railroad.

That meant, the Carrolls hoped, that Devereux and his party would feel safe enough to come into town openly, or that there would be some word or whisper of the fugitives. They could then follow Devereux and ambush him on his way to Lake Erie.

Ted's hand still pained him, and each time he tried unsuccessfully to use it, he cursed Devereux and the damned black man. He wondered if he would ever be able to fully use his hand again. The doctor who bandaged it had given him no guarantees.

But he could still balance a rifle on that arm. And in an ambush, he and John would have the advantage even with his game hand. Devereux owed him. Devereux owed him a great deal.

Two days went by, and they heard nothing, saw nothing suspicious. The town seemed peaceful enough, but the people were noticeably reticent. All attempts to draw any of them out, including a jocular storekeeper, came to naught.

Ted had tried to ingratiate himself, saying he and his brother might join John Brown's efforts to keep Kansas free of slavery. It was a tactic he devised after learning John Brown's father was a trustee of Oberlin College. But his overture met with silence and seeming indifference, as if everyone knew who he really was. After three more days, he was convinced something was wrong. Very wrong. It shouldn't have taken Devereux this long to get here.

Perhaps they had been mistaken about the route Devereux had taken. Perhaps the gambler had headed straight north to Wisconsin, or even further east. But the trail through Oberlin had seemed the straightest and most practical route. On the sixth day, they decided to ride up to Vermilion, a fishing village on Lake Erie. It was, they had been told, a frequent last stop on the Underground Railroad. Sympathetic fishermen could be hired to ferry fugitives to a steamer crossing to Canada.

With frustration and rage gnawing at their insides, the two brothers collected their horses. Five miles outside town, one of the horses started to go lame, and Ted had to dismount and walk him. He tried to trade the animal at a farmhouse, but the door was slammed in his face. A few miles farther, John's saddle started to slip. When he inspected it, he saw that the cinch straps had been frayed in two places. Another mile, and the same thing happened to the second saddle. There was no way of repairing them without assistance.

They turned back to Oberlin, only to find both the blacksmith and saddler out of town. No one knew when they would reopen. Not a horse in town was for sale, nor a saddle. A visit to the sheriff produced no better results. The man looked at the saddles and mildly observed that they should take better care of their equipment and animals.

The sheriff was treated to a long string of threats and curses, but he merely regarded his visitors benignly and shrugged. Defeated, the Carroll brothers started the walk to Wellington, the next town. They realized every bitter, painful step of the way that the people of Oberlin had outfoxed them, and that Devereux was probably well on his way to Canada.

Meredith looked over the peaceful grounds of Oberlin College. She and Lissa and Daphne occupied one room, and Quinn and Cam another. They had been here one day. Upon arriving they were told of the two strangers who looked like anything but what they said they were. The two men were altogether too curious for the cautious Ohioans. Meredith and Quinn immediately recognized the Carroll brothers from the descriptions.

The man who had led them there grinned and told them not to worry. The townspeople would take care of the slave catchers in their own way. Quinn winced, and Meredith knew he worried about getting more innocents involved, but his reservations were quickly swept aside. No one would get hurt, he was promised. Except perhaps the pride and temper of the two unwanted strangers.

The closer the fleeing party had come to Oberlin and Lake Erie, the more tense Quinn had become. Although he still held Meredith in his arms when they rested, he had not made love to her. True, there had been little privacy, but they had improvised very well in the past.

Meredith found it torture, plain torture, to be so near him

and yet have the invisible wall between them, one over which she could peek but not scale. If only Cam hadn't been hurt. Even though he was nearly well now, she knew Quinn still felt guilt over the incident. Guilt and blame. And fear that it would happen again.

If they could get to Canada without more trouble, perhaps then she could convince him that they belonged together, that he was protection, not danger. Life, not death.

Their new guide came that evening with a smile on his face. The Carrolls had informed the rooming-house proprietor they would be leaving on the morrow. Certain arrangements had been made to ensure that their upcoming journey would not be a trouble-free one. Their own party could leave at midmorning without fearing detection or interception.

They had dinner together that night, the five of them in a private room at the college. If all went well, they would be on a boat to Canada tomorrow night. There was an undeniable tension during the meal because everyone was hesitant to speak of the future. They were all waiting on Quinn, who had very little to say.

Only Lissa was firmly decided on her course. She had heard about the communities of ex-slaves in Canada and how badly they needed teachers and schools.

Her eyes bright with purpose and a shy smile on her lips, she announced that she wanted to teach. Meredith wanted to protest, wanted some way for Lissa to stay with her. What she really wanted was for all of them to go to California, as Quinn had once proposed. But he had changed his mind, and now her own life was uncertain and confused. Could she go back to Mississippi and forget everything? she wondered.

Quinn, she knew, was not safe any place. He had already told her he could not stay in Canada because of his murder conviction in England. Now he was also wanted in the States, although California was still the safest place for him.

Meredith looked up and caught his eyes on her. Dear God, but they were blue. So blue and so intense that she had to take her own eyes away for fear of being consumed by them. Her gaze wandered down to the bare skin exposed by the partially open buckskin shirt. She saw the barely healed cut that curved up to his neck, and her heart hurt for him. She thought of the other knife cuts on his chest, the whip scars on his back. He had endured so much. His body had endured so much. How could he ever be entirely free of his past suffering?

She dreaded tonight because they would be apart. Although it might be their last evening together, they could not sleep in each other's arms here. She wondered how she could get through the night alone, worrying whether tomorrow would be one of their last days together.

I love you, she said silently across the table.

He smiled, but it was a bittersweet smile that told her little. And then, abruptly, he left.

"What are we goin' do, Capt'n?"

"Go to Canada."

Cam gave him a disgusted look. "And then where?"

"You're a damn fool for wanting to go any place with me. What about Daphne?"

"She wants to go where I do. We're going to get married in Canada."

"Then you're even a bigger fool for going with me."

"I don't know about that. You freed me. You saved my life."

"And damned near got you killed."

Cam shook his head. "You think it wasn't worth it to me? You gave me something more important than life. You made it worthwhile. You gave that to your lady too. You goin' take it away now?"

Cam's eyes bored into him, and Quinn turned away. He wanted to believe. Christ, but he wanted to believe. He wanted Meredith so badly. He wanted to see her eyes dance with laughter, and hear her soft teasing. He wanted to bury himself in her until their souls touched and their hearts whispered with the same intimate language.

"You talk too much," he said, but Cam saw a light that hadn't been in his eyes before, and with a grunt of satisfaction he turned over and went to sleep.

They caught a fishing boat in Vermilion. Not until they pulled away from shore did Quinn relax. It had been a fast journey by horse from Oberlin to this small lakeside village. As if by magic or by someone's swift messenger, a fishing boat was waiting for them. There was no sign of the Carrolls, and Quinn, who had been told what had happened to the brothers, smiled wryly. The whole damned town. It seemed impossible. No violence, no one hurt. He still couldn't quite believe their luck until they were well out in the lake and all possibility of capture was gone.

They landed in Chatham, Canada, five days later. It had not been a pleasant voyage. A storm overtook them and the waters were rough. Meredith promptly got sick and stayed that way. Her intention to talk to Quinn, to convince him they should be together always, was impossible to carry out. It was all she could do to stand, much less convince a bear to raid a honeypot. She stayed in her cabin, reluctant to allow even Lissa inside. The giant paddlewheelers of the Mississippi had not prepared her for the storm-swept Great Lake.

She was still weak and miserable when they arrived in Canada, only to be met by a resplendently dressed member of the Royal Canadian Mounted Police. She saw Quinn stiffen at the sight of the uniform, an attitude that didn't change even as the man welcomed them pleasantly. She knew this would not be a good time to talk to him. But she had decided in the past days that she would not go back to Mississippi. If she had to follow him like an unwanted stray dog, she would do so.

Chatham was a small town, largely populated by escaped slaves, many of whom had become farmers and business owners. The five fugitives took rooms at a boardinghouse.

Daphne and Cam wasted no time in finding a minister. They were referred to a small Methodist church and a

Reverend Fargate, who greeted them joyfully, especially when he discovered that Lissa wished to teach.

"The need is very great," he said warmly, his bright blue eyes seemingly unable to move away from Lissa. When he finally forced his attention elsewhere, Meredith noted that Lissa's eyes had widened with interest of her own.

Reverend Fargate was a fine-looking man with curly brown hair and one of the kindest faces Meredith had ever seen. She would be leaving Lissa, she knew instinctively, in very good hands.

She tried not to listen to the rest of the conversation as Cam and Daphne approached the subject of marriage. It hurt too much.

Cam had his arm around Daphne. "Can you marry us? Soon?"

The minister's eyes warmed even more. "That," he said, "is my favorite duty. When would you like the ceremony to take place?"

Cam would have preferred that very moment, but he thought of Daphne and her travel-worn dress. "Tomorrow," he said. "Today I have to buy my bride a dress."

Reverend Fargate looked at Meredith and Quinn, watching as they avoided each other's eyes. Yet their faces told him a great deal. "You will be their witnesses?"

Quinn nodded slowly.

"Two o'clock tomorrow, then," the reverend said, his face turning back to Lissa. "You will come too?" There was a hopeful note in his voice, and she nodded shyly.

Meredith was filled with joy for Cam and Daphne, yet it was mixed with the old loneliness and uncertainty. She would be leaving Lissa.

And Quinn? She often caught his eyes upon her, but they were usually guarded and moved rapidly away when he caught her gaze on him. Tonight, drat it. Tonight she would go to his room.

In the meantime, she helped Daphne choose a dress for her wedding, and she and Lissa helped with the alterations. It was a lovely dress of beige silk, and Daphne looked beautiful in it. Daphne had protested at the cost, but Meredith had brought money with her, and she quickly swept aside the protests.

They ate dinner together. Quinn and Cam talked about the journey west, discussing various routes. They could travel overland, but it would be an extremely difficult journey, with Indian troubles along the way. They finally decided, instead, to travel by boat to Rochester, New York, then overland to Boston where they could catch a ship to California. Quinn felt that they would be safe in New York and Massachusetts since their pursuers believed them to be in Canada.

After dinner he held out a hand to Meredith. "Let's go for a walk."

It had been misting much of the day, but now the sun emerged long enough to paint the western sky a fiery red. Meredith moved close to Quinn and felt his body tremble as they touched. "I'm going with you," she announced.

"It will be hard. And dangerous."

"I'm used to hard. And dangerous."

He was silent a moment. "I don't want you to be."

"What about exciting, and adventurous and—"

"Deadly."

"Not with you. I have never felt so safe as I do with you."

He was silent. Since they had escaped from the Carroll brothers, he had felt a curious sense of freedom. And elation, particularly when he had learned of Oberlin's role in their escape. He was not alone. *They* were not alone.

For the first time in years, he felt released from the scourge he had so thoroughly believed he brought to others. But the trip through Canada and New York would be perilous. Did he have the right to endanger her again?

"I love you," she whispered.

He could no longer hold back his need, or his yearning. His arms went around her, and his lips hungrily sought hers. He felt a tornado of raw urgency rip through him. Caution met want and was tossed aside as easily as a leaf caught in a wind current. Their lips met in frantic wanting that had been building over the last uncertain, tormenting weeks.

Finally, he pulled away slightly, his eyes adoring her. "I love you," he said hoarsely, the words torn from his throat, unable to remain unsaid in his heart.

Their legs moved then. In concert and without conscious thought. They went inside and propelled their bodies past the still-sitting trio of friends in the dining room. They went up the steps to Quinn's room and through the door.

Neither knew who closed the door, or how they reached the bed. They only knew that they were, at last, together again.

Meredith woke slowly, lazily, until she realized something was wrong. The space beside her was empty, and she was filled with sudden panic.

Last night had been the most wonderful in her life. They had made love furiously, then tenderly as each tried to give the other ultimate pleasure and put aside the past. But they had spoken no more of the trip west, and now Meredith recalled he had never actually agreed to take her. What if he had gone on alone?

Meredith dressed quickly and ran down the steps of the boardinghouse. She threw open the front door, her eyes searching frantically, relaxing only when she saw him standing on a small hill nearby. He was looking away from her, toward the east where the sun was showering soft gold and rose colors in gentle layers across the horizon. She watched him, taking pleasure in his figure, in the familiar hard lean body now dressed in buckskins. His black hair ruffled in the breeze, and his stance was both watchful and . . . expectant, as if he were waiting for something, or someone.

He turned slightly, and she saw his profile and the beginning of a smile. Her eyes turned to where he was looking, and quivers of excitement, of profound wonderment, ran through her. A rainbow arced in the sky, one end reaching down to touch the path leading west.

Meredith walked over to him and put her hand in his, feeling his fingers tighten around her own.

"The rainbow of promise," she whispered.

He looked down at her, his blue eyes free as she had never seen them before, and they spoke of their own promise.

" 'Anguish and grief,' " he softly recited the words of Frederick Douglass, " 'like darkness and rain, can be described, but joy and gladness, like the rainbow of promise, defy alike the pen and pencil. . . .' "

He put his arms around her waist, and pulled her tightly against him. They both gazed ahead, the world, framed by their rainbow, now a gift before them, a gift to be lived and treasured.

Meredith felt his lips against her hair, soft and loving and needing. "Would you marry me today?" he said. "With Cam and Daphne?"

"Yes, oh yes," she answered softly as she turned and looked up at clear blue eyes, unshuttered and open.

He smiled, and his eyes finally joined his mouth in an expression of quiet elation. And she knew that Quinn, at last, was ready for his own joy and gladness.

E*pilogue*

BRETT DEVEREUX leaned forward in his seat as Elias Sprague was ushered in. He didn't observe the formalities.

"He's safe?"

"Both he and Cam, although Cam was wounded. Apparently he's well now."

"And Quinn?"

"From all reports, safely on his way to California. With his wife." There was a small beatific smile on Elias's face.

Brett stood suddenly, his chair swinging from the violence of his movement. "Wife? What wife?"

Elias savored his next words. He was enjoying this, although he knew it was neither kindly nor godly to tease. "A painter named M. Sabre."

Confusion crossed Brett's face, and his hand moved

toward the two paintings on his desk. The canvasses, along with a letter, had been delivered by Jamison, the pilot and now owner of the *Lucky Lady* weeks earlier, just after all hell had broken loose.

The paintings, one of a rainbow over the Mississippi, and the other of workers in a cotton field, were magnificent. The note had asked Brett to look after the paintings temporarily, that they would be sent for once Quinn had settled somewhere. Brett had studied them for a long time, wondering when his brother had started collecting art, and admiring their strength, color, and detail. He had kept them on his desk and looked at them frequently.

"How? Where?" The surprise in Brett's voice was evident.

Elias smiled. "The painter has been a very effective agent with the Railroad. You might know her by the name of Meredith Seaton."

Brett sat down slowly. Very slowly. He looked at Elias accusingly. "You knew?"

"She was one of our agents. Thee had no reason to know."

Brett leaned back and chuckled. The joke this time was on him. He had known about Quinn, had, in fact, been responsible for his being contacted initially about being a part of the Railroad. The idea had struck him after Quinn had bought Cam, and Brett noticed changes in his brother. The Underground Railroad, he had surmised privately, was what Quinn needed to give purpose to his life, to focus that rage that was so near the surface. He had never told Quinn of his own involvement, which, in fact, was small enough and usually involved only monetary contributions. Brett had felt Quinn needed to do this on his own, that he had needed to cure himself.

But Meredith? Plain, fussy, greedy Meredith?

Brett looked down at the paintings again and mentally compared them to the paintings she had given him.

What else had the prissy Miss Meredith hidden?

Knowing his brother, it was a great deal.

His grin spread, and he started laughing and laughing. Until tears ran down his face.

About the Author

PATRICIA POTTER has become one of the most highly praised writers of historical romance since her impressive debut in 1988, when she won the Maggie Award and a Reviewer's Choice Award from *Romantic Times* for her first novel. She most recently received a 1993 *Romantic Times* Career Achievement Award nomination for Storyteller of the Year and Reviewer's Choice nominations for her novel *Lightning* (Best Civil War Historical Romance), and the hero, Lobo, in *Lawless* (Knight in Shining Silver). She has worked as a newspaper reporter in Atlanta and was president of the Georgia Romance Writers Association from 1988 to 1990.

✳

*Don't miss Patricia Potter's next thrilling
historical novel,*

<u>NOTORIOUS</u>

*in which Marsh Canton, the mysterious black-
clad gunfighter from LAWLESS, faces the
biggest challenge of his life—and the most
dangerous threat to his guarded heart.*

COMING SOON FROM BANTAM.

Marsh Canton has been a hired gun almost all his
life. Now he's nearing forty, and he knows he's
pushed his luck to the limit. When he wins a San
Francisco saloon in a poker game, it seems a sign.
From now on, he'll be Taylor Canton, respectable
owner of the Glory Hole—but not if Catalina Hilliard
has anything to do about it. Cat's worked very hard
to make the Silver Slipper the most popular spot in
San Francisco, so hell would freeze first before she'd
let Canton take away any of her business. She's
determined to run him out of town, and once Canton
meets the exquisite, untamed beauty, it's a challenge
he accepts with relish. The war between them be-
comes the rage of San Francisco, but even more
notorious is the passion that burns between the cold-
blooded maverick and the woman who's wrapped
her heart with ice.

In the following excerpt, Cat has just walked into the
Glory Hole—and the astonishing sight of Canton
playing the piano.

"Miss Cat," he said as his eyes ran over her dress and shawl. "What a very pleasant surprise to have you visit again. Can't stay away?" His voice was low, and Cat didn't miss the taunt in it.

"I'm just returning your courtesy," she said sweetly. "A special invitation to sit at my table for the opening night of the Can Can." And then, because she realized that there was something about his musical ability he wished to hide, she remarked, "How interesting to discover you have . . . a talent. Are there any more I should know about?"

Something flickered in his eyes—anger, perhaps—before they clouded over as they had before, becoming like mirrors that reflected others but never himself. She wished she could do that. Her eyes could intimidate, but not like his. Never like his.

"Are you sure you want to know, Miss Cat?" Now his voice purred, but not like that of any cat she'd ever known. There was a sensual invitation in it that sent prickly shivers up and down her spine. She felt herself being expertly unclothed, piece by piece, by those damnable eyes. The shivers turned to raw, ragged heat that seemed to claw at her insides.

The air was alive with challenge . . . and that very same heat that had crawled inside her and was making her existence plain hell. It had reached outside her and grabbed him. She saw it plainly in the sudden tightness of his trousers. It was as if they were both caught in incandescent waves that burned and tormented. His dark gray eyes, usually as frigid as an ice-covered lake, were glittering with an internal fire of their own.

A muscle twitched in his cheek, and she took satisfaction in it. He wasn't nearly as indifferent as he wanted to appear. But then, as if through sheer force of will, the muscle quieted and a grim smile came to his lips. "I've forgotten my manners," he said in that natural way that told of breeding. "Catalina, this is Miss Jenny Davis, who will be entertaining here, and Jenny, this is Catalina Hilliard, our worthy competitor from the Silver Lady."

Jenny flushed and Cat wondered why. She'd seen the quick looks the girl had sent toward Canton, and a bubble of jealousy floated to the surface of her consciousness, even as she tried to disclaim it. Damn the man. Did he have every woman panting after him?

He didn't seem to notice as he turned to the girl. "I'll see you this evening, Jenny. I have some business to discuss with Miss Catalina." It was an abrupt dismissal, but a slight, practiced smile softened the impact, and the girl nodded, though her eyes were curious.

He directed his attention to Cat once more. She wasn't surprised when he took her arm and guided her toward the door. Nor was she capable at the moment of avoiding it without making a scene and making more of it than it might look to casual observers.

His fingers pressed into her arm in a possessive way, with a fierceness that indicated he wasn't going to let go. "Will you accompany me for a ride?" The question was not a question at all, but an order, and Cat bristled. She thought of pulling away, damn the consequences of a scene, but then he leaned down, his warm breath tickling her ear in a way that dulled her intent and excited . . . combustible parts of herself.

Before she could say no, he whispered, "Of course,

you will," as though he heard her unspoken denial. "We have some very important matters to discuss. A certain police captain, for instance."

"I'm not sure what you mean," she said with the composure she'd practiced over the years.

Canton smiled. "You're very good. You would have made one hell of a gunfighter."

She leaped on the words. "Is that what you are, Mr. Canton?"

His smile widened, and Cat realized it was no slip of a tongue on his part. He was offering a slice of temptation, a hint as to what she desperately wanted to know, as part of his invitation. Or order.

"I didn't say that. I merely said that you would have made a good one."

"And why is that?"

"You give very little away, Miss Cat. And then there's a certain ruthlessness."

"You're describing yourself, Mr. Canton."

"I thought we'd gone beyond Mr. Canton." That infernal chuckle was in his voice, that deep sensuousness that was one half invitation, one half challenge and all deadly. Her wayward body felt the craving she heard in his voice, the pure lust that astounded and horrified her.

She summoned every inch of willpower she had and tried to pull away, but his hand was like steel on her arm. "I have to get back."

"Then I'll have to abduct you," he said in a low voice no one else could hear. "I'll try to make it far more pleasant than the one you arranged for me."

"I have no idea what you're talking about."

"Of course, we could discuss it here." They had reached the door, away from Jenny Davis and customers, but all eyes in the establishment were fixed on them.

Cat lifted her chin. She didn't like the way he called her Cat. No one called her Cat, although a few had tried before she'd fixed them with the look that turned men into bumbling, apologetic fools. She had mastered it to perfection, but it didn't work on this man, seeming only to amuse him, as if he understood all the insecurity and pain that lay behind it, as if he knew it for the fraud it often was.

"We have nothing to discuss," she said coldly, even as she struggled to keep from trembling. All her thoughts were in disarray, and she wasn't sure whether it was because of her rage that he so easily penetrated all her defenses, that he was so adept at personal invasion, or because of that look in his eyes, that pure radiance of physical need that almost burned through her.

Fifteen years. Nearly fifteen years since a man had touched her so intimately. And he was doing it only with his eyes!

And, dear God, she was responding.

She'd thought herself immune from desire, that if she'd ever had any, it had been killed long ago by brutality and shame and utter abhorrence of an act that gave men power and left her little more than a thing to be used. She'd never felt this bubbling, boiling warmth inside, this craving that was more than physical but some kind of deeper hunger.

That's what frightened her most of all.

But she wouldn't show it. She would never show it, and eventually it would fade. She didn't even like Canton, devil take him. She didn't like anything about him. And she would send him back to wherever he came, tail between his legs, no matter what it took.

But now she had little choice, unless she wished to stand here all afternoon, his hand burning a brand into her. He wasn't going to let her go, and perhaps it was time to lay her cards on the table. She preferred open warfare to guerilla fighting. She hadn't felt right about the kidnapping and beating, she admitted to herself. She had soothed her somewhat jaded conscience with the fact that, after all, they hadn't achieved the desired result. Even if she did frequently regret that moment of mercy on her part.

She shrugged indifferently and his hand relaxed only slightly, still holding her like a steel manacle as he followed her out the door. He flagged down a carriage for hire and, with those elegant manners that still puzzled her, helped her inside with a grace that would put royalty to shame.

He left her for a moment and spoke to the driver, passng a few bills up to him, then returned and vaulted to the seat next to her. Not across, as she'd hoped but close . . . touching. Hard muscled thigh pushing against her leg; his tanned arm, made visible by the rolled up sleeve, brushing against her much smaller one, the wiry male hair sweeping over her skin with thousands of tiny electrical charges; his scent, a spicy mixture of bay and soap, teasing her senses. Everything about him—the strength and power and raw masculinity that he made no attempt to conceal—made her feel fragile as she'd not felt for years.

But not vulnerable, she told herself. Never vulnerable again. She would fight back, seize control and keep it.

She straightened her back and smiled, A seductive smile. A smile that had entranced men for the last ten years. A practiced smile that knew exactly how far to go. A kind of promise that left doors opened, while permitting retreat. It was a smile that kept men coming to the Silver Lady even as they understood they had no chance of realizing the dream. Hope sprang eternal with that smile. *Perhaps I will be the one.*

Canton raised an eyebrow. "You *are* very good," he said admiringly.

Cat didn't even try to pretend she didn't know what he meant. She shrugged. "It usually works."

"I imagine it does," he said. "Although I doubt if most of the men you . . . use it on have seen the thornier part of you."

"Most don't irritate me as you do."

"Irritate, Miss Cat?"

"Don't call me Cat. My name is Catalina."

"Is it?"

"Is yours really Taylor Canton?"

The last two questions were said softly, dangerously, both of them trying to probe weaknesses, and both recognizing the tactic of the other.

"I would swear to it on a bible," Marsh said, his mouth quirking upward, acknowledging the absurdity of the statement.

"I'm surprised you have one, or know what one is."

"I had a very good upbringing, Miss Cat." He emphasized the last word.

"And then what happened?" The question was caustic.

The sardonic amusement in his eyes faded slightly. "A great deal. And what is your story?"

Dear God, his voice was mesmerizing. An intimate song that said nothing but wanted everything. Deep and provocative. Compelling and irresistible. Almost.

"I had a very poor upbringing," she said. "And then a great deal happened."

For the first time since she'd met him, she saw real humor in his eyes. Not just that cynical amusement as if he were some higher being looking down on a world inhabited by silly children. "You're the first woman I've met with fewer scruples than myself," he said, admiration back in his voice.

She opened her eyes wide. "You have some?"

"As I told you that first night, I don't usually mistreat women."

"Usually?"

"Unless provoked."

"A threat, Mr. Canton?"

"I never threaten, Miss Cat. Neither do I turn down challenges."

"And you usually win?"

"Not usually, Miss Cat. Always." The last word was flat, almost ugly in its surety.

"So do I," she said complacently.

The heat in the closed carriage had escalated. Their voices had lowered into little more than husky whispers. The electricity between them was sparking, hissing, crackling, threatening to ignite. Her gaze couldn't move from his, nor his from hers. His hand moved to her arm, his fingers running up and down it in slow sensuous trails and she felt like a thousand nerve ends being singed. But she wouldn't move, wouldn't give him that satisfaction.

And then the heat was that of the bowels of a volcano. Intense and violent. She wondered very briefly if this was a version of hell. She had just decided it was when he bent toward her, his lips brushing over hers.

And heaven and hell collided.

The kiss had been as inevitable as day following night.

Marsh had known it from the moment he saw her in the Glory Hole.

The only way to get her out of his system was this, and

he was deadly determined to accomplish it. He'd thought the fireworks that constantly surrounded them were nothing more than that, a brief flurry of sound and fury, signifying nothing.

He hoped Shakespeare would forgive him for his literary liberties, but the mental diversion helped in re-establishing some kind of equilibrium.

Until his lips touched hers.

He hadn't really known what to expect. Ice that would cool the damned heat burning him inside out. Emptiness that would swallow his unexpected and disturbing need.

But there was no ice. No emptiness.

She was as unwilling a participant as he in the damnable attraction that engulfed them as if it were a hurricane and they were caught in the eye.

The eye that was every bit as dangerous as the wind that swirled around it. And explosive, filled with the hot expectancy of a pending lethal storm.

Her lips, at first reluctant and wary, suddenly yielded, yet she wasn't surrendering, was merely astonished and stunned. A part of him understood that, because he felt the same. He also felt the need to explore, to taste, to test. Even savor the currents of hot pleasure that surged through him as first their lips found common ground, and then their tongues and their hands.

He felt her arms go around him, just as he had wrapped her tightly against him. He felt every movement in her body, every quiver, every stiffening awareness as his own arousal pressed into her. How long hat it been since he'd felt this alive? Had he ever felt like this . . . even before war and hate and revenge had robbed him of feeling?

A low moan rumbled through his body as, unaccountably, his mouth gentled. He didn't understand where this very old tenderness came from, where it had been lurking to emerge at this inconvenient time. Still, it was . . . pleasant. More than pleasant, even, and some instinct told him it was as new and strange to her as it was to him.

Her mouth opened hesitantly under his lips, greeting him with an unexpected longing that went through to his core, and his tongue ran knowingly over the sensitive crevices of her mouth. He lifted his head slightly, his gaze moving to her eyes, and he was almost lost in the smoldering green depths of them, even as he sensed the hostility that was still there.

He closed his own eyes against them, against the confused yet heated emotion in them, and his lips hardened. He forced anger. He forced it because he *was* angry, angry that she was stirring things best left alone, angry because he knew he couldn't trust her. She was the woman who had had him beaten, almost shanghaied, who caused his imprisonment in a filthy cage. The gentleness changed to something harsh and bitter. Punishing.

He still felt her response, but now he knew it was unwilling, and he took a sudden cruel pleasure in the fact that she was as helpless against this attraction as he was.

His lust reached monumental proportions as he felt the surge of hot heat reach his loins. Christ, he hadn't meant this to happen. He'd wanted to punish her in some way for those two weeks of indignity and pain. He'd wanted to discomfort her, and now he was the one discomfited. He'd recognized her physical reaction to him and he'd wanted to tease and tempt and make her beg for more. But he was the one begging, damn her.

What was happening?

You don't even like her, he told himself.

But his hands wanted to be gentle, and he had to hold himself back. He could not betray this weakness, not to her. She would take that weakness and use it. Just as he would do the same to her.

After the one time in his life he'd lost his self-control, he had spent the rest of his life honing it. He had always been able to distance himself from events, even those he'd participated in as a principal, as if he were standing aside and watching himself do mechanical things.

But he was not standing away now, not any part of him. Every sense was engaged, every nerve ending tingling. The fact that they had been numb for so long only heightened the sensations.

His hand moved to one of her breasts, fondling it through the cloth. Heat radiated through the material, and his fingers moved up to caress her shoulders, then made their way under the material as his lips left her mouth and started nibbling at the soft vulnerable part of her neck. He felt shivers run through her body, almost like spasms. He felt similar spasms rock his body, and his hands became even more invasive. One started to unbutton the blouse in back while the other slipped down further until he found the soft flesh of her breast. It was firm, so firm, the nipple erect in its own excitement.

She suddenly wrenched away with a litle cry, staring at him with a kind of horror that stunned him into stillness. For the first time since he'd met her, he saw fear in her eyes. And vulnerability that struck him like a blacksmith's hammer.

He watched her fight for control. He should feel satisfaction, but didn't, only a greater emptiness that he inspired this . . . terror in her, even after she'd responded to him, after she'd been as aware as he of the physical attraction between them.

He watched her with narrowed eyes, wondering if this was some kind of game, even as his intuition told him it was not. No one could quite manage that look of humiliation, the struggle to hide it so gallantly. He half expected an explosion of cries of abuse, of blame, but it didn't come. But then she seldom did the expected; that, he knew, was part of his fascination with her.

Catalina's eyes met his directly. "That was a mistake," she said.

"Yours or mine?" His question was cool, as unemotional as her face was now, although his body was still caught in the storm of physical need. It ached unmercifully.

"Mine. I should never have come with you."

"I didn't give you any choice."

"I always have a choice, Mr. Canton."

He leaned back against the seat of the carriage, surveying her with eyes that were ruthless in their prying. "I would suspect that once you didn't." There was no sympathy in the statement, only an observation.

Her eyes went very cold. "You know nothing, Mr. Canton."

"I know you responded to me. I didn't imagine that . . . passion. I'm just not sure why you suddenly . . . ."

"Ah, you're not sure of something. What a surprise."

She was trying to divert him, and he had no intention of letting it happen, not when spasms of want still raked his body.

"The icy Miss Catalina," he said in a silky voice. "Fire and ice. Exactly what are you?"

"Nothing for you."

"That's not what your eyes were telling me minutes ago. You wanted me every bit as much as I wanted you."

"Male arrogance," she said superciliously, though he noticed the slightest tick in her cheek that gave her away. "You're not nearly as . . . interesting as you seem to think you are."

He raised an eyebrow. "No?" he asked in a low

rumbling voice. "Didn't anyone ever tell you what happens to little girls who lie?"

"Or you what happens to big boys who are arrogant bullies?" she retorted.

He chuckled mirthlessly. "They get shanghaied?"

She didn't blink. "That's a thought."

"I wouldn't try it," he warned softly. "Again."

"If I intended you to be shanghaied, you would be on your way to China," she said.

"Just beaten and jailed, then?"

"Do you always talk in riddles, Mr. Canton?"

He wished she didn't look so damn beautiful when she was angry. A lock of black hair had fallen from the twist that held her tresses back from her face, and it softened her expression.

"We could call a truce, Miss Cat." He hadn't meant to make the offer. She had started this war, and he had lost only one in his life. Actually others had lost that one for him. He'd never surrendered.

"No," she said flatly. "I've worked too hard to build the Silver Lady."

"So the war continues."

She shrugged. "Call it what you will."

"No more ambushes, Miss Cat," he warned quietly.

Her green eyes bored into him. "Who was it who said war was hell?"

His hand touched the soft flesh under her chin, lifting her face until her gaze locked into his. "A northern general, I think. But you don't know the beginning of hell, Miss Cat."

"And you do?" The electricity was there again, darting like heat lightning. Energy pulsed between them. Dare and counterdare. Thrust and counterthrust. Each searching out the other's weaknesses. He moved his fingers along her cheeks, watching as she colored from ivory to rose.

"Don't touch me," she said, jerking away.

"Why, Miss Cat?" He enjoyed using the name, knowing it provoked her, made the green eyes even greener as they glinted pure malice at him. "Does it disturb you? Burn you?"

It did, but Cat wasn't going to admit it. She felt like a rabbit hypnotized by the unblinking stare of a snake. If only her body didn't react to him in such unfamiliar ways. If only she didn't want to reach out and touch him. If only she didn't remember that moment when his lips first met hers, a moment unlike any she'd ever known. Rare and gentle. And she'd responded in a way that was unfathomable to her. But the sweetness was so quickly gone, she told herself that she'd simply imagined it.

He was pure devil.

"I don't like you, Mr. Canton."

"I don't think I asked if you liked me."

"Take me back."

"Not quite yet."

"Just what do you want?"

He leaned back and without asking her permission, lit a cheroot he'd taken from his shirt pocket. He inhaled deeply, then sent out lazy smoke rings to bounce against the ceiling of the carriage.

"Do you have any idea of what a jail cell is like?" he said after several moments of silence.

"No," she said, but I suspect you do and that you've been in one more than once."

"Only once, Miss Catalina. It wasn't much larger than this carriage, and not nearly as comfortable. I always give back in good measure what I get. I'm making this one exception."

"Another warning?"

"A promise."

She bristled. Catalina hadn't apologized to anyone in a number of years. It was a waste. You couldn't take back actions. She knew that better than anyone.

"You don't belong here, Mr. Canton."

He raised an eyebrow. "Where do I belong?" He really wanted to know.

Cat swallowed. There was just the faintest hint of wistfulness in the question. Not enough to invoke sympathy but enough to be intriguing. She remembered again that very brief instant of gentleness. It had to have been her imagination.

"Where did you come from?" It was the first truly personal question she'd posed. She thought he would brush it aside.

He shrugged carelessly, but she saw somthing flicker in his eyes, something like loss. "A place that no longer exists."

She shouldn't have asked the question. She didn't want to know. The conversation was too personal. She didn't want to like him, or feel the slightest interest. She just wanted him to disappear. She wanted the Silver Lady back like it was. She wanted her life back like it was. No complications. She wanted to be respected. She wanted to be rich. She wanted to . . . be safe. Which meant being alone.

Alone. The word had never hurt before. It had always represented Paradise. Why not now?

You can't trust him. You can't trust any man, the voice whispered to her.

"I want to go back," she said suddenly.

"Coward," he accused.

"I just don't like the company."

"But I do, and right now I'm in control."

"I'll have you arrested for kidnapping."

He moved his fingers across the skin of her arms. "Then I might as well make it worthwhile."

Don't miss these fabulous Bantam women's fiction titles on sale in April

---

Don't miss these fabulous Bantam women's fiction titles on sale in May

SACRED LIES

☐ 29063-0 $5.99/6.99 in Canada

by Dianne Edouard & Sandra Ware

Authors of MORTAL SINS

A beautiful agent is drawn into a web of betrayal and desire—where she must choose between who to believe...and who to love.

THE WIZARD OF SEATTLE

☐ 28999-3 $5.50/6.50 in Canada

by Kay Hooper

Co-author of THE DELANEY CHRISTMAS CAROL

A magical romantic fantasy!

From Seattle to Ancient Atlantis, Richard Patrick Merlin and Serena Smyth struggle for control of her spectacular gift of magic—defying a taboo so ancient that the reasons for its existence have been forgotten—risking all for an eternal love.

SILVER FLAME

☐ 29959-X $5.50/6.50 in Canada

by Susan Johnson

Bestselling author of SINFUL and FORBIDDEN

The Braddock-Black dynasty continues!
The fires of romance are white hot when Empress Jordan flees to the Montana wilderness...and finds a man as wild as the land around him.